RECURSION

BY BLAKE CROUCH

Wayward Pines

Pines
Wayward
The Last Town

Andrew Z. Thomas/Luther Kite Series

Desert Places
Locked Doors
Break You
Stirred
Serial Killers Uncut

Standalone Novels

Run
Abandon
Snow Bound
Famous
Eerie
Draculas
Dark Matter
Recursion

Letty Dobesh Series

The Pain of Others
Sunset Key
Grab

Other Stories And Novellas

*69
Remaking
On the Good, Red Road
Shining Rock
The Meteorologist
Unconditional
Perfect Little Town
Hunting Season

Story Collections

Fully Loaded
Thicker Than Blood
The Fear Trilogy

RECURSION

A Novel

BLAKE CROUCH

MACMILLAN

First published in the US 2019 by Crown, an imprint of the Crown
Publishing Group, a division of Penguin Random House LLC, New York

First published in the UK 2019 by Macmillan
an imprint of Pan Macmillan
20 New Wharf Road, London N1 9RR
Associated companies throughout the world
www.panmacmillan.com

ISBN 978-1-5098-6665-6

9 8 7 6 5 4 3 2 1

A CIP catalogue record for this book is available from the British Library.

Printed and bound by CPI Group (UK) Ltd, Croydon, CR0 4YY

Visit **www.panmacmillan.com** to read more about all our books
and to buy them. You will also find features, author interviews and
news of any author events, and you can sign up for e-newsletters
so that you're always first to hear about our new releases.

For Jacque

BOOK ONE

Time is but memory in the making.
–VLADIMIR NABOKOV

BARRY

Barry Sutton pulls over into the fire lane at the main entrance of the Poe Building, an Art Deco tower glowing white in the illumination of its exterior sconces. He climbs out of his Crown Vic, rushes across the sidewalk, and pushes through the revolving door into the lobby.

The night watchman is standing by the bank of elevators, holding one open as Barry hurries toward him, his shoes echoing off the marble.

"What floor?" Barry asks as he steps into the elevator car.

"Forty-one. When you get up there, take a right and go all the way down the hall."

"More cops will be here in a minute. Tell them I said to hang back until I give a signal."

The elevator races upward, belying the age of the building around it, and Barry's ears pop after a few seconds. When the doors finally part, he moves past a sign for a law firm. There's a light on here and there, but the floor stands mostly dark. He runs along the carpet, passing silent offices, a conference room, a break room, a library. The hallway finally opens into a reception area that's paired with the largest office.

In the dim light, the details are all in shades of gray. A sprawling mahogany desk buried under files and paperwork. A circular table covered in notepads and mugs of cold, bitter-smelling coffee. A wet bar stocked exclusively with bottles of Macallan Rare. A glowing aquarium that hums on the far side of the room and contains a small shark and several tropical fish.

As Barry approaches the French doors, he silences his phone and removes his shoes. Taking the handle, he eases the door open and slips out onto the terrace.

The surrounding skyscrapers of the Upper West Side look mystical in their luminous shrouds of fog. The noise of the city is loud and close—car horns ricocheting between the buildings and distant ambulances racing toward some other tragedy. The pinnacle of the Poe Building is less than fifty feet above—a crown of glass and steel and gothic masonry.

The woman sits fifteen feet away beside an eroding gargoyle, her back to Barry, her legs dangling over the edge.

He inches closer, the wet flagstones soaking through his socks. If he can get close enough without detection, he'll drag her off the edge before she knows what—

"I smell your cologne," she says without looking back.

He stops.

She looks back at him, says, "Another step and I'm gone."

It's difficult to tell in the ambient light, but she appears to be in the vicinity of forty. She wears a dark blazer and matching skirt, and she must have been sitting out here for a while, because her hair has been flattened by the mist.

"Who are you?" she asks.

"Barry Sutton. I'm a detective in the Central Robbery Division of NYPD."

"They sent someone from the Robbery—?"

"I happened to be closest. What's your name?"

"Ann Voss Peters."

"May I call you Ann?"

"Sure."

"Is there anyone I can call for you?"

She shakes her head.

"I'm going to step over here so you don't have to keep straining your neck to look at me."

Barry moves away from her at an angle that also brings him to the parapet, eight feet down from where she's sitting. He glances once over the edge, his insides contracting.

"All right, let's hear it," she says.

"I'm sorry?"

"Aren't you here to talk me off? Give it your best shot."

He decided what he would say riding up in the elevator, recalling his suicide training. Now, squarely in the moment, he feels less confident. The only thing he's sure of is that his feet are freezing.

"I know everything feels hopeless to you in this moment, but this is just a moment, and moments pass."

Ann stares straight down the side of the building, four hundred feet to the street below, her palms flat against the stone that has been weathered by decades of acid rain. All she would have to do is push off. He suspects she's walking herself through the motions, tiptoeing up to the thought of doing it. Amassing that final head of steam.

He notices she's shivering.

"May I give you my jacket?" he asks.

"I'm pretty sure you don't want to come any closer, Detective."

"Why is that?"

"I have FMS."

Barry resists the urge to run. Of course he's heard of False Memory Syndrome, but he's never known or met someone with the affliction. Never breathed the same air. He isn't sure he should attempt to grab her now. Doesn't even want to be this close. No, fuck that. If she moves to jump, he'll try to save her, and if he contracts FMS in the process, so be it. That's the risk you take becoming a cop.

"How long have you had it?" he asks.

"One morning, about a month ago, instead of my home in Middlebury, Vermont, I was suddenly in an apartment here in the city, with a stabbing pain in my head and a terrible nosebleed. At first, I had no idea where I was. Then I remembered . . . *this* life too. Here and now, I'm single, an investment banker, I live under my maiden name. But I have . . ."—she visibly braces herself against the emotion—"memories of my other life in Vermont. I was a mother to a nine-year-old boy named Sam. I ran a landscaping business with my husband, Joe Behrman. I was Ann Behrman. We were as happy as anyone has a right to be."

"What does it feel like?" Barry asks, taking a clandestine step closer.

"What does what feel like?"

"Your false memories of this Vermont life."

"I don't just remember my wedding. I remember the fight over the design for the cake. I remember the smallest details of our home. Our son. Every moment of his birth. His laugh. The birthmark on his left cheek. His first day of school and how he didn't want me to leave him. But when I try to picture Sam, he's in black and white. There's no color in his eyes. I tell myself they were blue. I only see black.

"All my memories from that life are in shades of gray, like film noir stills. They feel real, but they're haunted, phantom memories." She breaks down. "Everyone thinks FMS is just false memories of the big moments of your life, but what hurts so much more are the small ones. I don't just remember my husband. I remember the smell of his breath in the morning when he rolled over and faced me in bed. How every time he got up before I did to brush his teeth, I knew he'd come back to bed and try to have sex. That's the stuff that kills me. The tiniest, perfect details that make me know it happened."

"What about this life?" Barry asks. "Isn't it worth something to you?"

"Maybe some people get FMS and prefer their current memories to their false ones, but there's nothing about this life I want. I've tried, for four long weeks. I can't fake it anymore." Tears carve trails through her eyeliner. "My son never existed. Do you get that? He's just a beautiful misfire in my brain."

Barry ventures another step toward her, but she catches him this time.

"Don't come any closer."

"You are not alone."

"I am very fucking alone."

"I've only known you a few minutes, and I will be devastated if you do this. Think about the people in your life who love you. Think how they'll feel."

"I tracked Joe down," Ann says.

"Who?"

"My husband. He was living in a mansion out on Long Island. He acted like he didn't recognize me, but I know he did. He had a whole other life. He was married—I don't know to who. I don't know if he had kids. He acted like *I* was crazy."

"I'm sorry, Ann."

"This hurts too much."

"Look, I've been where you are. I've wanted to end everything. And I'm standing here right now telling you I'm glad I didn't. I'm glad I had the strength to ride it out. This low point isn't the book of your life. It's just a chapter."

"What happened to you?"

"I lost my daughter. Life has broken my heart too."

Ann looks at the incandescent skyline. "Do you have photos of her? Do you still talk with people about her?"

"Yes."

"At least she once existed."

There is simply nothing he can say to that.

Ann looks down through her legs again. She kicks off one of her pumps.

Watches it fall.

Then sends the other one plummeting after it.

"Ann, please."

"In my previous life, my false life, Joe's first wife, Franny, jumped from this building, from this ledge actually, fifteen years ago. She had clinical depression. I know he blamed himself. Before I left his house on Long Island, I told Joe I was going to jump from the Poe

Building tonight, just like Franny. It sounds silly and desperate, but I hoped he'd show up here tonight and save me. Like he failed to do for her. At first, I thought you might be him, but he never wore cologne." She smiles—wistful—then adds, "I'm thirsty."

Barry glances through the French doors and the dark office, sees two patrolmen standing at the ready by the reception desk. He looks back at Ann. "Then why don't you climb down from there, and we'll walk inside together and get you a glass of water."

"Would you bring it to me out here?"

"I can't leave you."

Her hands are shaking now, and he registers a sudden resolve in her eyes.

She looks at Barry. "This isn't your fault," she says. "It was always going to end this way."

"Ann, no—"

"My son has been erased."

And with a casual grace, she eases herself off the edge.

HELENA

October 22, 2007

Standing in the shower at six a.m., trying to wake up as the hot water sluices down her skin, Helena is struck with an intense sensation of having lived this exact moment before. It's nothing new. Déjà vu has plagued her since her twenties. Besides, there's nothing particularly special about this moment in the shower. She's wondering if Mountainside Capital has reviewed her proposal yet. It's been a week. She should've heard something by now. They should've at least called her in for a meeting if they were interested.

She brews a pot of coffee and makes her go-to breakfast—black beans, three eggs over-easy, drizzled with ketchup. Sits at the little table by the window, watching the sky fill with light over her neighborhood on the outskirts of San Jose.

She hasn't had a day to do laundry in over a month, and the floor of her bedroom is practically carpeted in dirty clothes. She digs through the piles until she finds a T-shirt and a pair of jeans she isn't totally ashamed to leave the house in.

The phone rings while she's brushing her teeth. She spits, rinses, and catches the call on the fourth ring in her bedroom.

"How's my girl?"

Her father's voice always makes her smile.

"Hey, Dad."

"I thought I'd missed you. I didn't want to bother you at the lab."

"No, it's fine, what's up?"

"Just thinking about you. Any word on your proposal?"

"Nothing yet."

"I have a really good feeling it's going to happen."

"I don't know. This is a tough town. Lots of competition. Lots of really smart people looking for money."

"But not as smart as my girl."

She can't take any more of her father's belief in her. Not on a morning like this, with the specter of failure looming large, sitting in a small, filthy bedroom of a blank-walled, undecorated house where she has not brought a single person in over a year.

"How's the weather?" she asks to change the subject.

"Snowed last night. First of the season."

"A lot?"

"Just an inch or two. But the mountains are white."

She can picture them—the Front Range of the Rockies, the mountains of her childhood.

"How's Mom?"

There's the briefest pause.

"Your mother's doing well."

"Dad."

"What?"

"How's Mom?"

She hears him exhale slowly. "We've had better days."

"Is she OK?"

"Yes. She's upstairs sleeping right now."

"What happened?"

"It's nothing."

"Tell me."

"Last night, we played gin rummy after dinner, like we always do. And she just . . . she didn't know the rules anymore. Sat at the kitchen table, staring at her cards, tears running down her face. We've been playing together for thirty years."

She hears his hand cover the receiver.

He's crying, a thousand miles away.

"Dad, I'm coming home."

"No, Helena."

"You need my help."

"We have good support here. We're going to the doctor this afternoon. If you want to help your mother, get your funding and build your chair."

She doesn't want to tell him, but the chair is still years away. *Light-years* away. It's a dream, a mirage.

Her eyes fill with tears. "You know I'm doing this for her."

"I know, sweetheart."

For a moment, they're both quiet, trying to cry without the other knowing, and failing miserably. She wants nothing more than to tell him it's going to happen, but that would be a lie.

"I'm going to call when I get home tonight," she says.

"OK."

"Please tell Mom I love her."

"I will. But she already knows."

———

Four hours later, deep in the neuroscience building in Palo Alto, Helena is examining the image of a mouse's memory of being afraid—fluorescently illuminated neurons interconnected by a spiderweb of synapses—when the stranger appears in her office doorway. She looks over the top of her monitor at a man dressed in chinos and a white T-shirt, with a smile several shades too bright.

"Helena Smith?" he asks.

"Yes?"

"I'm Jee-woon Chercover. Do you have a minute to speak with me?"

"This is a secure lab. You're not supposed to be down here."

"I apologize for the intrusion, but I think you'll want to hear what I have to say."

She could ask him to leave, or call security. But he doesn't look threatening.

"OK," she says, and it suddenly dawns on her that this man is bearing witness to the hoarder's dream that is her office—windowless, cramped, painted-over cinder-block walls, everything only made more claustrophobic by the bankers' boxes stacked three feet high and two deep around her desk, filled with thousands of abstracts and articles. "Sorry about the mess. Let me get you a chair."

"I got it."

Jee-woon drags a folding chair over and takes a seat across from her, his eyes passing over the walls, which are nearly covered in high-resolution images of mouse memories and the neuronal firings of dementia and Alzheimer's patients.

"What can I do for you?" she asks.

"My employer is very taken with the memory portraiture article you published in *Neuron*."

"Does your employer have a name?"

"Well, that depends."

"On . . . ?"

"How this conversation goes."

"Why would I even have a conversation with someone when I don't know who they're speaking for?"

"Because your Stanford money runs out in six weeks."

She raises an eyebrow.

He says, "My boss pays me very well to know everything about the people he finds interesting."

"You do realize what you just said is totally creepy, right?"

Reaching into his leather satchel, Jee-woon takes out a document in a navy binder.

Her proposal.

"Of course!" she says. "You're with Mountainside Capital!"

"No. And they're not going to fund you."

"Then how did you get that?"

"It doesn't matter. No one is going to fund you."

"How do you know?"

"Because this?" He tosses her grant proposal onto the wreckage of her desk. "Is timid. It's just more of what you've been doing at Stanford the last three years. It's not big-idea enough. You're thirty-eight years old, which is like ninety in academia. One morning in the not-too-distant future, you're going to wake up and realize your best days are behind you. That you wasted—"

"I think you should leave."

"I don't mean to insult you. If you don't mind my saying, your problem is that you're afraid to ask for what you really want." It occurs to her that, for some reason, this stranger is trolling her. She knows she shouldn't continue to engage, but she can't help herself.

"And why am I afraid to ask for what I really want?"

"Because what you really want is bank-breaking. You don't need seven figures. You need nine. Maybe ten. You need a team of coders to help you design an algorithm for complex memory cataloging and projection. The infrastructure for human trials."

She stares at him across the desk. "I never mentioned human trials in that proposal."

"What if I were to tell you that we will give you anything you ask for? No-limit funding. Would you be interested?"

Her heart is beating faster and faster.

Is this how it happens?

She thinks of the fifty-million-dollar chair she has dreamed of building since her mom started to forget life. Strangely, she never imagines it fully rendered, only as the technical drawings in the utility patent application she will one day file, entitled *Immersive Platform for Projection of Long-Term, Explicit, Episodic Memories.*

"Helena?"

"If I say yes, will you tell me who your boss is?"

"Yes."

"Yes."

He tells her.

As her jaw hits the desk, Jee-woon pulls another document out of his satchel and passes it to her over the bankers' boxes.

"What's this?" she asks.

"An employment and confidentiality agreement. Nonnegotiable. I think you'll find the financial terms to be very generous."

BARRY

November 4, 2018

The café occupies a picturesque spot on the banks of the Hudson, in the shadow of the West Side Highway. Barry arrives five minutes early to find Julia already seated at a table under an umbrella. They share a brief, fragile embrace, as if they're both made of glass.

"It's good to see you," he says.

"I'm glad you wanted to come."

They sit. A waiter swings by to take their drink orders.

"How's Anthony?" Barry asks.

"Great. Busy with the redesign of the Lewis Building lobby. Your work's good?"

He doesn't tell her about the suicide he failed to stop the night before last. Instead, they make small talk until the coffee arrives.

It's Sunday, and the brunch crowd is out in force. Every table in the vicinity seems to be a geyser of gregarious conversation and laughter, but they sip their coffees quietly in the shade.

Nothing and everything to say.

A butterfly flutters around Barry's head until he gently brushes it away.

Sometimes, late in the night, he imagines elaborate conversations with Julia. Exchanges where he says everything that has been festering all these years in his heart—the pain, the anger, the love—and then listens as she does the same. A clearing of air to the point where he finally understands her and she understands him.

But in person, it never feels right. He can't bring himself to say what's in his heart, which always feels clenched and locked up, encased in scar tissue. The awkwardness doesn't bother him like it used to. He has made peace with the idea that part of life is facing your failures, and sometimes those failures are people you once loved.

"I wonder what she'd be doing today," Julia says.

"I hope she'd be sitting here with us."

"I mean for work."

"Ah. A lawyer of course."

Julia laughs—one of the greatest sounds he's ever encountered—and he can't remember the last time he heard it. Beautiful but also crushing to experience. Like a secret window into the person he used to know.

"She would argue about anything," Julia says. "And she usually won."

"We were pushovers."

"One of us was."

"Me?" he says with faux outrage.

"By five years old, she had you pegged as the weak link."

"Remember the time she convinced us to let her practice backing up in the driveway—"

"Convinced you."

"—and she drove my car through the garage door?"

Julia snorts a laugh. "She was so upset."

"No, embarrassed." For a half second, his mind's eye conjures the memory. Or at least a piece of it. Meghan behind the wheel of his old Camry, the back half punched through the garage door, her face red and tears streaming down it as she white-knuckle-clenched the steering wheel. "She was tenacious and smart and would've done something interesting with her life." He finishes his coffee and pours another cup from the stainless-steel French press they're sharing.

"It's nice to talk about her," Julia says.

"I'm glad I finally can."

The waiter comes to take their food orders, and the butterfly returns, alighting on the surface of the table next to Barry's still-folded napkin. Stretching its wings. Preening. He tries to push the idea out of his mind that it's Meghan, somehow haunting him on today of all days. It's a stupid notion, of course, but the thought persists. Like the time a robin followed him for eight blocks in NoHo. Or on a recent walk with his dog in Fort Washington Park, when a ladybug kept landing on his wrist.

As the food arrives, Barry imagines Meghan sitting at the table with them. The rough edges of adolescence sanded down. Her entire life ahead of her. He can't see her face, no matter how hard he tries, only her hands, in constant motion as she talks, the same way her mother moves when she's confident and excited about something.

He isn't hungry, but he makes himself eat. It seems like there's something on Julia's mind, but she just picks at the remains of her frittata, and he takes a drink of water and another bite of his sandwich and stares at the river in the distance.

The Hudson comes from a pond in the Adirondacks called Lake Tear of the Clouds. They went there one summer when Meghan was eight or nine. Camped in the spruce trees. Watched the stars fall. Tried to wrap their minds around the notion that this tiny mountain lake was the source of the Hudson. It's a memory he returns to almost obsessively.

"You look thoughtful," Julia says.

"I was thinking of that trip we took to Lake Tear of the Clouds. Remember?"

"Of course. It took us two hours to get the tent up in a rainstorm."

"I thought it was clear."

She shakes her head. "No, we shivered in the tent all night and none of us slept."

"You sure about that?"

"Yes. That trip was the foundation of my never-again wilderness policy."

"Right."

"How could you forget that?"

"I don't know." The truth is he does it constantly. He is always looking back, living more in memories than the present, often altering them to make them prettier. To make them perfect. Nostalgia is as much an analgesic for him as alcohol. He says finally, "Maybe watching shooting stars with my girls felt like a better memory."

She tosses her napkin on her plate and leans back in her chair. "I went by our old house recently. Wow, it's changed. You ever do that?"

"Every now and then."

In actuality, he still drives past their old house anytime he has business in Jersey. He and Julia lost it in a foreclosure the year after Meghan died, and today it barely resembles the place they lived in. The trees are taller, fuller, greener. There's an addition above the garage, and a young family lives there now. The entire façade has been redone in stone, new windows added. The driveway widened and repaved. The rope swing that used to hang from the oak tree was taken down years ago, but the initials he and Meghan once carved at the base of the trunk remain. He touched them last summer—having somehow decided that a cab ride to Jersey at two in the morning after a night out with Gwen and the rest of Central Robbery Division was a good idea. A Jersey City cop had arrived after the new owners called 911 to report a vagrant in their front yard. Though stumbling drunk, he wasn't arrested. The cop knew of Barry, of what had happened to him. He called another taxi and helped Barry into the backseat. Paid the fare back to Manhattan in advance and sent him on his way.

The breeze coming off the water carries a cool bite, and the sun is warm on his shoulders—a pleasing contrast. Tourist boats go up and down the river. The noise of traffic is ceaseless on the highway above. The sky crisscrossed with the fading contrails of a thousand jets. It is late autumn in the city, one of the last good days of the year.

He thinks how it will be winter soon, and then another year gone by and another one on the chopping block, time flowing faster and faster. Life is nothing how he expected it would be when he was young and living under the delusion that things could be controlled. Nothing can be controlled. Only endured.

The check comes and Julia tries to pay, but he snatches it away and throws down his card.

"Thank you, Barry."

"Thank you for inviting me."

"Let's not go a year again without seeing each other." She raises her glass of ice water. "To our birthday girl."

"To our birthday girl." He can feel the cloud of grief coalescing in his chest, but he breathes through it, and when he speaks again his voice is almost normal. "Twenty-six years old."

After brunch, he walks to Central Park. The silence of his apartment feels like a threat on Meghan's birthday, the last five of which have not gone well.

Seeing Julia always upends him. For a long time after their marriage ended, he thought he missed his ex. Thought he would never get over her. He would often dream of her and wake to the ache of her absence eating him alive. The dreams cut him deeply—half memory, half fantasy—because in them, she felt like the Julia of old. The smile. The unhesitating laugh. The lightness of being. She was the person who stole his heart again. All through the following morning, she'd be on his mind, the totality of that loss staring him down, unblinking, until the emotional hangover of the dream finally released its hold on him like a slowly lifting fog. He saw Julia once, in the wake of one such dream—an unexpected bump-in at the party of an old friend. To his surprise, he felt nothing as they chatted stiffly on the veranda. Being in her presence slashed through the dream-withdrawal; he didn't want her. It was a liberating revelation, even as it devastated him. Liberating because it meant he didn't love this Julia—he loved the person she used to be. Devastating because the woman who haunted his dreams was truly gone. As unreachable as the dead.

The trees in the park are peaking after a hard freeze several nights ago, the leaves all frost-burned into late autumn brilliance.

He finds a spot in the Ramble, takes off his shoes and socks, and leans back against a perfectly slanted tree. He pulls out his phone and tries to read the biography he's been plodding through for nearly a year, but concentration is elusive.

Ann Voss Peters haunts him. The way she fell without a sound, her body rigid and upright. It took five seconds, and he didn't look away when she hit the Lincoln Town Car, parked on the curb below.

When he isn't replaying their conversation, he's grappling with the fear. Pressure-checking his memories. Testing their fidelity. Wondering—

How would I know if one had changed? What would it feel like?

Red and orange leaves drift down through the sunlight, accumulating all around him in the dappled shade. From his vantage in the trees, he watches people walking the trails, moseying by the lake. Most are with others, but some are alone like him.

His phone pops a text from his friend Gwendoline Archer, leader of the Hercules Team, a counterterrorism SWAT unit in the NYPD's Emergency Service Unit.

Thinking about you today. You OK?

He writes her back:

Yeah. Just saw Julia.

How was that?

Good. Hard. What are you up to?

Just finished a ride. Drinking at
Isaac's. Want some company?

God yes. OMW.

It's a forty-minute walk to the bar near Gwen's apartment in Hell's Kitchen, whose only apparent virtue is its forty-five-year longevity. Prickly bartenders serve boring domestics on tap and not a single whiskey whose bottle you couldn't buy in a store for under thirty bucks. The bathrooms are disgusting and still contain stocked condom dispensers. The jukebox plays '70s and '80s rock exclusively, and if no one feeds the box, there is no music.

Gwen is sitting at the far end of the bar, wearing biker shorts and a faded Brooklyn Marathon T-shirt, left-swiping on a dating app as Barry approaches.

He says, "I thought you gave up on that."

"For a while, I gave up on your gender entirely, but my therapist is all the way up my ass to try again."

She slides off the stool and embraces him, the faint smell of sweat from her ride combining with the remnants of body wash and deodorant, resulting in something like a salted caramel.

He says, "Thanks for checking in on me."

"You shouldn't be alone today."

She's fifteen years younger, in her mid-thirties, and at six feet, four inches, the tallest woman he knows personally. With short blond hair and Scandinavian features, she's not beautiful exactly, but regal. Often severe without trying. He once told her she had resting monarch face.

They met and bonded during a bank robbery turned hostage situation a few years back. The next Christmas, they hooked up in one of the more embarrassing moments of Barry's existence. It was one of the many NYPD holiday parties, and the night had gotten away from them both. He woke in her apartment at three in the morning with the room still spinning. His mistake was trying to sneak out when he wasn't ready for consciousness. He threw up on the floor beside her bed, and was in the midst of trying to clean it up when Gwen woke and yelled at him, "I will clean up your puke in the morning, just go!" He remembers nothing of the sex, if they had it or attempted to, and he can only hope she shares the same merciful gap in her memory.

Regardless, neither of them has acknowledged it since.

The bartender arrives to take Barry's order and deliver another Wild Turkey to Gwen. They drink and bullshit for a while, and as Barry finally registers the world beginning to loosen, Gwen says, "I heard you caught an FMS suicide Friday night."

"Yeah."

He fills her in on all the details.

"Be honest," she says. "How freaked out are you?"

"Well, I did make myself an Internet expert on FMS yesterday."

"And?"

"Eight months ago, the Centers for Disease Control identified sixty-four cases with similarities in the Northeast. In each case, a patient presented with complaints of acute false memories. Not just one or two. A fully imagined alternate history covering large swaths of their life up until that moment. Usually going back months or years. In some instances, decades."

"So do they lose their memories of their real life?"

"No, they suddenly have *two sets* of memories. One true, one false. In some cases, patients felt like their memories and consciousness had moved from one life into another. In others, patients experienced a sudden 'flash-in' of false memories from a life they never lived."

"What causes it?"

"Nobody knows. They haven't identified a single physiological or neurological abnormality in those who are affected. The only symptoms are the false memories themselves. Oh, and about ten percent of people who get it kill themselves."

"Jesus."

"The number could be higher. Way higher. That's the outcome of known cases."

"Suicides are up this year in the five boroughs."

Barry catches the bartender's eye, gives the signal for another round.

Gwen asks, "Contagious?"

"I couldn't find a definitive answer. The CDC hasn't found a pathogen, so it doesn't seem to be blood- or airborne. Yet. This article in *The New England Journal of Medicine* speculated that it actually spreads through a carrier's social network."

"Like Facebook? How is that even—"

"No, I mean when a person is infected with FMS, some of the people they know become infected. Their parents will share the same false memories, but to a lesser degree. Their brothers, sisters, close friends. There was this case study of a guy who woke up one day and had memories of an entirely different life. Being married to a different woman. Living in a different house, with different kids, working a different job. They reconstructed from his memory the guest list of his wedding—the one that he remembered, but never happened. They located thirteen from his list, and all of them also had memories of this wedding that never happened. Ever hear of something called the Mandela Effect?"

"I don't know. Maybe."

The next round comes. Barry drinks his shot of Old Grand-Dad and chases it with a Coors as the light through the front windows fades toward evening.

He says, "Apparently thousands of people remember Nelson Mandela dying in prison in the 1980s, even though he lived until 2013."

"I have heard of this. It's the whole Berenstain Bears thing."

"I don't know what that is."

"You're too old."

"Fuck you."

"There were these children's books when I was a kid, and a lot of people remember them being called *The Berenstein Bears*, S-T-E-I-N, when it's actually spelled Berenstain. S-T-A-I-N."

"Weird."

"Scary actually, since I remember Berenstein." Gwen shoots her whiskey.

"Also—and no one's sure if it's related to FMS—instances of acute déjà vu are on the rise."

"What does that mean?"

"People are struck, sometimes to a debilitating degree, with the sense that they're living entire sequences of their lives over."

"I get that sometimes."

"Me too."

Gwen says, "Didn't your jumper say that her husband's first wife had also thrown herself off the Poe Building?"

"Yeah, why?"

"I don't know. Just seems . . . unlikely."

Barry looks at her. The bar is getting full and loud.

"What are you getting at?" he asks.

"Maybe she didn't have False Memory Syndrome. Maybe this bitch was just crazy. Maybe don't worry so much."

———

Three hours later, he's wasted in a different bar—a wood-paneled, beer-lover's wet dream with the taxidermied heads of buffalo and deer protruding from the walls and a million taps lining the backlit shelves.

Gwen tries to take him to dinner, but the hostess sees him wavering on his feet in front of her podium and refuses them a table. Back outside, the city feels unmoored, and Barry is laser-focused on making the buildings not spin as Gwen holds him by his right arm, steering him down the street.

He suddenly realizes they're standing on a street corner Godknows-where, speaking to a cop. Gwen is showing the patrolman her star and explaining that she's trying to get Barry home but is afraid he'll throw up in a cab.

Then they're walking again, stumbling, the futuristic, nighttime brilliance of Times Square swirling like a bad carnival. He catches the time, 11:22 p.m., and wonders what black hole the last six hours fell into.

"I don't wannagohome," he says to no one.

Then he's staring at a digital clock that reads 4:15. It feels like someone caved his skull in while he slept, and his tongue is as dry as a strip of leather. This isn't his apartment. He's lying on the sofa in Gwen's living room.

He tries to go back and Scotch-tape the evening together but the pieces are shattered. He remembers Julia and the park. The first hour of the first bar with Gwen. But everything after is murky and tinged with regret.

His heart pounds in his ears. His mind races.

It is the lonely hour of the night, one with which he is all too familiar—when the city sleeps but you don't, and all the regrets of your life rage in your mind with an unbearable intensity.

Thinking about his father who died when he was young, and the enduring question—*Did he know that I loved him?*

And Meghan. Always Meghan.

When his daughter was a little girl, she was convinced a monster lived in the hope chest at the foot of her bed. It never crossed her mind in the daylight, but the moment the sun went down and he had tucked her in for the night, she would inevitably call out for him. And he'd hurry to her room and kneel beside her bed and remind her that everything seems scarier at night. It's just an illusion. A trick the darkness plays on us.

How strange then, decades later and his life so far off the course he charted, to find himself alone on a couch in a friend's apartment, attempting to assuage his fears with the same logic he used on his child all those years ago.

Everything will look better in the morning.

There will be hope again when the light returns.

The despair is only an illusion, a trick the darkness plays.

And he shuts his eyes and comforts himself with the memory of the camping trip to Lake Tear of the Clouds. To that perfect moment.

In it, the stars were shining.

He'd stay there forever if he could.

HELENA

November 1, 2007

Day 1

Her stomach is in knots as she watches the Northern California coastline dwindling away. She's sitting behind the pilot, under the roar of the rotors, watching the ocean stream beneath her, five hundred feet below the helicopter skids.

It is not a good day at sea. The clouds drape low; the water is gray and specked with whitecaps. And the farther from land they go, the darker the world becomes.

Through the helicopter's rain-streaked windshield, she sees

something materializing in the distance—a structure jutting out of the water, still a mile or two away.

She says into her microphone, "Is that it?"

"Yes ma'am."

Leaning forward against the shoulder harness, she watches with intense curiosity as the chopper begins its approach, slowing now, descending toward a colossus of iron, steel, and concrete that stands on three legs in the ocean like a giant tripod. The pilot pushes the stick and they bank left into a slow circle around the structure, whose main platform sits approximately twenty stories above the sea. A few cranes still overhang the sides—relics from the oil- and gas-drilling days. But otherwise, the rig has been stripped of its industrial trappings and transformed. On the primary platform, she sees a full basketball court. Swimming pool. Greenhouse. What appears to be a running track around the perimeter.

They land on a helipad. The turbo shaft begins to wind down, and through her window, Helena watches a man in a yellow bomber jacket jogging toward the helicopter. As he opens the cabin door, she fumbles with the three-point locking mechanism on her restraints until they finally unlatch.

The man helps her out of the chopper, down onto the skid, and then the landing surface. She follows him toward a set of stairs that descends from the helipad onto the main platform. The wind rips through her hoodie and T-shirt, and as she reaches the steps, the sound of the helicopter dies away, leaving the gaping silence of the open ocean.

They come off the last step onto a sprawling concrete surface, and there he is, moving toward them across the platform.

Her heart kicks.

His beard is unkempt, his dark hair wild and blowing in the wind. He is wearing a pair of blue jeans and a faded sweatshirt, and he is unmistakably Marcus Slade—inventor, philanthropist, business magnate, founder of more groundbreaking technology companies than she can name, touching sectors as diverse as cloud computing, transportation, space, and AI. He is one of the world's richest, most influential citizens. A high-school dropout. And only thirty-four years old.

He smiles and says, "We're doing this!"

His enthusiasm calms her nerves, and as they reach each other on the platform, she's unsure what's called for. A handshake? Polite hug? Slade makes the choice for her with a warm embrace.

"Welcome to Fawkes Station."

"Fawkes?"

"As in Guy Fawkes—remember, remember the fifth of November?"

"Oh. Right. Because memory?"

"Because disrupting the status quo is kind of my thing. You must be cold, let's get you inside." They're moving now, heading toward a five-story superstructure on the far side of the platform.

"Not quite what I was expecting," Helena says.

"I bought it a few years ago from ExxonMobil when the oil field ran dry. At first I was going to make this a new home for myself."

"You mean a fortress of solitude?"

"Totally. But then I realized I could live here and also use it as the perfect research facility."

"Why perfect?"

"A million reasons, but the most critical are privacy and security. I have my hands in a number of fields that are rife with corporate espionage, and this is about as controllable an environment as you can get, right?"

They pass the swimming pool, covered for the season, the tarp flapping violently in the November wind.

She says, "First off, thank you. Secondly, why me?"

"Because inside your head is a technology that could alter humanity."

"How so?"

"What's more precious than our memories?" he asks. "They define us and form our identities."

"Also, there will be a fifteen-billion-dollar market for Alzheimer's treatments in the next decade."

Marcus only smiles.

She says, "Just so you know, my primary goal is to help people. I want to find a way to save memories for deteriorating brains that can no longer retrieve them. A time capsule for core memories."

"I hear that. Can you think of any reason this can't be both a philanthropic and commercial endeavor?"

They pass the entrance to a large greenhouse, the walls inside steamed and dripping with condensation.

"How far offshore are we?" she asks, looking across the platform out to sea, where a dense cloud is rolling toward them.

"One hundred seventy-three miles. How'd your family and friends take the news that you were falling off the face of the Earth to do some super-secret research?"

She isn't sure how to answer that. Her life as of late has unspooled under the fluorescent lights of laboratories and revolved around the processing of raw data. She has never managed to achieve escape velocity from the irresistible gravity of her work—for her mom, but if she's honest, also for herself. Work is the only thing that makes her feel alive, and she's wondered, on more than one occasion, if that means she's broken.

"I work a lot," she says, "so I only had six people to tell. My dad cried, but he always cries. No one was really surprised. God, that sounds pathetic, doesn't it?"

Slade looks at her, says, "I think balance is for people who don't know why they're here."

She considers that. In high school, in college, she was encouraged again and again to find her passion—a reason to get out of bed and breathe. In her experience, few people ever found that raison d'être.

What teachers and professors never told her was about the dark side of finding your purpose. The part where it consumes you. Where it becomes a destroyer of relationships and happiness. And still, she wouldn't trade it. This is the only person she knows how to be.

They're approaching the entrance to the superstructure.

"Hold up a second," Slade says. "Watch." He points toward the wall of mist as it plows across the platform. The air becomes cold and silent. Helena can't even see to the helipad. They're caught in the heart of a cloud.

Slade looks at her. "Do you want to change the world with me?"

"That's why I'm here."

"Good. Let's go see what I've built for you."

BARRY

November 5, 2018

NEW YORK CITY POLICE DEPARTMENT

24TH PRECINCT, 151 W 100TH ST.

NEW YORK, NY 10025

* CHIEF OF POLICE   * TELEPHONE

JOHN R. POOLE   (212) 555-1811

[X] PRELIMINARY POLICE REPORT

[ ] SUPPLEMENTAL REPORT

CSRR	DATE	TIME	DAY	LOCATION
01457C	07/11/03	2130	FRI	2000 WEST 102ND
				41ST FLOOR

NATURE OF REPORT

POLICE—NARRATIVE

I, PO RIVELLI, WHILE ON PATROL, RESPONDED TO A 10-56A AT THE POE BUILDING ON THE TERRACE OF THE

HULTQUIST LLC OFFICES. I FOUND A WOMAN STANDING ON
THE LEDGE. I IDENTIFIED MYSELF AS A POLICE OFFICER
AND ASKED HER TO PLEASE STEP DOWN. SHE REFUSED TO
COMPLY AND WARNED ME NOT TO COME NEAR HER OR SHE
WOULD JUMP. I ASKED HER NAME AND SHE TOLD ME IT WAS
FRANNY BEHRMAN [W/F DOB 12/06/63 OF 509 E 110TH ST].
SHE DID NOT APPEAR TO BE UNDER THE INFLUENCE OF ANY
DRUGS OR ALCOHOL. I ASKED HER IF THERE WAS ANYONE I
COULD CALL FOR HER. SHE SAID "NO." I ASKED WHY SHE
WANTED TO END HER LIFE. SHE SAID NOTHING BROUGHT HER
HAPPINESS, AND THAT HER HUSBAND AND FAMILY WOULD BE
BETTER OFF WITHOUT HER. I ASSURED HER THIS WAS NOT
THE CASE.

AT THIS POINT, SHE STOPPED RESPONDING TO MY
QUESTIONS AND SEEMED TO BE BUILDING THE NERVE TO
JUMP. I WAS ON THE VERGE OF ATTEMPTING TO PHYSICALLY
REMOVE HER FROM THE LEDGE WHEN I RECEIVED A RADIO
COMMUNICATION FROM PO DECARLO, ADVISING THAT MRS.
BEHRMAN'S HUSBAND [JOE BEHRMAN, W/M DOB 3/12/61 OF
509 E 110TH ST.] WAS COMING UP THE ELEVATOR TO SEE
HIS WIFE. I ADVISED MRS. BEHRMAN OF THIS.

MR. BEHRMAN ARRIVED ON THE ROOF. HE APPROACHED HIS
WIFE AND CONVINCED HER TO STEP BACK ONTO THE TERRACE.

I ESCORTED MR. AND MRS. BEHRMAN DOWN TO THE
STREET, AND SHE WAS TRANSFERRED VIA AMBULANCE TO
SISTERS OF MERCY HOSPITAL FOR EVALUATION.

REPORT OF PO RIVELLI   OFFICER IN CHARGE SGT-DAWES

Massively hungover and sitting at his desk in the field of cubicles,
Barry reads the incident report for a third time. It's making his
brain itch in all the wrong ways, because it's the exact opposite of

what Ann Voss Peters said had happened between her husband and his first wife. She thought that Franny had jumped.

He sets the report aside, wakes his monitor, and logs into the New York State DMV database, his head throbbing behind his eyes.

His search for Joe and Franny Behrman turns up a last-known address of 6 Pinewood Lane in Montauk.

He should let this fall to the wayside. Forget about FMS and Ann Voss Peters and get on with the listing towers of paperwork and open case files that clutter his desk. There is no crime here to justify his time. Only . . . inconsistencies.

But the truth is—now he's madly curious.

He's been a detective for twenty-three years because he loves solving puzzles, and this one, this contradictory set of events, is whispering to him—a misalignment he feels a compulsion to put right.

He could get written up for driving his Crown Vic out to the end of Long Island on something that was decidedly not sanctioned, jurisdictional police business, and his head hurts too much to drive that far anyway.

So he pulls up the MTA website and studies the schedules.

There's a train leaving Penn Station for Montauk in just under an hour.

HELENA

January 18, 2008–October 29, 2008

Day 79

Living on Slade's decommissioned oil rig is like getting paid to stay at a five-star resort that also happens to be your office. She wakes each morning on the superstructure's top level, where all the crew quarters are located. Hers is a spacious corner apartment with floor-to-ceiling windows made of rain-repellant glass. They atomize water droplets so that even in the worst weather, her view of the endless sea remains unobstructed. Once a week, housekeepers clean her apartment and take out her laundry. A Michelin-starred chef prepares most meals, often using fresh-caught fish, and fruit and vegetables harvested from the greenhouse.

Marcus insists that she exercise five days a week to keep her spirits up and her mind sharp. There's a gym on the first level, which she uses when the weather is bad, and on the rare calm days of winter, she goes running on the track that circumnavigates the platform. She loves those runs the most, because it feels like she's doing laps at the top of the world.

Her research lab is 10,000 square feet—the entire third floor of the Fawkes Station superstructure—and she has made more progress in the last ten weeks than during her entire five-year stint at Stanford. Anything she needs, she gets. There are no bills to pay, no relationships to maintain. Nothing to do but single-mindedly pursue her research.

Up until now, she had been manipulating memories in mice, working with specific cell clusters that had been genetically engineered to be light-sensitive. Once a cell cluster had been labeled and associated with a stored memory (for instance, an electrical shock), she would then reactivate the memory of the mouse's fear by targeting those light-sensitive cell clusters with a special optogenetics laser inserted via filaments through the mouse's skull.

Her work on the oil platform is a whole other ball game.

Helena is leading the group tackling the main problem, which also happens to be her area of specialization—tagging and cataloging the neuron clusters connected to a particular memory, and then reconstructing a digital model of the brain that allows them to track memories and map them out.

In principle, it's no different from what she did with mouse brains, but orders of magnitude more complex.

The technology the other three teams are handling is challenging, but not groundbreaking—cutting-edge tech, yes, but with the right personnel and Marcus's giant checkbook, they should be able to re-create it with no serious roadblocks.

She has twenty people working under her across four groups. She's heading up the Mapping Team. The Imaging Team has been tasked with finding some way of filming neuronal firings that doesn't involve shoving a laser through a person's skull and into their brain. They've landed on building a device that utilizes an advanced form of magnetoencephalography, or MEG for short. A SQUID (superconducting quantum interference device) array will detect infinitesimal magnetic fields produced by individual neurons firing in the human brain, right down to the level of determining the position of each neuron. They call it the MEG microscope.

The Reactivation Team is building an apparatus that is essentially a vast network of electromagnetic stimulators that forms a shell around the head for 3D pinpoint accuracy and precision-targeting of the hundreds of millions of neurons that are required to reactivate a memory.

And finally, Infrastructure is building the chair for human trials.

It has been a good day. Perhaps even a great one. She met with Slade, Jee-woon, and the project managers to review progress, and everyone is ahead of schedule. It is four o'clock in the afternoon in late January, one of those fleeting winter days of warmth and blue. The sun is plunging into the ocean, turning the clouds and the sea into shades of gray and pink she has never seen before, and she's sitting on the edge of the platform, westward-facing, her legs swinging out over the water.

Two hundred feet below, waves swell and crash against the immense legs of this fortress in the sea.

She cannot believe she is here.

She cannot believe this is her life.

Day 225

The MEG microscope is nearly finished, and the reactivation apparatus has progressed as far as it can while everyone waits for mapping to get their arms around the cataloging problem.

Helena is frustrated with the delay. Over dinner with Slade in his palatial suite, she levels with him—the team is failing because their obstacle is a brute-force problem. Since they're scaling up from mice brains to human brains, the computing power they're working with is insufficient to map something as prodigiously complex as human memory structure. Unless she can figure out a shortcut, they simply don't have the CPU cycles to handle it.

"Ever heard of D-Wave?" Slade asks as Helena takes a sip of a white burgundy, the best wine she has ever tasted.

"Sorry, I haven't."

"It's a company out of British Columbia. A year ago, they released a prototype quantum processor. Its application is highly specific, but ideal for the sort of enormous data-set mapping problem we've run up against."

"How much are they?"

"Not cheap, but I was interested in the technology, so I ordered a few of their advanced prototypes for future projects last summer."

He smiles, and something about the way he studies her across the table leaves her with the unnerving sense that he knows more about her than she should be comfortable with. Her past. Her psychology. What makes her tick. But she can hardly blame him if in fact he has peeled back some of the layers. He's investing years and millions in her mind.

Through the window behind Slade, she sees a single speck of light, miles and miles out to sea, and is struck, not for the first time, by how utterly alone they are out here.

Day 270

The midsummer days are long and sunny, and progress has halted while they await the arrival of two quantum-annealing processors. Helena misses her parents desperately, and their once-a-week talks have become the highlight of her existence here. The distance is having an odd effect on her connection to her father. She feels closer to him than she has in years, since before high school. The smallest details of their lives in Colorado carry a sudden significance. She drinks in the minutiae, and the more boring the better.

Their weekend hikes in the foothills. Reports on how much snow still lingers in the high country. A concert they saw at Red Rocks. Results of her mom's neurologist appointments in Denver. Movies they've seen. Books read. The neighborhood gossip.

Most of the updates come from her dad.

Sometimes her mom is lucid, her old self, and they talk like they always have.

More often, Dorothy struggles to carry a conversation.

Helena is irrationally homesick for all things Colorado. For the long view from her parents' deck across the plain toward the Flatirons, the start of the Rockies. For the color green, since the only foliage to be seen on the rig is the small garden in the greenhouse. But mostly for her mother. She aches to be with her during what must be the scariest time of her life.

The hardest part is not being able to share any details of her tremendous progress on the chair, all of which is covered under an ironclad NDA. She suspects Slade listens in on every conversation. Of course, when she asked him, he denied it, but she still suspects.

Because of confidentiality concerns, no visitors are allowed on the rig, and no crew are given shore leave before their contracts are up, with the exception of family or medical emergencies.

Wednesday evenings have become designated party nights in

an attempt to develop some level of workplace camaraderie. It's a challenge for Helena, a hardcore introvert who, until recently, has led the life of a solitary scientist. They play paintball, volleyball, and basketball on the platform. Grill out by the pool and tap kegs of shipped-in beer. They blast music and get drunk. Sometimes they even dance. The courts and grilling area are enclosed by tall panels of glass to cut the near-constant barrage of wind. But even with the barriers, they often have to shout to be heard.

In foul weather, they gather in the communal wing off the cafeteria to play board games, or hide-and-seek in the superstructure.

As almost everyone's boss on the rig but Slade's, she's hesitant to get close to people on her team. But she's in a desert of water for as far as anyone can possibly see, stranded twenty stories above the ocean. Eschewing friendship and intimacy feels like it would lead her down the path of psychotic isolation.

It's during a game of hide-and-seek, in a top-floor linen closet, that she fucks Sergei—the genius electrical engineer and beautiful man who always destroys her at racquetball. They're standing too close in the dark as the seekers run past their hiding place, and suddenly she's kissing him and pulling him toward her and he's tugging her shorts down and pinning her against the wall.

Marcus brought Sergei over from Moscow. He might be the purest scientist in the group, and he's definitely the most competitive.

But he isn't her "rig crush." That would be Rajesh, the software engineer Slade recently hired in advance of the D-Wave's arrival. There's a warmth and honesty in his eyes that draw her in. He's soft-spoken and hugely intelligent. Over breakfast yesterday, he suggested they start a book club.

Day 302

The quantum processors arrive on a vast container ship. It's like Christmas morning, everyone standing on the deck, watching with a horrified fascination as the rig's crane hoists $30 million worth of computing power two hundred feet up onto the main platform.

Day 312

Mapping is back, the new processors up and running, code being written that will map a memory and upload its neural coordinates into the reactivation apparatus. The sense of having stalled has passed. There is momentum again, Helena's mood shifting from loneliness to exhilaration, but also a sense of wonder at Slade's prescience. Not just at the macro level in predicting the immensity of her vision, but more impressively at the granular—the fact that he knew the perfect tool for handling the vast amount of data associated with mapping human memory. And he knew one processor wouldn't be enough. He bought two.

At her weekly dinner with Slade, she informs him that if progress continues at this pace, they'll be ready for their first human trial in a month.

His face lights up. "Seriously?"

"Seriously. And I'm just letting you know now, I *will* be the first to try it out."

"Sorry. Way too dangerous."

"How is that your decision?"

"A thousand ways. Besides, without you, we'd be lost."

"Marcus, I insist."

"Look, we can discuss this later, but in the meantime let's celebrate."

He goes to his wine fridge and takes out a '47 Cheval Blanc. It takes him a moment to remove the delicate cork, and then he empties the bottle into a crystal decanter.

"Not too much of this left in the world," he says.

The moment Helena lifts the glass to her nose and inhales the sweet, spicy perfume of the ancient grapes, her concept of what wine can be is irrevocably altered.

"To you, and to this moment," Slade says, gently touching his glass against hers.

The taste of it is like what all the wine she's ever had has been aspiring to be, the scales of what is good, great, and transcendent recalibrating in her head.

It is otherworldly.

Warm, rich, opulent, stunningly fresh.

Stewed red fruits, flowers, chocolate, and—

"Been meaning to ask you something," Slade says, interrupting her reverie.

She looks at him across the table.

"Why memory? Obviously, you were into this before your mom got sick."

She swirls the wine in her glass, sees the reflection of them sitting at the table in the two-story windows that look out into oceanic darkness.

"Because memory . . . is everything. Physically speaking, a memory is nothing but a specific combination of neurons firing together—a symphony of neural activity. But in actuality, it's the filter between us and reality. You think you're tasting this wine, hearing the words I'm saying, *in the present*, but there's no such thing. The neural impulses from your taste buds and your ears get transmitted to your brain, which processes them and dumps them into working memory—so by the time you know you're experiencing something, it's already in the past. Already a memory." Helena leans forward, snaps her fingers. "Just what your brain does to interpret a simple stimulus like that is incredible. The visual and auditory information arrive at your eyes and ears at different speeds, and then are processed by your brain at different speeds. Your brain waits for the slowest bit of stimulus to be processed, then reorders the neural inputs correctly, and lets you experience them together, as a simultaneous event—about half a second after what actually happened. We think we're perceiving the world directly and immediately, but everything we experience is this carefully edited, tape-delayed reconstruction."

She lets him sit with that for a moment as she takes another glorious sip of wine.

Slade asks, "What about flashbulb memories? The super-vivid ones imbued with extreme personal significance and emotion?"

"Right. That gets at another illusion. The paradox of the specious present. What we think of as the 'present' isn't actually a moment. It's a stretch of recent time—an arbitrary one. The last two or three seconds, usually. But dump a load of adrenaline into your system, get the amygdala to rev up, and you create that hyper-vivid memory, where time seems to slow down, or stop entirely. If you change the way your brain processes an event, you change the duration of the 'now.' You actually change the point at which the present becomes the past. It's yet another way that the concept of the present is just an illusion, made out of memories and constructed by our brain."

Helena sits back, embarrassed by her enthusiasm, suddenly feeling the wine going to her head. "Which is why memory," she says. "Why neuroscience." She taps her temple. "If you want to understand the world, you have to start by understanding—truly understanding—how we experience it."

Slade nods, says, "'It is evident the mind does not know things immediately, but only by the intervention of the ideas it has of them.'"

Helena laughs with surprise. "So you've read John Locke."

"What?" Slade asks. "Just because I'm a tech guy, I never picked up a book? What you're talking about is using neuroscience to pierce the veil of perception—to see reality as it truly is."

"Which is, by definition, impossible. No matter how much we understand about how our perceptions work, ultimately we'll never escape our limitations."

Slade just smiles.

Day 364

Helena badges through the third-floor entrance and heads down a brightly lit corridor toward the main testing bay. She's as nervous as she's been since her first day here, her stomach so unsettled she only had coffee and a few pieces of pineapple for breakfast.

Overnight, Infrastructure moved the chair they've been building from their workshop into the main testing bay, where Helena now stops in the threshold. John and Rachel are bolting the base of the chair into the floor.

She knew this would be an emotional moment, but the intensity of seeing her chair for the first time takes her by storm. Until now, her work product has consisted of images of neuron clusters, sophisticated software programs, and a shit-ton of uncertainty. But the chair is a thing. Something she can touch. The physical manifestation of the goal she has been driving toward for ten long years, accelerated by her mother's illness.

"What do you think?" Rachel asks. "Slade had us alter the blueprints to surprise you."

Helena would be furious at Slade for this unilateral design change if what they had built weren't so perfect. She's stunned. In her mind, the chair was always a utilitarian device, a means to an end. What they've built for her is artful and elegant, reminiscent of an Eames lounge chair, except all one piece.

The two engineers are looking at her now, no doubt trying to ascertain her reaction, to see if their boss is pleased with their work.

"You've outdone yourselves," she says.

By lunch, the chair has been fully installed. The MEG microscope, mounted seamlessly to the headrest, resembles an overhanging helmet. The bundle of cords running out of it has been threaded down the back of the chair and into a port in the floor, so the overall appearance is of a sleek, clean-lined device.

Helena won her fight with Slade to be the chair's first occupant by withholding her knowledge about how high a synaptic number they would need in order to properly reactivate a memory. Slade pushed back, of course, arguing her mind and memory were far too valuable to take the risk, but that wasn't a fight he or anybody ever had a chance of winning.

And so, at 1:07 p.m., she eases down onto the soft leather and leans back. Lenore, one of the imaging technicians, carefully lowers the microscope onto Helena's head, the padding forming a snug fit. Then she fastens the chin strap. Slade watches from a corner of the room, recording on a handheld video camera with a big grin, as if he's filming the birth of his first child.

"Does that feel OK?" Lenore asks.

"Yeah."

"I'm going to lock you in now."

Lenore opens two compartments embedded in the headrest and unfolds a series of telescoping titanium rods, which she screws into housings on the exterior of the microscope to stabilize it.

"Try to move your head now," Lenore says.

"I can't."

"How does it feel to be sitting in your chair?" Slade asks.

"I kind of want to throw up."

Helena watches as everyone files out of the testing bay and into an adjacent control room that is visually connected by a wall of glass. After a moment, Slade's voice comes through a speaker in the headrest: "Can you hear me?"

"Yes."

"We're going to dim the lights now."

Soon all she can see are the faces of her team, glowing a faint blue in the light of a dozen monitors.

"Try to relax," Slade says.

She takes in a deep breath through her nose and lets it out slowly as the geometric array of SQUID detectors begins to hum softly above her, a soft whirring that feels like a billion nano-massages against her scalp.

They have endlessly debated what type of memory should be the first one they map. Something simple? Complex? Recent? Old? Happy? Tragic? Yesterday, Helena decided they were overthinking it. How does one define a "simple" memory anyway? Is there even such a thing when it comes to the human condition? Consider the albatross that landed on the platform during her run this morning. It's a mere flicker of thought in her mind that will one day be cast out into that wasteland of oblivion where forgotten memories die. And yet it contains the smell of the sea. The white, wet feathers of the bird glistening in the early sun. The pounding of her heart from the exertion of the run. The cold slide of sweat down her sides and the burn of it in her eyes. Her wondering in that moment where the bird considered home in the unending sameness of the sea.

When every memory contains a universe, what does simple even mean?

Slade's voice: "Helena? Are you ready?"

"I am."

"You have a memory picked out?"

"Yes."

"Then I'm going to count down from five, and when you hear the tone . . . remember."

BARRY

November 5, 2018

In summer, the train would be standing room only, packed with Manhattanites heading for the Hamptons. But it is a cold November afternoon, the gun-gray clouds threatening the season's first snow, and Barry has the coach car on the Long Island Railroad almost entirely to himself.

As he stares through the window, watching the lights of Brooklyn shrink away through the dirty glass, his eyes grow heavy.

When he wakes, night has fallen. The view out the window is now darkness, points of light, and his own reflection in the glass.

Montauk is the last stop on the line, and he steps off the train at a little before eight p.m. into a frigid rain sheeting down through the illumination of the streetlamps. He tightens the belt of his woolen trench coat and turns up the collar, his breath steaming in the chill. He walks alongside the tracks to the station house, which has been shuttered for the night, and climbs into the taxi he ordered from the train.

Most of downtown Montauk has been closed for the season. He was here once before, twenty years ago, with Julia and Meghan, on a crowded summer weekend when the streets and beaches were jammed with vacationers.

Pinewood Lane is a secluded, sand-dusted road, cracked and buckled by tree roots. A half mile in, the cab's headlights strike a gated entrance, where a plaque with the Roman numeral "VI" is affixed to one of the stone pillars.

"Pull up to the box," he tells the driver.

The car edges forward, Barry's window humming down into the door.

He reaches out, presses the call button. He knows they're home. Before he left New York, he called, pretending to be FedEx trying to schedule a late delivery.

A woman answers, "Behrman residence."

"This is Detective Sutton with the New York Police Department. Is your husband at home, ma'am?"

"Is everything OK?"

"Yes. I need to speak with him."

There's a pause, followed by the sound of hushed conversation.

Then a man's voice comes through the speaker. "This is Joe. What's this regarding?"

"I'd rather tell you in person. And in private."

"We were about to sit down to dinner."

"I apologize for the intrusion, but I just took a train here from the city."

The private drive is a one-laner that winds through stretches of grassland and forest on a gradual ascent toward a residence that's perched atop a gentle bluff. From a distance, the house appears to be constructed entirely of glass, the interior glowing like an oasis in the night.

Barry pays the driver in cash, including an extra $20 to wait for him. Then he steps out into the rain and climbs the steps toward the entrance. The front door swings open as he reaches the stoop. Joe Behrman looks older than his driver's license photograph, his hair now streaked with silver and carrying just enough weight in his sun-damaged face to make his jowls sag.

Franny has aged more gracefully.

For three long seconds, he's unsure if they're going to invite him in, but then Franny finally steps back, offers a forced smile, and ushers him into their home.

The open-concept space is a marvel of perfectly apportioned design and comfort. In daylight, he imagines the curtain of windows affords a spectacular view of the sea and surrounding forest preserve. The smell of something baking in the kitchen permeates the house and reminds Barry of what it was like to have things cooked from scratch instead of reheated in a microwave or brought to him in plastic bags by strangers.

Franny squeezes her husband's hand, says, "I'll keep everything in the warming drawer." Then she turns to Barry. "May I take your coat?"

Joe leads Barry back into a study with glass on one wall and the rest covered in books. As they sit across from each other in the vicinity of a gas-log fireplace, Joe says, "I have to tell you, it's a little unnerving to get an unannounced visit from a detective at dinnertime."

"Sorry if I spooked you. You're not in trouble or anything."

Joe smiles. "You might have led with that."

"I'll get right to it. Fifteen years ago, your wife went up to the forty-first floor of the Poe Building on the Upper West Side and—"

"She's much better now. A completely different person." A flicker of annoyance, or fear, crosses Joe's face, which has taken on a measure of color. "Why are you here? Why are you in my house on what should be a peaceful night with my wife, digging up our past?"

"Three days ago, I was driving home, and a call came in over the radio for a 10-56A—that's a suicide attempt. I responded and found a woman sitting out on the ledge on the forty-first floor of the Poe Building. She said she was suffering from FMS. You know what that is?"

"The false-memory thing."

"She described to me this entire life that never happened. She had a husband and a son. They lived in Vermont. Ran a landscaping business together. She said his name was Joe. Joe Behrman."

Joe becomes very still.

"Her name was Ann Voss Peters. She thought that Franny had *jumped* from the place where she was sitting. She told me she came here and spoke to you, but that you didn't know her. The reason she had chosen that ledge was because she held out hope that you would come to her rescue, making up for your failure to save Franny. But obviously, Ann's memory was flawed, because you *did* save Franny. I read the police report this afternoon."

"What happened to Ann?"

"I wasn't able to save her."

Joe closes his eyes, opens them. "What do you want from me?" he asks, his voice just above a whisper.

"Did you know Ann Voss Peters?"

"No."

"So how does Ann know you? How did she know your wife had gone up on that same ledge with the intention of committing suicide? Why did she believe she had been your wife? That the two of you had a boy named Sam?"

"I have no idea, but I would like you to leave now."

"Mr. Behrman—"

"Please. I have answered your questions. I have done nothing wrong. Go."

While he can't begin to guess why, he is certain of one thing— Joe Behrman is lying.

Barry rises from the chair. He reaches into his jacket and pulls out a business card, which he places on the table between the chairs. "If you change your mind, I hope you'll call me."

Joe doesn't respond, doesn't get up, doesn't even look at Barry. He's holding his hands in his lap—to stop them from trembling, Barry knows—and staring intently into the fire.

As Barry rides into Montauk, he checks the schedules on his MTA app. He should have just enough time to grab a bite and make the 9:50 p.m. back into the city.

The diner is nearly empty, and he slides onto a stool at the counter, still running on the adrenaline of his conversation with Joe.

Before his food comes, a man with a shaved head enters and claims one of the booths. Orders coffee and sits there reading something on his phone.

No.

Pretending to read something on his phone.

His eyes are too alert, and the bulge beneath his leather jacket suggests a shoulder holster. He has the concealed intensity of a cop or a soldier—eyes never still, always darting, always processing, even though his head never moves. It's conditioning you can't unlearn.

But he never looks at Barry.

You're just being paranoid.

Barry is halfway through his huevos rancheros and thinking about Joe and Franny Behrman when a glint of pain flashes behind his eyes.

His nose begins to bleed, and as he catches the blood in a napkin, a completely different set of memories of the last three days crowds into his mind. He was driving home on Friday night, but no 10-56A ever came over the radio. He never rode up to the forty-first floor of the Poe Building. Never met Ann Voss Peters. Never watched her fall. Never looked at the police report regarding the attempted suicide of Franny Behrman. Never bought a train ticket to Montauk. Never interviewed Joe Behrman.

Considered from a certain perspective, he was just sitting in his recliner in his one-bedroom apartment in Washington Heights, watching a Knicks game, and now he's suddenly in a Montauk diner with a bloody nose.

When he tries to look these alternate memories squarely in the eye, he finds that they carry a different feel from any memory he's ever known. They're lifeless and static, draped in hues of black and gray, just as Ann Voss Peters described.

Did I catch this from her?

His nose has stopped bleeding, but his hands have begun to shake. Throwing some money on the counter, he heads out into the night, trying to stay calm, but he's reeling.

There are so few things in our existence we can count on to give us the sense of permanence, of the ground beneath our feet. People fail us. Our bodies fail us. We fail ourselves. He's experienced all of that. But what do you cling to, moment to moment, if memories can simply change. What, then, is real? And if the answer is nothing, where does that leave us?

He wonders if he's going mad, if this is what it feels like to lose your mind.

It's four blocks to the train station. There are no cars out, the town is dead, and as a creature of a city that never sleeps, he finds the silence of this off-season hamlet unnerving.

He leans against a streetlamp, waiting for the doors of the train to open, one of four people on the platform, including the man from the diner.

The rain striking his hands is turning to slush, his fingers are freezing, but he wants them that way.

The cold is the only thing keeping him tethered to reality.

HELENA

Day 366

Two days after the first use of the chair, Helena sits in the control room, surrounded by the Imaging Team, staring at a huge monitor that shows a static, 3D image of her brain, the synaptic activity represented by varying shades of luminous blue.

She says, "The spatial resolution is stunning, guys. Beyond what I ever dreamed of."

"Just wait," Rajesh says.

He taps the space bar, and the image comes alive. Neurons glowing and fading like a trillion lightning bugs brightening a summer evening. Like the smoldering of stars.

As the memory plays, Rajesh magnifies the image to the level of individual neurons. Threads of electricity arcing from synapse to synapse. He slows it down to show the activity over the span of a millisecond, and still the complexity remains unfathomable.

When the memory ends, he says, "You promised you'd tell us what we've been looking at."

Helena smiles. "I was six years old. My father had taken me fly-fishing to this stream he loved in Rocky Mountain National Park."

Rajesh asks, "Can you be specific in terms of exactly what you were remembering during these fifteen seconds? Was it the entire afternoon? Certain moments?"

"I would describe it as flashes, which, in the aggregate, comprise the emotional return to the memory."

"For instance . . ."

"The sound of water babbling over the rocks in the streambed. Yellow aspen leaves floating in the current, and how they look like gold coins. My father's rough hands tying a fly. The anticipation of hooking a fish. Lying in the grass on the bank, staring down into the water. Bright-blue sky and the sun coming through the trees in shards of light. A fish my father caught quivering in his hands and his explaining that the red coloration under its lower jaw is why they call it a cutthroat trout. Later that afternoon, a hook going into my thumb." Helena holds up the finger in question to show them the tiny white scar. "It wouldn't come out because of the barb, so my father opened his pocket knife and cut the skin. I remember crying, his telling me to hold still, and when the hook was finally out, he held my thumb in the freezing water until it went numb. I watched the blood flowing out of the cut into the current."

"What is your emotional connection to that memory?" Rajesh asks. "The reason you chose it."

Helena looks into his big, dark eyes, says, "The pain of the fish-hook, but mainly because it's my favorite memory of my father. The moment when he was most quintessentially *him*."

Day 370

They put Helena back in the chair and have her recall the memory again and again, breaking it down into segments until Rajesh's team is able to assign individual synaptic patterns to specific moments.

Day 420

The first reactivation attempt occurs on Helena's second Christmas Eve on the rig. They put her into the chair and fit her with a head-piece embedded with the network of electromagnetic stimulators.

Sergei has programmed the apparatus with the synaptic coordinates of a single segment of Helena's fly-fishing memory. When the lights go down in the main testing bay, Helena hears Slade's voice in the headrest speaker.

"You ready?"

"Yes."

They've all decided not to tell Helena when the reactivation apparatus will fire, or which memory segment they've selected, the concern being if she's anticipating the memory, chances are she may inadvertently retrieve it on her own.

Helena closes her eyes and begins the mind-clearing exercise she's been practicing for a week now. She sees herself walking into a room. There's a bench in the middle, the kind one might find in an art museum. She takes a seat and studies the wall in front of her. From floor to ceiling, it transitions imperceptibly from white to black, passing through shades of subtly deepening gray. She starts at the bottom, taking her time scanning slowly up the length of the wall, fully observing the color of one section before moving on to the next, each subsequent region barely darker than the one before—

The sudden pinch of a barbed hook jabbing into her thumb, her voice a shriek of pain, a red bubble of blood filling in around the hook as her father comes running.

"Did you do it?" Helena asks, her heart slamming in her chest.

"Did you experience something?" Slade asks.

"Yes, just now."

"Describe it."

"A vivid memory flash of the hook puncturing my thumb. Was that you guys?"

Cheers erupt from the control room.

Helena begins to cry.

Day 422

They begin recording and cataloging the autobiographical memories of everyone on the rig, keeping strictly to flashbulb memories.

Day 424

Lenore allows them to record her memory of the morning of January 28, 1986.

She was eight years old on a visit to the dentist's office. The office manager had brought a television from home and set it up in the waiting room. Lenore was sitting with her mother before her appointment, watching coverage of the historic shuttle launch when the spacecraft disintegrated over the Atlantic Ocean.

The information that encoded most strongly for her was the small television sitting on a rolling stand. The camera footage of the looping white clouds moments after the explosion. Her mother saying, "Oh dear God." The severe concern in Dr. Hunter's eyes. And one of the dental hygienists coming out of the back to stare at the television as tears ran down her face and under the surgical mask she still wore.

Day 448

Rajesh remembers the last time he saw his father before moving to America. They had taken a safari, just the two of them, in Spiti Valley, high in the Himalayas.

He remembers the smell of the yaks. The sharp intensity of mountain sunlight. The frigid bite of the river. The light-headedness that plagued him from the 4,000-meter, oxygen-deprived air. Everything brown and barren, except the lakes like pale-blue eyes, and the temples with their vibrantly colored prayer flags, and the upper reaches of the highest peaks gleaming with bright snow.

But especially the night Raj's father told him what he really thought about life, about Raj, Raj's mother, everything, in a fleeting moment of vulnerability as the two of them sat before a dying campfire.

Day 452

Sergei sits in the chair remembering the moment a motorcycle clipped the back of his car. The sudden impact of metal on metal. Seeing the bike somersault down the highway out the driver-side window. The fear, the terror, the taste of rust in the back of his throat and a sense of time slowing to a crawl.

Then bringing his car to a stop in the middle of the busy Moscow street and stepping out into the smell of oil and gas leaking from the crushed motorcycle, and the biker sitting in the middle of the road, his chaps shredded down to skin, staring dumbfounded at his hands, most of the fingers shaved off, then shouting when he saw Sergei, the biker trying to stand and fight, then screaming when his leg, twisted impossibly underneath him, refused to work.

Day 500

It is one of the first temperate days of the year. All winter, the rig has been pounded by storm after storm, testing the limit of even Helena's threshold for claustrophobic working environments. But today is warm and blue, and the sea calm enough for the entire surface to lie glittering beneath the platform.

She and Slade move leisurely around the running track.

"How do you feel about the progress we've made?" he asks.

"Great. It's gone much faster than I had hoped. I think we should publish something."

"Really."

"I'm ready to take what we've learned and start changing people's lives."

He looks at her, leaner and harder since they first met almost a year and a half ago. Then again, she's changed too. She's in the greatest physical shape of her life, and her work has never been more engaging.

Nothing about Slade's involvement in this project has matched her expectations. Since her arrival on the rig, he has left only once, and he's been intimately involved during every step of the process. Both he and Jee-woon have attended every team meeting. Consulted on every material decision. She had assumed a man as busy as Slade would only parachute in occasionally, but his obsession has rivaled hers.

Now he says, "You're talking about publishing, and I feel like we've hit a wall." They turn the northeast corner of the track and head west. "The experience of reactivating a memory is a disappointment."

"I'm shocked to hear you say that. Everyone who has undergone reactivation has come out reporting a memory experience far more vivid and intense than anything they've recalled on their own. Reactivation raises all vital signs, sometimes to the point of intense stress. You've seen their medical charts. You've had your memories lit up. You disagree?"

"I don't disagree that it's a more intense experience than remembering something on my own, but it isn't nearly as dynamic as I'd hoped."

She feels a flush of anger color her face. "We're making progress at a blinding rate, and scientific breakthroughs in our understanding of memory and engrams that would light up the world if you agreed to let me publish. I want to start mapping memories of test subjects with stage-three Alzheimer's, and when they hit stage five or six, reactivate the memories we've saved for them. What if that's the path to synaptic regeneration? To a cure? Or at the very least, to preserving core memories for a person whose brain is failing them?"

"Are you making this about your mom, Helena?"

"Of course I am! She's going to reach a point in the next year when there won't be any memories left to map. What do you think I'm doing here? Why do you think I've devoted my life to this?"

"I love your passion, and I want to destroy this disease too. But first, I want: *Immersive platform for projection of long-term, explicit, episodic memories.*" The exact title of her dream patent application from years ago, the one she hasn't filed yet.

"How'd you know about my patent?"

Instead of answering her, he asks another question: "Do you think what you've built so far is anywhere close to immersive?"

"I've given this project everything I have."

"Please stop being so defensive. The technology you've built is perfect. I just want to help you make it everything it can be."

They turn the northwest corner, heading south now. Teams Imaging and Mapping are battling it out on the volleyball court. Rajesh is painting a watercolor en plein air beside the tarped-over pool. Sergei shoots free throws on the basketball court.

Slade stops walking and looks at Helena. "Instruct Infrastructure to build a deprivation tank. They'll need to coordinate with Sergei to find a way to waterproof and stabilize the reactivation apparatus on a test subject who's floating inside."

"Why?"

"Because it will create the pure-heroin version of memory reactivation that I'm looking for."

"How could you possibly know—?"

"Once you've accomplished that, devise a method for stopping a test subject's heart once they're inside the deprivation tank."

She looks at Slade as if he's lost his mind.

He says, "The more stress the human body endures during reactivation, the more intense their experience of the memory. Buried deep inside our brain is a rice-size gland called the pineal, which plays a role in the creation of a chemical called dimethyltriptamine, or DMT. You've heard of it?"

"It's one of the most potent psychedelics known to man."

"In tiny doses, released into our brains at night, DMT is responsible for our dreams. But at the moment of death, the pineal gland releases a veritable flood of DMT. A going-out-of-business sale. It's the reason people see things when they die, such as racing through a tunnel toward a light, or their entire life flashing before their eyes. To have an immersive, dreamlike memory, we need bigger dreams. Or, if you will, a lot more DMT."

"No one knows what our conscious minds experience when we die. You can't be sure this will have any effect on the memory immersion. We might just kill people."

"When did you become such a pessimist?"

"Who exactly do you think is going to volunteer to die for this project?"

"We'll bring them back to life. Poll your team. I'll pay well considering the risk. And if you don't have enough sign-ups for trials, I'll look elsewhere."

"Will you volunteer to go inside the deprivation tank and have your heart stopped?"

Slade smiles, dark. "When the procedure is perfected? Absolutely. Then, and only then, you can bring your mother to the rig, and use all of my equipment and all of your knowledge to map and save her memories."

"Marcus, please—"

"Then, and only then."

"She's running out of time."

"So get to work."

She watches him go. Before, it was always just far enough below the surface of consciousness to ignore. Now it's staring her in the face. She doesn't know how, but Slade knows things he shouldn't, that he couldn't possibly—the full details of her vision for memory projection, right down to the name of the patent application she would've one day filed. The quantum processors he somehow knew would solve the mapping problem. And now this mad notion of stopping the heart as a means to deepen the immersive experience. Even more alarming, the way Slade drops these little hints, it's almost like he wants her to know that he knows things he shouldn't. Like he wants her to be worried about the scope of his power and knowledge. It occurs to her that, if this friction continues, a day may come when Slade revokes her access to the memory platform. Perhaps she can persuade Raj to build her a clandestine, secondary user account just in case.

For the first time since setting foot on this rig, she wonders if she's safe here.

BARRY

"Sir? Excuse me, sir?"

Barry rouses from sleep, eyes opening, everything momentarily blurry and no idea for five disorienting seconds where he is. Then he registers the rocking motion of the train. Light poles streaking past through the window across the aisle. The face of the elderly conductor.

"May I see your ticket?" the old man asks in a courtly manner refined in another age. Barry rifles through his coat until he finds his phone in the bottom of an inner pocket. Opening the MTA app, he holds his ticket up so the conductor can scan the bar code.

"Thank you, Mr. Sutton. Sorry to wake you."

As the conductor moves on to the next car, Barry notices four missed call notifications on his phone's display screen—all from the same 934 area code.

And one voicemail.

He presses Play, brings the phone to his ear. *"Hi, it's Joe . . . Joe*

*Behrman. Um . . . can you please call me as soon as you get this? I really
need to talk to you."*

Barry immediately returns the call, and Joe answers before the
second ring, "Detective Sutton?"

"Yes."

"Where are you?"

"On the train back to New York."

"You have to understand, I never thought anyone would find
out. They promised me it would never happen."

"What are you talking about?"

"I was scared." Joe is crying now. "Can you come back?"

"Joe. I'm on a train. But you can talk to me right now."

For a moment, the man just breathes heavily into the phone.
Barry thinks he hears a woman also crying in the background, but
he isn't sure.

"I shouldn't have done it," Joe says. "I know that now. I had this
great life with a beautiful son, but I couldn't look myself in the
mirror."

"Why?"

"Because I wasn't there for her, and she jumped. I couldn't for-
give my—"

"Who jumped?"

"Franny."

"What are you talking about? Franny didn't jump. I just saw her
at your house."

Over the static-laced connection, Barry hears Joe breaking
down.

"Joe, did you know Ann Voss Peters?"

"Yes."

"How?"

"I was married to her."

"What?"

"It's my fault Ann jumped. I saw an ad in the classifieds. It said,

'Would you like a do-over?' There was a phone number and I called it. Ann told you she had False Memory Syndrome?"

"Correct." *And now I have it.* "It sounds like you may have it too. They say it travels in social circles."

Joe laughs, but the sound is full of regret and self-hatred. "FMS isn't what people think it is."

"You know what FMS is?"

"Of course."

"Tell me."

It becomes quiet over the line, and for a moment, Barry thinks he's lost the signal.

"Joe, are you there? Did I lose you?"

"I'm here."

"What is FMS?"

"It's people like me, who've done what I did. And it's only going to get worse."

"Why?"

"I . . ." There's a long pause. "I can't explain. It's insane. You need to go see for yourself."

"How do I do that?"

"After I called that number, they interviewed me over the phone, and then took me to a hotel in Manhattan."

"There are a lot of hotels in Manhattan, Joe."

"Not like this one. You can't just go there. *They* invite you. The only access is through an underground garage."

"Do you know the street address?"

"It's on East Fiftieth, between Lexington and Third. There's an all-night diner on the same block."

"Joe—"

"These are powerful people. Franny had a breakdown when she remembered, and they knew. They showed up. They threatened me."

"Who are *they*?"

There's no answer.

"Joe? Joe?"

He hung up.

Barry tries to call him back, but it goes straight to voicemail.

He looks out the window—nothing to see but darkness occasionally broken by the lights of a house or a station scrolling past.

He turns his focus toward those alternate memories that found him at the diner. They're still there. They never happened, but they feel just as real as the rest of his memories, and he can't square the paradox in his mind.

He looks around the car—he's the sole passenger.

The only sound is the steady heartbeat of the train speeding along the track.

He touches the seat, runs his fingers across the fabric.

He opens his wallet and looks at his New York State driver's license, and then his NYPD badge.

Taking a breath, he tells himself—*You are Barry Sutton. You are on a train from Montauk to New York City. Your past is your past. It cannot change. What is real is this moment. The train. The coldness of the window glass. The rain streaking across the other side of it. And you. There is a logical explanation for your false memories, for whatever happened to Joe and Ann Voss Peters. To all of it. It's just a puzzle to be solved. And you are very good at solving puzzles.*

All that's bullshit.

He's never been more afraid in his life.

When he steps out of Penn Station, it's after midnight. Snow is pouring out of a pink sky, an inch already collected on the streets.

He turns up his collar, raises his umbrella, and heads north from Thirty-Fourth.

The streets and sidewalks empty.

The snow dampening the noise of Manhattan to a rare hush.

Fifteen minutes of fast walking brings him to the intersection of Eighth Avenue and West Fiftieth, where he cuts east across the avenues, colder now that he's walking into the storm, the umbrella tilted like a shield against the wind and snow.

He stops at Lexington to let three snowplows pass and stares at a red neon sign across the street:

McLachlan's Restaurant
Breakfast
Lunch
Dinner
Open 7 Days
24 Hours

Barry crosses, and then he's standing under it, watching the snow fall through the red illumination and thinking this has to be the all-night diner Joe mentioned on the phone.

He's been walking for nearly forty minutes, and he's beginning to shiver, the snow soaking through his shoes. Beyond the restaurant, he passes an alcove where a homeless man sits muttering to himself and rocking back and forth, his arms wrapped around his legs. Then a bodega, a liquor store, a luxury women's clothing store, and a bank—all shuttered for the night.

Near the end of the block, he stops at the entrance to a darkened driveway, which tunnels down into the subterranean space beneath a neo-gothic building wedged between two higher skyscrapers built of steel and glass.

Lowering his umbrella, he walks down the driveway, into the low-lit gloom below street level. After forty feet, it terminates at a garage door constructed of reinforced steel. There's a keypad, and above it, a surveillance camera.

Well, shit. This would appear to be the end of the line for tonight. He'll come back tomorrow, stake out the entrance, see if he can catch anyone coming or—

The sound of gears beginning to turn gives his heart a jolt. He looks back at the garage door, which is slowly lifting off the ground, light from the other side stretching across the pavement, already reaching the tips of Barry's wet shoes.

Leave?

Stay?

This may not even be the right place.

The door is halfway up and still rising, and there's no one on the other side.

He hesitates, then crosses the threshold into a modest, underground parking structure, occupied by a dozen vehicles.

His footsteps reverberate off the concrete as the halogen lights burn down from overhead.

He sees an elevator, and beside it, a door presumably leading to a stairwell.

The light above the elevator illuminates.

A bell dings.

Barry ducks behind a Lincoln MKX and watches through the tinted glass of the front passenger window as the elevator doors part.

Empty.

What the hell is this?

He shouldn't be here. None of this has anything to do with his actual caseload, and no crime, as far as he can tell, has been committed. Technically, *he's* trespassing.

Fuck it.

The walls inside are smooth, featureless metal, the elevator apparently controlled from an external source.

The doors close.

The elevator climbs.

His heart pounds.

Barry swallows twice to clear the pressure from his ears, and after thirty seconds, the car comes to a shuddering stop.

The first thing he hears, as the doors spread, is Miles Davis— one of the perfect slow songs off *Kind of Blue*—drifting on a lonesome echo through what appears to be the lobby of a hotel.

He steps off the elevator onto the marble floor. There's dark, brooding woodwork everywhere. Leather couches, black lacquered chairs. A trace of cigar smoke in the air.

Something timeless about the space.

Straight ahead stands an unmanned reception desk with a backdrop of vintage mailboxes that would've been used in another era, and the letters *HM* emblazoned on the brick above it all.

He hears the fragile clink of ice cubes settling in glassware, and then voices drifting over from a bar that's nestled against a curtain of windows. Two men, seated on leather-cushioned stools, are in conversation as a black-vested barkeep polishes glassware.

As Barry moves toward the bar, the smell of the cigar grows stronger, the air becoming hazy with smoke.

Barry climbs onto one of the stools and leans against the solid mahogany bar. Through the nearby windows, the buildings and lights of the city are shrouded in a whiteout.

The bartender comes over.

She's beautiful—dark eyes and prematurely gray hair held up by chopsticks. Her name tag reads TONYA.

"What are you drinking?" Tonya asks.

"Could I get a whiskey?"

"Looking for anything in particular?"

"Dealer's choice."

She goes to pour his drink, and Barry glances at the men several seats down. They're drinking bourbon from a half-empty bottle that's sitting between them on the bar.

The one closest to him looks to be in his early seventies, with gray, thinning hair and an emaciation that suggests terminal illness. Smoke spirals up from the cigar in his hand, which smells like rain falling on a desert.

The other man is closer to Barry's age—bland, clean-shaven face, tired eyes. He asks the older man, "How long have you been here, Amor?"

"About a week."

"Have they given you a date yet?"

"Tomorrow actually."

"No shit. Congratulations."

They touch glasses.

"Nervous?" the young man asks.

"I mean, it's on my mind what's coming. But they do a really thorough job preparing you for everything."

"Is it true—no anesthesia?"

"Unfortunately, yes. When'd you get here?"

"Yesterday." Amor takes a puff off his cigar.

Tonya appears with a whiskey, which she sets on a napkin in front of Barry with HOTEL MEMORY embossed in gold on the paper.

"Have you decided what you're going to do when you get back?" the younger man asks.

Barry sips the scotch—sherry, caramel, dried fruits, and alcohol.

"I have some ideas." Amor raises his cigar hand. "No more of this." He points at the whiskey. "Less of that. I used to be an architect, and there was this building I always regretted not pursuing. Could've been my magnum opus. You?"

"I'm not sure. I feel so guilty."

"Why?"

"Isn't this selfish?"

"These are *our* memories. No one else has a claim on them." Amor polishes off the last of his whiskey. "I better hit the hay. Big day tomorrow."

"Yeah, me too."

Sliding off their respective stools, the men shake hands and wish each other luck. Barry watches them wander away from the bar to a bank of elevators.

When he turns back toward the bar, the bartender is facing him.

"What is this place, Tonya?" he asks, but his mouth feels odd and his words emerge with a sluggish clumsiness.

"Sir, you're not looking so well."

He feels something loosen behind his eyes.

An untethering.

He looks at his drink. He looks at Tonya.

"Vince will help you to a room," she says.

Barry steps down off the stool, swaying slightly on his feet, and turns to meet the dead-eyed stare of the man from the diner. Around his neck is an ornate tattoo of a woman's hands strangling the life out of him.

Barry reaches for his gun, but it's like moving through syrup, and Vince's hands are already inside his coat, deftly unsnapping the shoulder holster that secures his service weapon, and slipping the gun down the back of his jeans. He digs Barry's phone out of his pocket, tosses it to Tonya.

"I'm NYPD," Barry slurs.

"So was I."

"What is this place?"

"You're about to find out."

The wooziness is intensifying.

Vince grabs Barry by the arm and leads him away from the bar toward the bank of elevators beyond the reception desk. He calls the elevator and drags Barry inside.

Then Barry is stumbling through a hotel corridor as the world melts around him.

He weaves down the soft red carpeting, passing sconces made of old lamps that cast an antique light on the wainscoting between the doors.

1414 is projected onto the door by a light in the opposite wall that moves the number in the pattern of a slow figure eight around the peephole.

Vince lets them inside and steers Barry toward the expansive four-poster, shoving him onto the bed, where Barry curls up in the fetal position.

Fading fast and thinking, *You fucked up now, didn't you?*

The door to the room slams shut.

He's alone, unable to move.

The lights of the snowbound city bleed through the sheer curtain at the wall of windows, and the last thing he sees before losing consciousness are the ornamented chevrons of the Chrysler Building, glowing like jewels in the storm.

His mouth is dry.

Left arm sore.

The surroundings crystallizing into focus.

Barry is reclined in a leather chair—black, elegant, ultramodern—to which he's also been strapped. His ankles, his wrists, one across his waist, another over his chest. There's an IV port in his left forearm—hence the pain—and a metal cart beside his chair, out of which runs the plastic tube that's plugged into his bloodstream.

The wall facing him is lined with a computer terminal and an assortment of medical equipment, including (and to his considerable alarm) a crash cart. Tucked away in an alcove on the far side of the room, he sees a smooth, white object with tubes and wires running into it, which looks like a giant egg.

A man Barry has never seen before is seated on a stool beside him. He has a long, wild beard, stark blue eyes that radiate intelligence, and an uncomfortable intensity.

Barry opens his mouth, but he's still too drowsy to form words.

"Still feeling groggy?"

Barry nods.

The man touches a button on the cart beside the chair. Barry watches as a clear liquid pushes through the IV line into his arm. The room brightens. He feels instantly alert, as if he just mainlined a shot of espresso, and with the awareness comes fear.

"Better?" the man asks.

Barry tries to move his head, but it has been immobilized. He can't even turn a millimeter in either direction.

"I'm a cop," Barry says.

"I know. I know quite a lot about you, Detective Sutton, including the fact that you are a very lucky man."

"Why do you say that?"

"Because of your past, I've decided not to kill you."

Is that a good thing? Or is this man just toying with him?

"Who are you?" Barry asks.

"It doesn't matter. I'm about to give you the greatest gift of your life. The greatest gift a person could ever hope to receive. If you don't mind," he says, the courtesy paradoxically alarming, "I have a few questions before we get started."

Barry is growing more alert by the minute, the confusion fading as his last piece of memory returns—stumbling down the hotel corridor and into Room 1414.

The man asks, "Did you go to the home of Joe and Franny Behrman in an official capacity?"

"How'd you know I went there?"

"Just answer the question."

"No. I was satisfying my own curiosity."

"Did any of your colleagues or superiors know about your trip to Montauk?"

"No one did."

"Did you discuss with anyone your interest in Ann Voss Peters and Joe Behrman?"

Though he spoke to Gwen about FMS on Sunday, he feels confident in his assumption that no one could possibly know about their conversation.

So he lies. "No."

Barry has the tracking software activated on his phone. He has no idea how long he's been unconscious, but assuming it's still early Tuesday morning, his absence from work won't be noticed until late afternoon. In theory, hours from now. He has no appointments scheduled. No drink or dinner plans. It could be several days before his absence pings on anyone's radar.

"People will come looking for me," Barry says.

"They'll never find you."

Barry breathes in slowly, steeling himself against the rising panic. He needs to convince this man to release him, with nothing but words and logic.

Barry says, "I don't know who you are. I don't know what any of this is about. But if you release me now, you will never hear from me again. I swear to you."

The man slides off the stool and moves across the room to the computer terminal. Standing before an immense monitor, he types on a keyboard. After a moment, Barry hears whatever apparatus is attached to his head begin to make a barely discernible whirring, like the wings of a mosquito.

"What is this?" Barry asks again, his heart rate ticking up a notch, fear occluding his better thinking. "What do you want with me?"

"I want you to tell me about the last time you saw your daughter alive."

In a pure and blinding rage, Barry strains against the leather straps, struggling with everything he has to disengage his head from whatever is holding it in place. The leather creaks. His head doesn't budge. Sweat beads on his face and runs down into his eyes with a salty burn he is powerless to wipe away.

"I'll kill you," Barry says.

The man leans forward, inches away, a blue-flame coldness in his eyes. Barry smells his expensive cologne, the toasted sourness of coffee on his breath.

"I'm not trying to taunt you," the man says. "I'm trying to help you."

"Fuck you."

"You came to *my* hotel."

"Yeah, and I'm sure you told Joe Behrman exactly what to say to lure me here."

"Tell you what—let's make this choice as straightforward as

possible. You answer honestly when I ask a question, or you'll die where you sit."

Trapped in this chair, Barry has no choice but to play along, to keep staying alive until he sees an opening, a chance, no matter how small, to get free.

"Fine."

The man lifts his head to the ceiling and says, "Computer, start session."

An automated, feminine voice responds, *New session beginning now.*

The man looks into Barry's eyes.

"Now, tell me about the last time you saw your daughter alive, and don't leave out a single detail."

HELENA

March 29, 2009–June 20, 2009

Day 515

Standing in the vestibule of the superstructure's western loading bay, Helena zips into her foul-weather gear, thinking the wind sounds like a deep-voiced ghost, roaring on the other side of the door. All morning, it's been gusting to eighty—hard enough to blow someone her size off the platform.

Dragging the door open, she stares into a grayed-out world of sideways-blowing rain and connects the carabiner on her harness to the cable that's been strung across the platform. Despite anticipating the power of the wind, she isn't ready for the sheer force that almost sweeps her off her feet. She leans into it, bracing herself, and moves outside.

The platform is cloaked in gray, and all she can hear is the raving madness of the wind and the needles of rain slamming into the hood of her jacket like ball bearings.

It takes ten minutes to cross the platform, a series of hard-fought steps against a constant loss of balance. She finally reaches her favorite spot on the rig—the northwest corner—and sits down with her legs hanging over the side, watching sixty-foot waves smash into the platform legs.

The last two members of Infrastructure left yesterday, before the storm's arrival. Her people didn't just object to Slade's new directive to "put people in a deprivation tank and stop their heart." With the exception of her and Sergei, they resigned en masse and demanded to be returned to the mainland immediately. Whenever she feels guilty for staying, she thinks of her mom and others like her, but it's a small consolation.

Besides, she's pretty sure Slade wouldn't let her leave regardless.

Jee-woon has flown inland to find personnel for the medical team and new engineers to build the deprivation tank, leaving Helena alone on the rig with Slade and a skeleton crew.

Out here on the platform, it's like the world is screaming in her ear.

Lifting her face to the sky, she screams back.

Day 598

Someone is knocking at her door. Reaching out in the darkness, she turns on the lamp and climbs out of bed in pajama bottoms and a black tank top. The alarm clock on her desk shows 9:50 a.m.

She moves into the living room and toward the door, hitting the button on the wall to raise the blackout curtains.

Slade is standing in the corridor in jeans and a hoodie—first time she's laid eyes on him in weeks.

He says, "Shit, I woke you."

She squints at him under the glare of the light panels in the ceiling.

"Mind if I come in?" he asks.

"Do I have a choice?"

"Please, Helena."

She takes a step back and lets him enter, following him down the short entryway, past the powder room, and into the main living space.

"What do you want?" she asks.

He takes a seat on the ottoman of an oversize chair, beside the windows that look out into a world of infinite sea.

He says, "They tell me you aren't eating or exercising. That you haven't spoken to anyone or gone outside in days."

"Why won't you let me talk to my parents? Why won't you let me leave?"

"You aren't well, Helena. You're in no state of mind to protect the secrecy of this place."

"I told you I wanted out. My mom's in a facility. I don't know how she's doing. My dad hasn't heard my voice in a month. I'm sure he's worried—"

"I know you can't see it right now, but I am saving you from yourself."

"Oh, fuck you."

"You checked out, because you disagreed with the direction I was taking this project. All I've been doing is giving you time to reconsider throwing everything away."

"It was *my* project."

"It's my money."

Her hands tremble. With fear. With rage.

She says, "I don't want to do this anymore. You have ruined my dream. You have blocked me from trying to help my mom and others. I want to go home. Are you going to continue keeping me here against my will?"

"Of course not."

"So I can leave?"

"Do you remember what I asked you the first day you got here?"

She shakes her head, tears coming.

"I asked if you wanted to change the world with me. We are standing on the shoulders of all the brilliant work you've done, and I came here this morning to tell you that we're almost there. Forget everything that's happened in the past. Let's cross the finish line together."

She stares at him across the coffee table, tears gliding down her face.

"What are you feeling?" he asks. "Talk to me."

"Like you stole this thing away from me."

"Nothing could be further from the truth. I stepped in when your vision flagged. That's what partners do. Today is the biggest day of my life and yours. It's everything we've been working toward. That's why I came up here. The deprivation tank is ready. The reactivation apparatus has been retrofitted to work inside. We're running a new test in ten minutes, and this is the big one."

"Who's the test subject?"

"It doesn't matter."

"It does to me."

"Just a guy getting paid twenty grand a week to make the ultimate sacrifice for science."

"And you told him how dangerous this research is?"

"He's fully aware of the risks. Look, if you want to go home, pack your bags and be at the helipad at noon."

"What about my contract?"

"You promised me three years. You'll be in breach. You'll forfeit your compensation, profit participation, everything. You knew the ground rules going in. But if you want to finish what we started, come down to the lab with me right now. It's going to be a day for the record books."

BARRY

November 6, 2018

Strapped into a chair in a waking nightmare, Barry says, "It was October twenty-fifth. Eleven years ago."

"What's the first thing you remember when you think of it?" the man asks. "The most potent image or feeling?"

Barry is caught in the strangest juxtaposition of emotion. He wants to break this man in half, but the thought of Meghan that night is on the verge of breaking him.

He answers in monotone, "Finding her body."

"I'm sorry if I wasn't clear. Not after she was gone. Before."

"The last time I spoke to her."

"That's what I want you to talk about."

Barry stares across the room, gritting his teeth.

"Please continue, Detective Sutton."

"I'm sitting in my chair in my living room, watching the World Series."

"Do you remember who was playing?"

"Red Sox and Rockies. Game two. The Sox had won the first game. They would take the series in four straight."

"Who were you rooting for?"

"I didn't really care. I guess I wanted to see the Rockies tie it up, keep the series interesting. Why are you doing this to me? What purpose does—"

"So you're sitting in your chair . . ."

"I'm probably drinking a beer."

"Would Julia have been watching with you?"

Jesus. He knows her name.

"No. I think she was watching TV in our bedroom. We'd already eaten dinner."

"As a family?"

"I don't remember. Probably." Barry is suddenly aware of a pressure in his chest, the intensity of which is nearly crushing. He says, "I haven't talked about that night in years."

The man just sits there on his stool, running his fingers through his beard and coolly studying him, waiting for Barry to push on.

"I see Meghan coming out of the hallway. I don't remember for sure what she was wearing, but for some reason, I see her in this pair of jeans and a turquoise sweater she always wore."

"How old is your daughter?"

"Ten days shy of sixteen. And she stops in front of the coffee table—I know this happened for sure—and she's standing between me and the television with her hands on her hips and this quasi-severe look on her face."

Tears fill in at the edges of his eyes.

"It's still incredibly emotional for you," the man says. "This is good."

"Please," Barry says. "Don't make me do this."

"Continue."

Barry takes a breath, blindly groping for some handhold of emotional balance.

He says finally, "It was the last time I would look into my daughter's eyes. And I didn't know it. I kept trying to look around her to see the television."

He doesn't want to cry in front of this man. Jesus, anything but that.

"Continue."

"She asked if she could go to DQ. She usually went there a couple of nights a week to do her homework, hang out with friends. I went through the standard questioning. Did your mother say it was OK? No, she had come to me instead. Is your homework finished? No, but part of the reason she wanted to go was to meet up with Mindy, her lab partner in biology, to discuss a project they were working on. Who else was going to be there? A list of names, most of which I knew. I remember checking my watch—it was eight thirty and still in the early innings of the game—and I told her she could go, but that I wanted her home no later than ten. She made her arguments for eleven. I said, 'No, it's a school night, you know your curfew,' and then she let it go and headed for the door.

"I remember calling out to her just before she left, telling her I loved her."

Tears release, his body shaking with emotion, but the straps hold him tight against the chair.

Barry says, "The truth is, I don't know if I called out to her. I think probably I didn't, that I simply went back to watching the game and didn't think of her again until ten p.m. had come and gone, and I wondered why she wasn't home yet."

The man says, "Computer, stop session." And then: "Thank you, Barry."

He leans forward and wipes the tears from Barry's face with the back of his hand.

"What was the point of all that?" Barry asks, broken. "That was worse than any physical torture."

"I'll show you."

The man taps a button on the medical cart.

Barry glances at the tube in his arm as a stream of clear liquid rushes into his vein.

HELENA

June 20, 2009

Day 598

The man is wiry and tall, his thin arms streaked with needle tracks. On his left shoulder is a tattoo of the name *Miranda*, which looks fresh—still red and inflamed. He wears a silver headpiece that fits him as snugly as a skullcap, only slightly thicker, and a second device the size of a whiteboard eraser has been affixed to his left forearm. Otherwise, he stands naked before a white, shell-like structure reminiscent of an egg. A man and a woman wait in the wings beside a crash cart.

Helena is watching it all through one-way glass from a seat at the main console in the adjacent control room, between Marcus Slade and Dr. Paul Wilson, project manager for the medical team. To the left of Slade sits Sergei, the only member of the original crew who stayed.

Someone touches her shoulder. She glances back at Jee-woon, who has just slipped into the control room to take a seat behind her.

Leaning forward, he whispers in her ear, "I'm really glad you decided to join us for this. The lab hasn't been the same without you."

Slade looks over at Sergei, who's studying a screen displaying a high-resolution image of the test subject's skull.

"How we looking on those reactivation coordinates?" Slade asks.

"Locked and loaded."

Slade turns to the doctor. "Paul?"

"Ready when you are."

Slade taps a button on the headset he's wearing, says, "Reed, we're all set on our end. Why don't you go ahead and climb inside."

For a moment, the wiry man doesn't move. Just stands there shivering, staring into the tank through the open hatch. The lights give his skin a bluish hue, except for the needle scars, which glow red against his sickly pallor.

"Reed? Can you hear me?"

"Yeah." The man's voice comes through four speakers positioned in the corners of the control room.

"Ready to do this?"

"It's just . . . What if I feel pain? I'm not totally sure what to expect."

He stares toward the one-way glass—haggard and emaciated, his ribs showing through sallow skin.

"You can expect what we talked about," Slade says. "Dr. Wilson is sitting here beside me. You want to say something, Paul?"

The man with wavy silver hair dons his headset. "Reed, I have all your vital signs in front of me, which I'll be monitoring in real time, and a full contingency plan if I see that you're in distress."

Slade says, "Don't forget the bonus I'm going to pay you if today's test is successful."

Reed focuses his hollowed-out stare back on the tank.

"OK," he says, psyching himself up. "OK, let's do this." He grabs the handles on the sides of the deprivation tank and climbs unsteadily inside, the slosh of water audible through the speakers.

Slade says, "Reed, let us know when you're comfortably settled in."

After a moment, the man says, "I'm floating."

"If it's all right with you, I'm going to go ahead and close the hatch now."

Ten tense seconds elapse.

"Is that OK with you, Reed?"

"Yeah, all right."

Slade keys in a command. The hatch slowly lowers into place, closing seamlessly.

"Reed, we're ready to turn out the lights and get started. How you feeling?"

"I think I'm ready."

"Do you remember everything you and I discussed this morning?"

"I think so."

"I need you to be sure."

"I'm sure."

"Good. Everything's going to be fine. When you see me next, tell me my mother's name is Susan. That way I'll know."

Slade dims away the light. A previously dormant monitor glows to life, displaying a live feed of a night-vision camera looking straight down on Reed from the ceiling of the tank. It shows him floating on his back in the heavily salinized water. Slade pulls up a timer on the primary monitor, sets it for five minutes.

"Reed, this is the last you'll hear from me. We're going to give you a few minutes to relax and center yourself. Then we'll be under way."

"Got it."

"Godspeed. You're going to make history today."

Slade starts the countdown and removes his headset.

Helena asks, "What type of memory are you reactivating?"

"Did you notice the tattoo on his left shoulder?"

"Yeah."

"We inked that yesterday morning. Last night, we mapped the memory of the event."

"Why a tattoo?"

"Because of the pain. I wanted a strong, recent encoding experience."

"And a heroin addict is the best you could come up with for a test subject?"

Slade makes no response. His transformation is astounding. He's pushing this project farther than she was ever willing to go. She never imagined she'd encounter someone more driven and single-minded than herself.

"Does he even know what he's gotten himself into?" she asks.

"Yes."

Helena watches the time wind down. Seconds and minutes slipping away.

She looks at Slade and says, "This is way outside the bounds of responsible scientific testing."

"I agree."

"And you just don't care?"

"The kind of breakthrough I'm looking for today doesn't happen in the shallow end of the pool."

Helena studies the screen that shows Reed floating motionless in the tank.

"So you're willing to risk this man's life?" she asks.

"Yes. But so is he. He understands the state he's in. I think it's heroic. Besides, when we're finished, he'll go into rehab at a luxury clinic. And if this works, you and I will be drinking Champagne in your apartment . . ." He glances at his Rolex. "In ten minutes."

"What are you talking about?"

"You'll see."

They all wait in a strained silence for the final two minutes, and when the timer chimes, Slade says, "Paul?"

"Standing by."

Slade stares down the length of the console to the man in control of the stimulators. "Sergei?"

"Ready when you are."

"Resuscitation?"

"Paddles charged, standing by."

Slade looks at Paul and nods.

The doctor releases a breath, presses a key, says, "One milligram push of Rocuronium, away."

"What's that?" Helena asks.

"A neuromuscular blocking agent," Dr. Wilson says.

Slade says, "Whatever happens, we can't have him thrashing around in there, destroying that headpiece."

"He knows he's being temporarily paralyzed?"

"Of course."

"How are these drugs being administered?"

"Through a wireless IV port embedded in his left forearm. It's basically just a version of the lethal injection cocktail, minus the sedative."

The doctor says, "Two-point-two-milligram push of sodium thiopental, away."

Helena divides her attention between the night-vision feed of the tank's interior, and the screen the doctor is studying, which shows Reed's pulse rate, blood pressure, EKG, and a dozen other metrics.

"Blood pressure dropping," Dr. Wilson says. "Heart rate descending through fifty beats per minute."

"Is he suffering?" Helena asks.

"No," Slade says.

"How can you be sure?"

"Twenty-five beats per minute."

Helena leans in close to the monitor, watching Reed's face in tones of night-vision green. His eyes are closed, and he displays no visible signs of pain. He actually looks peaceful.

"Ten beats per minute. BP—thirty over five."

Suddenly the control room fills with the sustained tone of a flatline.

The doctor shuts it off and says, "Time of death: 10:13 a.m."

Reed looks no different in the tank, still floating in the saltwater.

"When do you revive him?" Helena asks.

Slade doesn't answer.

"Standing by," Sergei says.

A new window has appeared on the doctor's primary monitor. *Time Since Heart Death: 15 seconds.*

When the clock passes one minute, the doctor says, "DMT release detected."

Slade says, "Sergei."

"Initiating memory-reactivation program. Firing the stimulators . . ."

The doctor continues to read off the levels of various vital signs, now mainly associated with cerebral oxygen levels and activity. Sergei also gives an update every ten seconds or so, but for Helena, the din of their voices fades away. She can't take her eyes off the man in the tank, wondering what he's seeing and feeling. Wondering if she would be willing to die to experience the full power of her invention.

At the two-minute, thirty-second mark, Sergei says, "Memory program complete."

"Run it again," Slade says.

Sergei looks at him.

The doctor says, "Marcus, at five minutes, the chances of bringing him back are virtually nonexistent. The cells in his brain are dying rapidly."

"Reed and I talked about it this morning. He's ready to face this."

Helena says, "Pull him out."

"I'm not comfortable with this either," Sergei says.

"Please just trust me. Run the program one more time."

Sergei sighs and quickly types something. "Initiating memory-reactivation program. Firing the stimulators."

As Helena glares at Slade, he says, "Jee-woon pulled that man out of a drug house in one of the worst neighborhoods in San Francisco. He was unconscious, the needle still hanging out of his arm. He would probably be dead right now if it weren't—"

"That is no justification for this," she says.

"I understand how you could feel that way. I would again ask, *all of you*, to please just trust me for a little while longer. Reed will be perfectly fine."

Dr. Wilson says, "Marcus, if you have any intention of reviving Mr. King, I would suggest you tell my doctors to pull him out of the chamber immediately. Even if we get his heart to start beating again, if his cognitive functioning is gone, he'll be of no use to you."

"We aren't pulling him out of the tank."

Sergei rises and heads for the exit.

Helena leaves her chair, following right behind him.

"The door is locked from the outside," Slade says. "And even if you were to get through, my security detail is waiting in the hall. I'm sorry. I had a feeling you'd lose your nerve when we reached this moment."

The doctor says into his microphone, "Dana, Aaron, pull Mr. King out of the tank and begin resuscitation immediately."

Helena stares through the wall of glass. The doctors standing by the crash cart aren't moving.

"Aaron! Dana!"

"They can't hear you," Slade says. "I muted the testing-bay inter-coms right after you started the drug sequence."

Sergei charges the door, ramming his shoulder into the metal.

"You want to change the world?" Slade asks. "This is what it takes. This is what it feels like. Moments of steel, unflinching resolve."

On the night-vision feed from inside the tank, Reed isn't moving a muscle.

The water is perfectly calm.

Helena looks at the doctor's monitor. *Time Since Heart Death: 304 seconds.*

"We're past the five-minute mark," she says to Dr. Wilson. "Is there hope?"

"I don't know."

Helena rushes to an empty chair and lifts it off the ground, Jee-woon and Slade realizing what she's doing a half second too late, both men launching from their seats to stop her.

She brings the chair back over her shoulder and hurls it at the one-way window.

But it never reaches the glass.

BARRY

November 6, 2018

His eyes open, but he sees nothing. His sense of time is gone. Years could have passed. Or seconds. He blinks, but nothing changes. He wonders, *Am I dead?* Draws in a breath, his chest expanding, then lets it out. When he lifts his arm, he hears water moving and feels something sliding down the surface of his skin.

He realizes he's floating on his back, with no effort, in a pool of water that is the exact temperature of his skin. When he's motionless, he can't sense it, and even as he becomes still again, he's struck by the sensation of his body having no end and no beginning.

No . . . there is one sensation. Something has been affixed to his left forearm.

Reaching over with his right hand, he touches what feels like a hard plastic case. An inch wide, maybe four inches long. He tries to pull it off, but it's either been glued to or embedded in his skin.

"Barry." It's the voice of the man from before. The one who was sitting on the stool making him talk about Meghan as Barry was strapped to that chair.

"Where am I? What's happening?"

"I need you to calm down. Just breathe."

"Am I dead?"

"Would I be telling you to breathe if you were? You aren't dead, and where you are is irrelevant at this point."

Barry reaches a hand straight up out of the water, his fingers touching a surface two feet above his face. He searches for a lever, a button, something to open whatever he's been placed inside, but the walls are smooth and seamless.

He feels a slight vibration in the device on his forearm, reaches over to touch it again, but nothing happens. His right arm will no longer move.

He tries to lift his left—nothing.

Then his legs, his head, his fingers.

He can't even blink, and when he tries to speak, his lips refuse to part.

"What you're experiencing is a paralytic agent," the man says from somewhere in the darkness above. "That was the vibration you just felt—the device injecting the drug. Unfortunately, we need to keep you conscious. I won't lie to you, Barry. The next few moments are going to be very uncomfortable."

Terror swallows him—the most profound fear he has ever known. His eyes are locked open, and he keeps trying to move—

arms, legs, fingers, anything—but nothing responds. He might as well be trying to control a single strand of hair. And that's all before the real horror hits: he is unable to contract his diaphragm.

Which means he can't draw breath.

A maelstrom of panic washes over him, and finally pain, everything distilling down to a second-by-second escalation of the desperate need to inhale oxygen. But he is locked out of the controls of his own body. He cannot cry out or flail or beg for his life, which he would be more than willing to do if he could only speak.

"You've probably realized by now that you no longer have the ability to breathe. This isn't sadism, Barry. I promise you that. It will all be over soon."

He can only lie in the utter darkness, listening to the screaming of his mind and the torrent of racing thoughts while the sole sound is the thunderous pounding of his heart as it beats faster and faster.

The device on his forearm vibrates again.

Now a white-hot pain courses through his veins, and that jackhammer thudding of his heart responds instantly to whatever was just blasted into his bloodstream.

Slowing.

Slowing.

Slowing.

And then he no longer hears or feels it beating.

The silence of wherever he is becomes complete.

In this moment, he knows that blood is no longer circulating in his body.

I cannot breathe and my heart has stopped beating. I'm dead. Clinically dead. So how am I still thinking? How am I aware? How long will this last? How bad will the pain get? Is this really the end of me?

"I just stopped your heart, Barry. Please listen. You have to maintain focus during the next few moments, or we will lose you. If you make it to the other side, remember what I did for you. Don't let it happen this time. You can change it."

Explosions of color detonate in Barry's oxygen- and blood-starved brain—a light show for a dead man, each flash closer and brighter than the one before.

Until all he sees is a blinding whiteness that is already beginning to fade through shades of gray toward black, and he knows what lies at the end of that spectrum—unbeing. But maybe an end to the pain. To this brutal thirst for air. He's ready for it. Ready for anything that makes this stop.

And then he smells something. It's odd, because it conjures an emotional response he can't quite name, but which carries the ache of nostalgia. It takes a moment, but he realizes it's what his house used to smell like after he and Julia and Meghan had finished dinner. In particular, Julia's meatloaf and roasted carrots and potatoes. Next he catches the scent of yeast and malt and barley. Beer, but not just any beer. The Rolling Rocks he used to drink out of those green bottles.

Other smells emerge and merge in an aroma more complex than any wine. It's one he would recognize anywhere—the house in Jersey City he once lived in with his ex-wife and his dead daughter.

The smell of home.

Suddenly, he tastes the beer and the constant presence in his mouth of the cigarettes he used to smoke.

His brain fires an image that cuts through the dying whiteout—blurry and fuzzy at the edges, but quickly sharpening into focus. A television. And on the screen, a baseball game. The image in his mind's eye as clear as sight, gray-scale at first, but then color bleeding into everything he sees.

Fenway Park.

The green grass under the burn of the stadium lights.

The crowd.

The players.

The red clay of the pitcher's mound and Curt Schilling standing there with his hand in his glove, staring down Todd Helton at the plate.

It's as if a memory is being built before him. First the foundation of smell and taste. Then the scaffolding of visuals. Next comes an overlay of touch as he feels, actually *feels*, the cool softness of the leather chair he's sitting in, his feet propped up on the extended footrest, his head turning, and a hand—*his hand*—reaching for the bottle of Rolling Rock resting on a coaster on the table beside the chair.

As he touches the bottle, he can feel the cold wetness of the condensation on the green glass, and as he brings it to his lips and tilts it back, the taste and the smell overwhelm him with the power of actuality. Not of a mere memory, but an event that is happening *now*.

And he is keenly aware, not just of the memory itself, but of his perspective of the memory. It is unlike any recollection he has ever experienced, because he is *in* it, peering through the eyes of his younger self and watching the movie of his old life unfold before him as a fully immersed observer.

The pain of dying has become a dim and distant star, and now he begins to hear sounds, just brushstrokes at first, muffled and indistinct, but slowly gaining in volume and clarity, as if someone were slowing turning up the dials.

The announcers on the television.

A telephone ringing in their house.

Footsteps moving down the hardwood floor of the hallway.

And then Meghan is standing in front of him. He's staring up into her face, and her mouth is moving, and he hears her voice— too faint, too distant to make out any specific words, only to hear that familiar tone that has been quietly fading in his memory for eleven years.

She is beautiful. She is vital. Standing in front of the television, blocking the screen, with her backpack slung over one shoulder, blue jeans, a turquoise sweater, her hair pulled back into a ponytail.

This is too intense. Worse than the torture of asphyxiating and equally out of his control, because this is not a memory he is retrieving of his own volition. It's somehow being projected for him, against his will, and he thinks perhaps there's a reason our memories are kept hazy and out of focus. Maybe their abstraction serves as an anesthetic, a buffer protecting us from the agony of time and all that it steals and erases.

He wants out of his memory, but he can't leave. All senses are fully engaged. Everything as clear and vivid as existence. Except he has no control. He can do nothing but stare through the eyes of his eleven-years-younger self and listen to the last conversation he ever had with his daughter, feeling the vibration of his larynx, and then the movement of his mouth and lips forming words.

"You talked to Mom about this?" His voice doesn't sound strange at all. It feels and sounds exactly the way it does when he speaks.

"No, I came to you."

"Is your homework done?"

"No, that's why I want to go."

Barry feels his younger self leaning to see around Meghan as Todd Helton gets a piece of the next pitch. The third-base runner scores, but it's a groundout for Helton.

"Dad, you're not even listening to me."

"I am listening to you."

Now he's looking at her again.

"Mindy is my lab partner, and we have this thing due next Wednesday."

"For what?"

"Biology."

"Who else is going to be there?"

"Oh my God, it's me, Mindy, maybe Jacob, definitely Kevin and Sarah."

Now he watches himself lift his left arm to glance at his watch—one he will lose when he moves out of this house ten months from now in the wake of Meghan's death and the explosive decompression of his marriage.

It's a hair past 8:30 p.m.

"So can I go?"

Say no.

Younger Barry watches the next Rockies player walking to the plate.

Say no!

"You'll be back no later than ten?"

"Eleven."

"Eleven is for weekends, you know that."

"Ten thirty."

"OK, forget it."

"Fine, ten fifteen."

"Are you kidding me with this?"

"It takes ten minutes to walk there. Unless you want to drive me." Wow. He had repressed this moment because it was too painful. She had suggested he drive her, and he had refused. If he had, she would still be alive.

Yes! Drive her! Drive her, you idiot!

"Honey, I'm watching the game."

"So ten thirty then?"

He feels his lips curling up in a smile, remembers acutely the long-lost feeling of losing a negotiation with his daughter. The annoyance, but also the pride that he was raising a woman of grit, who knew her own mind and fought for the things she wanted. Remembered hoping she would carry that fire into her adult life.

"Fine." Meghan starts for the door. "But not a minute later. I have your word?"

Stop her.

Stop her!

"Yes, Dad." Her last words. Now he remembers. *Yes, Dad.*

Barry's younger self is staring at the television again, watching Brad Hawpe rifle a ball straight up the middle. He can hear Meghan's footsteps moving away from him, and he's screaming inside, but nothing's happening. It's as if he's inhabiting a body over which he exerts no control.

His younger self isn't even watching Meghan as she moves

toward the door. Only cares about the game, and he doesn't know he just looked into his daughter's eyes for the last time, that he could stop this from happening with a word.

He hears the front door open and slam shut.

Then she's gone, walking away from her house, from him, to her death. And he's sitting in a recliner watching a baseball game.

The pain of not being able to breathe has left him. He has no sense of floating in that warm water or of his heart lodged dormant in his chest. Nothing matters but this excruciating memory he is being forced to endure for reasons beyond his comprehension and the fact that his daughter has just left his house for the last—

His left pinkie moves.

Or rather, he is aware of having moved it. Of the action being a result of his intention.

He tries again. The entire hand moves.

He extends one arm, then the other.

He blinks. Takes a breath.

He opens his mouth and makes a sound like a grunt—guttural and meaningless—but *he* made it.

What does this mean? Before, he was experiencing the memory as an observer scrolls through a read-only file. Like watching a movie. Now he can move and make sound and interact with his environment, and every second, he is feeling more in control of this body.

Reaching down, he lowers the recliner's footrest. Then he's standing, looking around this house he lived in more than a decade ago and marveling at how exquisitely real it is.

Moving across the living room, he stops in front of the mirror beside the front door and studies his reflection in the glass. His hair is thicker and back to the color of sand, devoid of the silver, which, over the last few years, has been claiming more and more real estate on his thinning head of hair.

His jawline is sharp. No sagging jowls. No puffy bags under his eyes or gin blossoms on the side of his nose, and he realizes he let his body go to absolute shit since Meghan's death.

He looks at the door. The door his daughter just walked out of.

What the hell is happening? He was in a hotel in Manhattan, being killed in some kind of deprivation tank.

Is this real?

Is this happening?

It can't be, and yet it feels exactly like living.

He opens the door and steps out into the autumn evening.

If this isn't real, it's torture of the worst possible kind. But what if what the man said to him was true? *I'm about to give you the greatest gift of your life. The greatest gift a person could ever hope to receive.*

Barry slams back into the moment. Those are questions for later. Right now, he is standing on the front porch of his house, listening to the leaves of the oak tree in his front yard twittering in a gentle breeze that also moves the rope swing. By all appearances, it is, impossibly, October 25, 2007, the night his daughter was killed in a hit-and-run. She never made it to Dairy Queen to meet up with her friends, which means this tragedy will happen in the next ten minutes.

And she already has a two-minute head start.

He isn't wearing shoes, but he's wasted enough time already.

Pulling the front door to the house closed, he steps down into the lawn, leaves crunching under his bare feet, and heads off into the night.

HELENA

June 20, 2009

Day 598

Someone is knocking at her door. Reaching out in the darkness, she turns on the lamp and climbs out of bed in pajama bottoms and a black tank top. The alarm clock on her desk shows 9:50 a.m.

As she moves through the living room and toward the door, hitting the button on the wall to raise the blackout curtains, she's gripped by a powerful sense of déjà vu.

Slade is standing in the corridor in jeans and a hoodie, holding a bottle of Champagne, two glasses, and a DVD. First time she's laid eyes on him in weeks.

He says, "Shit, I woke you."

She squints at him under the glare of the light panels in the ceiling.

"Mind if I come in?" he asks.

"Do I have a choice?"

"Please, Helena."

She takes a step back and lets him enter, following him down the short entryway, past the powder room, and into the main living space.

"What do you want?" she asks.

He takes a seat on the ottoman of an oversize chair, beside the windows that look out into a world of infinite sea.

He says, "They tell me you aren't eating or exercising. That you haven't spoken to anyone or gone outside in days."

"Why won't you let me talk to my parents? Why won't you let me leave?"

"You aren't well, Helena. You're in no state of mind to protect the secrecy of this place."

"I told you I wanted out. My mom's in a facility. I don't know how she's doing. My dad hasn't heard my voice in a month. I'm sure he's worried—"

"I know you can't see it right now, but I am saving you from yourself."

"Oh, fuck you."

"You checked out because you disagreed with the direction I was taking this project. All I've been doing is giving you time to reconsider throwing everything away."

"It was *my* project."

"It's my money."

Her hands tremble. With fear. With rage.

She says, "I don't want to do this anymore. You have ruined my dream. You have blocked me from trying to help people like my mom. I want to go home. Are you going to continue keeping me here against my will?"

"Of course not."

"So I can leave?"

"Do you remember what I asked you the first day you got here?"

She shakes her head, tears coming.

"I asked if you wanted to change the world with me. We're standing on the shoulders of all the brilliant work you've done, and I came here this morning to tell you that we did it."

She stares at him across the coffee table, tears gliding down her face.

"What are you talking about?"

"Today is the biggest day of my life and yours. It's everything we've been working toward. So I came up here to celebrate with you."

Slade begins to untwist the wire holding the muselet to the bottle of Dom Perignon. When he gets it off, he tosses the wire cage on the coffee table. Then, gripping the bottle between his legs, he carefully pops the cork. Helena watches him pour the Champagne into the glasses, carefully filling each flute to the brim.

"You've lost your mind," she says.

"We can't drink these yet. We have to wait until . . ." He checks his watch. "Ten fifteen, give or take. While we wait, I want to show you something that happened yesterday."

Slade takes the DVD from the coffee table to the entertainment center. He loads it into the player and turns up the volume.

Onscreen: a tall, emaciated man she has never seen before is reclined in the memory chair. Jee-woon Chercover is leaning over him, inking a tattoo of letters—*M-i-r-a-n*—into his left shoulder. The emaciated man lifts an arm and says, *"Stop."*

Slade steps into the frame. *"What is it, Reed?"*

"I'm back. I'm here. Oh my God."

"What are you talking about?"

"The experiment worked."

"Prove it to me."

"Your mother's name is Susan. You told me to tell you that right before I got into the egg."

Onscreen, a huge grin spreads across Slade's face. He asks, "What time did we do the experiment tomorrow?"

"Ten a.m."

Slade turns off the television and looks at Helena.

She says, "Was that supposed to make any sense to me?"

"I guess we'll know in a minute."

They sit in awkward silence, Helena watching the Champagne bubbles effervesce.

"I want to go home," she says.

"You can leave today if you want."

She looks at the wall clock—10:10 a.m. It's so quiet in her apartment, she can hear the hiss of gas escaping the flutes. She stares at the sea, thinking whatever this is about, she's over it. She'll leave the rig, her research, everything. Forfeit her money, her profit participation, because no dream, no ambition, is worth what Slade has done to her. She'll go back home to Colorado and help take care of her mother. She couldn't preserve her fading memories or stop the disease, but at least she can be with her for however much time she has left.

Ten fifteen comes and goes.

Slade keeps looking at his watch, a bit of worry now creeping into his eyes.

Helena says, "Look, whatever this was supposed to be, I'm ready for you to leave. What time can the helicopter fly me back to California?"

Blood slides out of Slade's nose.

Now she tastes rust, realizes blood is trickling out of hers as well. Reaching up, she tries to catch it in her hands, but it seeps through her fingers and onto her shirt. She rushes into the powder room, grabs a couple of washcloths out of the drawer, and holds one to her nose as she carries the other back out to Slade.

As she hands it to him, she feels a stabbing agony behind her eyes, like the worst ice-cream headache of her life, and she can see by the look on his face that Slade is experiencing the same sensation.

He's smiling now, blood between his teeth. Rising from the ottoman, he wipes his nose and tosses the towel away.

"Do you feel them coming?" he asks.

At first, she thinks he's talking about the pain, but it's not that. She is suddenly aware of an entirely new memory of the last half hour. A gray, haunted-looking memory. In it, Slade didn't come here with a bottle of Champagne. He invited her to come down to the testing bay with him. She remembers sitting in the control room and watching a heroin addict climb into the deprivation tank. They fired a memory of him getting a tattoo, and then they killed him. She was trying to throw a chair through the window between the control room and the testing bay when, suddenly, she's here instead—standing in her apartment with a nosebleed and a killer headache.

"I don't understand," she says. "What just happened?"

Slade lifts his Champagne glass, clinks it against hers, and takes a long sip.

"Helena, you didn't just build a chair that helps people relive their memories. You made something that can return them to the past."

BARRY

October 25, 2007

The windows of neighboring houses seem to flicker from the illumination of television screens inside, and there's no one out except Barry, who's running down the middle of a street that is empty and plastered with fallen leaves from the oaks that line the block. He feels stronger than he has in ages. There's no pain in his left knee from the ill-advised slide across home plate during a softball game in Central Park that will not happen for another five years. And he's so much lighter on his feet, by thirty pounds at least.

A half mile in the distance, he sees the glow of restaurants and motel signs, Dairy Queen among them. He detects something in the left front pocket of his jeans. Slowing to a fast walk, he reaches in and pulls out a first-generation iPhone whose screensaver is a photo of Meghan crossing the finish line at a cross-country meet.

It takes four attempts to unlock it, and then he scrolls contacts until he finds Meghan, calling her as he begins to jog again.

It rings once.

Voicemail.

He calls again.

Voicemail again.

And he's running down the broken sidewalk past a collection of old buildings that will gentrify into loft space, a coffee shop, and a distillery in the coming decade. But for now, they loom dark and abandoned.

Several hundred yards away, he sees a figure emerge from the darkness of this undeveloped area and into the well-lit outer edge of the business district.

Turquoise sweater. Ponytail.

He shouts his daughter's name. She doesn't look back, and he's sprinting now, running as hard as he's ever run in his life, screaming her name between gulps of air, even as he wonders—

Is any of this real? How many times has he fantasized about this moment? Being given a shot at preventing her death . . .

"Meghan!" She's fifty yards ahead of him now, and he's close enough to see that she's talking on her phone, oblivious.

Tires squeal somewhere behind him. He glances back at fast-approaching headlights and registers the growl of a revving engine. The restaurant Meghan never reached is in the distance, on the opposite side of the street, and now she takes a step into the road to cross.

"Meghan! Meghan! *Meghan!*"

Three feet into the street, she stops and looks back in Barry's direction, the phone still held to her ear. He's close enough now to see the pure confusion on her face, the noise of the approaching car right on his heels.

A black Mustang blurs past at sixty miles per hour, the car streaking down the middle of the street and weaving across the centerline.

And then it's gone.

Meghan is still by the curb.

Barry reaches her, out of breath, his legs burning from the half-mile sprint.

She lowers her phone. "Dad? What are you doing?"

He looks up and down the road. It's just the two of them standing in the yellow light of an overhanging streetlamp, no cars coming, and quiet enough to hear dead leaves scraping across the pavement.

Was that Mustang the car that hit her eleven years ago, which is also, impossibly, tonight? Did he just stop it from happening?

Meghan says, "You're not wearing shoes."

He hugs her fiercely, still gasping for air, but there are sobs mixing in now, and he can't hold them back. It's too much. Her smell. Her voice. The sheer presence of her.

"What happened?" Meghan asked. "Why are you here? Why are you crying?"

"That car . . . it would've . . ."

"Jesus, Dad, I'm fine."

If this isn't real, it's the cruelest thing a person could ever do to him, because this doesn't feel like some virtual-reality experience or whatever that man subjected him to. This feels *real*. This is living. You don't come back from this.

He looks at her, touches her face, vital and perfect in the streetlight.

"Are you real?" he asks.

"Are you drunk?" she asks.

"No, I was . . ."

"What?"

"I was worried about you."

"Why?"

"Because, because that's what fathers do. They worry about their daughters."

"Well, here I am." She smiles uncomfortably, clearly and rightly questioning his sanity in this moment. "Safe and sound."

He thinks about the night he found her, not far from where they're standing. He had been calling her for an hour, and her phone just kept ringing before going to voicemail. It was while walking down this street that he'd seen the cracked screen of her phone lighting up where it had been dropped in the middle of the road. And then he'd found her body, broken and sprawled in the shadows beyond the sidewalk, the trauma indicating she'd been thrown a great distance after having been struck at a high rate of speed.

It's a memory that will never leave him, but which now possesses a gray and fading quality, just like the false memory that plagued him in that Montauk diner. Has he somehow changed what happened? That can't possibly be.

Meghan looks up at him for a long moment. Not annoyed anymore. Kind. Concerned. He keeps wiping his eyes, trying not to cry, and she seems simultaneously freaked out and moved.

She says, "It's OK if you cry. Sarah's dad gets emotional about everything."

"I'm very proud of you."

"I know." And then, "Dad, my friends are waiting on me."

"OK."

"But I'll see you later?" she asks.

"Definitely."

"We still going to the movies this weekend? For our date?"

"Yes, of course." He doesn't want her to go. He could hold her in his arms for a solid week and it wouldn't be enough. But he says, "Please be careful tonight."

She turns away and continues walking up the street. He calls her name. She looks back.

"I love you, Meghan."

"Love you too, Dad."

And he stands there trembling and trying to understand what just happened, watching her move away from him and then across the street, and then into Dairy Queen, where she joins her friends at a table by the window.

Footsteps approach from behind.

Barry turns, sees a man dressed in black coming toward him. Even from a distance, he looks vaguely familiar, and as he draws near, the full recognition hits. He's the man from the diner, Vince, who escorted him to the room after he'd been drugged in the hotel bar. The one with the neck tattoo, except he doesn't have it anymore. Or yet. Now, he has a full head of hair, a leaner build. And looks *ten years* younger.

Barry instinctively backs away, but Vince holds up his hands in a show of peace.

They face each other on the empty sidewalk under the street-lamp.

"What's happening to me?" Barry asks.

"I know you're confused and disoriented, but that won't last. I'm here to fulfill the final piece of my employment contract. Are you getting it yet?"

"Getting what?"

"What my boss did for you."

"This is real?"

"This is real."

"How?"

"You're with your daughter again, and she's alive. Does it matter? You won't see me after tonight, but I have to tell you something. There are ground rules, and they're simple. Don't try to game the larger system with your knowledge of what's to come. Just live your life again. Live it a little better. And tell no one. Not your wife. Not your daughter. *No one.*"

"What if I want to go back?"

"The technology that brought you here hasn't even been invented yet."

Vince turns to go.

"How do I thank him for this?" Barry asks, his eyes filling with tears again.

"Right now, in 2018, he's looking in on you and your family. Hopefully, he's seeing that you made the most of this chance. That you're happy. That your daughter is well. And most importantly, that you kept your mouth shut and played by the rules I just explained to you. That's how you can thank him."

"What do you mean, 'Right now, in 2018'?"

He shrugs. "Time is an illusion, a construct made out of human memory. There's no such thing as the past, the present, or the future. It's all happening now."

Barry tries to let that sink in, but it's too much to process. "You went back too, huh?"

"A bit further than you. I've been reliving my life for three years already."

"Why?"

"I messed up when I was a cop. Got in business with the wrong people. I own a fly-fishing shop now, and life is beautiful. Good luck with your second chance."

Vince turns away and walks off into the night.

BOOK TWO

We are homesick most for the places we have never known.

−CARSON MCCULLERS

HELENA

Day 598

Helena sits on the sofa in her apartment, trying to comprehend the magnitude of the last thirty minutes of her life. Her knee-jerk reaction is that it can't possibly be true, that it's some trick or illusion. But she keeps seeing the finished tattoo of *Miranda* on the heroin addict's shoulder; the unfinished tattoo of it in the video Slade just showed her. And she knows that somehow, even though she has a rich and detailed memory of the experiment this morning—right down to throwing a chair at a window—none of it happened. It exists as a dead branch of memory in the neuronal structure of her brain. The only thing she can compare it to is the remembrance of a very detailed dream.

"Tell me what's going through your mind right now," Slade says.

She fixes her stare on him. "Can this procedure—dying in the deprivation tank as a memory reactivates—actually alter the past?"

"There is no past."

"That's crazy."

"What? You can have your theories, but I can't have mine?"

"Explain."

"You said it yourself. 'Now' is just an illusion, an accident of how our brains process reality."

"That's just . . . freshman philosophy shit."

"Our ancestors lived in the oceans. Because of how light travels through water versus air, their sensory volume—the region in which they could scan for prey—was limited to their motor volume—the region they could actually reach and interact with. What do you think the result of that might be?"

She considers the question. "They could only react to immediate stimuli."

"OK. Now, what do you think happened when those fish finally crawled out of the ocean four hundred million years ago?"

"Their sensory volume increased, since light travels farther in air than in seawater."

"Some evolutionary biologists believe this terrestrial disparity between motor and sensory volume set the stage for the evolution of consciousness. If we can see ahead, then we can think ahead; we can plan. And then we can envision the future, even if it doesn't exist."

"So what's your point?"

"That consciousness is a result of environment. Our cognitions—our idea of reality—are shaped by what we can perceive, by the limitations of our senses. We think we're seeing the world as it really is, but you of all people know . . . it's all just shadows on the cave's wall. We're just as blinkered as our water-dwelling ancestors, the boundaries of our brains just as much an accident of evolution. And like them, by definition, we can't see what we're missing. Or . . . we couldn't, until now."

Helena remembers Slade's mysterious smile that night at dinner, so many months ago. "Piercing the veil of perception," she says.

"Exactly. To a two-dimensional being, traveling along a third dimension wouldn't just be impossible, it'd be something they couldn't conceive of. Just as our brains fail us here. Imagine if you could see the world through the eyes of more advanced beings—in four dimensions. You could experience events in your life in any order. Relive any memory you want."

"But that's . . . it's . . . ridiculous. And it breaks cause and effect."

Slade smiles that superior smile again. Still one step ahead. "Quantum physics is on my side here, I'm afraid. We already know that on the particle level, the arrow of time isn't as simple as humans think it is."

"You really believe time is an illusion?"

"More like our perception of it is so flawed that it may as well be an illusion. Every moment is equally real and happening now, but the nature of our consciousness only gives us access to one slice at a time. Think of our life like a book. Each page a distinct moment. But in the same way we read a book, we can only perceive one moment, one page, at a time. Our flawed perception shuts off access to all the others. Until now."

"But how?"

"You once told me that memory is our only true access to reality. I think you were right. Some other moment, an old memory, is just as much *now* as this sentence I'm speaking, just as accessible as walking into the room next door. We just needed a way to convince our brains of that. To short-circuit our evolutionary limitations and expand our consciousness beyond our sensory volume."

Her head is spinning.

"Did you know?" she asks.

"Did I know what?"

"What we were actually working toward from the beginning. That it was so much more than memory immersion."

Slade looks at the floor, then up at her again. "I respect you too much to lie to you."

"So . . . yes."

"Before we get to what I've done, can we just take a moment to relish what you've accomplished? You are now the greatest scientist and inventor who ever lived. You're responsible for the most important breakthrough of our time. Of any time."

"And the most dangerous."

"In the wrong hands, certainly."

"My God, you're arrogant. In any hands. How did you know what the chair could do?"

Slade sets his Champagne on the coffee table, gets up, and moves to the window. Several miles out to sea, storm clouds are billowing toward the platform.

"First time we met," he says, "you were leading an R&D group for a company in San Francisco called Ion."

"What do you mean 'the first time'? I've never worked—"

"Just let me finish. You hired me on as a research assistant. I would type up reports based on your dictation, track down articles you wanted to read. Manage your calendar and travel. Keep your coffee hot and your office clean. Or at least navigable." He smiles with something that approximates nostalgia. "I think my official title was lab bitch. But you were good to me. You made me feel included in the research, like I was a real part of your team. Before we met, I was in a bad way with drugs. You might have saved my life.

"You built a great MEG microscope and a decent electromagnetic stimulation network. You had far superior quantum processors to what we're using here, since Qbit technology was much further along. You had figured out the deprivation tank and how to make the reactivation apparatus operational inside. But you weren't satisfied. Your theory all along was that the tank would put a test subject into such an intense state of sensory deprivation that when we stimulated the neural coordinates for a memory, the experience would escalate into this completely immersive, transcendental event."

"Wait, so this all happened when?"

"On the original timeline."

It takes a moment for the magnitude of what he's saying to hit her.

"Was I pursuing my Alzheimer's time capsule application?" she asks.

"I don't think so. Ion was keen on pursuing the entertainment application of the chair, and that's what we were working on. But much like what we've discovered here, all you could do is give someone a slightly more vivid experience of a memory, without them having to retrieve it themselves. Tens of millions had been spent, and this technology you had staked your career on wasn't materializing." Slade turns away from the glass and looks at her. "Until November second, 2018."

"The *year* 2018."

"Yes."

"As in, nine years in the future."

"Correct. On that morning, something tragic and accidental and amazing happened. You were running a memory reactivation on a new test subject named Jon Jordan. The retrieval event was a car accident where he had lost his wife. Everything was humming along, and then he coded inside the deprivation tank. It was a massive cardiac arrest. As the medical team rushed to pull him out, something extraordinary happened. Before they could get the tank open, everyone in the lab was suddenly standing in a slightly different position. Our noses were all bleeding, some of us had splitting headaches, and instead of Jon Jordan in the tank, you were running an experiment on a guy named Michael Dillman. It all happened in the blink of an eye, like someone had flipped a switch.

"No one understood what had happened. We had no records of Jordan ever setting foot in our lab. We were rattled, trying to make sense of it all. Call it misguided curiosity, but I couldn't let it go. I tried to locate Jordan, to see what had happened to him, where he had gone, and it was the strangest thing—that car-accident memory we were reactivating? Turns out he had actually died in that wreck alongside his wife, fifteen years earlier."

Rain begins to strike the glass with a ticking sound that is just barely perceptible from inside Helena's apartment.

Slade returns to the ottoman.

"I think I was the first one to realize what had happened, to understand that you had somehow sent Jon Jordan's consciousness back into a memory. Of course, we'll never know, but I'm guessing the disorientation of returning to his younger self altered the outcome of the accident to kill both him and his wife."

Helena looks up from the patch of carpeting she's been staring into while she braced against the horror of this revelation.

"What did you do, Marcus?"

"I was forty-six years old. An addict. I had squandered my time. I was afraid you'd destroy the chair if you figured out what it was capable of."

"What did you do?"

"Three days later, the night of November fifth, 2018, I went to the lab and reloaded one of *my* memories into the stimulators. Then I climbed into the tank and shot a lethal dose of potassium chloride into my bloodstream. Christ, it burned like fire in my veins. Worst pain I have ever experienced. My heart stopped, and when the DMT hit, my consciousness shot back into a memory I'd made when I was twenty years old. And that was the start of a new timeline that branched off from the original in 1992."

"For the entire world?"

"Apparently."

"And that's the one we're living?"

"Yes."

"What happened to the original?"

"I don't know. When I think about it, those memories are gray and haunted. It's like all the life was sucked out of it."

"So you still remember the original timeline, where you were my forty-six-year-old lab assistant?"

"Yeah. Those memories traveled with me."

"Why don't I have them?"

"Think about our experiment just now. You and I had no memory of it until we caught back up to the precise moment when Reed died in the egg and traveled back into his tattoo memory. Only then did your memories and consciousness from that previous timeline, where you tried to throw a chair through the glass, slide into this one."

"So in nine years, on the night of November 5, 2018, I'm going to remember this whole other life?"

"I believe so. Your consciousness and memories from that original timeline will merge into this one. You'll have two sets of memories—one live, one dead."

Rain is sheeting down the glass, blurring away the world beyond.

Helena says, "You needed me to make the chair a second time."

"That's true."

"And with your knowledge of the future, you built an empire on this timeline, and lured me with the promise of unlimited funding once I'd made my initial breakthroughs at Stanford."

He nods.

"So you could completely control the creation of the chair and how it was used."

He says nothing.

"You've basically been stalking me since you started this second timeline."

"I think 'stalking' is a bit hyperbolic."

"I'm sorry, are we on a decommissioned oil rig in the middle of the Pacific that you built solely for me, or did I miss something?"

Slade lifts his Champagne glass and polishes off the rest.

"You stole that other life from me."

"Helena—"

"Was I married? Did I have kids?"

"Do you really want to know? It doesn't matter now. It never happened."

"You're a monster."

She gets up, goes to the window, and stares through the glass at a thousand shades of gray—the ocean near and the ocean far, stratified layers of cloud, an incoming squall. Over the last year, this apartment has felt more and more like a prison, but never more so than now. And it occurs to her as hot, angry tears run down her face that it was her own self-destructive ambition that carried her to this moment, and probably the one in 2018.

Hindsight is also having a clarifying effect on Slade's behavior, especially with regards to his ultimatum several months ago that they start killing test subjects to heighten the memory-reactivation experience. At the time, she thought it was reckless on his part. It had resulted in the mass exodus of almost everyone on the rig. Now she sees it for what it was—meticulously calculated. He knew they were in the homestretch and wanted nothing but a dedicated skeleton crew to witness the chair's true function. Now that she thinks about it, she isn't even certain the rest of her colleagues made it back to shore.

Up until now, she has suspected her life might be in danger.

Now she's sure of it.

"Talk to me, Helena. Don't go inward again."

Her response to Slade's revelation will probably be the determining factor in what he decides to do with her.

"I'm angry," she says.

"That's fair. I would be too."

Prior to this moment, she had assumed Slade possessed an immense intellect, that he was a master manipulator of people, as all industry leaders tend to be. Perhaps that's still true, but the lion's share of his success and fortune is simply attributable to his knowledge of future events. And *her* intellect.

The invention of the chair can't just be about money for him. He already has more money, fame, and power than God.

"Now that you've got your chair," she says, "what do you plan to do with it?"

"I don't know yet. I was thinking we could figure that out together."

Bullshit. You know. You've had twenty-six years leading up to this moment to figure it out.

"Help me streamline the chair," he says. "Help me test it safely. I couldn't tell you what I meant the first time, or even the second when I asked this question, but now you know the truth, so now I'm asking for a third time, and I hope the answer will be yes."

"What question?"

He comes over and takes hold of her hands, close enough now that she can smell the Champagne on his breath.

"Helena, do you want to change the world with me?"

BARRY

He walks into his house and closes the front door, stopping again at the mirror by the coat rack to stare at the reflection of his younger self.

This isn't real.

This can't be real.

Julia is calling his name from the bedroom. He moves past the television, where the World Series is still on, and turns down the hallway, the floor creaking under his bare feet in all the familiar places. Past Meghan's room, and then a guestroom that doubles as a home office, until he's standing in the doorway of his and Julia's room.

His ex is sitting in bed with a book opened across her lap and a cup of tea steaming on her bedside table.

"Did I hear you go out?" she asks.

She looks so different.

"Yeah."

"Where's Meghan?"

"She went to Dairy Queen."

"It's a school night."

"She'll be back by ten thirty."

"Knew who to ask, didn't she?"

Julia smiles and pats the bedspread beside her, and Barry enters their room, his eyes drifting over wedding photos, a black-and-white of Julia holding Meghan on the night of her birth, and finally a print over the bed of Van Gogh's *The Starry Night*, which they bought at MoMA ten years ago after seeing the original. He climbs onto the bed and sits against the headboard next to Julia. Up close, she looks airbrushed, her skin too smooth, only beginning to suggest the wrinkles he saw at brunch two days ago.

"Why aren't you watching your game?" she asks. The last time they sat on this bed together was the night she left him. Stared into his eyes and said, *I'm sorry, but I can't separate you from all this pain.* "Honey. What's wrong? You look like someone died."

He hasn't heard her call him *honey* in ages, and no he doesn't feel like anyone died. He feels . . . an intense sense of disorientation and disconnect. Like his own body is an avatar for which he's still getting a feel for the functionality.

"I'm fine."

"Wow, you want to try that again, but more convincing this time?"

Is it possible that the loss he's carried since Meghan's death is bleeding from his soul through his eyes and into this impossible moment? That on some lower frequency, Julia senses that shift in him? Because the absence of tragedy is having an inverse, proportional effect on what he sees when he looks into her eyes. They astound him. Bright and present and clear. The eyes of the woman he fell in love with. And it hits him all over again—the ruinous power of grief.

Julia runs her fingers down the back of his neck, which puts a shiver through his spine and raises gooseflesh. He hasn't been touched by his wife in a decade.

"What's the matter? Something happen at work?"

Technically, his last day of work consisted of getting killed in a deprivation tank, and sent back into whatever this is, so . . .

"Yeah, actually."

The sensory experience of it is what's killing him. The smell of their room. The softness of Julia's hands. All the things he'd forgotten. Everything he lost.

"Do you want to talk about it?" she asks.

"Would you mind if I just lie here while you read?"

"Of course not."

And so he rests his head on her lap. He has imagined this a thousand times, usually at three a.m., lying in bed in his Washington Heights apartment, caught in that wearisome handoff between intoxication and hangover, wondering—

What if his daughter had lived? What if his marriage had survived? What if everything had not derailed? What if . . .

This isn't real.

This can't be real.

The only sound in the room is the soft scratch of Julia turning the page every minute or so. His eyes are closed, he's just breathing now, and as she runs her fingers through his hair the way she used to, he turns onto his side to hide the tears in his eyes.

Inside, he's a quivering heap of protoplasm, and it takes a herculean effort to maintain his mental composure. The pure emotion is staggering, but Julia doesn't seem to notice the handful of times his back heaves with a barely suppressed sob.

He was just reunited *with his dead child.*

He saw her, heard her voice, held her.

Now he's somehow back in his old bedroom with Julia, and it's too much to take.

A terrifying thought creeps in—*What if this is just a psychotic break?*

What if it all goes away?

What if I lose Meghan again?

Hyperventilating—

What if—

"Barry, you OK?"

Quit thinking.

Breathe.

"Yeah."

Just breathe.

"You sure?"

"Yeah."

Go to sleep.

Don't dream.

And see if all of this still exists in the morning.

He is woken early by light coming through the blinds. Finds himself lying beside Julia, still wearing his clothes from last night. He climbs out of bed without disturbing her and pads down the hallway to Meghan's room. The door is closed. He cracks it open, peers inside. His daughter sleeps under a mound of blankets, and it is quiet enough in the house at this hour for him to hear her breathing.

She is alive. She is safe. She is right there.

He and Julia should be in a state of grief and shock, just getting back to their house after spending all night in the morgue. The image of Meghan's body on the slab—her crushed-in torso covered in a black bruise—has never left him, although his memory of it has taken on the same haunted complexion as the other false memories.

But there she is, and here he is, feeling more at home in this body with every passing second. That clipped line of memories of his other life is receding, as if he's just woken from the longest, most horrific nightmare. An eleven-year-long nightmare.

That's exactly what it is, he thinks—*a nightmare.* Because this is feeling more and more like his reality now.

He slips into Meghan's room and stands next to the bed, watching her sleep. Bearing witness to the formation of the universe couldn't fill him with a more profound sense of wonder and joy and overwhelming gratitude at whatever force remade the world for Meghan and for him.

But a cold terror is also breathing down his neck at the thought that this might be a delusion.

A piece of inexplicable perfection waiting to be snatched away.

He wanders through the house like a ghost through a past life, re-discovering spaces and objects all but lost in his memory. The alcove in the living room where every Christmas they put up the tree. The small table by the front door where he stashed his personal effects. A coffee mug he favored. The roll-top desk in the guestroom where he paid the bills. The chair in the living room where every Sunday he read the *Washington Post* and *New York Times* cover to cover.

It is a museum of memories.

His heart is beating faster than normal, keeping time with a low-level headache behind his eyes. He wants a cigarette. Not psy-chologically—he finally quit five years ago after numerous failed attempts—but apparently his thirty-nine-year-old body physically needs a nicotine bump.

He goes into the kitchen and fills a glass with water from the tap. Stands at the sink, watching the early light brushstroke the backyard into being.

Opening the cabinet to the right of the sink, he pulls out the cof-fee he used to drink. He brews a pot and loads what he can of yes-terday's dishes into the dishwasher, then sets to work completing the task that was his for the duration of their marriage—washing the remaining dishes by hand in the sink.

When he finishes, the cigarettes are still calling to him. He goes to the table by the front door and grabs the carton of Camels and throws them in the garbage bin outside. Then he sits on the porch drinking his coffee in the cold, hoping his head will clear and wondering if the man responsible for sending him here is watch-ing him right now. Perhaps from some higher plane of existence? From beyond time? The fear returns. Will he be suddenly ripped out of this moment and thrown back into his old life? Or is this permanent?

He tamps down the rising panic. Tells himself he didn't imagine FMS and the future. This is far too elaborate, even for his detective's mind, to have dreamed up.

This is real.

This is now.

This *is*.

Meghan is alive, and nothing will ever take her away from him again.

He says aloud, the closest thing to a prayer he's ever made, *"If you can hear me right now, please don't take me away from this. I will do anything."*

There is no response in the dawn silence.

He takes another sip of coffee and watches the sunlight stream through the branches of the oak tree, striking the frosted grass, which begins to steam.

HELENA

July 5, 2009

Day 613

As she descends the stairwell toward the superstructure's third level, her parents—Mom especially—are on her mind.

Last night, she dreamed of her mother's voice.

The subtle Western twang.

The lilting softness.

They were sitting in a field adjacent to the old farmhouse where she grew up. A fall day. The air crisp and everything tinged with the golden light of late afternoon as the sun slipped behind the mountains. Dorothy was young, her hair still auburn and blowing in the wind. Even though her lips weren't moving, her voice was clear and strong. Helena can't remember a word she said, only the feeling her mother's voice conjured inside of her—pure and unconditional love coupled with the bite of an intense nostalgia that made her heart ache.

She's desperate to talk to them, but since the revelation two weeks ago that she and Slade built something far more powerful than a memory-immersion device, she hasn't felt comfortable broaching the subject of communicating with her mom and dad again. She will when the time comes, but everything is still too fresh and raw.

She's having a hard time coming to grips with what she thinks about her accidental invention, how Slade manipulated her, and what lies ahead.

But she's working in the lab again.

Exercising.

Putting on a good face.

Trying to be useful.

As she leaves the stairwell for the lab, a bump of adrenaline plows through her system. They're running test number nine on Reed King today, a new one. She's going to experience reality shifting beneath her feet again, and there's no denying the thrill.

As she approaches the testing bay, Slade swings around the corner.

"Morning," she says.

"Come with me."

"What's wrong?"

"Change of plan."

Looking tense and disturbed, he leads her into a conference room and closes the door. Reed is already seated at the table, wearing torn jeans and a knit sweater, his hands clutching a steaming cup of coffee. His time on the rig seems to be putting some meat on his bones and erasing the junkie hollowness from his stare.

"Experiment's off," Slade says, taking a seat at the head of the table.

Reed says, "I had fifty thousand coming to me for this one."

"You'll still get your money. The thing is, we already performed the experiment."

"What are you talking about?" Helena asks.

Slade checks his watch. "We ran the experiment five minutes ago." He looks at Reed. "You died."

"Isn't that what was supposed to happen?" Reed asks.

"You died in the tank, but there was no reality shift," Slade says. "You actually just died."

"How do you know all this?" Helena asks.

"After Reed died, I got in the chair and recorded an earlier memory of cutting myself while shaving this morning." Slade lifts his head, touches a nasty slice along his neckline. "We pulled Reed out of the tank. Then I climbed in, died, and returned to my shaving moment so I could come down here and stop the experiment from going forward."

"Why didn't it work?" she asks. "Was the synaptic number not high—"

"The synaptic number was well into the green."

"What was the memory?"

"Fifteen days ago. June twentieth. The first time Reed climbed into the tank, with the full tattoo of *Miranda* on his arm."

It's like something just detonated inside Helena's brain.

"No shit he died," she says. "That isn't a real memory."

"What do you mean?"

"That version of events never happened. Reed never got a tattoo. He changed that memory when he died in the tank." Now she looks at Reed, starting to put the pieces together. "Which means there was nothing for you to return to."

"But I remember it," Reed says.

"What does it look like in your mind's eye?" she asks. "Dark? Static? Shades of gray?"

"Like time had been frozen."

"Then it's not a real memory. It's . . . I don't know what to call it. Fake. False."

"Dead," Slade says, glancing at his watch again.

"So this wasn't an accident." She glares at Slade across the table. "You knew."

"Dead memories fascinate me."

"Why?"

"They represent . . . another dimension of movement."

"I don't know what the fuck that means, but we agreed yesterday that you wouldn't try to map a—"

"Every time Reed dies in the tank, he orphans a string of memories that become dead in our minds after we shift. But what really happens to those timelines? Have they truly been destroyed, or are they still out there somewhere, beyond our reach?" Slade looks at his watch again. "I remember everything from the experiment we did this morning, and the two of you will gain those dead memories any second now."

They sit in silence at the table, a coldness enveloping Helena.

We are fucking with things that shouldn't be fucked with.

She feels the pain coming behind her eyes. Reaching forward, she grabs a few tissues from the box of Kleenex to stop the nosebleed.

The dead memory of their failed test comes crashing through.

Reed coding in the tank.

Five minutes dead.

Ten minutes.

Fifteen.

Her yelling at Slade to do something.

Rushing into the testing bay, tearing open the hatch of the deprivation tank.

Reed floating peacefully inside.

Death-still.

Pulling him out with Slade and setting him dripping wet on the floor.

Performing CPR as Dr. Wilson says over the intercom, "There's no point, Helena. He's been gone too long."

Continuing anyway, sweat pouring into her eyes as Slade vanishes across the hall, into the room with the chair.

She's given up on saving Reed by the time Slade reenters—sitting in the corner and trying to come to terms with the fact that they really killed a man. Not just a man. He was her responsibility. Here because of something she built.

Slade begins to strip.

"What are you doing?" she asks.

"Fixing this." Then he looks toward the one-way glass between the testing bay and control room. "Will somebody get her out of here, please?"

Slade's men burst in as he climbs naked into the tank.

"Please come with us, Dr. Smith."

Rising slowly, walking out of her own volition into the control room, where she sits behind Sergei and Dr. Wilson as they reactivate Slade's shaving-cut memory.

All the time thinking, This is wrong, this is wrong, this is wrong, until . . .

She's suddenly sitting right here, in this conference room, catching blood with the Kleenex.

Helena looks at Slade.

He's watching Reed, who's staring with a kind of entranced smile into nothing.

"Reed?" Slade asks.

The man doesn't answer.

"Reed, can you hear me?"

Reed turns his head slowly until he's staring at Slade, blood running over his lips, dripping on the table.

"I died," Reed says.

"I know. I went back into a memory to save—"

"And it was the most beautiful thing I've ever seen."

"What did you see?" Slade asks.

"I saw . . ." He struggles to put it into words. "Everything."

"I don't know what that means, Reed."

"Every moment of my life. I was rushing through this tunnel that was filled with them, and it was so lovely. I found one I'd forgotten. An exquisite memory. I think it was my first."

"Of what?" Helena asks.

"I was two, maybe three. I was sitting on someone's lap on a beach, and I couldn't turn around to see their face, but I knew that it was my father. We were in Cape May on the Jersey Shore, where we used to vacation. I couldn't see her, but I knew my mother was behind me too, and my brother, Will, was standing in the distance in the surf, letting the waves hit him. It smelled like the ocean and sunscreen and the funnel cakes someone was selling behind us on the boardwalk." Tears running down his face now. "I have never felt such love in my entire life. Everything good. Safe. It was a perfect moment before . . ."

"What?" Slade asks.

"Before I became me." He wipes his eyes, looks at Slade. "You shouldn't have saved me. You shouldn't have brought me back."

"What are you talking about?"

"I could've stayed in that moment forever."

BARRY

November 2007

Each day is a revelation, every moment a gift. The simple act of sitting across the dinner table from his daughter and listening to her talk about her day feels like a pardon. How could he ever have taken even one second of it for granted?

He drinks in every moment—the way Meghan's eyes roll when

he asks about boys, the way they light up when they talk about the colleges she wants to visit. He cries spontaneously in her presence, but it's easy enough to blame on quitting the cigarettes, on watching his little girl become a woman.

Julia's antennae are slightly up. In these moments, he notices her watching him the way one might examine a painting hanging not quite straight.

Every morning, when consciousness first returns, he lies in bed afraid to open his eyes, fearing he'll find himself back in his one-bedroom apartment in Washington Heights, with this second chance fading into oblivion.

But he's always next to Julia, always watching the light come through the blinds, and his only connection to that other life exists in false memories, which he would love to forget.

HELENA

July 5, 2009

Day 613

After dinner, as Helena washes her face and gets ready for bed, she hears a knock at her door, finds Slade standing in the hallway, eyes dark and troubled.

"What happened?" she asks.

"Reed hanged himself in his room."

"Oh God. Because of the dead memory?"

"Let's not make any assumptions. The brain of an addict is wired differently from ours. Who knows what he really saw when he died.

Anyway, I just thought you should know. But don't worry. I'll get him back tomorrow."

"Get him back?"

"With the chair. I'll be honest, I'm not looking forward to dying again. As you can imagine, it's deeply unpleasant."

"He made a choice to end his life," Helena says, trying to keep her emotion in check. "I think we should respect that."

"Not while he's still under my employ."

Lying in bed, hours later, she tosses and turns.

Thoughts rip through her mind, and she can't shut them off.

Slade has lied to her.

Manipulated her.

Kept her from communicating with her parents.

Stolen a life from her.

While nothing has ever intellectually intrigued her more than the mysterious power of the chair, she doesn't trust Slade with it. They have altered memories. Changed reality. Brought a man back from the dead. And yet he keeps pushing boundaries with an obsessive determination that makes her wonder what his real endgame is with all of this.

She climbs out of bed and walks over to the window, sweeps away the blackout curtains.

The moon is high and full and shining down on the sea, whose surface is a gleaming, blue-black lacquer, as still as a frozen moment.

There will never be a day when she flies her mother here and puts her in the chair to map whatever is left of her mind.

That was never going to happen. It's time to let the dream die and get the fuck out.

But she can't. Even if she made it out on one of the supply ships, the moment Slade realized she was gone, he'd simply return to a memory before she escaped and stop her.

He could stop you before you even tried to escape. Before the idea even occurred to you. Before this moment.

All of which means—there's only one way off the platform now.

BARRY

December 2007

He is better at his job, partly because he remembers some of the cases and suspects, but mainly because he gives a shit. The powers that be try to promote him to a better-paying, supervisory desk job, but he declines. He wants to be a great detective, nothing more.

He stays off cigarettes, drinks only on weekends, runs three times a week, and takes Julia out every Friday night. It isn't quite perfect between them. She doesn't carry the trauma of Meghan's death and the destruction of their marriage, but for him there is no escaping how those events corroded their bond. In his previous life, it took him a long time to stop being in love with Julia, and even though he's back to before everything imploded, it's not just a light switch he can flip back on.

He watches the news every morning, reads the papers every Sunday, and while he remembers the big moments—the candidate who will become president, the first tremors of a recession—the majority of it is granular and insignificant enough as to feel brand-new all over again.

He sees his mom every week now. She is sixty-six years old and in five years will exhibit the first symptoms of the glioblastoma brain cancer that will kill her. In six, she won't recognize him or be able to carry a conversation, and she will die in hospice care soon after, a wasted husk of herself. He will hold her bony hand in her final moments, wondering if she is even capable of registering the sensation of human touch in the annihilated landscape of her brain.

Oddly, he finds no sadness or despair knowing how and when her life will end. Those last days feel untouchably remote as he sits in her Queens apartment the week before Christmas. In fact, he considers the foreknowledge a gift. His father died when Barry was fifteen from an aortic aneurysm, sudden and unexpected. With his mom, he has years to say goodbye, to make certain she knows he loves her, to say all the things that are in his heart, and there is immeasurable comfort in that. He has wondered lately if that's all living really is—one long goodbye to those we love.

He's brought Meghan along with him today, and his daughter and mother are playing chess while he sits by the window, his mother singing in that delicate falsetto that always stirs something deep inside of him, his attention divided between their game and the passersby on the street below.

Despite the old technology all around him and the occasionally familiar news headline, he doesn't feel like he's living in the past. This moment feels very much like *now*. The experience is having a philosophical impact on his perception of time. Perhaps Vince was right. Maybe it is all happening at once.

"Barry?"

"Yes, Mom?"

"When did you become so introspective?"

He smiles. "I don't know. Maybe turning forty did it to me."

She watches him for a moment, turning her attention back to the chessboard only when Meghan makes her next move.

———

He lives his days and sleeps his nights.

Goes to parties he's already been to, watches games he's already seen, solves cases he's already solved.

It makes him wonder about the déjà vu that haunted his previous life—the perpetual sense that he was doing or seeing something he'd already seen before.

And he wonders—is déjà vu actually the specter of false timelines that never happened but did, casting their shadows upon reality?

HELENA

October 22, 2007

She is sitting at her old desk again in the musty depths of the neuroscience building in Palo Alto, caught in a transition between memory and reality.

The pain of dying in the tank is still fresh—the burn in her oxygen-starved lungs, the excruciating weight of her paralyzed heart, the panic and the fear, wondering if her plan would work. And then, when the memory-reactivation program finally engaged and the stimulators fired—pure exhilaration and release. Slade was right. Absent DMT, the experience of reactivating a memory was nothing more than watching a movie we've already seen a thousand times before. This is like living it.

Jee-woon is sitting across from her, his face coming into hard focus, and she wonders if he notices anything off about her, since she doesn't have control of her body yet. But she's catching words here and there—pieces of a familiar conversation.

". . . very taken with the memory-portraiture article you published in *Neuron*."

Her muscular control starts at her fingertips and toes, then works inward, up her arms and legs, until she can control her ability to blink and swallow. Suddenly, her body feels like something that belongs to her, and she is flooded with control, with the thrill of full possession, completely back inside her younger self again.

She looks around her office, the walls covered in high-resolution images of mice memories. A moment ago, she was 173 miles off the northern California coast, almost two years in the future, dying in the deprivation tank on the third floor of Slade's oil platform.

"Everything OK?" Jee-woon asks.

It worked. My God, it worked.

"Yeah. I'm sorry. You were saying?"

"My employer is very impressed with your work."

"Does your employer have a name?" she asks.

"Well, that depends."

"On . . . ?"

"How this conversation goes."

Having this conversation for a second time feels both perfectly normal and mind-bogglingly surreal. It is, without question, the strangest moment of her entire existence, and she has to force herself to focus.

She looks at Jee-woon and says, "Why would I even have a conversation with someone when I don't know who they're speaking for?"

"Because your Stanford money runs out in six weeks." He reaches into his leather satchel and takes out a document in a navy binder—her grant proposal.

As Jee-woon pitches her on coming to work for his boss for no-limit funding, she stares at that grant proposal, thinking, *I did it. I built my chair, and it is so much more powerful than I ever imagined it could be.*

"You need a team of coders to help you design an algorithm for complex memory cataloging and projection. The infrastructure for human trials."

Immersive platform for projection of long-term, explicit, episodic memories.

She built it. And it worked.

"Helena?" Now Jee-woon is staring at her across the disaster zone that is her desk.

"Yes?"

"Do you want to come work with Marcus Slade?"

The night Reed killed himself, she crept down to the lab, and using a back-door access into the system she'd convinced Raj to embed before he left, mapped a memory of this moment—Jee-woon showing up at her Stanford lab. It had left a strong-enough neuronal footprint to be viable for return. Then she programmed the memory-reactivation sequence, the drug cocktail, and climbed into the tank at three thirty in the morning.

Jee-woon says, "Helena? What do you say?"

"I would love to work with Mr. Slade."

He pulls another document out of his satchel and passes it to her.

"What's this?" she asks, though she already knows. She signed it in what is now a dead memory.

"An employment and confidentiality agreement. Nonnegotiable. I think you'll find the financial terms to be very generous."

BARRY

January 2008–May 2010

And then life feels like life again, the days running together with a sense of sameness and acceleration, more and more of them passing without him ever thinking about the fact that he is living his life all over again.

HELENA

The smell of Jee-woon's cologne still lingers in the elevator as Helena rides up to the first floor of the neuroscience building. It's been almost two years since she set foot on the Stanford campus. Since she set foot on land. The green of the trees and the grass almost moves her to tears. The way sunlight passes through trembling leaves. The smell of flowers. The sound of birds that don't live at sea.

The fall day is bright and warm, and she keeps looking at the screen on her flip phone, staring at the date because a part of her still doesn't believe it's October 22, 2007.

Her Jeep is waiting for her in the faculty parking lot. She climbs onto the sun-warmed seat and digs the key out of her backpack.

Soon, she's burning down the interstate, the wind screaming over the roll bars. The oil platform feels like a gray, fading dream, and even more so the chair, the tank, Slade, and the last two years, which have, because of something *she* built, not even happened yet.

At her house in San Jose, she packs a suitcase with clothes, a framed photograph of her parents, and six books that mean the world to her: *On the Fabric of the Human Body* by Andreas Vesalius, *Physica* by Aristotle, *The Mathematical Principles of Natural Philosophy* by Isaac Newton, Darwin's *On the Origin of Species*, and two novels—Camus's *The Stranger*, and Gabriel García Márquez's *One Hundred Years of Solitude*.

At the bank, she closes her savings and checking accounts—a little under $50,000. She takes $10,000 in cash, puts the remaining $40,000 into a brokerage account, then walks out into the noonday sun with a white envelope that feels woefully slim.

Near Highway 1, she stops at a convenience store to gas up her Jeep. When the transaction is complete, she throws her credit card in the trash, lowers the soft-top, and climbs in behind the wheel. She doesn't know where she's going. This is as far as she planned last night on the rig, and her mind is racing with both exhilaration and terror.

There's a dime in one of the cup holders. She flips it in the air and catches it against the top of her left hand.

Heads, she goes south.

Tails, she goes north.

The road winds along the craggy coastline, the sea yawning out into gray mist several hundred feet below.

She speeds through cedar forests.

Past coastal headlands.

Across windswept balds.

Through towns that barely warrant a name—tiny outposts on the edge of the world.

Her first night, she stops a couple hours north of San Francisco at a refurbished roadside motel called Timber Cove, which is perched on a cliff that overlooks the sea.

Sits alone by a fire pit with a glass of wine from a bottle that was made just twenty miles inland, watching the sun drop and considering what her life has become.

She takes out her phone to call her parents but hesitates.

At this moment, Marcus Slade is expecting her imminent arrival on his decommissioned oil platform to begin work on the chair, no doubt believing that the knowledge of its true, mind-blowing capability rests solely with him. When she fails to show up, he'll not only suspect what she's done, he'll turn the world inside out looking for her, because without her, he doesn't have a prayer of building—or, in a sense, of rebuilding—the chair.

He might even use her parents to get to her.

She sets the phone on the ground and crushes it under the heel of her boot.

———

She pushes north up Highway 1, taking a short detour to a place she's always wanted to see on the Lost Coast—Black Sands Beach in Shelter Cove.

Then on through redwood groves and quiet seaside communities and into the Pacific Northwest.

A couple days later, she's in Vancouver, heading up the coast of British Columbia, from city to town to village to some of the most beautifully desolate country she's ever laid eyes on.

Three weeks later, while meandering through the wilds of northern Canada, a storm catches up with her as night is falling.

She stops at a roadside tavern on the outskirts of a village that's a relic from the Gold Rush days, settles onto a stool at a wood-paneled bar, and drinks beer and bullshits with the locals as a fire burns in a massive stone hearth and the first snow of the season whisks against the window glass.

In some ways, the village of Haines Junction, Yukon, feels every bit as remote as Slade's oil rig—this hamlet in the farthest reaches of Canada, tucked into an evergreen forest at the foot of a glaciated mountain range. To everyone in the village, her name is Marie Iden—first name inspired by the first woman to win a Nobel Prize and whose work led to the discovery of radioactivity, the last name by one of her favorite thriller writers.

She lives in a room above the tavern and gets paid under the table to tend bar on weekends. She doesn't need the money. Her knowledge of future markets will turn her investments into millions in the years to come. But it's good to keep busy, and it might cause questions if she has no apparent source of income.

Her room isn't much—a bed, a dresser, and one window that

overlooks the emptiest highway she's ever seen. But for now at least, it's all she needs. She makes acquaintances, no friends, and enough wanderers pass through the bar and the town to afford the occasional twenty-four-hour-lonely-heart liaison.

And she is lonely, but that emotion appears to be the norm here. It didn't take her long to clock Haines Junction as a refuge for a distinct class of people.

Those looking for peace.

Those looking to hide.

And, of course, those hoping for both.

She misses the mental stimulation of her work. Misses being in a laboratory. Misses having a goal. It eats her up inside to wonder what her parents must make of her disappearance. She feels guilty every hour of every day that she isn't building the memory chair that could preserve core memories for people like her mom.

It has crossed her mind that one solution to all of this would be to kill Slade. It'd be easy enough to get close to him—she could call Jee-woon, say she's reconsidered the offer. But she doesn't have it in her. For better or worse, she simply isn't that person.

So she comforts herself with the knowledge that every day she remains in this secluded corner of the world, undiscovered by Slade, is a day she keeps the world safe from what she has the potential to create.

After two years, she procures fake credentials and identification documents from the Dark Web and moves to Anchorage, Alaska, where she volunteers as a research assistant for a neuroscientist at the university—a kind man who has no idea that one of his underlings is the preeminent research scientist in the world. She spends her days interviewing Alzheimer's patients and recording their deteriorating memories over weeks and months as the disease progresses through its cruel, dehumanizing stages. The work is hardly groundbreaking, but at least she's lending her intellect to a field of study she's passionate about. The boredom and purposelessness of her time in the Yukon had driven her to the brink of depression.

There are days she wants desperately to start building the MEG microscope and the reactivation apparatus as a means for capturing and preserving the memories of the people she interviews, who are slowly losing themselves and the memories that define them. But the risk is too great. It could alert Slade to her work, or someone might, as she apparently did, accidentally make the leap from memory reactivation to memory travel. Humans cannot be trusted with technology of such power—with the splitting of the atom came the atomic bomb. The ability to change memory, and thereby reality, would be at least that dangerous, in part because it would be so seductive. Was she herself not changing the past now, and at her first opportunity?

But the chair has been unmade, she has vanished, and there is no threat to memory and time but the knowledge in her own mind, which she will take to the grave.

The thought of killing herself has occurred to her on more than one occasion. It would be the ultimate insurance policy against Slade finding her and forcing her cooperation. She's gone so far as to make potassium chloride tablets in the event that day ever comes.

She keeps them with her at all times, in a silver locket around her neck.

Helena parks in a visitor's space near the entrance and steps out into the sweltering August heat. The grounds are well kept. There are gazebos and water features and picnic areas. She wonders how her father is affording this place.

She checks in at the main desk and has to write her name on a visitor's sign-in form. As the admin makes a copy of her driver's license, Helena looks around, nervous.

She's been three years on this new timeline. Slade's false memories of their time together on his oil platform would have found him early in the morning on July 6, 2009, the same moment (in the previous timeline) when she died in the deprivation tank and returned to the memory of Jee-woon coming to her lab at Stanford.

If Slade wasn't looking for her prior to that, he will be now. In all likelihood, he's paid off someone here to alert him if Helena ever turns up.

Which she just has.

But she didn't come here ignorant of the risk.

If Slade or one of his men tracks her down, she's prepared to handle it.

Reaching up, she clutches the locket hanging from her neck.

"Here you are, hon." The admin hands Helena a visitor's badge. "Dorothy's in Room 117, end of the hall. I'll buzz you through."

Helena waits as the doors to the Memory Care wing slowly open.

The smells of cleaning products and urine and cafeteria food comingle to conjure the memory of the last time she set foot in an adult-care facility—twenty years ago, during the final months of her grandfather's life.

She passes a common area, where residents in a heavily medicated stupor sit around a television showing a nature program.

The door to 117 is ajar, and she eases it open.

By Helena's math, it's been five years since she last saw her mother.

Dorothy is sitting in a wheelchair with a blanket over her legs, staring out the window toward the foothills of the Rocky Mountains. She must have seen Helena in her peripheral vision, because she turns her head slowly toward the doorway.

Helena smiles.

"Hi."

Her mother stares at her, unblinking.

No sign of recognition.

"Is it all right if I come in?"

Her mother lowers her head in a gesture that Helena takes for assent. Moving inside, she shuts the door after her.

"I like your room very much," Helena says. There's a muted television showing a news channel. Photographs *everywhere*. Of her parents in younger, better times. Of her as a baby, as a child, as a just-turned-sixteen-year-old sitting behind the wheel of their family's Chevy Silverado, on the day she got her driver's license.

According to the CaringBridge page her father made, they moved Dorothy into memory care after last Christmas, when she left the stove on and nearly caught the kitchen on fire.

Helena sits down beside her mother at the small, circular table by the window. There's a bouquet of flowers that's old enough to have shed a carpet of leaves and petals around the vase.

Her mother's frailness is birdlike, and the late-morning light that strikes her face makes it look as thin as paper. Though only sixty-five, she looks much older. Her silver hair is thinning. Liver spots cover her hands, which still look remarkably feminine and graceful.

"I'm Helena. Your daughter."

Her mother looks at her, skeptical.

"You have a really nice view of the mountains."

"Have you seen Nance?" her mother asks. She doesn't sound anything like herself—her words coming slowly, and with considerable effort. Nancy was Dorothy's older sister. She died in childbirth more than forty years ago, before Helena was born.

"I haven't," Helena says. "She's been gone a while now."

Her mom looks out the window. While it's clear over the plains and the foothills, farther back, black clouds have begun to coalesce around the high peaks. Helena thinking—this disease is some sadistic, schizophrenic form of memory travel, flinging its victims across the expanse of their life, tricking them into thinking they're living in the past. Cutting them adrift in time.

"I'm sorry I haven't been around to see you," Helena says. "It's not because I didn't want to—I think about you and Dad every day.

But these last few years have been . . . really hard. You're the only person in the world I can tell this to, but I was given a chance to build my memory chair. I told you about it once, I think. You were the reason I built it. I wanted to save your memories. I thought I was going to change the world. I thought I'd gotten everything I ever dreamed of. But I failed. I failed you. And all the people like you, who could've used my chair to save a part of themselves from this . . . fucking disease." Helena wipes her eyes. She can't tell if her mother is listening. Maybe it doesn't matter. "I brought something awful into the world, Mama. I didn't mean to, but I did, and now I have to spend the rest of my life in hiding. I shouldn't have come here, but . . . I needed to see you one last time. I need you to hear me say I—"

"It's going to storm in the mountains today," Dorothy says, still watching the black clouds.

Helena lets out a deep, trembling breath. "Looks that way, doesn't it?"

"I used to hike in those mountains with my family to a place called Lost Lake."

"I remember that. I was there with you, Mom."

"We would swim in the freezing water, and then lie out on the warm rocks. The sky was so blue it was almost purple. There were wildflowers in the meadows. It doesn't seem that long ago."

They sit in the silence.

Lightning touches the summit of Longs Peak.

Too distant to hear the thunder.

Helena wonders how often her father comes to visit. Wonders how hard it must be for him. She'd give anything to see him again.

Helena brings all of the photos over and takes her time showing each one to her mother, pointing to faces, saying names, recalling moments from her own memory. She starts to pick out memories she thinks her mother would count as her most special and important, and then realizes it's far too intimate a choice to make for another person. She can only share her own.

And then the oddest thing happens.

Dorothy looks at her, and for a moment, her eyes have become clear, lucid, and fierce—as if the woman Helena has always known has somehow fought through the tangle of dementia and ruined neural pathways to see her daughter for a fleeting breath.

"I was always proud of you," her mother says.

"You were?"

"You are the best thing I ever did."

Helena wraps her arms around her mother, tears streaming.

"I'm sorry I couldn't save you, Mom."

But when she pulls away, the moment of clarity has passed.

She's staring into the eyes of a stranger.

BARRY

June 2010–November 6, 2018

One morning, he wakes up and it's Meghan's high school graduation.

She is salutatorian; she gives a great speech.

He cries.

And then an autumn comes when it's just him and Julia and a very quiet house.

One night in bed, she turns to him and says, "Is this how you want to spend the rest of your life?"

He doesn't know what to say to her. Strike that. He knows. He had always blamed Meghan's death for his and Julia's demise. It was their family—the *three* of them—that united him and Julia. When Meghan died, that bond disintegrated in the span of a year.

Only now is he able to admit that they were always doomed. His second journey through their marriage has just been a slower, less dramatic death, brought on by Meghan growing up and pulling back and making her own way in life.

So yes, he knows. He just doesn't want to say it.

This relationship was meant for a specific time, and no longer.

His mother dies exactly the way he remembers.

Meghan is already at the bar when he arrives, sipping a martini and texting someone. For a moment, he doesn't see her, because she is just another beautiful woman at a chic Manhattan bar, having an early evening cocktail.

"Hi, Megs."

She sets her phone facedown and slides off the stool, embracing him harder than usual, pulling him in close, not letting go.

"How are you doing?" she asks.

"It's fine, I'm fine."

"Are you sure?"

"Yeah."

She studies him dubiously as he takes his seat at the bar and orders a San Pellegrino with a small dish of limes.

"How's work?" he asks. She's in her first year as a community organizer for a nonprofit.

"Insanely busy and amazing, but I don't want to talk about work."

"You know I'm proud of you, right?"

"Yes, you tell me every time you see me. Look, I need to ask you something."

"OK." He sips his limey mineral water.

"How long were you unhappy?"

"I don't know. A while. Years maybe."

"Did you and Mom stay married because of me?"

"No."

"You swear?"

"I swear. I wanted it to work out. I know your mother did too. Sometimes it just takes a while to finally call it a day. You may have contributed to our not noticing how unhappy we were, but you were *never* the reason we stayed."

"Have you been crying?"

"No."

"Bullshit."

She's good. He signed the separation agreement in his lawyer's office an hour ago, and barring something unforeseen, a judge will sign a divorce decree within the month.

It was a long walk here, and, yes, for much of it he was crying. That's one of the great things about New York—no one cares about your emotional state as long as there's no blood involved. Crying on the sidewalk in the middle of the day is no less private than crying in your bedroom in the middle of the night. Maybe it's because no one cares. Maybe it's because it's a brutal city, and they've all been there at one time or another.

"How's Max?" Barry asks.

"Bye, Max."

"What happened?"

"He saw the writing on the wall."

"What writing is that?"

"'Meghan is a workaholic.'"

Barry orders another mineral water.

"You look really good, Dad."

"You think?"

"Yeah. I can't wait to start hearing your terrible dating stories."

"I can't wait to start experiencing them."

Meghan laughs, and something about the way her mouth moves

makes him see the little girl in her face again, though only for a fleeting second.

Barry says, "It's your birthday Sunday."

"I know."

"Mom and I still want to take you out for brunch."

"Are you sure it won't be weird?"

"Oh, it will be, but we want to do it anyway if you're up for it. We want to be OK again."

"I'm in," Meghan says.

"Yeah?"

"Yeah. I want us to be OK too."

After drinks with Meghan, he grabs a bite at his favorite pizza joint in the city—an Upper West Side hole-in-the-wall that's not too far from his precinct. It's a midnight kind of place with attitude, bad lighting, and no seating—just a bar that lines the perimeter of the restaurant, everyone standing, holding greasy paper plates with massive slices and giant cups of oversweetened soft drinks.

It's Friday night and loud and perfect.

He considers a drink, but decides drinking alone post-signing-divorce-papers is too pathetic, and heads for his car instead. Drives the streets of his city feeling happy and emotional and overwhelmed by the sheer mystery of being alive. He hopes Julia is OK. He texted her after he signed the papers. Wrote that he was glad they were going to be friends, and he would always be there for her.

As he sits in traffic, he checks his phone again to see if she responded.

Now there's a text from her:

Here for you always. That will never change.

His heart is full in a way it hasn't been in as long as he can remember.

He looks up through the windshield. Traffic still isn't moving, even though the light ahead is green. Cops are diverting cars away from the street ahead.

He rolls down his window and shouts to the nearest cop, "What's going on?"

The man motions for him to move along.

Barry hits his grille lights and bloops his siren. That gets the young patrolman's attention. He comes running over, all apologies. "Sorry, they got us closing down the street ahead. It's pretty chaotic."

"What happened?"

"Lady jumped off the building on the next block."

"Which one?"

"That skyscraper right there."

Barry looks up at a white Art Deco tower with a crown of glass and steel, a knot forming in the pit of his stomach.

"What floor?" he asks.

"I'm sorry?"

"What floor did she jump from?"

An ambulance screams past, lights and sirens blaring as it barrels through the intersection straight ahead.

"Forty-one. Looks like another FMS suicide."

Barry pulls his car over to the curb and climbs out. He jogs across the street, flashing his badge at the patrolmen cordoning off the area.

He slows down as he approaches a circle of cops, EMTs, and firemen, all gathered around a black Lincoln Town Car whose roof has been spectacularly crushed.

Walking over, he had steeled himself to see the grotesque effects a four-hundred-foot fall wreaks on the human body, but Ann Voss Peters looks almost serene. The only visible external damage is a small trickle of blood from her ears and mouth. She landed on her back, and in such a way that the smashed roof of the Town Car appears to be cradling her. Her legs are crossed at her ankles, and her left arm is crossed over her chest and resting against her face, as if she's merely sleeping.

An angel fallen from the sky.

It wasn't that he'd forgotten. His remembrance of Hotel Memory, his death in the deprivation tank, and return to the night Meghan died was always there, on the outskirts of awareness—a bundle of grayed-out memories.

But there was also a dreamlike quality to the last eleven years. He was swept up in the minutiae of living, and with no tangible connection to the life he'd been ripped out of, it was all too easy to relegate what had happened to the deepest recesses of consciousness and memory.

But now, sitting in a café on the banks of the Hudson River with Julia and Meghan on the morning of his daughter's twenty-sixth birthday, he has a blinding awareness of being in this moment for a second time. It all comes back to him in a rush of memory as clear as water. He and Julia sat at a table not far from this spot, imagining what Meghan would be doing if she were alive today. He had posited she would be a lawyer. They had laughed about that and reminisced about the time she drove his car through the garage door, before comparing memories of a family vacation to the headwaters of the Hudson.

Now his daughter is sitting across from him, and for the first time in a long while, he is floored by her presence. By the fact that she exists. The feeling is as strong as the early days of his return to the memory, when every second shone like a gift.

Barry shudders into consciousness at three in the morning, roused by a pounding in his apartment. He rolls out of bed, slowly emerging from a shroud of sleep as he staggers out of his room. Jim-Bob, his rescue, is barking fiercely at the door.

A glance through the peephole snaps him wide-awake—Julia is standing in the bleary light of the hall. He turns the dead bolt, throws the chain, pulls the door open. Her eyes are swollen from crying, her hair is catastrophic, and she's wearing a trench coat over a pair of pajamas, her shoulders dusted with snow.

She says, "I tried to call. Your phone was off."

"What happened?"

"Can I come in?"

He steps back, and she enters his apartment, a manic intensity in her eyes. Gently taking her arm, he guides her over to the sofa.

"You're scaring me, Jules. What's wrong?"

She looks at him, trembling. "Have you heard of False Memory Syndrome?"

"Yes, why?"

"I think I have it."

His stomach tightens. "What makes you say that?"

"An hour ago, I woke up with a splitting headache and a headful of memories of this other life. Gray, listless memories." Her eyes fill with tears. "Meghan died in a hit-and-run when she was in high school. You and I divorced a year later. I married a man named Anthony. It was all so real. Like I had really lived it. You and I had brunch yesterday at that same café on the river, only Meghan wasn't there. She'd been dead eleven years. I woke up tonight, alone in my bed, no Anthony, realizing that, in actuality, you and I had lunch with her yesterday. That she's alive." Julia's hands are shaking violently. "What's real, Barry? Which set of memories is the truth?" She breaks down. "Is our daughter alive?"

"Yes."

"But I remember going to the morgue with you. I saw her broken body. She was gone. I remember like it happened yesterday. They had to carry me out. I was screaming. You remember, don't you? Did it happen? Do you remember her dying?"

Barry sits on the couch in his boxers, coming to the realization that this all makes some terrible kind of sense. Ann Voss Peters jumped off the Poe Building three nights ago. He had brunch with Meghan and Julia yesterday. Which means that tonight is the night he was sent back into the memory of the last time he saw his daughter alive. Catching back up to this moment must have unleashed all of Julia's memories of that lifeless timeline when Meghan died.

"Barry, am I losing my mind?"

And then it hits him—if Julia has those memories, so does Meghan.

He looks at Julia. "We have to go."

"Why?"

He stands. "Right now."

"Barry—"

"Listen to me—you're not losing your mind, you're not crazy."

"You remember her dying too?"

"Yes."

"How is that possible?"

"I promise I will explain everything, but right now, we have to go to Meghan."

"Why?"

"Because she's experiencing the same thing you are. She's remembering her own death."

Barry takes the West Side Highway, heading south through a snowstorm out of Washington Heights and the northern reaches of Manhattan, the road abandoned at this time of night.

Julia is holding her phone to her ear, saying, "Meghan, please call me when you get this. I'm worried about you. Your father and I are coming over right now." She looks across the center console at Barry, says, "She's probably just sleeping. It is the middle of the night."

They ride through the empty streets of lower Manhattan, cutting across the island into NoHo, the tires sliding on the slick pavement.

Barry pulls to a stop in front of Meghan's building, and they climb out into the pouring snow.

At the entrance, he presses the buzzer for Meghan's apartment five times, but she doesn't answer.

He turns to Julia. "Do you have a key?"

"No."

He starts ringing other apartments until someone finally buzzes them in.

Meghan's building is a sketchy-looking prewar walk-up. He and Julia race up six flights of a gloomy stairwell to the top floor and run down a dimly lit hall. Apartment J is at the end—Meghan's bicycle is leaning against the window to the fire escape.

He bangs on the door with his fist. No answer. Taking a step back, he raises his right leg and front-kicks the door. A spike of pain shoots up his leg, but the door only shudders.

He kicks it again, harder this time.

It bursts open, and they rush inside into darkness.

"Meghan!" His hand fumbles across the wall and hits the lights, which illuminate a tiny studio. There's a sleeping alcove on the right—empty. An efficiency kitchen to the left. A short hallway leading to the bathroom.

He starts toward it, but Julia rushes past him, shouting her daughter's name.

At the end of the hall, she drops to her knees, says, "Honey, oh God, I'm right here."

Barry reaches the end of the hall, and his heart falls. Meghan is lying on the linoleum floor and Julia is down on the ground next to her, running her hand across her head. Meghan's eyes are open, and for an agonizing second, he thinks she's dead.

She blinks.

Barry carefully lifts Meghan's right arm, checking the pulse in her radial artery. It's strong, maybe too strong, and quite fast. He wonders—does she recall the trauma of being struck by a two-ton object traveling sixty miles per hour? The moment her consciousness stopped? Whatever came after? What would it be like to remember your own death? How would someone even recall a state of unbeing? As blackness? Nothingness? It strikes him, like dividing by zero, as an impossibility.

"Meghan," he says softly, "can you hear me?"

She stirs, staring up at him now, and her eyes look full, as if she actually sees him.

"Dad?"

"Mom and I are right here, honey."

"Where am I?"

"In your apartment, on the floor of your bathroom."

"Am I dead?"

"No, of course not."

"I have this memory. It wasn't there before. I was fifteen, walking to Dairy Queen to see my friends. I was on the phone, wasn't thinking, went to cross the street. I remember the sound of a car engine. I turned and stared into the oncoming headlights. I remember the car hitting me and then lying on my back, thinking how stupid I was. I didn't hurt that much, but I couldn't move, and everything was going dark. I couldn't see, and I knew what was coming. I knew it meant the end of everything. Are you sure I'm not dead?"

"You are here with me and Mom," Barry says. "You are very much alive."

Meghan's eyes flit back and forth, like a computer processing data.

She says, "I don't know what's real."

"You're real. I'm real. This moment is real." But even as he says it, he isn't sure. Barry studies his ex, thinking how she looks like the Julia of old, that black weight of Meghan's death back in her eyes.

"Which set of memories feels more real to you?" he asks Julia.

"One isn't more real than the other," she says. "It's just that I'm living in a world that aligns with my daughter being alive. Thank God. But I feel like I've lived through both of them. What's happening to us?"

Barry releases a long exhale and leans back against the shower door.

"In the . . . I don't even know what to call it . . . the past life where Meghan died, I was investigating a case involving False Memory Syndrome. There were things that didn't add up. One night—this night, actually—I found this strange hotel. I was drugged, and when I woke up, I was strapped into this chair and facing a man who threatened to kill me if I didn't recount the night Meghan died."

"Why?"

"I have no idea. I don't even know his name. Later, I was put into a deprivation chamber. He paralyzed me, and then stopped my heart. As I was dying, I started experiencing these intense flashes of the memory I had described to him. I don't know how, but my fifty-year-old consciousness was . . . *returned* to the body of my thirty-nine-year-old self."

Julia's eyes go a mile wide; Meghan sits up.

He says, "I know it sounds crazy, but I was suddenly back in the night Meghan died." He looks at his daughter. "You had just walked out the door. I rushed after you and caught up to you seconds before you would've crossed the street and been hit by a speeding Mustang. Do you remember that?"

"I think so. You were weirdly emotional."

"You saved her," Julia says.

"I kept thinking it was all a dream, or some strange experiment I would be pulled out of at any moment. But days went by. Then months. Then years. And I just . . . I fell into the grooves of our life. It all felt so normal, and after a while, I never really thought about what had happened to me. Until three days ago."

"What happened three days ago?" Meghan asks.

"This woman jumped off a building on the Upper West Side, which was the event that had set me down the road of that false-memory case to begin with. It was like waking up from a long dream. A lifetime of a dream. Tonight was the night I was sent back into that other life."

Whether the expression on Julia's face is disbelief or shock, he can't tell.

Meghan's eyes have gone glassy. She says, "I should be dead."

He brushes her hair behind her ears the way he used to when she was a little girl.

"No, you're right where you should be. You're alive. This is what is real."

He skips work that morning, and not just because he only got back to his apartment at seven a.m. He fears his colleagues' memories of Meghan's death will also have emerged last night—an eleven-year stretch of false memories where his daughter wasn't alive.

When he wakes, his phone is blowing up with notifications from half his contacts list—missed calls and voicemails, frantic texts about Meghan. He doesn't respond to any of them. He needs to talk with Julia and Meghan first. They should be on the same page with what they're telling people, although he can't imagine what that page might look like.

He walks into the NoHo bar around the corner from Meghan's apartment to meet his daughter and his ex, finds them waiting for him in a corner booth, close enough to the open kitchen to feel the heat of the stove and hear the clang of pots and pans and food sizzling on a griddle.

Barry slides in next to Meghan and tosses his coat across the bench.

She looks worn out, bewildered, shell-shocked.

Julia isn't much better.

"How you doing, Megs?" he asks, but his daughter just stares back at him, her face a blank wall.

He looks at Julia. "Have you spoken to Anthony?"

"I tried to call him but haven't been able to get through."

"You OK?"

She shakes her head, eyes shimmering. "But this isn't about me today."

They order food and a round of drinks.

"What do we tell people?" Julia asks. "I've gotten over a dozen calls today."

"Same here," Barry says. "I think for now we stay with the idea that this is FMS. At least that's something they might've heard of."

"Shouldn't we tell people what happened to you, Barry?" Julia asks. "About that strange hotel and the chair and you living those eleven years for a second time?"

Barry remembers the warning he was given on the night he returned to the memory of Meghan's death.

Tell no one. Not your wife. Not your daughter. No one.

"This knowledge we have is actually dangerous," he says. "We have to keep all of this to ourselves for now. Just try to live a normal life again."

"How?" Meghan asks, her voice unraveling. "I don't even know how to think about my life anymore."

"Things will be weird at first," Barry says, "but we'll fall back into the grooves of our existence. If you can say nothing else about our species, we're adaptable, right?"

Nearby, a waiter drops a tray of drinks.

Meghan's nose begins to bleed.

He feels a glint of pain behind his eyes, and across the table, Julia is clearly experiencing something similar.

The bar goes silent, no one talking, everyone sitting frozen at their tables.

The only sound is the music coming through the speakers and the drone of a television.

Meghan's hands are trembling.

So are Julia's.

And his.

On the television above the bar, a news anchor is staring into the camera, blood running down his face as he searches for words. *"I, um . . . I'm going to be honest, I don't exactly know what just happened. But something clearly has."*

The image changes to a live shot that overlooks the southern border of Central Park.

There's a building on West Fifty-Ninth Street that wasn't there a moment ago.

At well over two thousand feet, it's easily the tallest thing in the city, and constructed of two towers, one on Sixth Avenue, the other on Seventh, which connect at the top to form an elongated, upside-down *U*.

Meghan makes a sound like a whimper.

Barry grabs his coat, slides out of the booth.

"Where are you going?" Julia asks.

"Just come with me."

They move through the stunned restaurant and back outside, where they pile into Barry's Crown Vic. He fires the sirens and they speed north up Broadway, then onto Seventh Avenue. Barry can only get them as close as West Fifty-Third before the street becomes impassable with traffic.

All around them, people are getting out of their cars.

They abandon Barry's cruiser and walk with the crowd.

After several blocks, they finally stop in the middle of the street to see it with their own eyes. There are thousands of New Yorkers all around them, faces lifted skyward, many holding up their phones to take photos and videos of the new addition to the Manhattan skyline—the U-shaped tower standing on the southern end of Central Park.

Meghan says, "That wasn't there a moment ago. Right?"

"No," Barry says. "It wasn't. But at the same time . . ."

"It's been there for years," Julia says.

They stare at the marvel of engineering called the Big Bend, Barry thinking that, up until this moment, FMS has flown largely under the radar—isolated cases wreaking havoc on the lives of strangers.

But this will affect everyone in the city, and many around the world.

This will change everything.

The glass and steel of the building's west tower is catching parting rays of the setting sun, and memories of Barry's existence with this building in the city are flooding in.

"I've been to the top of it," Meghan says, tears running down her face.

It's true.

"With you, Dad. It was the best meal of my life."

When she finished her bachelor's degree in social work, he took her to dinner at Curve, the restaurant at the top with spectacular views of the park. It wasn't just the view that attracted them; Meghan had a food crush on the chef, Joseph Hart. Barry distinctly remembers riding an elevator that transitioned from a vertical ascent to a forty-five-degree climb through the initial angle of the curve to a horizontal traverse across the top of the tower.

The longer he stares at it, the more it feels like an object that is a part of this reality.

His reality.

Whatever that even means anymore.

"Dad?"

"Yes?" His heart is pounding; he feels unwell.

"Is this moment real?"

He looks down at her. "I don't know."

———

Two hours later, Barry walks into the low-rent bar near Gwen's place in Hell's Kitchen and climbs onto the stool beside her.

"You all right?" Gwen asks.

"Is anybody?"

"I tried to call you this morning. I woke up with this alternate history of our friendship. One where Meghan died in a hit-and-run when she was fifteen. She's alive, right?"

"I just came from seeing her."

"How's she doing?"

"Honestly? I don't know. She remembered her own death last night."

"How is that possible?"

He waits for their drinks to come, and then tells her everything, including his extraordinary experience in the chair.

"You went back into a memory?" she whispers, leaning in close.

She smells like a combination of Wild Turkey, whatever shampoo she uses, and gunpowder, Barry wondering if she came straight here from the range, where she is a sight to behold. He's never seen anyone shoot like Gwen.

"Yes, and then I started living it, but with Meghan alive this time. Right up to this moment."

"You think that's what FMS really is?" she asks. "Changing memories to change reality?"

"I know it is."

On the muted television above the bar, Barry sees a photograph of a man he recognizes from somewhere. At first, he can't tie the recognition to a memory.

Barry reads the closed captioning of the news anchor's reporting.

[AMOR TOWLES, RENOWNED ARCHITECT OF THE BIG BEND, WAS FOUND MURDERED IN HIS APARTMENT ONE HOUR AGO WHEN—]

"Is this Big Bend building a product of the chair?" Gwen asks.

"Yes. When I was in that weird hotel, there was this guy, older gentleman. I believe he was dying. I overheard this conversation where he said that he was an architect, and when he got back into his memory, he was going to follow through on a building he always regretted not pursuing. In fact, he was scheduled to go in the chair today, which is when reality changed for all of us. I'm guessing they killed him for breaking the rules."

"What rules?"

"They told me I was only supposed to live my life a little better. No gaming of the system. No sweeping changes."

"Do you know why he's letting people redo their lives? This man who built the chair?"

Barry slugs back the rest of his beer. "No idea."

Gwen sips her whiskey. The jukebox has been turned off, and now the bartender unmutes the television and switches channels. Every network has been running nonstop coverage since the building appeared this afternoon. On CNN, an "expert" on False Memory Syndrome has been dredged up to speculate on what they're calling the "memory malfunction" in Manhattan. She's saying, *"If memory is unreliable, if the past and the present can simply change without warning, then fact and truth will cease to exist. How do we live in a world like that? This is why we're seeing an epidemic of suicides."*

"You know where this hotel is?" Gwen asks.

"It's been eleven years—at least in my mind—but I could probably find it again. I know it's in Midtown, assuming it's still there."

"Our minds aren't built to handle a reality that's constantly changing our memories and shifting our present," Gwen says. "What if this is only the beginning?"

Barry's phone vibrates in his pocket against his leg.

"Sorry about this."

He pulls it out and reads a text from Meghan:

> Dad. I can't do this anymore.
> I don't know who I am. I don't
> know anything except I don't
> belong here. I'm so sorry.
> I love you always.

He slides off the stool.

"What's wrong?" Gwen asks.

And starts running for the door.

Meghan's cell keeps going straight to voicemail, and in the aftermath of the Big Bend's appearance, the city streets are still clogged.

As Barry drives toward NoHo, he grabs his radio's hand mic and calls New York One to request that a unit in the vicinity of Meghan's apartment stop by for a welfare check.

"New York One, 158, are you talking about the 904B on Bond Street? We have multiple units and fire companies already on scene and ambulances en route."

"What are you talking about? Which building?"

"Twelve Bond Street."

"That's my daughter's building."

There's silence over the airwaves.

Barry tosses the hand mic, hits the lights, and screams through traffic, weaving in and out of cars, around buses, tearing through intersections.

As he turns onto Bond Street several minutes later, he abandons his car at the police barricade and runs toward fire engines shooting streams of water at the façade of Meghan's building, where flames are curling out of windows on the sixth floor. The scene is pure chaos—an array of emergency lights and cops putting up tape to keep the residents of neighboring buildings at a safe distance while the occupants of Meghan's building flood out of the front entrance.

A cop tries to stop him, but Barry rips his arm away, flashes his badge, and pushes on toward the fire engines and the entrance to the building, the heat of the flames making his face break out in beads of sweat.

A firefighter staggers out of the entrance, whose door has been ripped off its hinges. He's carrying an older man, and both their faces are blackened.

A fire lieutenant—a bearded giant of a man—steps in front of Barry, blocking his path. "Get back behind the tape."

"I'm a cop, and that's my daughter's building!" He points up at the flames peeling out of the top floor window at the far end. "That's her apartment flames are coming out of!"

The lieutenant's face falls. He takes Barry by the arm and pulls him out of the way of a train of firefighters carrying a hose toward the nearest hydrant.

"What?" Barry asks. "Just tell me."

"The fire started in that apartment in the kitchen. It's spreading through the fifth and sixth floors right now."

"Where's my daughter?"

The man takes a breath, glances over his shoulder.

"Where's my fucking daughter?"

"Look at me," the man says.

"Did you get her out?"

"Yes. I am very sorry to tell you this, but she died."

Barry staggers back. "How?"

"There was a bottle of vodka and some pills on her bed. We think she took them and then tried to make tea, but lost consciousness soon after. Something on the counter got too close to the burner. It was accidental, but—"

"Where is she?"

"Let's go sit down and—"

"Where is she?"

"On the sidewalk, on the other side of that truck."

Barry starts toward her, but suddenly the man's arms are gripping him from behind in a bear hug.

"Sure you want to do that, brother?"

"Get off!"

The man lets him go, Barry stepping over hoses, moving in front of the truck, closer to the fire. The commotion dies away. All he sees are Meghan's bare feet poking out from underneath the white sheet that's covering her, which is soaking wet and almost translucent from the spray of the fire hoses.

His legs fail him.

He sinks down onto the curb and breaks as the water rains down on him.

People try to talk to him, to get him to come with them, to move, but he doesn't hear them. He stares straight through them.

Into nothing.

Thinking—*I've lost her twice now.*

It's been two hours since Meghan died, and his clothes are still damp.

Barry parks at Penn Station and starts walking north from Thirty-Fourth Street, just like he did after returning from Montauk on a midnight train, the night he stumbled into Hotel Memory.

That night, it had been snowing.

Now it's raining, the buildings cloaked in mist above their fiftieth floors, and the air cold enough to cloud his breath.

The city stands strangely silent.

Few cars on the road.

Fewer people on the sidewalks.

The tears are cold on his face.

He pops his umbrella after three blocks. In his mind, it's been eleven years since the night he wandered into Hotel Memory. Chronologically, it happened today, just in a false memory.

As Barry reaches West Fiftieth, it's raining harder, the cloud deck lowering. He's confident the hotel was on Fiftieth, and he's pretty sure he headed east.

He keeps catching glimpses of the two bases of the Big Bend, luminous in the rain. The curve is hidden in the clouds a couple thousand feet above.

He's trying not to think of Meghan in this moment, because when he does, he crumbles all over again, and he needs to be strong, needs his wits about him.

Cold and so tired, he's beginning to wonder if perhaps he walked west that night, instead of east, when a red neon sign in the distance catches his attention.

McLachlan's Restaurant
Breakfast
Lunch
Dinner
Open 7 Days
24 Hours

Barry moves toward the sign until he's standing under it, watching the rain fall through the red illumination.

He picks up his pace.

Past the bodega, which he remembers, and then the liquor store, a women's clothing store, a bank—all closed—until, near the end of the block, he stops at the entrance to the dark driveway, which slopes down into the subterranean space beneath a neo-gothic building, wedged between two higher skyscrapers.

If he walked down that driveway, he'd arrive at a garage door built of reinforced steel.

This is how he entered Hotel Memory all those years ago.

He's absolutely sure of it.

There's a part of him that wants to run down there, charge through, and shoot every fucking person he sees inside that hotel, ending with the man who put him in the chair. Meghan's brain broke because of him. She is dead because of him. Hotel Memory needs to end.

But that would most likely only get him killed.

No, he'll call Gwen instead, propose an off-the-books, under-the-radar op with a handful of SWAT colleagues. If she insists, he'll take an affidavit to a judge. They'll cut power to the building, go in with night-vision gear, do a floor-to-floor sweep.

Clearly, some minds, like Meghan's, cannot handle the changing of their reality, and the collateral damage is also tragic—in addition to his daughter, three people died in her building from the fire, and over the radio on his drive to Penn Station, he heard more reports of people—unbalanced by the appearance of the Big Bend—wreaking havoc in the city.

Healthy minds are being made unwell; unwell minds are being driven over the edge.

He pulls out his phone, opens contacts, scrolls to the g's.

As his finger hovers over *Gwen*, someone shouts his name.

He glances across the street, sees someone running toward him.

A woman's voice yells, "Don't make that call!"

He's already reaching into his jacket, thumbing off the button to his shoulder holster, getting a solid grip on his subcompact Glock, thinking she probably works for whoever built the chair, which means—*fuck!*—they know he's scoping the building.

"Barry, don't shoot, please."

She slows to a walk, raises her hands.

They're open, empty.

She approaches cautiously, barely five feet tall, wearing boots and a black leather jacket beaded with raindrops. A shock of red hair comes to her chin, but it's damp. She's been waiting for him in the rain. The thing that disarms him is the kindness in her green eyes, and something else, which strikes him—oddly—as familiarity.

She says, "I know you were sent back into the worst memory of your life. The man who did that is Marcus Slade. He owns that building. And I know what just happened to Meghan. I'm so sorry, Barry. I know you want to do something about it."

"You work for them?"

"No."

"Are you a mind reader?"

"No."

"Then how could you possibly know what happened to me?"

"You told me."

"I've never seen you before in my life."

"You told me in the future, four months from now."

He lowers the pistol, his brain twisting itself in knots. "You used that chair?"

She looks up into his eyes with an intensity that sends a cool electricity down his spine. "I invented the chair."

"Who are you?"

"Helena Smith, and if you go into Slade's building with Gwen, it will lead to the end of everything."

BOOK THREE

Time is what keeps everything from happening at once.

−RAY CUMMINGS

BARRY

The woman with fiery hair takes Barry by the arm and pulls him down the sidewalk, away from the entrance to the subterranean garage.

"We're not safe here," she says. "Let's walk to your car. Penn Station, right?"

Barry pulls his arm away from her and starts moving in the opposite direction.

She calls after him, "Standing on the driveway of your home in Portland, watching a total solar eclipse with your father. Spending summers with your grandparents at their farmhouse in New Hampshire. You'd sit in the apple orchard and tell yourself elaborate stories."

He stops and looks back at her.

She continues, "While you were devastated when your mother died, you were also grateful, because you knew when her time was coming, and you had a proper chance to say goodbye. To make sure she knew you loved her. You didn't have that with your father, who died suddenly when you were fifteen. You still wake up in the middle of the night sometimes, wondering if he knew."

He's shivering by the time they reach his Crown Vic. Helena gets down on her knees on the wet pavement and runs her hands across the car's undercarriage.

"What are you doing?" Barry asks.

"Making sure there's no tracking device on your car."

They climb in out of the rain, and he turns on the heat and waits for the engine to warm the frigid air blowing through the vents.

On the forty-minute walk down from Fiftieth, she told him a crazy story he isn't completely sure he believes, about how she accidentally built the chair on a decommissioned oil platform in a previous timeline.

"I have so much more to tell you," Helena says, buckling her seat belt.

"We can go to my apartment."

"It isn't safe there. Marcus Slade is aware of you, of where you live. If, at any point in the future, he realizes you and I are working together, he'll use you to get to me. He could use his chair to return to tonight and find us in this moment. You have to stop thinking linearly. You have no idea what he's capable of."

The lights of the Battery Tunnel stream past overhead, and Helena is explaining how she escaped Slade's oil rig into her own memory, and fled to Canada.

"I was prepared to live out the rest of my life under the radar. Or kill myself if Slade ever found me. I was totally on my own—my mom died in 2011, my dad not long after. Then in 2016, the very first reports of a mysterious, new disease started surfacing."

"False Memory Syndrome."

"FMS didn't come into the full public consciousness until recently, but I knew right away it was Slade. The first two years I was in hiding, he would've had no memory of our time together on the rig. In his mind, I had vanished after Jee-woon approached me with the job offer. But when we returned to 2009, specifically the night I escaped using the chair, Slade gained all of the memories of our time together. They were dead memories, of course, but—and here's where I miscalculated—they contained enough information for him to eventually build the chair and all its components himself.

"I came to New York, which seemed to be ground zero for the FMS outbreak, figuring Slade had built his new lab in the city and was testing the chair on people. But I couldn't find him. We're almost here."

Deep in Red Hook, Barry drives slowly past a row of warehouses along the water. Helena points out her building, but she makes Barry park five blocks away in a dark alley, backing into the shadows between a pair of overflowing dumpsters.

The rain has stopped.

Outside, it's unnervingly quiet, the air redolent of wet garbage and standing puddles of rainwater. His mind's eye keeps conjuring his last glimpse of Meghan—lying on the dirty sidewalk in front of her building, her bare feet sticking out from under the wet sheet.

Barry chokes down the grief, pops the trunk, and grabs his tactical shotgun and a box of shells.

They walk broken sidewalks for a quarter mile, Barry on alert for approaching vehicles or footsteps, but the only noise comes from the distant drone of helicopters circling the city and the deep-voiced horns of barges on the East River.

Helena leads him to a nondescript metal door in the side of a waterfront building that still bears the brewery signage of its former occupant.

She punches in the door code, lets them inside, and hits the lights. The warehouse reeks of spent grain, and the echo of their footsteps fills the space like a derelict cathedral. They move past rows of stainless-steel brewing tanks, a rusted-out mash tun, and finally the remnants of a bottling line.

They climb four flights to a sprawling loft with floor-to-ceiling windows overlooking the river, Governors Island, and the shimmering southern tip of Manhattan.

The floor is tracked with cables and a maze of disassembled

circuit boards. There's a rack of custom-built servers humming along an old brick wall, and what appears to be a chair in the throes of construction—a raw-wood frame with bundles of exposed wires running up the arms and legs. An object that vaguely resembles a helmet is clamped to a workbench and subsumed in a riot of unfinished circuitry.

"You're building your own chair?" Barry asks.

"I outsource some coding and engineering work, but I've built it twice already, so I have some shortcuts up my sleeve and plenty from my investments. Advancements in computer processing have brought costs way down since my time on the rig. You hungry?"

"No."

"Well, I'm starving."

Beyond the servers, there's a modest kitchen, and across from it, positioned along the windows, a dresser and a bed. With no real delineation between work and living space, the loft feels like exactly what it is—the lab of a desperate, possibly mad scientist.

Barry washes his face at the bathroom sink, and when he emerges, finds Helena at the stove, attending to a pair of skillets.

He says, "I love huevos rancheros."

"I know. And you *really* love mine, well, technically my mother's recipe. Sit."

He takes a seat at a small Formica table, and she brings over a plate.

Barry isn't hungry, but he knows he should eat. He cuts into one of the over-easy eggs, the yolk running into the beans and salsa verde. He takes a big bite. She was right—they're the best he's ever had.

Helena says, "Now I have to tell you about things that haven't happened yet."

Barry stares at her across the table, thinking there's a haunted quality to her eyes, which look unmoored.

She says, "After the Big Bend, FMS mania will hit a fever pitch. Shockingly, it will still be viewed as a mysterious epidemic with no identifiable pathogen, although a handful of theoretical physicists will begin floating ideas about miniature wormholes and the possibility that someone is experimenting with space-time.

"Day after tomorrow, you will take a SWAT team into Slade's hotel. He and most of his team will die in the raid. Newspapers will report that Slade has been disseminating a neurological virus that attacks areas of the brain that store memory. The news cycle will obsess on this for a while, but in a month, the public hysteria will die down. It will appear as though the mystery has been solved, order restored, and there will be no new cases of FMS."

As Helena scarfs down a few bites, it dawns on Barry that he's sitting across the table from a woman who is telling him the future. But that isn't even the strangest part. The strangest part is that he's starting to believe her.

Helena sets her fork down.

She says, "But I know it's not over. I imagine the worst—that after your SWAT raid, the chair fell into the hands of someone else. So a month from now, I'll come and find you. I'll prove my bona fides by telling you exactly what you found in Slade's lab."

"And I believe you?"

"Eventually. You tell me that during the raid, before Slade was killed, he tried to destroy the chair and the processors, but that some of it was salvaged. Government agents—you don't know who they worked for—came in and took everything. I have no way of knowing, but I assume they don't know what the chair is, or how it works. Most of it is damaged, but they're working day and night to reverse-engineer everything. Can you imagine if they're successful?"

Barry goes to the refrigerator, a tremor in his hand as he pulls open the door and takes out a couple of cold longneck bottles.

He sits back down. "So my action of raiding Slade's lab leads to this."

"Yes. You've experienced the chair. You know its power. From what I can tell, Slade is just using it to send a select few back into their memories. Who knows why? But look at the fear and panic it's causing. Won't take much of messing with reality for humanity to go completely off the rails. We have to stop him."

"With your chair?"

"It won't be operational for another four months. The longer we wait, the greater the chance someone finds Slade's lab before we get in there. You've already put it on Gwen's radar. And once people know the chair exists, their memories of it will always return, no matter how many times a timeline is changed. The same way Julia and Meghan remembered Meghan dying in a hit-and-run last night."

"Their memories only arrived when we reached the moment I had used the chair in the last timeline. Does it always work that way?"

"Yes, because that was the moment their consciousness and memories from the prior timeline merged into this one. I think of it as a timeline anniversary."

"So what are you proposing we do?"

"You and I take control of Slade's lab tomorrow. Destroy the chair, the software, all the infrastructure, all trace of its existence. I have a virus ready to upload to his stand-alone network once we're inside. It'll reformat everything."

Barry drinks his beer, a tightness ratcheting down in his stomach.

"Did Future Me agree with this plan?"

Helena smiles. "In fact, we came up with it together."

"Did I think you and I have a chance?"

"Honestly? No."

"What do you think?"

Helena leans back in her chair. She looks bone weary. "I think we're the best chance the world has."

Barry stands at the wall of windows near Helena's bed, looking across the ink-black river to the city. He hopes Julia is OK, but he doubts it. When he called her, she broke down crying on the phone, hung up, and refused to take his calls. He's guessing there's a part of her that blames him.

The Big Bend now dominates the skyline, and he wonders if he'll ever grow used to it, or if it will always—for him and others—represent the unreliability of reality.

Helena comes up beside him.

"You OK?" she asks.

"I keep seeing Meghan dead on the sidewalk. I could almost see her face through the wet sheet they had draped over her. Going back and living those eleven years again—it ultimately fixed nothing for my family."

"I'm so sorry, Barry."

He looks at her.

Breathes in, breathes out.

"Have you ever handled a gun?" he asks.

"Yes."

"Recently?"

"Future You knew it would just be you and me charging into Slade's building, so you started taking me to the range."

"You sure you're up for this?"

"I built the chair because my mom got Alzheimer's. I wanted to help her and others like her. I thought if we could figure out how to capture memories, it would lead us to understanding how to stop them from erasing altogether. I didn't mean for the chair to become what it became. It's not only destroyed my life, now it's destroying the lives of others. People have lost their loved ones. Have had entire lifetimes erased. *Children* erased."

"You didn't mean for any of this to happen."

"Yet here we are, and it was my ambition that put this device in the hands of Slade, and later, others." She looks at Barry. "You're here because of me. The world is losing its collective mind because of me. There's a fucking building out there that wasn't there yesterday because of me. So I don't really care what happens to me tomorrow so long as we destroy every trace of the chair's existence. I'm ready to die if that's what it takes."

He didn't see it until this moment—the weight she carries. The self-hate and regret. What must it feel like to create a thing that could destroy the structure of memory and time? What must it cost her to repress the weight of all that guilt and horror and terror and anxiety?

Barry says, "No matter what, I got to see my daughter grow up because of you."

"I don't mean this to sound the way it will, but you shouldn't have. If we can't rely on memory, our species will unravel. And it's already beginning."

Helena stares at the city across the water, Barry thinking there's something overwhelming about her vulnerability in this moment.

"We should probably get some sleep," she says. "You can have my bed."

"I'm not taking your bed from you."

"I sleep on the couch most nights anyway, so I can fall asleep to the sound of the television."

She turns to go.

"Helena."

"What?"

"I know I don't really know you, but I'm certain your life is more than that chair."

"No. It defines me. First part of my life I spent trying to build it. I'll spend the rest of whatever's left trying to destroy it."

HELENA

She lies facing the television, the light of the screen flickering against her closed eyelids and the volume just high enough to engage her ever-restless mind. Something drags her into full and sudden consciousness. She jerks up into a seated position on the couch. It's just Barry, crying softly across the room. She wishes she could climb into bed and comfort him, but it would be too soon—they're essentially strangers. Perhaps he needs to grieve alone for now anyway.

She settles back down on the cushions, the couch springs creaking as she pulls the blankets to her neck. It isn't lost on her how strange it is to remember the future. The memory of her and Barry's goodbye in this very room, four months from now, is still a throbbing ache. She was floating in the deprivation tank, and Barry leaned down and kissed her. There were tears in his eyes as he closed the hatch. In hers too. Their future seemed so full of promise, and she was killing it.

The Barry she left behind already knows if she's been successful. He'll have known the moment she died in the tank, his reality instantly shifting to align with this new reality she's creating.

She resists the urge to wake the Barry of the present and tell him. It would only make breaking into Slade's lab more difficult tomorrow, throwing an emotional wrench into things. And what would she say? There were sparks? Chemistry? Best to keep to the plan. All that matters is that tomorrow goes well. She can't undo the damage her mind has wrought on the world, but perhaps she can seal the wound, stanch the bleeding.

She once had such immense dreams—eradicating the effects of memory-ravaging disease. Now, with her mom and dad gone and no real friends to speak of besides a man four months in the unreachable future, her dreams have reset from world-changing to the desperately personal.

She would simply like to be able to lie down at night, in peace, with a quiet mind.

She tries to sleep, knowing that she needs it more tonight than perhaps any other night of her life.

So of course sleep eludes her.

In the evening, they slip out the back of her building, taking a moment to study the nearby streets before venturing into the open. The district is mostly abandoned industrial buildings, and there's little traffic to speak of, and nothing that looks suspicious.

As Barry takes them on a route through Brooklyn Heights, he glances at her across the center console. "When you were showing me the chair last night, you mentioned you had built it twice before. When was the first time?"

She takes a sip of the coffee she brought along—her talisman against the previous night of sleepless misery.

"In the original timeline, I was head of this R&D group for a San Francisco–based company called Ion. They weren't interested in the medical applications of my chair. They only saw the entertainment value and the dollar signs that came with it.

"I was spinning my wheels, burned out, getting nowhere. Ion was on the verge of pulling the plug on my research when a test subject had a heart attack and died inside the deprivation tank. We all experienced a slight reality shift, but no one understood what had happened. No one except my assistant, Marcus Slade. Got to hand it to him—he realized what I'd created even before I did."

"What happened?"

"A few days later, he asked to meet me at the lab. Said it was an emergency. When I showed up, he had a gun. He forced me to log into the system and load a reactivation program for a memory we had mapped for him. And when I had done that, he killed me."

"When was this?"

"Two days ago. November 5, 2018. But, of course, it happened several timelines ago."

Barry takes the exit for the Brooklyn Bridge.

"I don't mean to second-guess you," he says, "but couldn't you have gone back into a different memory?"

"Like stop myself from being born so the chair was never made?"

"That's not what I meant."

"*I* can't go back and stop myself from being born. Someone else can, and then I become a dead memory. But there's no grandfather paradox or any temporal paradox when it comes to the chair. Everything that happens, even if it's changed or undone, lives on in dead memories. Cause and effect are still alive and well."

"OK, then what about returning to a memory on the oil rig? You could've pushed Slade off the platform or something."

"Everything that happened on the rig exists in dead memories. You can't return to them. We've tried—with disastrous results. But yes. I should've killed him when I had the chance."

They're halfway across the river now, the overhanging cross-bars rushing past overhead. Maybe it's the coffee, probably it's their proximity to the city, but she is suddenly wide-awake.

"What are dead memories?" Barry asks.

"It's what everyone thinks of as false memories. Except they aren't false. They just happened on a timeline that someone ended. For instance, the timeline where your daughter was hit by a car is now a dead memory. You ended that timeline and started this one when Slade killed you in the deprivation chamber."

They ride into Midtown, head north up Third Avenue, and then left onto East Forty-Ninth before finally pulling over onto the curb just shy of the ostensible entrance to Slade's building—a false-fronted lobby with a bank of elevators that go nowhere. The only real way inside is through the underground parking structure on Fiftieth.

It's raining bullets when they step out of the car. Barry pulls a black duffel bag out of the trunk, and Helena follows him onto the sidewalk and a little ways down to the entrance of a bar they've been in once before, four months from now, when they came to scope out the tunnel access to Slade's building and discuss their plans for this exact moment.

The rancid-smelling Diplomat is surprisingly busy, and every bit as soulless as she remembers. Barry's badge gets the diminutive bartender's attention. It's the same guy she and Barry met four months from now in a dead future—an asshole with a Napoleon complex, but one who helpfully carries a healthy fear of cops. She stands next to Barry as he introduces himself, and then Helena as his partner, explaining they need access to the cellar because a sexual assault was reported to have taken place there late last night.

For five seconds, Helena thinks this isn't going to work. The bartender stares at her like he's not totally buying her place in all of this. He could ask to see a warrant. He could cover his ass and call the owner. But instead, he yells for someone named Carla.

A waitress sets a bus tray of empty pint glasses on the bar and wanders over.

The bartender says, "These are cops. They need to see the cellar."

Carla shrugs, then turns without a word and heads down the length of the bar into a room of cold storage. She leads them through a maze of silver kegs to a narrow door in the farthest corner of the refrigerated room.

Plucking a key off a nail in the wall, she opens the padlock on the door. "Word of warning—there are no lights down there."

Barry unzips the duffel, pulls out a flashlight.

She says, "The man came prepared. Well, then, I'll leave you to it."

Barry waits until she's gone to open the cellar door.

The flashlight beam reveals a claustrophobic stairwell of questionable integrity, descending into darkness. The old, pervasive dampness is overwhelming—the smell of a long-forgotten place. Helena takes a deep breath to still the frenzy of her racing pulse.

"This is it?" Barry asks.

"This is it."

She follows him down the creaking steps, which spill into a cellar containing racks of collapsed shelving and a rusted-out oil drum filled with burnt garbage.

At the far end of the room, Barry pulls another door open with a nerve-shattering creak. They cross the threshold into an arched corridor with walls of crumbling brick.

It's colder down here beneath the city streets, the air dank with mildew and restless with the trickle of running water and the distant, unseen scratching of what she fears are rats.

Helena leads the way.

Their footsteps make echoing splashes.

Every fifty feet, they pass disintegrating doors leading into the underbellies of other buildings.

At the second junction, she turns down a new passage, and after a hundred feet or so, stops and shows Barry a door like all the rest. It takes a fair amount of pressure to get the handle to turn, and when it does, he forces his shoulder into the door, jarring it open.

They move out of the tunnel, into another cellar, where Barry drops the duffel bag onto the stone floor and unzips it. Out comes a crowbar, a package of zip ties, a box of twelve-gauge shells, a shotgun, and four spare magazines for his Glock.

He says, "Grab as many extra cartridges as you can carry."

Helena tears open the box and starts cramming shells into the inner pockets of her leather jacket. Barry checks the load on the Glock, removes his trench coat, and jams the extra magazines into his pockets. Then he takes up the crowbar and crosses the room toward a newer door. It's locked from the other side. He works the end of the crowbar deep into the jamb and torques back as hard as he can.

At first, there's nothing but the sound of him straining. Then comes the deep splintering of wood and the shriek of metal failing. When the door cracks open, Barry reaches through the opening and pulls off a broken, rusted padlock. Then he carefully opens the door wide enough for them to squeeze through.

They emerge into the hotel's old boiler room, which looks to have been out of commission for at least the last half century. Threading their way through a labyrinth of ancient machinery and gauges, they finally pass the massive boiler itself, then move through a doorway to the bottom of a service stairwell that spirals up into darkness.

"What floor is Slade's penthouse again?" Barry whispers.

"Twenty-four. The lab is on seventeen, servers on sixteen. You ready?"

"Wish we were taking the elevators."

Their plan is to go straight for Slade, hoping he'll be in his residence in the penthouse. The moment he hears gunfire or catches wind of anything suspicious, he'll likely be running for the chair so he can go back and stop them before they even set foot inside his building.

Barry begins the ascent, keeping the flashlight trained on their feet. Helena follows closely behind, trying to step as softly as she can, but the old wood of the stairs flexes and groans under their weight.

After several minutes, Barry stops at a door with the number 8 painted on the wall beside it, and turns off the light.

"What is it?" Helena whispers.

"Heard something."

They stand listening in the dark, her heart pounding and the shotgun growing heavier by the second. She can't see a thing, can't hear a thing but a faint, low moan that's like breath passing over the opening of a bottle.

From high above, a single beam of light shoots down the center of the stairwell and slants toward them across the checkered floor.

"Come on," Barry whispers, opening the door and pulling her into a corridor.

They move quickly down a red-carpeted hall of hotel rooms, whose numbers are projected onto the doors by lights in the opposing wall.

Halfway down the corridor, the door to Room 825 swings inward and a middle-aged woman steps out, wearing a navy robe with "HM" embossed on the lapel and carrying a silver ice bucket.

Barry glances over at Helena, who nods.

They're ten feet from the hotel guest now, who hasn't seen them yet.

Barry says, "Ma'am?"

When she looks in their direction, he aims his gun at her.

The ice bucket falls to the floor.

Barry brings a finger to his lips as they quickly close in.

"Not a word," he says, and they push her back through the doorway and follow her into the room.

Helena locks the dead bolt, hooks the chain.

"I have some money and credit cards—"

"We're not here for that. Sit on the floor and keep your mouth shut," Barry says.

The woman must've just stepped out of the shower. Her black hair is damp, and there's not a speck of makeup on her face. Helena doesn't meet her eyes.

Dropping the duffel bag on the floor, Barry unzips it and pulls out the zip ties.

"Please," she begs. "I don't want to die."

"No one's going to hurt you," Helena says.

"Did my husband send you?"

"No," Barry says. He looks at Helena. "Go put some pillows in the bathtub."

Helena grabs three pillows off the decadent four-poster bed and lays them in the claw-foot tub, which stands on a small platform with a view of dusk falling on the city and the buildings beginning to glow.

When she walks back out into the bedroom, Barry has the woman on her stomach and is binding her wrists and ankles. He finally lifts her over his shoulder and carries her into the bathroom, where he lays her gently in the tub.

"Why were you here?" he asks.

"You know what this place is?"

"Yes."

Tears run down her face. "I made a bad mistake fifteen years ago."

"What?" Helena asks.

"I didn't leave my husband when I should've. I wasted the best years of my life."

"Someone will come for you," Barry says. Then he rips a piece from the roll of duct tape and pats it over her mouth.

They close the door to the bathroom. The gas-log fireplace is putting out a welcome heat. The bottle of Champagne the woman was apparently about to drink stands on the coffee table beside a single glass and an open journal, both pages filled with handwriting.

Helena can't help herself. She glances at the elegant scrawl and realizes it's the narrative of a memory, perhaps the one the woman in the bathtub was going back to.

It begins—*The first time he hit me I was standing in the kitchen at ten p.m., asking him where he'd been. I remember the redness on his face and the smell of bourbon on his breath and his watery eyes*

Helena closes the journal and goes to the window, sweeping aside the curtain.

Anemic light creeps in.

Peering eight stories down onto East Forty-Ninth, she can see Barry's car a little ways down the block.

The city is wet, dreary.

The woman is crying in the bathroom.

Barry walks over, says, "I don't know if we've been made. Regardless, we should go after Slade right now. I say we take our chances with the elevator."

"Do you have a knife?"

"Yeah."

"May I see it?"

Barry reaches into his pocket and pulls out a folding knife as Helena removes her leather jacket and rolls up the sleeves of her gray shirt.

She takes it from him, sits down in one of the armchairs, and opens the blade.

"What are you doing?" he asks.

"Making a save point."

"A what?"

She inserts the tip of the knife into the side of her left arm above the elbow and draws the blade across her skin.

As the pain comes and the blood begins to flow—

BARRY

November 7, 2018

"What the hell are you doing?" Barry asks.

Helena's eyes are shut, her mouth hanging slightly open, perfectly still.

Barry carefully pries the knife out of her hands. For a long moment, nothing happens. Then her bright-green eyes snap open.

Something in them has changed. They exude a newfound fear and intensity.

"You OK?" Barry asks.

Helena surveys the room, glances at her wristwatch, and then wraps her arms around Barry with a startling ferocity.

"You're alive."

"Of course I'm alive. What happened to you?"

She leads him over to the bed. They sit, and Helena removes one of the pillowcases and tears off a strip of cloth, which she begins to tie around her self-inflicted wound to stop the bleeding.

"I just used the chair to return to this moment," she says. "I'm starting a new timeline."

"Your chair?"

"No, the one up on seventeen. Slade's chair."

"I don't understand."

"I've already lived the next fifteen minutes. The pain of cutting myself just now was a breadcrumb back to this moment. It left me a vivid, short-term memory to return to."

"So you know what's about to happen?"

"If we go to the penthouse, yes. Slade knows we're coming. He'll be waiting for us. We won't even make it out of the elevator before a bullet goes through your eye. There's so much blood, and I start shooting. I must hit Slade, because suddenly he's crawling across his living room.

"I take the elevator down to seventeen, find the lab, and shoot the door open as Jee-woon is climbing into the tank. He starts toward me, saying he knows I would never hurt him after all he did for me, but he's never been more wrong about anything in his life.

"At the terminal, I log in with some backdoor credentials. Then I map a memory, climb into the tank, and return to the memory of cutting myself in this room."

"You didn't have to come back for me."

"To be completely honest, I wouldn't have. But I didn't know where Sergei was, and there wasn't enough time to destroy all the equipment. But I am very glad you're alive." She looks at her watch again. "You're going to have an awful memory of all of this in about twelve minutes, and so is everyone else in the building, which is a problem."

Barry rises from the bed, gives Helena a hand up.

She lifts the shotgun.

He says, "So Slade is in the penthouse, anticipating that's where we'll go first—which we did the first time around."

"Correct."

"Jee-woon is already heading for the chair on seventeen, probably waiting to hear if there's been a security breach so he can jump into the deprivation chamber and overwrite this timeline. And Sergei is . . ."

"Unknown. I say we go straight to the lab and deal with Jee-woon first. No matter what, he can't be allowed to get in the tank."

They head out of the room and into the corridor. Barry keeps compulsively touching the extra magazines in his pockets.

At the bank of elevators, he calls for a car, listening to the gears turning on the other side of the doors and holding his Glock at the ready.

Helena says, "We've done this part already. There's no one coming down."

As the light above the elevator illuminates, the bell dings.

Barry raises his gun, finger on the trigger.

The doors part.

Empty.

They step into the small car, and Helena presses the button for 17. The walls of this elevator are old, smoke-stained mirrors, and staring into them creates a recursive illusion—an infinite number of Barrys and Helenas in elevator cars bending away through space.

As they begin to climb, Barry says, "Let's stand against the wall. Want to offer the smallest targets possible when the doors open. What weapon did Slade have?"

"A handgun. It was silver."

"Jee-woon?"

"There was a gun that looked more like yours by the terminal."

The button for each floor illuminates as they pass through it.

Nine.

Ten.

A wave of nausea hits him—nerves. There's a taste of fear in his mouth from the adrenaline dumping into his bloodstream.

Eleven.

Twelve.

Thirteen.

He marvels that Helena doesn't look as scared as he feels. Then again, from her perspective, she's already waded into the fray once before.

"Thank you for coming back for me," he says.

Fourteen.

"Just, you know, try not to die this time."

Fifteen.

Sixteen.

"Here we go," she says.

The elevator grinds to a halt at seventeen.

Barry raises the Glock.

Helena shoulders the shotgun.

The doors slide apart to reveal an empty corridor that runs the length of the building, with other hallways branching off a little ways down.

Barry steps carefully over the threshold.

The faint hum of lights burning overhead is the only sound.

Helena comes alongside him, and as she brushes her hair out of her face, Barry is overcome by a savage, protective impulse that terrifies and bewilders him. He's known her barely twenty-four hours.

They advance.

The lab is a sleek, white space, filled with recessed lighting and glass. They pass a window that peers into a room containing more than a dozen MEG microscopes, where a young scientist is soldering a circuit board. She doesn't see them slip past.

As they approach the first junction, a door closes somewhere nearby. Barry stops, listening for the sound of footsteps, but all he can hear are those lights.

Helena leads them down another corridor that ends at a long

wall of windows overlooking the blue Manhattan gloom of this raw evening, the lights of surrounding buildings shining through the misty dusk.

"The lab is just ahead," Helena whispers.

Barry's hands are sweating. He wipes his palms on the sides of his pants to get a better grip on the Glock.

They stop at a door equipped with keypad entry.

"He may already be inside," she whispers.

"You don't know the code?"

She shakes her head, raises the shotgun. "But this worked last time."

Barry catches movement swinging around the corner at the end of the corridor.

He steps in front of Helena, who screams, "Jee-woon, no!"

Gunshots explode the silence, the muzzle flash bursting from a barrel aimed at Barry, who empties his Glock in a blitzkrieg of noise.

Jee-woon has vanished.

It all happened in five seconds.

Barry ejects the empty magazine, slams in a fresh one, thumbs the slide.

He looks at Helena. "You OK?"

"Yes. Because you stepped in front of . . . oh God, you're shot."

Barry staggers back, blood pouring down his abdomen, down his leg under his pants, flowing across the top of his shoe and onto the floor in a long, burgundy smear. The pain is coming, but he's too jacked on adrenaline to register its full effect—only an intensifying pressure in the middle-right section of his torso.

"We have to get out of this corridor," he groans, thinking, *There's a bullet in my liver.*

Helena drags him back around the corner.

Barry sinks to the floor.

Bleeding profusely now, the blood nearly black.

He looks up at Helena, says, "Make sure . . . he isn't coming."

She peeks around the corner.

Barry lifts his gun, which he hadn't noticed slip from his grasp, off the floor.

"They could already be in the lab," he says.

"I'll stop them."

"I'm not going to make it."

There's movement on his left; he tries to raise the Glock, but Helena beats him to the punch, firing an earsplitting blast from the shotgun that forces a man he hasn't seen before back into the corridor.

"Go," Barry says. "Hurry."

The world is darkening, his ears ringing. Then he's lying with his face against the floor and the life rushing out of him.

He hears more gunfire.

Helena shouting, "Sergei, don't make me do this. You know me!"

Then two shotgun blasts.

Followed by screaming.

From his sideways perspective, he sees several people run through the intersection of corridors, heading back toward the elevators—guests and other crew members fleeing the mayhem.

He tries to get up, but he can barely move his hand. His body feels cemented to the ground.

The end is coming.

It's the hardest thing he's ever done to simply rise up onto his elbows. He somehow manages to crawl, dragging himself back around the corner of the windowed corridor that leads to the lab.

He hears more gunshots.

His vision swings in and out of focus, the glass shards on the floor from the shot-out windows slicing into his arms and a cold rain blowing into the building. The walls are peppered with bullet holes, and a haze of smoke permeates the air with a taste like metal and sulfur in the back of his throat.

Barry crawls through a scattering of his .40-caliber shell casings, and he tries to call out to Helena, but her name leaves his lips as nothing but a whimper.

He pulls himself the rest of the way to the entrance. It takes a moment for his vision to sharpen into focus. Helena stands at the terminal, her fingers flying across an array of keyboards and touch-screens. Summoning his voice, he wills it to project her name.

She glances back at him. "I know you're hurting. I'm going as fast as I can."

"What are you doing?" Barry asks, each breath more agonizing than the one before it, and carrying less oxygen to his brain.

"I'm going back to the memory of cutting myself in that hotel room."

"Jee-woon and Sergei are gone." He coughs up blood. "Just . . . destroy everything now."

"Slade's still out there," Helena says. "If he escapes, he could build another chair. I need you to guard the door. I know you're hurting, but can you do that? Let me know if he comes." She moves away from the terminal, climbing onto the curved body of the memory chair.

"I'll try," Barry says.

He rests his head against the cool floor.

"We'll get the next one right," Helena says. Reaching up, she carefully pulls down the MEG microscope.

As she secures the chin strap, Barry fights to keep his eyes on the corridor, knowing if Slade comes, there's nothing he can do to stop him. He doesn't even have the strength to raise his weapon.

The dead memories of him dying in the last timeline finally shred into his consciousness.

The elevator doors opening to the entryway of Slade's penthouse.

Slade standing in his immaculate living room of windows pointing a revolver into the elevator car.

Barry thinking, Fuck. He knew.

A burst of light without sound.

Then—nothing.

Through the fog of death, Barry struggles to glance one last time into the lab, sees Helena tearing off her shirt, sliding her jeans down her legs, and climbing into the deprivation tank.

Barry is sprinting down a corridor, his nose bleeding, head throbbing. The pain of getting shot in the previous timeline is gone, the memories of this new one cascading into place.

He and Helena came up from Room 825.

Stepped off the elevator onto 17, took a different route to the lab, intending to catch Jee-woon and Slade coming off the elevator.

But they ran into Sergei instead and lost way too much time getting through him.

Now they're racing for the lab.

Barry wipes the blood from his nose and blinks through the saltwater sting of sweat in his eyes.

They round a corner and reach the door to the lab, which Helena opens with a shotgun blast. Barry charges in first, two thunderous gunshots erupting that miss his head by less than a foot. To his surprise, the shots came from a man he's seen once before—eleven years ago, on the night he was sent back into a memory.

Marcus Slade is standing twenty feet away by the terminal, wearing a white tank top and gray shorts, as if he just came from the gym, his curly, dark hair slicked back with sweat.

He's holding a satin stainless revolver and staring at Barry with total recognition.

Barry puts a round through his right shoulder, Slade stumbling back into the array of control panels, the gun slipping from his grasp as he slides down onto the floor.

Helena rushes to the deprivation tank and pulls the emergency release lever.

By the time Barry reaches the tank, she's already opening the hatch to expose Jee-woon floating on his back in the saltwater, desperately trying to pull the IV port out of his left forearm.

Barry holsters the Glock, reaches into the warm water, and hauls Jee-woon out, throwing him across the room.

Jee-woon hits the floor and rights himself, looking up at Barry and Helena, on his hands and knees, naked and dripping on the tile. He looks at Slade's gun, eight feet away, and lunges for it, Barry tracking him, and as he fires, so does Helena, the full load of buckshot slamming Jee-woon against the wall, his chest a gaping wound, and his strength rushing out of him apace with his blood.

Barry moves carefully toward him, keeping the gun trained on the man's ruined center mass, but Jee-woon is gone by the time he reaches him—eyes glassing over with that final emptiness.

HELENA

November 7, 2018

It is one of the most gratifying moments of her fragmented existence to site Slade down the barrel of the shotgun.

She reaches into her pocket and pulls out a thumb drive. "I'm going to wipe every line of code. Then I'm going to dismantle the chair, the microscope—"

"Helena—"

"*I'm* talking now! The stimulators. Every piece of hardware and software in the building. It's going to be like the chair never existed."

Slade is leaning against the base of the terminal, pain in his eyes. "It's been a minute, huh?"

"Thirteen years for me," she says. "How long for you?"

He seems to consider the question as Barry moves toward him and kicks the revolver across the room.

"Who knows?" he says finally. "After you ghosted off my oil platform—well done, by the way, never understood exactly how you pulled that off—it took me years to rebuild the chair. But since then, I've lived more lifetimes than you can possibly fathom."

"Doing what?" she asks.

"Most of them were quiet explorations of who I am, who I could be, in different places, with different people. Some were . . . louder. But this last timeline, I discovered that I could no longer generate a sufficient synaptic number to map my own memory. I've traveled too much. Filled my mind with too many lives. Too many experiences. It's beginning to fracture. There are entire lifetimes I've never remembered, that I only experience in flashes. This hotel isn't the first thing I did. It's the last. I built it to let others experience the power of what is still, what will always be, *your* creation."

He takes a strained breath and looks at Barry, Helena thinking that his eyes, even through the obvious pain, contain the composed depth of a man who has lived a long, long time.

"Helluva way to thank the man who gave you your daughter back," Slade says.

"Well, now she's dead again, you fucking asshole. The shock of remembering her own death and that building appearing yesterday pushed her over the edge."

"I'm truly sorry to hear that."

"You're using the chair destructively."

"Yes," Slade says. "It will be destructive at first, like all progress. Just as the industrial age ushered in two world wars. Just as *Homo sapiens* supplanted the Neanderthal. But would you turn back the clock on all that comes with it? Could you? Progress is inevitable. And it's a force for good."

Slade glances at the entry wound in his shoulder, touches it, grimaces, then looks back at Barry. "You want to talk about destructive? How about being locked in our little fishbowls, in this joke of an existence imposed on us by the limits of our primate senses? Life is suffering. But it doesn't have to be. Why should you be forced to accept your daughter's death when you can change it? Why shouldn't a dying man go back to his youth with full wisdom and knowledge instead of gasping out his last hours in agony? Why let a tragedy unfold when you could go back and prevent it? What you're defending isn't reality—it's a prison, a lie." Slade looks at Helena. "You *know* this. You have to see this. You've ushered in a new age for humanity. One where we no longer have to suffer and die. Where we can experience *so much*. Trust me, your perspective changes when you've lived countless lives. You've allowed us to escape the limitations of our senses. You've saved us all. *That's* your legacy."

"I know what you did to me in San Francisco," Helena says. "In the original timeline." Slade stares back at her, unblinking. "When you told me about accidentally discovering what the chair could do, you left out the part where you murdered me."

"And yet here you are. Death no longer has any hold over us. This is your life's work, Helena. Embrace it."

She says, "You can't possibly think humanity can be trusted with the memory chair."

"Think of the good it could do. I know you wanted to use this technology to help people. To help your mom. You could go back and be with her before she died, before her mind destroyed itself. You could save her memories. We can undo the killings of Jee-woon and Sergei. It'd be like none of this happened." His smile is filled with pain. "Can't you see how beautiful a world that would be?"

She takes a step toward him. "You might be right. Maybe there is a world where the chair makes all our lives better. But that's not the point. The point is, you might be *wrong* too. The point is, we don't know what people would do with this knowledge. All we know is that once enough people know about the chair, or how to build it, there's no going back. We'll never escape the loop of universal knowledge of the chair. It will live on in every subsequent timeline.

We'll have doomed humanity forever. I'd rather take the chance at passing up something glorious than risk everything on one roll of the dice."

Slade smiles that *I-know-more-than-you-realize* smile that takes her back to her years with him on the oil platform.

He says, "You're still being blinded by your limitations. Still not seeing the whole picture. And maybe you never will, unless you can travel the way I've traveled. . . ."

"What does that mean?"

He shakes his head.

"What are you talking about, Marcus? What do you mean, 'the way I've traveled'?"

Slade just stares at her, bleeding, and then the hum of the quantum processors fades away, the room suddenly silent.

One by one, the monitors in the terminal go dark, and as Barry looks quizzically at Helena, all of the lights flicker out.

BARRY

November 7, 2018

He sees the afterimages of Helena, Slade, and the chair.

Then nothing.

The lab stands pitch-black.

No sound but the thrumming of his heart.

Straight ahead, where Slade sat just seconds ago, Barry hears the noise of someone scrambling across the floor.

A shotgun blast illuminates the room for a deafening splinter of a second—enough time for Barry to see Slade disappear through the doorway.

Barry takes a tentative step forward, his retinas still reeling from the muzzle flash of Helena's gun, the darkness tinged with orange. The doorway materializes into view as lights from the surrounding buildings slink in through the windows of the hallway.

His hearing has recovered just enough from the gunshot to register the sound of quick footsteps rushing away down the corridor. Barry doesn't think Slade had time, in those few seconds of darkness, to get his hands on the revolver, but he can't be certain. More likely—Slade's making a mad dash for one of the stairwells.

Helena's voice emerges from the doorway, a whisper: "You see him?"

"No. Hang back until I figure out what's going on."

He jogs past the windows that peer out into a rainy, Manhattan night. From somewhere on the floor comes a *rat-a-tat* like a snare drum being played.

He turns the next corner into pure darkness, and as he approaches the main corridor, his foot strikes something on the floor.

Bending down, he touches the bloodied cloth of Slade's tank top. He still can't see a thing, but he recognizes the high-pitched wheezing of a punctured lung failing to fully inflate, and the softer gurgles of Slade drowning in his own blood.

A cold terror engulfs him. Running his hand along the wall, he reaches the junction of corridors.

For a moment, the only sound is Slade dying right behind him.

Something whips past the tip of his nose and *thunks* into the wall behind him.

Suppressed gunshots and muzzle fire reveal a half dozen officers by the bank of elevators, all in full tactical helmets and body armor, assault weapons shouldered.

Barry pulls back around the corner, shouts, "Detective Sutton, NYPD! Twenty-fourth precinct!"

"Barry?"

He knows that voice.

"Gwen?"

"What the fuck is going on, Barry?" Then to those around her: "I know him, I know him!"

"What are you doing here?" Barry asks.

"We had a report of shots fired in this building. What are *you* doing here?"

"Gwen, you have to get your team out of here and let me—"

"It's not my team."

"Whose is it?"

A male voice booms down the hall, "Our drone is showing a heat signature in one of the rooms behind you."

"They aren't a threat," Barry says.

"Barry, you need to let these guys do their job," Gwen says.

"Who are they?" Barry asks.

"Why don't you step out and talk to us? I'll make the introductions. You're making everyone very nervous."

He hopes Helena has realized what's happening and fled. He needs to buy her more time. If she can get to her Red Hook lab, in four months, she can finish building the chair and return to this day and fix this.

"You're not hearing me, Gwen. Take everyone back down to the garage and leave." Barry turns and screams down the corridor toward the lab, "Helena, run!"

The sound of rattling gear starts down the corridor—they're moving toward him.

Barry juts around the corner and fires a shot at the ceiling.

The return of gunfire is an instantaneous overreaction—a maelstrom of bullets strafing the corridor all around him.

Gwen screaming, *"Are you trying to get yourself killed?"*

"Helena, go! Get out of the building!"

Now something rolls down the corridor and stops three feet from Barry. Before he even has time to wonder what it is, the flashbang cracks open, a blinding ribbon of light and smoke unfurling, his vision bright white and the high-pitched tone of temporary hearing loss blocking out all other noise.

When the first bullet hits him, he doesn't feel any pain—only impact.

Then comes another and another, tearing into his sides, his leg, his arm, and as the pain comes, it occurs to him that Helena won't be saving him this time.

BOOK FOUR

He who controls the past controls the future.
He who controls the present controls the past.

−GEORGE ORWELL, *1984*

HELENA

Day 8

It is the strangest captivity.

The apartment is a one-bedroom near Sutton Place, spacious and high-ceilinged, with a million-dollar view of the Fifty-Ninth Street Bridge, East River, and the distant sprawl of Brooklyn and Queens.

She doesn't have access to a phone, Internet connection, or any other mode of contact with the outside world.

Four cameras, mounted to the walls, keep watch over every square inch of space, their red recording lights glowing above her even while she sleeps.

Her captors, a couple named Alonzo and Jessica, carry themselves with a calm collectedness. In the beginning, it eased her nerves.

Day one, they sat her down in the living room and said, "We know you have questions, but we aren't the ones to answer them."

Helena asked anyway.

What happened to Barry?

Who raided Marcus Slade's building?

Who's keeping me here?

Jessica leaned forward and said, "We're expensive prison guards, OK? Nothing more. We don't know why you're here. We don't *want* to know why you're here. But if you're cool, we, and the other people working with us, who you will never meet, will be cool."

They provide her meals.

Every other day, they make a run to the grocery store and bring back whatever she writes down on a piece of paper.

On a surface level, they're friendly enough, but there's an undeniable hardness in their eyes—no, a detachment—which makes her fairly certain they would hurt her, or worse, if the order ever came down.

She watches the news first thing in the mornings, and with each passing cycle, FMS occupies less bandwidth in the endless parade of tragedies and scandals and celebrity gossip.

When another school shooting takes nineteen lives, it is the first day since the Big Bend appeared that FMS isn't mentioned in the top headlines.

Her eighth day in the apartment, Helena sits at the kitchen island, eating a breakfast of huevos rancheros and watching sunlight pour through the window that overlooks the river.

This morning, in the reflection of the bathroom mirror, she inspected the row of stitches across her forehead and the fading, black-and-yellow bruise from the SWAT officer who knocked her unconscious on the stairwell of Slade's building while she was trying to escape.

Each day, the pain lessens as the fear and uncertainty grow.

She eats slowly, trying not to think of Barry, because when she imagines his face, the abject helplessness of her situation becomes unbearable, and the not knowing what's happening makes her want to scream.

The dead bolt turns, and Helena looks down the short hall into the foyer as the door swings open to reveal a man who, up until now, has existed only in a dead memory.

Rajesh Anand says to someone in the hall, "Close the door and turn off the cameras."

"Holy shit, Raj?" She leaves her stool at the island and meets him where the hall opens into the living room. "What are you doing here?"

"Came to see you." He stares at Helena with an air of confidence he didn't have when they worked together on the rig, looking better with age, his clean-shaven features at once delicate and handsome. He's wearing a suit and holding a briefcase in his left hand. The corners of his brown eyes crinkle with a genuine smile.

They move into the living room and sit across from each other on a pair of leather sofas.

"You're comfortable here?" he asks.

"Raj, what's happening?"

"You're being held in a safe house."

"Under whose authority?"

"The Defense Advanced Research Projects Agency."

Her stomach tightens. "DARPA?"

"Is there anything I can get for you, Helena?"

"Answers. Am I under arrest?"

"No."

"So I'm being detained."

He nods.

"I want a lawyer."

"Not possible."

"How is that not possible? I'm an American citizen. Isn't this illegal?"

"Possibly."

Raj lifts his briefcase and sets it on the table. The black leather has worn through in places and the brass hardware is deeply tarnished. "I know it's not much to look at," he says. "It was my father's. He gave it to me the day I left for America."

As he begins to fumble with the locking mechanism, Helena says, "There was a man with me on the seventeenth floor of that—"

"Barry Sutton?"

"They won't tell me what happened to him."

"Because they don't know. He was killed."

She knew it.

Felt it in her bones all week locked in this luxurious prison.

And still it breaks her.

As she cries, her face screws up with grief, and she can feel the stitches pulling across her forehead.

"I'm very sorry," Raj says. "He shot at the SWAT team."

Helena wipes her eyes and glares across the table.

"How are you mixed up in all of this?"

"It was the mistake of my life abandoning our project on Slade's oil platform. I thought he was mad. We all did. Sixteen months later, I woke up one night with a nosebleed. I didn't know how, or what it meant, but our entire time together on the rig had turned into false memories. I realized you'd achieved something incredible."

"So you knew what the chair was even then?"

"No. I only suspected you had figured out some way to alter memories. I wanted to be a part of it. I tried to find you and Slade, but you'd both vanished. When False Memory Syndrome first cropped up on a mass scale, I went to the one place I knew would be interested in my story."

"DARPA? You seriously thought that was a *good* idea?"

"All the government agencies were discombobulated. The CDC was trying to find a pathogen that didn't exist. A RAND physicist wrote a memo theorizing FMS could be micro changes in space-time. But DARPA believed me. We started tracking down victims of FMS and interviewing them. Last month, I found someone who claimed to have been put into a chair and sent back into a memory. All they knew was that it had happened in a hotel somewhere in Manhattan. I knew it had to be you or Slade, or the two of you working together."

"Why would you go to DARPA with something like this?"

"Money and resources. I brought a team to New York. We started looking for this hotel, but we couldn't find it. Then after Big Bend appeared, we heard chatter that an NYPD SWAT team was planning a raid on a building in Midtown that might have some connection to FMS. My team took over."

Helena looks out the window across the river, the sun warm on her face.

"Were you working with Slade?" Raj asks.

"I was trying to stop him."

"Why?"

"Because the chair is dangerous. Have you used it?"

"I've run a few diagnostics. Mainly I've been getting myself up to speed on the functionality." Raj pops the lock on the briefcase. "Look, I hear your concerns, but we could really use you. There's so much we don't know." From the briefcase, he pulls out a sheaf of paper and tosses it on the coffee table.

"What's this?" she asks.

"Employment contract."

She looks up at Raj. "Didn't you hear what I just said?"

"They know the chair is capable of memory return. Do you actually think they're not going to use it? That genie is never going back into the bottle."

"Doesn't mean I have to help them."

"But if you are willing, you'll be treated with the respect that's owed to the genius who invented this technology. You'll have a seat at the table. Be a part of making history. That's my pitch. Can I count you in?"

Helena looks across the table with a razor-blade smile. "You can get fucked."

Day 10

It's snowing outside, a fragile inch already collected on the windowsill. Traffic creeps along on the Fifty-Ninth Street Bridge, which appears to pass in and out of existence depending upon the intensity of the snowfall.

After breakfast, Jessica unlocks the dead bolt and tells her to get dressed.

"Why?" Helena asks.

"Now," Jessica says, with the first hint of menace Helena has heard from either of them in the ten days they've been together.

Down the freight elevator to the underground parking garage and a row of pristine black Suburbans.

They take the Queens-Midtown Tunnel like they're heading out to LaGuardia, Helena wondering if they're flying somewhere, but not daring to ask. They pass by the airport and continue into Flushing, past the rainbow-colored storefronts of Chinatown, then finally pull into a collection of low-rise office buildings that defines nondescript.

Once outside, Alonzo takes Helena by the arm and escorts her up the walkway to the main entrance, through the double doors, then deposits her by the front desk, where a very tall man—at least six and a half feet—stands waiting.

He dismisses Alonzo with a deep-voiced "I'll text you," and turns his focus on Helena.

"So you're the genius?" the man asks. He has a magnificent beard and thick, dark eyebrows that run together like a hedge below his forehead. He extends his hand. "I'm John Shaw. Welcome to DARPA."

"What do you do here, Mr. Shaw?"

"I suppose you could say I'm in charge. Come with me." He starts toward the security checkpoint, but she doesn't move. After five steps, he glances back at her. "That wasn't a suggestion, Dr. Smith."

He badges them both through sliding glass doors and leads her down a hallway of baize carpeting. While from the outside the building resembled a sad office park, the interior, with its grim lighting and utilitarian design, is a soulless government labyrinth to the bone.

He says, "We gutted Slade's lab and brought everything here so we could properly secure it."

"Did Raj not convey my thoughts on helping you?"

"He did."

"So why am I here?"

"I want to show you what we're doing."

"If it involves using the chair, I'm not interested."

They arrive at a revolving door of impenetrable-looking glass and a biometric security system.

Shaw looks down at Helena, towering over her by more than a foot. His face might be friendly under different circumstances, but in this moment, he looks intensely annoyed.

The smell of cinnamon-flavored Altoids wafts over her as he says, "I want you to know, there is no place safer in the width and breadth of the entire world than the other side of that glass. It may not look like it, but this building is a goddamn fortress, and at DARPA, we keep our secrets."

"That glass can't contain the chair. Nothing can. Why do you want it anyway?"

The right side of his mouth curls up, and for an instant, she glimpses the steel cunning in his eyes.

"Do me one favor, Dr. Smith," Shaw says.

"What's that?"

"For the next hour of your life, try to keep an open mind."

The chair and deprivation chamber stand side by side as center-pieces under the burn of the floodlights, in the most exquisite lab Helena has ever seen.

Raj is already seated at the terminal when they enter, and behind him stands a woman in her mid-twenties in black military fatigues and boots, her arms sleeved with tattoos and her black hair pulled back into a ponytail.

Shaw brings Helena over to the terminal.

"This is Timoney Rodriguez."

The soldier nods to Helena. "Who's this?"

"Helena Smith. She created all of this. Raj, how're we doing?"

"Full steam ahead." He swivels his chair around and looks up at Timoney. "You ready?"

"I think so."

Helena looks at Shaw. "What's happening?"

"We're sending Timoney back into a memory."

"For what purpose?"

"You'll see."

Helena turns to Timoney. "You realize they're about to kill you in that tank?"

"John and Raj briefed me on everything when they brought me on board."

"They're going to paralyze you and stop your heart. Having experienced it four times, I can assure you it's an agonizing process, and there's no way to circumvent the pain."

"Cool, cool."

"The changes you make will affect other people and cause all kinds of pain for them. Pain they're not ready for. Do you think you have a right to do that?"

No one acknowledges Helena's question.

Raj rises and motions to the chair. "Take a seat, Timoney."

He grabs one of the silver skullcaps in the cabinet beside the terminal and carries it over to the chair. Then he fits it on Timoney's head and begins to fasten the chin strap.

"This is the reactivation apparatus?" Timoney asks.

"Exactly. It works with the MEG microscope to record the memory. Then when you move over to the tank, it saves the neural pattern for reactivation by the stimulators." He lowers the MEG over the skullcap. "Have you thought about which memory you want to record?"

"John said he'd give me some guidance."

"Only parameter on my end is that it needs to be three days old," Shaw says.

Raj opens the compartments embedded in the chair's headrest and unfolds the telescoping titanium rods, which he locks into housings on the exterior of the microscope.

He says, "The memory doesn't have to be extensive. It just needs to be vivid. Pain and pleasure are good markers. So is strong emotion. Right, Helena?"

She says nothing. She's watching her worst nightmare unfold— the chair in a government laboratory.

Raj walks over to the terminal, tees up a new recording file, and carries over the tablet that functions as a remote control.

Taking a seat on the stool beside Timoney, he says, "Best way to record a memory, especially in the beginning, is to talk your way through it. Try to go deeper than just what you saw and felt. The memory of sounds, tastes, and smells are all critical for a vivid retrieval. Whenever you're ready."

Timoney closes her eyes, takes a deep breath.

She recalls standing at the copper-topped bar of a whiskey place she frequents in the Village, waiting for a bourbon she ordered. A woman squeezed in beside her to flag down the bartender, and bumped into Timoney, close enough for Timoney to smell the fragrance she wore. The woman looked over to apologize, and they locked eyes for three seconds. Timoney knew that any day now, she'd be climbing into the tank to die. She was excited and terrified by the prospect. In fact, the reason she'd gone out that evening was because she needed some physical connection.

"Her skin was the color of coffee and cream, and her lips just slayed me. I wanted to touch her so badly. God, I needed to get ragdolled, but I just smiled and said, 'It's fine, don't worry about it.' Life's made up of a thousand little regrets like that, isn't it?"

Timoney opens her eyes. "How was that?"

Raj holds up the tablet to show everyone—SYNAPTIC NUMBER: 156.

"Is that sufficient?" Shaw asks.

"Anything above 120 is in the safe zone."

He runs an IV line into Timoney's left forearm and mounts the injection port. Then Timoney strips out of her fatigues and heads over to the tank.

Raj opens the hatch, and Shaw gives her a hand as she climbs in.

Looking down at his soldier floating in the saltwater, Shaw says, "You remember everything we discussed?"

"Yes. I'm not sure what to expect."

"To be honest, none of us are. We'll see you on the other side."

Raj closes the hatch and moves to the terminal. Shaw sits beside him, and Helena comes over to study the monitors. The reactivation protocol is already initiating, Raj double-checking the dosages for the Rocuronium and sodium thiopental.

"Mr. Shaw?" Helena says.

He looks up at her.

"Right now, we are the only people in the world who control the chair."

"I would hope so."

"I am begging you. Show restraint. Its use has only ever caused mayhem and pain."

"Maybe the wrong people were at the controls."

"Humanity doesn't have the wisdom to handle this sort of power."

"I'm about to prove you wrong."

She needs to stop this, but there are two armed guards just outside the door. If she tried anything, they'd be on her in a matter of seconds.

Raj lifts the headset and speaks into the microphone, "We're starting in ten seconds, Timoney."

The woman's breathing comes fast over the speaker. *"I'm ready."*

Raj activates the injection port. Slade's equipment has improved vastly since their days on the rig, when it required a medical doctor to be on hand to monitor test subjects and advise when the stimulators should be fired. This new software automates the drug sequence based on real-time vital sign reporting and engages the electromagnetic stimulators only when the dimethyltriptamine release is detected.

"How long before the shift?" Shaw asks.

"Depends on how her body responds to the drugs."

The Rocuronium fires, followed thirty seconds later by the sodium thiopental.

Shaw leans in toward a split-screen that displays Timoney's vital signs on the left, and a night-vision camera feed of her inside the tank on the right.

"Her heart rate is off the charts, but she looks so calm."

"Yours would be too if you were suffocating while your heart was stopped," Helena says.

They all watch Timoney's heart rate flatline.

Minutes elapse.

A line of sweat runs down the side of Shaw's face.

"Should it be taking this long?" he asks.

"Yes," Helena says. "This is how long it takes to die after your heart quits beating. I promise you it feels much longer to her."

The monitor that shows the status of the stimulators flashes an alert—DMT RELEASE DETECTED. The previously dark image of Timoney's brain explodes with a light show of activity.

"Stimulators are firing," Raj says.

After ten seconds, a new alert replaces the DMT notice—MEMORY REACTIVATION COMPLETE.

Raj looks over at Shaw and says, "Any moment—"

Instead of the terminal, Helena is suddenly at the conference table on the other side of the lab. Her nose is bleeding, head throbbing.

Shaw, Raj, and Timoney are also seated around the table, everyone's nose bleeding except for Timoney's.

Shaw laughs. "My God." He looks at Raj. "It worked. It fucking worked!"

"What did you do?" Helena asks, still trying to sort out dead memories from the new, real ones.

"Think about the school shooting two days ago," Raj says.

Helena tries to remember the news coverage she watched the last few mornings in her apartment—hordes of students evacuating the school, horrifying videos taken on students' phones showing the rampage as it unfolded inside the cafeteria, devastated parents pleading for politicians to do something, to never let this happen again, law enforcement briefings and vigils and—

But none of that happened.

Those are dead memories now.

Instead, as the shooter walked up the steps of the school, an AR-15 slung over his shoulder and carrying a black duffel bag loaded with homemade bombs, handguns, and fifty high-capacity magazines, a 7.62 NATO round fired from an M40 rifle at a distance of approximately 300 yards entered the back of his head and exited through his left sinus cavity.

More than twenty-four hours later, the identity of the would-be school shooter's killer remains unknown, but the anonymous vigilante who snuffed him out is being heralded across the world as a hero.

Shaw looks at Helena. "Your chair saved nineteen lives."

She's speechless.

He says, "Look, I know there's an argument to be made that the chair should be eradicated from the face of the Earth. That it's an affront to the natural order of things. But it just saved nineteen kids and erased the unfathomable pain of their families."

"That's . . ."

"Playing God?"

"Yeah."

"But isn't it also playing God *not* to intervene when you have that power?"

"We shouldn't have that power."

"But we do. Because of something you created."

She's reeling.

"It's like you only see the harm your chair might do," Shaw says. "When you were first starting out with your research, way back when you were experimenting on mice, what was your guiding purpose?"

"I'd always been interested in memory. When my mom got Alzheimer's, I wanted to build something that could save core memories."

"You've gone way beyond that," Timoney says. "You didn't just save memories. You saved lives."

"You asked me why I wanted the chair," Shaw says. "I hope today has given you a window into who I am, what I'm about. Go home, enjoy this moment. Those kids are alive because of you."

Back at the apartment, she sits in bed all afternoon, watching breaking news coverage of the school shooting that "unhappened." Students who were murdered stand in front of cameras, recounting false memories of being gunned down. A weeping father speaks of going to the morgue to identify his dead son, a broken mother tells of being in the midst of planning her daughter's funeral only to shift into a moment of driving her to school instead.

Helena wonders if she's the only one who sees the slight unhinging behind the eyes of one of the previously murdered students.

As she witnesses the world attempting to come to terms with the impossible, she wonders what the masses make of it.

Religious scholars speak of ancient times, when miracles happened with great frequency. They speculate that we have returned to such an era, that this could be a precursor to the Second Coming.

While people flock to churches in droves, the best scientists can come up with is that the world experienced another "mass memory incident." And though they talk of alternate realities and the fragmenting of space-time, they look more baffled and rattled than the men of God.

She keeps coming back to something Shaw said to her in the lab. *It's like you only see the harm your chair might do.* It's true. All she's ever considered is the potential damage, and that fear has informed the trajectory of her life since her time on Slade's oil rig.

As night falls on Manhattan, she stands by the floor-to-ceiling window, looking out at the Fifty-Ninth Street Bridge, its trusses illuminated and spectacularly reflected in a swirl of shimmering color on the surface of the East River.

Tasting what it feels like to change the world.

Day 11

The next morning, she's delivered to the DARPA building in Queens, where Shaw is waiting for her again outside security.

As they head back toward the lab, he asks, "Did you watch the news last night?"

"A bit of it."

"Felt pretty good, didn't it?"

In the lab, Timoney, Raj, and two men Helena has never seen before are seated at the conference table. Shaw introduces her to the newcomers—a young Navy SEAL named Steve, whom he describes as Timoney's counterpart, and an impeccably groomed man in a bespoke black suit named Albert Kinney.

"Albert's defected here from RAND," Shaw says.

"You designed the chair?" Albert asks, shaking her hand.

"Unfortunately," Helena says.

"It's astonishing."

She takes one of the last unoccupied seats as Shaw moves to the head of the table, where he stands, surveying the group.

"Welcome," he says. "I've spoken to each of you individually over the last week about the memory chair my team recovered. Yesterday afternoon, we successfully used the chair to revise the outcome of the school shooting in Maryland. Now, there is a philosophy, which I respect, that says we can't trust ourselves with something of such raw power. I don't mean to speak for you, Dr. Smith, but even you, the chair's creator, hold that opinion."

"That's right."

"I have a different perspective, emboldened by what we achieved yesterday. I believe that, as technology arises in the world, we're entrusted to find its best use for the continuation and betterment of our species. I believe the chair contains an awesome potential to bring good into the world.

"In addition to Dr. Smith, we have at this table Timoney Rodriguez and Steve Crowder, two of the bravest, most capable soldiers ever produced by the US military. Raj Anand, the man responsible for finding the chair. Albert Kinney, a RAND systems theorist with a mind like a diamond. And me. As deputy director for DARPA, I have the resources to create, under the veil of absolute secrecy, a new program, which we're starting today."

"You intend to keep using the chair?" Helena asks.

"Indeed."

"To what end?"

"The mission statement for our group is something we'll craft together."

Albert asks, "So you're thinking of us as a kind of brain trust?"

"Precisely. And the parameters of use are also something we'll decide on together."

Helena pushes her chair back and rises. "I won't be a part of this."

Shaw looks up at her from the head of the table, his jaw tensing.

"This group needs your voice. Your skepticism."

"It's not skepticism. Yes, we saved lives yesterday, but in doing so, we created false memories and confusion in the minds of millions of people. Every time you use the chair, you'll be changing the way human beings process reality. We have no idea what those long-term effects might be."

"Let me ask you something," Shaw says. "Do you think any decent person is sad right now that nineteen students *weren't*, in fact, murdered? We aren't talking about swapping out good memories for bad or randomly altering reality. We're here for one purpose—the undoing of human misery."

Helena leans forward. "This is no different from how Marcus Slade was using the chair. He wanted to change how we experienced reality, but on a practical level, he was letting people go back and fix their lives, which was good for some people, and *catastrophic* for others."

Albert says, "Helena raises a legitimate concern. There's already quite a bit of literature out there on the effects of FMS on the brain, issues of excess memory storage, and false memories in people with mental disorders. I'd recommend we have a team research every serious paper that's been published on the subject, so we can stay informed moving forward. In theory, if we limit the age of the memories we send our agents back to, we'll limit the cognitive dissonance between the real and false timelines."

"In theory?" Helena asks. "Shouldn't you move forward on better information than the theoretical if you're talking about changing the nature of reality?"

"Albert, are you proposing we take travel into the distant past off the table?" Shaw asks. "Because I have a list here"—he touches a black leather notebook—"of atrocities and disasters from the twentieth and twenty-first centuries. I'm just spitballing, but what if we found a ninety-five-year-old with sniper training in their past. A sharp mind. Clear recollection. Helena, what's the earliest age you'd feel comfortable sending someone back into a memory?"

"I can't believe we're even discussing this."

"We're just talking here. There are no bad ideas at this table."

"The female brain is fully mature at twenty-one," she says. "The male brain, a few years later. Sixteen could probably handle it, but we'd need testing to be sure. There's a potential that if we sent someone back into their memories at too young an age, their cognitive functioning would simply collapse. An adult consciousness being shoved into an underdeveloped brain could be disastrous."

"Are you suggesting what I think you are, John?" Albert asks. "That we send agents forty, fifty, sixty years back to assassinate dictators before they go on to murder millions?"

"Or to *stop* a killing that's the catalyst for an epic tragedy—for instance, when Gavrilo Princip, a Bosnian Serb, murdered Archduke Franz Ferdinand in 1914, and in so doing, tipped over the first domino in a chain that would ultimately trigger the First World War. I'm simply raising the possibility for discussion. We are sitting in a room with a machine of incredible power."

A sobering silence falls on the group.

Helena sits back down. Her heart is racing, her mouth gone dry.

She says, "The only reason I'm still at this table is because someone needs to be a voice of reason."

"I couldn't agree more," Shaw says.

"It's one thing to change the events of the last few days. Don't get me wrong, that's still dangerous and you should never do it again. It's another entirely to save the lives of millions half a century ago. For the sake of argument, what if we figured out some way to stop World War Two from happening? What if, because of our actions, thirty million people lived who would've otherwise died? Maybe you think that sounds amazing. Look closer. How do you begin to calculate the good and the evil potential of those who died? Who's to say that the actions of a monster like Hitler or Stalin or Pol Pot didn't prevent the rise of a much greater monster? At the very least, an alteration on this scale would certainly change our present beyond comprehension. It would undo the marriages and births of millions of people. Without Hitler, an entire generation of immigrants would never have come to the US. Or, simpler still, if your great-grandmother's high school sweetheart doesn't die in the war, she marries him instead of your great-grandfather. Your grandparents are never born, your parents are never born, and—fucking obviously—neither are you." She looks across the table at Albert. "You're a systems theorist? Is there any modeling you can conceive of that would even begin to extrapolate the changes to the population of the planet at this level of magnitude?"

"Yes, I could develop some models, but to your point, tracking cause and effect with such an immense dataset is virtually impossible. I agree with you that we're flying dangerously close to the law of unintended consequences. Here's a thought experiment off the top of my head.

"If England didn't go to war with Germany because of something we did, then Alan Turing, the father of the computer and artificial intelligence, wouldn't have been pushed to break Germany's ciphering technology. Now, maybe he still would've gone on to lay a foundation for the modern, microchip-driven world we live in. Then again, maybe not. Or to a lesser degree. And how many lives have been saved based on all this technology that protects us? More than the lives lost in the Second World War? The 'what-ifs' snowball out into infinity."

Shaw says, "Point taken. These are the types of discussions we need to be having." He looks at Helena. "This is why I want you here. You aren't going to stop me from using the chair, but maybe you can help us use it wisely."

Day 17

They spend the first week hammering out ground rules, among them—

The only people allowed to use the chair are trained agents, such as Timoney and Steve.

The chair can never be used to alter events in the personal histories of the team members, or their friends and families.

The chair can never be used to send agents further back than five days into the past.

The chair's sole use is for the undoing of unthinkable tragedies and disasters, which can be circumvented easily and anonymously by one agent.

All decisions to use the chair will be put to a vote.

Albert has taken to calling their group the Department of Undoing Particularly Awful Shit, and like many names that start as a bad joke without a quick replacement, the name sticks.

Day 25

A week later, Shaw submits the next mission candidate for the group's consideration, even bringing in a photograph to make his case.

Twenty-four hours ago, in Lander, Wyoming, an eleven-year-old girl was found murdered in her bedroom, with the MO eerily similar to five previous murders that had occurred over an eight-week period in remote towns across the American west.

The perpetrator had broken into the bedroom at some point between eleven p.m. and four a.m. using a glass cutter. He gagged his victim and violated her while her parents slept unknowing in a room across the hall.

"Unlike previous crimes," Shaw says, "where the victims weren't found until days or weeks later, this time he left her in her bed, tucked in under the covers for her parents to find her the next morning. Which means we have a definitive window of time for when the murder occurred, and we also know the precise place. There seems to be little question this monster will do this again. I'd like to propose a vote to use the chair, and I vote yes."

Timoney and Steve are instant yeses.

Albert asks, "How would you propose Steve dispatch the killer?"

"What do you mean?"

"Well, there's a quiet way of doing it, where he intercepts the guy and takes him out into the middle of nowhere and puts him in a hole in the ground where no one will ever find him. And then there's the noisy way, where the would-be killer is found with his throat slit in the bushes under the very window he was on the verge of climbing through, with the glass cutter and knife still in his possession. With the noisy version, we would be, in effect, announcing the existence of the Department of Undoing Particularly Awful Shit. Maybe we want to make that announcement, maybe we don't. I'm merely raising the question."

Helena has been staring at the most disturbing photograph she's ever seen, and rational thought is disintegrating beneath her. In this moment, all she wants is for the person who did this to suffer.

She says, "My vote is that we take this lab apart and wipe the servers. But if you decide to go through with this—I realize I can't stop you—then kill this animal and leave him with his incriminating tools under the girl's window."

"Why, Helena?" Shaw asks.

"Because if people know that someone, some entity, is behind these reality shifts, then the awareness of your work begins to take on a mythic stature."

"You mean like Batman?" Albert asks, smirking.

Helena rolls her eyes, says, "If your aim is to repair the evil that men do, maybe it's in your interest for evil men to fear you. Also, if they find this guy near the scene of the crime, ready to break into a house, authorities will link him to the other murders, and hopefully give closure to the other families."

Timoney says, "You're saying we become the bogeyman?"

"If someone chooses not to commit an atrocity because they fear a shadow group with the ability to manipulate memory and time, that's a mission you'll never have to face, and false memories you'll never have to create. So yes. Become the bogeyman."

Day 24

Steve finds the child murderer at 1:35 a.m. as he's beginning to cut a hole in the window of Daisy Robinson's bedroom. He tapes his mouth and wrists and cuts him slowly ear to ear, watching as he writhes and bleeds out in the dirt beside the house.

Day 31

The following week, they decline to intervene in a train derailment in the Texas hill country that kills nine people and injures many more.

Day 54

When a regional jet crashes in the evergreen forest south of Seattle, they again opt not to use the chair, the group reasoning that, as in the case of the derailment, by the time the cause of the accident is determined, too much time will have passed to send Steve or Timoney back.

Day 58

Day by day, it's becoming clearer the types of tragedies they are most suited to fix, and if there's any hesitation, any doubt whatsoever, to Helena's relief, they err on the side of noninterference.

She continues to be held captive in the apartment building near Sutton Place. Alonzo and Jessica have allowed her to begin taking walks at night. One of them trails a half block behind; the other stays half a block ahead.

It's the first week of January, and the air whipping between the buildings is a polar blast in her face. But she basks in the faux-freedom of walking in New York at night, imagining she is truly on her own.

She becomes contemplative, thinking of her parents, of Barry. She keeps returning to the last image she holds of him—standing in Slade's lab just before the lights went down. And then a minute later, the sound of his voice, screaming at her to go.

Tears run cold across her face.

The three most important people in her life are gone, and she will never see them again. The stark loneliness of that knowledge cuts her to the bone.

She is forty-nine, and she wonders if this is what feeling old really means—not just a physical deterioration, but an interpersonal. A growing silence caused by the people you most love, who have shaped you and defined your world, going on ahead into whatever comes after.

With no way out, no endgame in sight, and everyone she loves gone, she is unsure how much longer she will keep doing this.

Day 61

Timoney returns to a memory to stop a deranged fifty-two-year-old insurance salesman from walking into a political demonstration at Berkeley and massacring twenty-eight students with an assault rifle.

Day 70

Steve breaks into an apartment in Leeds while the man is assembling his vest, slides the blade of a combat knife through the base of his skull, and scrambles his medulla oblongata, leaving him facedown on the table atop a pile of nails, screws, and bolts that would've torn twelve people to shreds in the London Underground the following morning.

Day 90

On the program's three-month anniversary, a report in the *New York Times* profiles their eight missions, speculating that the deaths of would-be murderers, school shooters, and one suicide bomber suggest the work of an enigmatic organization in possession of a technology beyond all understanding.

Day 115

Helena is in bed, right on the cusp of sleep, when a hard knocking on the front door sets her heart racing. If this were her apartment, she could pretend to be out and wait for the latecomer to go away, but alas, she lives under surveillance, and the dead bolt is already turning.

She climbs out of bed, dons her terrycloth robe, and emerges into the living room as John Shaw is opening the front door.

"Come right in," she says. "By all means."

"Sorry, and sorry about the late visit." He moves down the hall into the living room. "Nice apartment."

She can smell the cinnamon-spiced fire of bourbon on his breath—a fair amount of it. "Yeah, it's rent-controlled and everything."

She could offer him a beer or something; she doesn't.

Shaw climbs onto one of the cushioned stools at the kitchen island, and she stands across from him, thinking he looks more pensive and troubled than she's ever seen him.

"What can I do for you, John?"

"I know you have never believed in what we're doing."

"That's true."

"But I'm glad you're in the conversation. You make us better. You don't know me that well, but I haven't always . . . hey, do you have anything to drink?"

She goes to the Sub-Zero, pulls out a couple of bottles from Brooklyn Brewery, and pops the caps.

Shaw takes a long swig and says, "I build shit for the military to help them kill people as efficiently as possible. I've been behind some truly horrific technology. But these last few months have been the best of my life. Every night, while I fall asleep, I think about the grief we're erasing. I see the faces of the people whose lives or loved ones we're saving. I think about Daisy Robinson. I think about all of them."

"I know you're trying to do what's right."

"I am. First time in my life, maybe." He drinks his beer. "I haven't said anything to the team, but I'm getting pressure from people in high places."

"What kind of pressure?"

"Because of my history, I'm afforded a long leash and minimal oversight. But I still have my masters. I don't know if they suspect something, but they want to know what I'm working on."

"What can you do?" she asks.

"There's a few ways to play it. We could create a false-front program, give them something shiny to look at, which bears no actual resemblance to what we're doing. It'd probably buy us a little time. The better play is just telling them."

"You can't do that."

"DARPA's primary objective is to make breakthroughs in technologies that will strengthen our national security, with a focus on military applications. It's only a matter of time, Helena. I can't hide it from them forever."

"How would the military use the chair?"

"How wouldn't they? Yesterday, a platoon from the 101st was ambushed in Kandahar Province. Eight marines KIA. That's not public information yet. Last month, a Black Hawk crashed on a night training mission in Hawaii. Five dead. You know how many missions fail because you missed the enemy by a few days or hours?

Right place, wrong time? They would see the chair as a tool that would give commanders the ability to edit warfare."

"What if they don't share your perspective on how the chair should be used?"

"Oh, they won't." Shaw polishes off his beer. He unbuttons his collar, loosens his tie. "I don't want to freak you out, but it isn't just the DoD who would exploit the chair. The CIA, NSA, FBI—every agency will want a piece of it if word gets out. We are a DoD agency, and that'll provide some cover, but they'll all demand a seat in the chair."

"Jesus. Will word get out?"

"Hard to say, but can you imagine if the Justice Department had this tech? They'd turn this country into *Minority Report*."

"Destroy the chair."

"Helena . . ."

"What? How hard is this? Destroy it before any of this happens."

"Its potential for good is too high. We've already proven that. We can't destroy it because of fear for what *might* happen."

It becomes silent in the apartment. Helena wraps her fingers around the cold, sweating bottle of beer.

"So what's your plan?" she asks.

"I don't have one. Not yet. I just needed you to know what's coming."

Day 136

It begins sooner than anyone anticipates.

Shaw walks into the lab on March 22 for their daily briefing of all the horrible shit that's happened in the world in the past twenty-four hours and says, "We have our first mandated assignment."

"From whom?" Raj asks.

"Way up the food chain."

"So they know?" Helena asks.

"Yes." He opens a manila file with Top Secret stamped in red on the cover. "This has not been in the news. On January fifth, seventy-five days ago, a sixth-generation fighter jet malfunctioned and went down near the Ukraine/Belarus border. They don't think the aircraft was destroyed, and they're pretty sure the pilot was captured. We're talking about a Boeing F/A-XX, which is still in development, highly classified, and loaded with all sorts of bells and whistles we'd prefer the Russians not have.

"They've asked me to send an agent back to January fourth to tell me about this crash. Then I'm to deliver a message to the Deputy SecDef, who will make sure word gets down through the ranks so the aircraft is inspected before the test flight and not flown anywhere near Russian territory."

"Seventy-six days?" Helena asks.

"Correct."

Albert says, "Did you tell them we don't use the chair to go back that far?"

"I didn't put it quite that stridently, but yes."

"And?"

"They said, 'Do as you're fucking told.'"

They send Timoney back at ten a.m. on March 22.

By eleven a.m., Helena and the team are in front of the TV, glued to CNN in shock. This is the first time they've used the chair to go back *before* the date of a previous intervention, and as far as they can gather from reports, it's had an extraordinary effect. Until now, the false memory phenomenon has obeyed its predictable pattern, sticking to its individual timeline anniversaries. In other words, when an operative alters a timeline, the false memories of that "dead" timeline always arrive at the exact moment the operative died in the tank. This time, however, it seems those anniversary points have been overridden—not erased, but pushed back to ten a.m. this morning, the moment of the chair's latest use when Timoney went back to give Shaw the message about the downed fighter jet. So instead of recalling each dead timeline as it happened, the public received the full hit of dead memories in a single gulp, at ten a.m. today, everyone simultaneously remembering all the averted massacres since January fourth, including Berkeley and the London Underground suicide bombing.

Inflicting these false memories one by one, over the course of several months, was disruptive enough. Hitting everyone with all of them, in a single instant, is exponentially more so.

So far, the media isn't reporting any deaths or breakdowns as a result of the sudden onslaught, but for Helena it's a stark reminder that her machine is far too mysterious, dangerous, and unknowable to exist.

Day 140

Shaw is still given free rein to intervene in civilian tragedies, but their work is becoming increasingly military-facing.

They use the chair to go back and undo a drone strike that hit a wedding, killing mostly Afghan women and children, and completely missing the intended target, who wasn't even in attendance.

Day 146

They revise an airstrike from a B-1 Lancer bomber that misdirected its payload and killed an entire spec-ops team in Zabul Province instead of the Taliban force it had been called in to hit.

Day 152

Four dead soldiers, attacked by Islamic militants while on patrol in the Niger desert, are resurrected when Timoney dies in the tank and gives Shaw the details of the upcoming ambush.

They're using the chair with such frequency—at least once a week now—that Shaw brings on a new agent to lighten the burden on Steve and Timoney, who are beginning to experience the first signs of mental degradation from the stress of dying again and again.

Day 160

Helena rides down to the parking garage of her building and heads for the black Suburban with Alonzo and Jessica, feeling more hopeless than she can ever recall. She can't keep doing this. The military is using her chair, and she is powerless to stop them. The chair itself is kept under 24/7 surveillance, and she doesn't have access to the system. Even if she managed to escape from Alonzo and Jessica, considering what she knows, the government would never stop hunting her. Besides, Shaw could simply send an agent back into a memory to prevent her escape from ever happening.

Dark thoughts are whispering to her again.

Her phone vibrates in her pocket as they head south on FDR Drive—Shaw calling.

She answers, "Hey, I'm on my way in."

"I wanted to tell you first."

"What?"

"We got a new assignment this morning."

"What is it?"

The sky disappears as they pass through the Manhattan portal of the Queens-Midtown Tunnel.

"They want us to send someone back almost a year."

"Why? For what?"

Jessica hits the brake pedal hard enough for Helena to jerk forward against her shoulder harness. Through the windshield, a sea of red taillights illuminates the tunnel ahead, accompanied by the cacophony of drivers beginning to honk their horns.

"An assassination."

There's a distant burst of light, followed by a sound like thunder, deeper in the tunnel.

The windows rattle; the car shudders beneath her; the overhead lights wink out for a terrifying second before flickering back on.

"The hell was that?" Alonzo asks.

"John, I'll call you right back." Helena lowers her phone. "What's going on?"

"I think there was a wreck up ahead."

People are beginning to get out of their cars.

Alonzo opens his door, steps out into the tunnel.

Jessica follows him.

The odor of smoke pushing through the vents snaps Helena into the present. She glances back through the rear window at the cars gridlocked behind them.

A man runs past her window, sprinting for daylight, and the first flicker of fear slides down Helena's spine.

More people are coming now, and they all look terrified, rushing between the cars back toward Manhattan, trying to get away from something.

Helena opens her door, steps outside.

The commotion of human fear and despair echoes off the tunnel walls, and it's rising, drowning out the idling of a thousand car engines.

"Alonzo?"

"I don't know what happened," he says, "but it's something bad."

The air smells wrong—not just of engine exhaust but of gasoline and melting things.

Smoke rolls out of the tunnel ahead, and the people stumbling toward her look shell-shocked, their faces bleeding and blackened.

The air quality is deteriorating fast, her eyes beginning to burn, and now she can barely see what lies ahead.

Jessica says, "We need to get out of here, Alonzo. Right now."

As they turn to go, a man emerges from the smoke, limping and holding his side, in obvious pain.

Helena rushes toward him, coughing now, and as she draws near she sees that he's holding a fragment of glass that's embedded in his side. His hands are drenched in blood, and his face is smoke-blackened and wrenched in agony.

"Helena!" Jessica yells. "We are leaving!"

"He needs our help."

The man falls into Helena, gasping for breath. Alonzo hurries over, and he and Helena each take one of his arms and drape it around their shoulders. He's a big man, at least two-fifty, and he wears a half-incinerated shirt with the name and logo of a courier service across the lapel pocket.

It's a relief to be heading for the exit. With every step, the man's left foot squishes in his shoe, which is filling up with blood.

"Did you see what happened?" Helena asks.

"These two semis stopped in traffic. They were blocking both lanes a little ways ahead of me. Everyone was laying on their horns. It didn't take long for people to start getting out of their cars and approaching the trucks to see what was wrong. Just as this guy stepped up onto one of the rigs, I saw a bright flash and then the loudest sound I ever heard. Suddenly this ball of fire is rushing over the tops of all the cars. I got down in the floorboard a second before it reached my van. The windshield exploded and then the inside was on fire. I thought I was going to burn to death, but somehow I . . ."

The man stops talking.

Helena stares down at the pavement, which is vibrating under her feet, and then they all look down the tunnel toward Queens.

It's hard to tell at first because of the smoke, but soon the movement in the distance becomes clear—people are running toward them, the sound of screams rising and reverberating off the walls.

Helena looks up as a fracture opens down the middle of the ceiling, twelve feet overhead and breaking at right angles, chunks of concrete falling all around her, smashing windshields and people. There's a cool wind in her face, and now, over the screams of terror, a sound like white noise and thunder, growing exponentially louder with every passing second.

The deliveryman whimpers.

Alonzo says, "Fuck."

Helena feels mist on her face, and then a wall of water blasts out of the smoke carrying cars and people.

It hits Helena like a wall of freezing bricks, sweeping her off her feet, and she's tumbling in a vortex of frigid violence, slamming into walls, the ceiling, then crashing into a woman in a business suit, their eyes meeting for two surreal seconds before Helena is speared through the windshield of a FedEx truck.

Helena stands at the window in her living room, her nose bleeding, head throbbing, trying to process what just happened.

Though she can still feel the terror of being swept through the tube in a debris-wave of water, cars, and people, her death in the tunnel never happened.

It's all a dead memory.

She woke up, made breakfast, got ready, and was heading out the door when she heard two explosions so loud and close they shook the floor and rattled the glass.

She ran back into the living room, and through the window, watched in stunned amazement as the Fifty-Ninth Street Bridge burned. After five minutes, she gained the false memories of dying in the tunnel.

Now, the two towers of the Fifty-Ninth Street Bridge that frame Roosevelt Island are engulfed in twisting columns of flame reaching hundreds of feet into the air and burning hot enough for her to feel the heat, even from a thousand feet away and through the window.

What the fuck is happening?

The span of bridge between Manhattan and Roosevelt Island is draped across the East River like a severed tendon, its trusses still clinging to the Manhattan tower. Cars are sliding down the steep pavement into the river, people clinging to the railing as the current slowly pulls the bridge segment out of socket with a torqueing shriek she can feel in her fillings.

She wipes the blood from her nose as it hits her—*I experienced a reality shift. I died in the tunnel. Now I'm here. Someone is using the chair.*

The span connecting Roosevelt Island and Queens has already torn completely off, and downriver, she sees a thousand-foot section of burning roadway crash into a container ship, impaling its hull with spearlike jags of sheared-off metal trussing.

Even inside the apartment, the air smells of things burning that shouldn't be able to burn, and the wail of the sirens of hundreds of incoming emergency vehicles is deafening.

As her phone vibrates behind her on the kitchen island, the last threads of metal pull loose from the Manhattan tower like whips cracking, and with a tremendous groan, the bridge segment breaks free, plummeting a hundred and thirty feet, the double-decker roadway smashing through concrete into FDR Drive, crushing traffic, leveling trees by the shoreline, then scraping slowly across the eastern terminus of Fifty-Ninth and Fifty-Eighth Streets, gouging out the entire northeast aspect of a skyscraper, and just missing Helena's building before sliding into the East River.

She rushes into the kitchen and answers the phone with, "Who's using the chair?"

"It's not us," John says.

"Bullshit. I just shifted from dying in the Midtown Tunnel to standing in my apartment, watching this bridge burn."

"Just get here as fast as you can."

"Why?"

"We're fucked, Helena. We are so fucked."

The door to her apartment bursts open. Alonzo and Jessica rush inside, noses bleeding, looking scared out of their minds.

Helena senses a deceleration of all movement.

Another shift coming?

Jessica says, "What the hell is—"

Now Helena is staring through the tinted glass of the backseat window, looking north up the East River toward Harlem and the Bronx.

She never died in the tunnel.

The destruction of the Fifty-Ninth Street Bridge didn't happen.

In fact, they're halfway across the upper level of the Fifty-Ninth Street Bridge, which stands fully intact at this moment.

From behind the wheel, Jessica says, "Oh God."

The Suburban swerves into the adjacent lane, and Alonzo reaches over, grabs the steering wheel from the passenger seat, and whips the vehicle back into its lane.

Straight ahead, a bus drifts into their lane, sideswiping three cars and crushing them into the divider in a spray of sparks and shattering glass.

Jessica cranks the steering wheel, just missing the pileup as the car momentarily leans over on two wheels.

"Look behind us," she says.

Helena glances back, sees massive columns of smoke rising out of Midtown.

"It's some false-memory thing, isn't it?" Jessica says.

Helena dials Shaw, holds the phone to her ear, thinking, *Someone's using the chair to shift reality from one disaster to the next.*

"All circuits are busy, please try your call again."

Alonzo turns on the radio.

"—getting reports that two semitrucks exploded near Grand Central Terminal. There's quite a bit of confusion. There were reports earlier of some type of accident at the Queens-Midtown Tunnel, and I remember

seeing the Fifty-Ninth Street Bridge go down, but . . . I don't know how this is possible—I see it standing in perfect condition on our tower cam right—"

—and they're stopped on East Fifty-Seventh Street, the air choked with smoke, her ears ringing.

Another headache.

Another nosebleed.

Another shift.

The tunnel never happened.

The bridge never happened.

Grand Central Terminal was never bombed.

Only the dead memories of those events remain, stacked in her mind like the memories of dreams.

She woke up, made breakfast, got dressed, and rode down to the parking garage under her building with Jessica and Alonzo, just like every other morning. They were heading west on East Fifty-Seventh to loop around onto the bridge when a blinding flash split the sky, coupled with a sound like a thousand synchronized cannon blasts ricocheting off the surrounding buildings.

They're stuck in traffic now, and all around her, people are standing on the sidewalk, looking in horror at Trump Tower, which is billowing clouds of smoke and flame.

The lower ten floors are sagging like a melting face, the interiors of individual rooms exposed like cubbyholes. The ones higher up are still largely intact, with people inside of them staring over the newly made precipice into the crater that used to be the intersection of Fifty-Seventh and Fifth Avenue.

As the city screams with incoming sirens, Jessica shrieks, "What's happening? What is *happening*?"

Straight ahead, a human being falls out of the sky and crushes in the roof of a cab.

Another person crashes through a car windshield directly behind the Suburban.

A third plummets through the awning of a private sports club, Helena wondering if people are throwing themselves off buildings because this is too much for their psyches to bear. It wouldn't surprise her. If she didn't know about the chair, what would she think was happening to the city, to time, to reality itself?

Jessica is crying.

Alonzo says, "It feels like the end of everything."

Helena looks up at the building out her window as a blond-haired woman leaps from an office whose glass was shattered by the blast. She falls like a rocket, headfirst, screaming toward impact, and Helena starts to turn away, but she can't.

The movement of everything decelerates again.

The roiling smoke.

The flames.

The falling woman grinding down into extreme slow-motion, her head inching closer and closer to the pavement.

Everything stops.

This timeline dying.

Jessica's hands eternally clutch the steering wheel.

Helena can never look away from the jumper, who will never hit the ground, because she's frozen in midair, the top of her head one foot from the pavement, her yellow hair splayed out, eyes closed, face in a perpetual grimace, bracing for impact—

And Helena is walking through the double doors of the DARPA building, where Shaw stands just outside security.

They stare at each other, processing this new reality as the accompanying set of replacement memories clicks in.

None of it happened.

Not the tunnel, the bridge, Grand Central, or Trump Tower.

Helena woke up, got ready, and was driven here like every other morning, without incident.

She opens her mouth to speak, but Shaw says, "Not out here."

Raj and Albert are sitting at the conference table in the lab, watching the news on a television embedded in the wall. The screen has been divided into four live images from tower cams showing the Fifty-Ninth Street Bridge, Grand Central Terminal, Trump Tower, and the Queens-Midtown Tunnel, all untouched, over the banner, "MASS MEMORY MALFUNCTION IN MANHATTAN."

"What the fuck is going on?" Helena asks.

She's physically shaking, because, although it never happened, she can still feel the impact from the wall of water slamming into her. She can hear the bodies striking cars all around her. She can hear the shriek of the bridge tearing itself apart.

"Sit down," Shaw says.

She takes the chair across from Raj, who looks completely shell-shocked.

Shaw remains standing, says, "The schematics for the chair, the tank, our software, the protocol—it all leaked."

Helena points at the screen. "Someone else is doing this?"

"Yes."

"Who?"

"I don't know."

"It would take more than a couple of months to build the chair if you were just working from blueprints," she says.

"It leaked a year ago."

"How is that possible? You didn't even have the chair a year—"

"Marcus was operating out of that hotel for more than a year. Someone got curious about what he was doing and hacked his servers. Raj just found evidence of the incursion."

"It was a massive data breach," Raj says. "They hid it well, and they got everything."

Shaw looks at Albert. "Tell her what you found."

"Other instances of reality shifts."

"Where?"

"Hong Kong, Seoul, Tokyo, Moscow, four in Paris, two in Glasgow, one in Oslo. Very similar to the way FMS stories first appeared in America last year."

"So people are using the chair, and you know this for sure."

"Yes. I even found a company in São Paulo using it for tourism."

"Jesus Christ. How long has all this been happening?"

"Goes back almost three months."

Shaw says, "The Chinese and Russian governments have both reached out to say they have this technology."

"It's like every new sentence you say is more terrifying than the one before it."

"Well, in keeping with that trend . . ." He opens a laptop on the table and types in a URL. "This went live five minutes ago. No press coverage yet."

She leans in toward the screen.

It's the WikiLeaks homepage.

Under the "War & Military" heading, she sees a graphic of a soldier sitting in a chair that looks exactly like the one in the middle of this room, over the headline:

> **US Military Memory Machine.** Thousands of pages
> containing full schematics to an apparatus that purports
> to send soldiers back into their memories may explain
> the spate of reversed tragedies over the last six months.

Her chest becomes tight.

Black stars burning across her field of vision.

She asks, "How is WikiLeaks connecting the chair to our government?"

"Unknown."

Albert says, "To recap, Slade's servers were hacked. Contents probably sold to multiple buyers. From one or more of those buyers, or the hackers themselves, the plans continued to leak. There are likely multiple chairs in use in many countries throughout the world at this moment. China and Russia have the chair, and now, with WikiLeaks publishing the schematics, any corporation, dictator, or wealthy individual with twenty-five million dollars lying around can build their own private memory machine."

Raj says, "Don't forget—a terrorist group of some sort appears to be one of the proud new owners of a chair, and they're using it to repeat the same attack on different landmarks in one of the most densely populated cities in the world."

Helena looks over at the chair.

The tank.

The terminal.

The air has a faint humming quality.

On the television screen, the news is now covering a new attack in San Francisco, where the Golden Gate Bridge is sending up plumes of black smoke into the early morning sky. Her mind is trying to wrap itself around the situation, but it's too immense, too tangled, too fucked.

"What's the worst-case scenario, Albert?" Shaw asks.

"I believe we're experiencing it."

"No, I mean in terms of what could happen next."

Albert has always been unflappable, as if his great intelligence shielded and lifted him above it all. But not today. Today he looks scared.

He says, "It's unclear whether Russia or China only have the blueprints to the chair, or if they've already built one. If it's the former, rest assured they are racing to construct a chair, along with every other country in the world."

"Why?" Helena asks.

"Because it's a weapon. It's the ultimate weapon. Remember our first meeting at this table, when we talked about sending a ninety-five-year-old sniper into a memory to change the outcome of a war?

Who among our enemies—hell, even our friends—would benefit from using the chair against us?"

"Who wouldn't?" Shaw says.

"So this is analogous to a nuclear standoff?" Raj asks.

"Quite the opposite. Governments don't use nuclear weapons, because the moment they press the button, their opponent will do the same. The threat of retaliation is too great a deterrent. But there *is* no threat of retaliation or assured mutual destruction with the chair. The first government, or corporation, or individual, to successfully and strategically use it—whether by changing the outcome of a war or assassinating a long-dead dictator or whatever—wins."

Helena says, "You're saying it's in everyone's best interest to use the chair."

"Exactly. And as soon as possible. Whoever rewrites history in their own interest first, wins. It's too big a gamble to let someone else get there first."

Helena glances at the television again.

Now the Transamerica Pyramid in San Francisco's financial district is burning.

"Could be a foreign government behind these attacks," Helena says.

"Nope," Albert says, studying his phone. "An anonymous group just claimed responsibility on Twitter."

"What do they want?"

"No idea. Often, the mere creation of mayhem and terror is itself the endgame."

Now a woman is onscreen at the news-anchor desk, looking shaken as she speaks to the camera.

"Turn it up, Albert," Shaw says.

"Amidst conflicting reports of terrorist attacks in New York and San Francisco, a report from The Guardian's Glenn Greenwald has just been published, alleging that the US government has been in possession of a new technology called a memory chair for at least six months, which it pirated from a private corporation. Mr. Greenwald contends the memory

chair allows for the consciousness of its occupant to travel into the past, and according to his confidential sources, this chair is the actual cause of False Memory Syndrome, the mysterious—"

Albert mutes the television.

"We have to do something right now," he says. "Any moment, reality could shift us into a completely different world, or out of existence altogether."

Shaw has been pacing, but now he slumps down in his chair and looks at Helena. "I should've listened to you."

"Now isn't the time for—"

"I thought we could use it for good. I was ready to dedicate the rest of my—"

"It doesn't matter. If you'd done what I said and destroyed the chair, we'd be helpless right now."

Shaw glances at his phone. "My superiors are on their way."

"How long do we have?" Helena asks.

"They're on a jet up from DC, so about thirty minutes. They'll take over everything."

"We'll never be allowed back in here," Albert says.

"Let's send Timoney back," Shaw says.

"To when?" Albert asks.

"To before Slade's lab was hacked. Now that we know the location of his building, we can raid it earlier. There will be no cyber theft, and we'll be the sole custodians of the chair."

"Until we arrive back at this moment," Albert says. "And then the world will remember all the mayhem that happened this morning."

Helena says, "And the people who currently have the chair will just rebuild it from a false memory. Like Slade did. It'll be harder without blueprints, but not impossible. What we need is more time."

Helena rises and heads over to the terminal, where she takes down a skullcap and climbs into the chair.

"What are you doing?" Shaw asks.

"What does it look like? Raj? Come give me a hand? I need to map a memory."

Raj, Shaw, and Albert exchange glances across the table.

"What are you doing, Helena?" Shaw asks again.

"Getting us out of this jam."

"How?"

"Will you just fucking trust me, John?" she shouts. "We are out of time. I have stood by, offered counsel, played by *your* rules. Now it's your turn to play by mine."

Shaw sighs, deflated. She knows the pain of letting go of the promise of the chair. It isn't just the disappointment of all the unrealized scientific and humanitarian uses to which it might be put under ideal conditions. It's the realization that, as a deeply flawed species, we will never be ready to wield such power.

"OK," he says finally. "Raj, fire up the chair."

It is the first real taste of freedom the girl has ever known.

In the early evening, she walks out of the two-story farmhouse and climbs into the blue-and-white '78 Chevy Silverado that is her family's only vehicle.

She never expected her parents to give her one when she turned sixteen two days ago. Her plan is to work next summer lifeguarding and babysitting, and hopefully earn enough money to buy her own car.

Her parents are standing on the ever-so-slightly sagging front porch, watching proudly as she slides the key into the ignition.

Her mother takes a Polaroid.

As the engine roars to life, what strikes her most is the emptiness in the truck.

No Dad sitting in the passenger seat.

No Mom between them.

It's just her.

She can listen to any music she wants, as loud as she wants. She can go anywhere she wants, drive as fast as she wants.

Of course, she won't.

On her maiden voyage, her plan is to venture into the dangerous and distant wilds of the convenience store, a mile and a half down the road.

Buzzing with energy, she shifts the truck into drive and accelerates slowly down the long driveway, hanging her left arm out the window to wave at her parents.

The country road that runs in front of her home is empty.

She pulls out into the road and turns on the radio. The new song, "Faith," by George Michael is playing on the college radio station out of Boulder, and she sings at the top of her voice as the open fields race past, the future feeling closer than ever. Like it might have actually arrived.

The lights of the gas station glow in the distance, and as she takes her foot off the brake pedal, she registers a piercing pain behind her eyes.

Her vision blurs, her head pounds, and she just avoids crashing the truck into the pumps.

In a parking space beside the store, she kills the engine and pushes her thumbs into her temples against the searing pain, but it keeps building and building—so intense she's afraid she's going to be sick.

And then the strangest thing happens.

Her right arm moves toward the steering column and grasps the keys. She says, "What the hell?"

Because she didn't move her arm.

Next, she watches as her wrist turns the key and restarts the engine, and now her hand is moving over to the gear shift and sliding the lever into reverse.

Against her own will, she looks over her shoulder, out the rear window, backing the truck through the parking lot, and then shifting into drive.

She keeps thinking, I'm not driving, I'm not doing any of this, *as the truck speeds down the highway, back toward home.*

A darkness is creeping in at the edges of her vision, the Front Range and the lights of Boulder dimming away and getting smaller, as if she's falling slowly into a deep well. She wants to scream, to stop this from happening, but she's just a passenger in her own body now, unable to speak or smell or feel a thing.

The sound of the radio is little more than a dying whisper, and all at once, the pinprick of light that was her awareness of the world winks out.

HELENA

Helena turns off the country road into the driveway of the two-story farmhouse where she grew up, feeling more at home with each passing moment in this younger version of herself.

The farmhouse looks smaller, so much more insignificant than how she remembered it in her mind's eye, and undeniably fragile standing against the blue wall of mountains that sweep up from the plains, ten miles away.

She parks and turns off the engine and looks in the rearview mirror at her sixteen-year-old face.

No lines.

Many freckles.

Eyes clear and green and bright.

Still a child.

The door creaks as she shoulders it open and steps down into the grass. The sweet, dank richness of a nearby dairy farm is on the breeze, and it is unquestionably the smell she most associates with home.

She feels so light on her feet walking up the weathered steps of the porch.

The low din of the television is the first thing she hears as she pulls the front door open and steps inside. Down the hallway, which runs past the stairs, she hears movement in the kitchen—stirring, mixing, pots clanging, water running. The whole house smells of a chicken roasting in the oven.

Helena peers into the living room.

Her father is sitting in his recliner with his feet up, doing what he did every weekday evening of her youth—watching *World News Tonight*.

Peter Jennings is reporting that Elie Wiesel has won the Nobel Peace Prize.

"How was your drive?" her father asks.

She realizes that children are always too young and self-absorbed to really see their parents in the prime of their lives. But she sees her father in this moment like she never has before.

He's so young and handsome.

Not even forty.

She can't take her eyes off him.

"It was a lot of fun." Her voice sounds odd to her—high and delicate.

He looks back at the television set and misses seeing her wipe tears from her eyes.

"I don't need the truck tomorrow, so check with Mom, and if she doesn't either, you can take it to school."

This reality is feeling sturdier by the second.

She approaches the recliner, leans down, and wraps her arms around his neck.

"What's this for?" he asks.

The scent of Old Spice and the faint sandpaper scratchiness of his beard just beginning to come in nearly breaks her.

"For being my dad," she whispers.

She walks through the dining room and into the kitchen, finds her mother leaning back against the counter, smoking a cigarette and reading a paperback romance.

Last time Helena saw her she was in an adult care center near

Boulder, twenty-four years from now, her body frail, her mind destroyed.

All of that will still happen, but in this moment, she's wearing a pair of blue jeans and a button-down blouse. She has an '80s perm and bangs, and she is in the absolute peak of her life.

Helena crosses the small kitchen and pulls her mother into a hard embrace.

She's crying again, and she can't stop.

"What's wrong, Helena?"

"Nothing."

"Did something happen on your drive?"

Helena shakes her head. "I'm just emotional."

"About what?"

"I don't even know."

She feels her mother's hands running through her hair and smells the perfume she always wore—Estée Lauder's White Linen— against the bite of cigarette smoke.

"Getting older can be scary," her mom says.

It feels impossible that she is here. Moments ago, she was suffocating in a deprivation tank, fifteen hundred miles away and thirty-three years in the future.

"Do you need help with dinner?" Helena asks, finally pulling away.

"No, the chicken still has a little ways to go. You're sure you're OK?"

"Yeah."

"I'll call up when it's ready."

Helena heads through the kitchen and down the hall to the foot of the stairs. They're steeper than she remembers, and much creakier.

Her room is a wreck.

Like it always was.

Like all of her future apartments and offices will be.

She sees articles of clothing she had forgotten about.

A one-armed teddy bear she will lose in college.

A Walkman, which she opens to see the clear cassette of INXS's *Listen Like Thieves*.

She sits down at the small desk and stares through the charmingly distorted glass of the old windowpane. The view is of the lights of Denver, twenty miles away, and the purple plains to the east, the big, wild world looming unseen beyond. She would often sit here, daydreaming of what her life might become.

She could never have fathomed.

A science textbook lies open beside a take-home test on cellular biology that she will have to finish tonight.

In the middle drawer, she finds a black-and-white composition book with "Helena" written on the front.

This, she remembers.

She opens the book to page after page of her cursive, teenage scrawl.

While she never lost her memories of previous timelines after prior uses of the chair, she harbors a fear that it could happen now. These are uncharted waters—she's never traveled back so far, or into herself at so young an age. There's a chance she could forget what she came from, why she's here.

She takes a pen and turns to a blank page in the diary, writes down the date, and begins a note to herself to explain everything that has happened in her previous lives:

Dear Helena—On April 16, 2019, the world will remember a memory chair you created. You have 33 years to find some way to stop this from happening. You are the only one who can stop this from happening . . .

BOOK FIVE

When a person dies, he only appears to die. He is still very much alive in the past . . . All moments, past, present and future, always have existed, always will exist. It is just an illusion we have here on Earth that one moment follows another one, like beads on a string, and that once a moment is gone it is gone forever.

–KURT VONNEGUT, *SLAUGHTERHOUSE-FIVE*

BARRY

April 16, 2019

Barry is sitting in a chair in the shade, looking out across a forest of saguaro at a desert catching morning light.

The sharp pain behind his eyes is mercifully retreating.

He was lying on the seventeenth floor of a building in Manhattan, bullets whizzing past and riddling his body and the blood rushing out of him as he pictured his daughter's face.

Then a bullet struck his head and now he's here.

"Barry." He turns to look at the woman sitting beside him—short red hair, green eyes, Celtic paleness. Helena. "You're bleeding."

She hands him a napkin, which he holds to his nose to catch the blood.

"Talk to me, honey, she says. "This is new territory. Thirty-three years' worth of dead memories coming at you. What's going through your mind right now?"

"I don't know. I was . . . it feels like I was just in that hotel."

"Marcus Slade's?"

"Yeah, I was shot. I was dying. I still feel the bullets hitting me. I was yelling at you to run. Then I was suddenly here. Like no time had passed at all. But my memories of that hotel feel dead now. Black and gray."

"Do you feel more like the Barry from that timeline or this one?"

"That one. I have no idea where I am. The only familiar thing to me is you."

"You'll have the memories of this timeline soon."

"A lot of them?"

"A lifetime of them. I'm not sure what to expect for you. It may be jarring."

He looks at the range of brown mountains. The desert is flowering. Birds are singing. There is no wind, and the chill of the night lingers in the air.

"I've never seen this place before."

"This is our home, Barry."

He takes a moment to let that hit him.

"What's today?"

"April 16, 2019. In the timeline where you died, I used a DARPA deprivation tank to go back thirty-three years to 1986. And then I lived my life all over again, right up to this moment, trying to find a way to stop today from happening."

"What happens today?"

"After you died in Slade's hotel, knowledge of the chair leaked to the public, and the world went insane. Today is the day that the world will remember all of it. Until now, you and I are the only ones who knew."

"I feel . . . strange," he says.

He lifts a glass of ice water from the table and drinks it down.

His hands begin to shake.

Helena notices, says, "If it gets bad, I have this." She lifts a capped syringe off the table.

"What is it?"

"A sedative. Only if you need it."

It starts like a summer storm.

Just a super-cooled drop of rain here and there.

The rumble of distant thunder.

Dry lightning sparking across the horizon.

The initial memory of this timeline finds him.

First time he ever saw Helena she climbed onto the barstool beside him in a dive bar in Portland, Oregon, and said, "You look like you want to buy me a drink." It was late, he was drunk, and she was like no one he had met—early twenties but an old soul with the most brilliant mind he'd ever encountered. The instant familiarity of being in her presence felt, not just like he'd known her all his life but as if he were waking up for the first time. They bullshitted until last call, and then she took him back to the motel where she was staying and fucked him like it was the last day on Earth.

Another one—

They had been together several months, and he was already in love with her when she told him she could tell the future.

He said, "Bullshit."

She said, "I'll prove it one day."

She didn't make a big deal out of it. Said it in passing, almost like a joke, and he forgot all about her claim until December of 1990. They were watching the news one night, and she told him that next month the US would drive Iraqi forces out of Kuwait in a mission called Operation Desert Storm.

There were other instances.

Walking into a theater to see The Silence of the Lambs, *she told him the film would sweep the Oscars this time next year.*

That spring, she sat him down in the small apartment they were living in, gave him a handheld tape recorder, and sang the chorus to Nirvana's "Smells Like Teen Spirit" two months before the song released. Then she recorded herself telling him that the governor of Arkansas would announce his candidacy for president of the United States by year's end, and that he would win next year, defeating the incumbent and a strong third-party challenger.

They had been together almost two years when he demanded she tell him how she could possibly know these things. It wasn't the first time he'd asked. They were sitting at a bar in Seattle, watching the 1992 general election returns come in. And because of how she had gone about it—proving her bona fides before ever asking Barry to believe an insane story about a memory chair and a future they had already lived—he believed her, even when she told him he wouldn't remember any of his past lives for another twenty-seven years, and that technology sufficient for her to build the chair wouldn't exist for another fifteen.

"Are you OK?" Helena asks.

His focus is back in the moment, sitting on their concrete patio, watching a bee helicoptering around the remains of breakfast.

"It's the weirdest feeling," he says.

"Can you try to describe it?"

"It's like . . . two separate people, two distinct consciousnesses, with vastly different histories and experiences, are merging inside of me."

"Is one more dominant than the other?"

"No. At first I felt like the me who was shot in the hotel, but now I'm feeling equally at home in this reality."

Remembering a lifetime in the span of sixty seconds is a hell of a thing.

He faces a tsunami of memories, but it's the quiet moments that hit with the most force—

A snowy Christmas with Helena and her parents at their farmhouse in Boulder, Dorothy forgetting to put the turkey in the oven and everyone but Helena laughing it off, because she knew it was the beginning of her mother's mental deterioration.

Their wedding in Aruba.

A trip, just the two of them, to Antarctica in the summer of 2001 to witness the migration of emperor penguins, which they would both come to see as the best moment of their life together—a respite from the ever-present race to fix the looming future.

Several bitter fights about having children and Helena's insistence that they not bring a child into a world that would likely destroy itself in two decades.

The funerals of his mother, her mother, and most recently, her father.

The time she asked Barry if he wanted to know anything about his old life, and Barry saying that he didn't want to know any reality but this one.

The first time she demonstrated the power of the chair.

Now the full arc of their time together is coming into focus.

They spent their lives constructing the memory chair in secret and

trying to find a way to prevent the world from remembering how to build
it. Although the chair had been used on countless occasions on prior time-
lines, the most "recent" use of the chair by Helena (in the DARPA lab)
overrode all of the other false memory anniversary points. Which meant
no one, not even Slade, would have knowledge of those prior timelines.

Until April 16, 2019.

Then, and only then, would the false memories of all that had hap-
pened come crashing down on everyone.

With a fortune amassed by 2001, they had an operational chair by
2007.

Once the chair was built, they spent a decade running experiments
with it and imaging each other's brains, studying neural activity at the
moment a reality shift occurred and dead memories flooded in, searching
for the accompanying neuron cascade of new information.

Their hope was to find a way to prevent dead memories from older
timelines from flashing in without harming the brain. But all they ac-
complished was the recording of neural activity associated with dead
memories. They made no progress toward finding a method of shielding
the brain from those memories.

Barry looks over at his wife of twenty-four years, a completely
different man from who he was just moments ago.

"We failed," he says.

"Yeah."

The other half of his duality, the one that lived every moment of
this timeline, has just experienced the false memories of Meghan
and Julia. His life as a detective in New York City. The death of his
daughter, his divorce and descent into depression and regret. Meeting Slade and going back eleven years to save Meghan. Losing her
a second time. Helena coming into his life. Their connection. His
death in Slade's hotel.

"You're crying," Helena says.

"It's a lot."

She reaches over, takes his hand in hers.

He says, "I finally remember it."

"What?"

"Those handful of months in New York with you after I raided Slade's hotel with Gwen the first time. I remember the end of that timeline, leaning down and kissing you as you floated in the deprivation tank, about to die. I was in love with you."

"You were?"

"Madly."

They're quiet for a moment, looking out across the Sonoran desert, a landscape they have come to love together—so different from the lush, Pacific Northwest woods of his youth and the evergreen forests of Helena's.

This has been a good place for them.

"We should look at the news," Helena says.

"Let's wait," Barry says.

"What good will waiting do?"

"Let us live a little while longer with the hope that no one else remembered?"

"You know that's not going to happen."

"You always were the realist."

Helena smiles, tears glistening in the corners of her eyes.

Barry rises from the chair and turns to face the back of their sprawling desert home. Built of rammed earth and expansive panes of glass, it blends seamlessly into its environment.

He heads inside through the kitchen, past the dining-room table, to the sitting area by the television. Lifting the remote, he hesitates as Helena's barefooted steps move toward him across the cool tile.

She takes the remote out of his hand and presses the Power button.

The first thing he reads is a banner across the bottom of the screen.

MASS SUICIDES REPORTED ACROSS THE WORLD.

Helena lets out a pained sigh.

Cell-phone footage from a city street shows bodies bouncing off the pavement like some kind of horrific hailstorm.

Like Barry, the world just remembered the previous timeline when the chair's existence became public knowledge. The attacks on New York City. WikiLeaks. Widespread usage of the chair across the globe.

Barry says, "Maybe it'll all be OK. Maybe Slade was right. Maybe humanity will adapt and evolve to accept this."

Helena turns the channel.

A frazzled-looking anchor is trying to maintain some vestige of professionalism. *"Russia and China have just released a joint statement at the UN, accusing the United States of reality theft in an effort to prevent other nations from using the memory chair. They have vowed to rebuild the technology immediately and warned that any further use of the chair will be seen as an act of war. The US has not yet responded—"*

She turns the channel again.

Another shell-shocked anchor: *"In addition to the mass suicides, hospitals in all major cities are reporting an influx of patients suffering catatonia—a state of unresponsive stupor brought about by—"*

The co-anchor cuts him off: *"I'm sorry to interrupt you, David. The FAA is reporting . . . Jesus . . . Forty commercial jet crashes in United States airspace in the last fifteen—"*

Helena turns off the television, drops the remote on the sofa, and walks into the foyer. Barry follows her to the front door, which she pulls open.

The view from the porch overlooks the gravel driveway and the gentle decline of the desert as it slopes for twelve miles toward the city of Tucson, shimmering like a mirage in the distance.

"It's still so quiet," she says. "Hard to believe everything is falling apart out there."

The last thirty-three years of Barry's existence is putting down roots in his mind, feeling more real with every breath. He isn't the man he was in Slade's hotel. He isn't the man who spent the last twenty-four years with Helena, trying to save the world from experiencing this day. He's, somehow, both of them.

He says, "There was a part of me that didn't believe it would happen."

"Yeah."

Helena turns and embraces him with a sudden force that drives him back several steps toward the door.

"I'm sorry," he whispers.

"I don't want to do this."

"What?"

"This! My life! Go back to 1986, find you, convince you I'm not crazy. Amass a fortune. Build the chair. Try to prevent dead memories. Fail. Watch the world remember. Rinse, repeat. Are the rest of my many lives nothing more than trying to figure a way out of this inescapable loop?"

He looks down at her, framing her jaw in his hands. "I have an idea," he says. "Let's forget all of this."

"What are you talking about?"

"Let's just be together today. Let's just live."

"We can't. This is all happening. This is what is real."

"I know, but we can wait until tonight for you to go back to '86. We know what comes next. What has to happen. We don't need to obsess over it. Let's just be present for the time we have left together."

They set off on their favorite hike through the desert to force themselves to stay away from the news.

The trail is one they've blazed over the years, right out the back of their house and up into the saguaro-covered hills.

Sweat is pouring out of Barry, but the exertion is exactly what he needed—something to burn through the surreal shock of the morning.

At midday, they top out on the rock outcropping several hundred feet above their house, which is practically invisible from this height, camouflaged against the floor of the desert.

Barry opens his backpack and takes out a liter of water. They pass it back and forth and try to catch their breath.

There is no movement anywhere.

The desert as silent as a cathedral.

Barry is thinking there's something about the rock and the ancient cacti that suggests the frozen, timeless permanence of a dead memory.

He looks at Helena.

She pours a little water over her face and hands him the bottle.

"I could do this on my own next time," she says.

"That's what you're sitting here thinking during our last hours together?"

She touches the side of his face. "For decades, you've shared the burden of the chair with me. You've known this day was coming, that it would probably mean the end of everything, and I'd have to go back to 1986 and try it all over again."

"Helena—"

"You wanted kids, I didn't. You sacrificed your interests to help me."

"Those were all my choices."

"Next time around, you could have a different life, without the knowledge of what's coming. That's all I'm saying. You could have the things you—"

"You want to do this without me?"

"No. I want to breathe the same air as you every minute of every day of my life, no matter how many timelines I live. That's why I found you in the first place. But this chair is my cross to bear."

"You don't need me."

"That is not what I'm saying. Of course I need you. I need your love, I need your mind, your support, all of it. But I need you to know—"

"Helena, don't."

"Let me say this! It's enough that I have to see the chair destroying the entire world. People throwing themselves off of buildings because of something I made. It's another to see it ruin the life of the man I love."

"Life with you isn't a life ruined."

"But you know this is all it can ever be. Stuck in this thirty-three-year loop, trying to find a way to stop this day from coming. All I'm saying is that if you want to just live your fucking life without the pressure of trying to keep the world intact, that's OK."

"Look at me."

The water she dribbled on her face has beaded up on the layer of sunscreen. He stares into her emerald eyes, clear and bright in the sun.

"I don't know how you do this, H. I don't know how you carry this weight. But as long as it's on your shoulders, it's also on mine. We will find a way to solve this. If not in the next life, then the one after. And if not in that one, then the one—"

She kisses him on top of their mountain.

They're a hundred yards from the house when the sound of a helicopter builds behind them, and then streaks across the early-afternoon sky.

Barry stops and watches it cruise toward Tucson.

"That's a Black Hawk," he says. "Wonder what's going on in town."

The chopper banks hard to the left and slows its groundspeed, now drifting back in their direction as it lowers from five hundred feet toward the ground.

Helena says, "They're here for us."

They take off sprinting toward the house, the Black Hawk now hovering seventy-five feet above the desert floor, the rotors roaring and swirling up a cloud of dust and sand, Barry close enough to see three pairs of legs hanging off each side of the open cabin above the skids.

The tip of Helena's boot strikes a half-buried rock and she goes down hard on the trail. Barry grabs her under both arms and heaves her back onto her feet, blood now running down her right knee.

"Come on!" he screams.

They pass the saltwater pool and reach the patio where they had breakfast.

Thick ropes drop out of the Black Hawk like tentacles, the soldiers already descending them.

Barry slides open the rear door, and they rush through the kitchen and turn down the hallway. Through the windows that look out into the desert on the other side of the house, he sees a cluster of heavily armed and armored soldiers in desert camo jogging up through the landscaping in a tactical formation toward their front door.

Helena is ahead of him, limping from her fall.

They race past the home office and guestroom, and through another window, Barry glimpses the Black Hawk setting down on his driveway behind their cars.

They stop where the hall ends, and Helena presses against one of the rocks in the river-stone wall, which opens to reveal its secret utility as a hidden door.

She and Barry slip inside as the sound of a small explosion shudders through the house.

Then it's just the two of them, gasping for breath in the pitch-black.

"They're in the house," Barry whispers.

"Can you hit the light?"

He feels around until his fingers graze the switch.

"You sure they won't see it?"

"No, but I can't do this in the dark."

Barry flicks the switch. A single, unshaded bulb burns down

from overhead. They're standing in a kind of anteroom, barely larger than a kitchen pantry. The inner door is the basic size and shape of a standard door, except that it weighs six hundred pounds, is built of steel plates layered to a thickness of two inches, and when activated, shoots ten massive bolts into a jamb.

Helena is typing in the code on the keypad, and the footsteps of at least half a dozen soldiers are moving toward them down the hallway, Barry picturing them closing in on the river-stone terminus, the sound of whispered voices and boot-falls and jostling gear getting closer and closer.

A shouted voice from the far side of the house—probably in their master suite—echoes down the long hall.

"Clear on the east side!"

"Impossible. We saw them enter the house. Everyone check closets? Under beds?"

On the illuminated display, Barry watches as Helena keys in the last number.

The high-pitched whirring of internal gears becomes audible inside the anteroom, and possibly beyond, Barry and Helena holding each other's stare as the ten bolts retract one by one like muffled gunshots.

A woman's voice comes through the other side of the hidden door: "You hear that?"

"It came from inside this wall."

He hears what sounds like hands running across the faux stones. Helena drags open the heavy door. Barry follows her across the threshold into another place of darkness, just as the hidden door cracks open.

A soldier shouts, "There's something back here!"

Helena pulls the vault door closed, types the locking code into the keypad on this side, and the ten dead bolts shoot home again.

When she hits the lights, they reveal a claustrophobic metal staircase, spiraling thirty feet down into the earth.

The temperature drops as they descend.

The soldiers pound on the vault door.

"They'll find a way through," Barry says.

"Then let's hurry."

Three stories underground, the staircase ends at a doorway that leads into a two-thousand-square-foot lab, where they've spent most of their waking hours for the last fifteen years. It is, for all intents and purposes, a bunker, with a dedicated air recirculation and filtration system, stand-alone solar-powered electrical system, a galley and sleeping quarters, and food and water rations for one year.

"How's your leg?" Barry asks.

"It doesn't matter."

She limps past the Eames lounge chair, which they retrofitted into a memory chair, and then a region of the lab they used for brain imaging, and their study of dead-memory processing.

Helena sits down at the terminal and uploads the memory-reactivation program they always keep idling in case of emergencies. Since she already mapped the memory of her first solo drive when she turned sixteen, she can go straight to the deprivation chamber.

"I thought we'd have more time today," Barry says.

"Me too."

A detonation above them shakes the floor and rattles the walls. Plaster dust rains down from the ceiling like fine snow.

Barry rushes back through the lab to the foot of the stairwell. The air is full of dust, but he doesn't hear incoming voices or footsteps yet.

As he moves back into the lab, he sees Helena pulling off her shirt and sports bra, and then sliding her shorts down her legs.

She stands naked before him, strapping on the skullcap, her right leg bleeding, tears streaming down her face.

He goes to his wife and embraces her as another blast shakes the foundation of their subterranean lab.

"Don't let them in here," she says.

She wipes her eyes and kisses him, and then Barry helps her into the tank.

When she's floating in the water, he looks down at her, says, "I'll be in that Portland bar in October of 1990, waiting for you."

"You won't even recognize me."

"My soul knows your soul. In any time."

He closes the hatch and moves over to the terminal. It's gone quiet for a moment, no sound but the humming of the servers.

He initiates the reactivation program and leans back in the chair, trying to wrap his mind around what comes next.

An earth-shaking blast cracks the walls and the concrete floor beneath his feet, Barry wondering if the Black Hawk dropped a bomb on their house.

Smoke is pouring through the vents, and the light panels are flickering, but the reactivation program continues to run.

He goes to the stairwell again—the only way in or out of the lab.

Now he hears voices above and sees beams of light swinging through the dust-choked smoke.

They've breached the vault door, their boots clanging down the metal steps.

Barry slams the door to the lab and turns the dead bolt. It's just a metal fire door—they could probably kick it in.

He returns to the terminal and studies the readout of Helena's vitals. She's been flatlined now for several minutes.

Something hits the other side of the door.

Again.

And again.

A machine gun fires and another boot or shoulder or battering ram slams into the metal.

Miraculously, it holds.

"Come on," Barry says.

He hears voices yelling in the stairwell and then a deafening blast that sets his ears ringing—a grenade or a charge.

A wall of smoke appears where the door had been, and a soldier steps through over the flattened door, pointing an automatic rifle at Barry.

Barry raises his arms over his head and rises slowly from the chair as more soldiers pour into the lab.

The screen at the terminal, which shows the status of the stimulators, flashes an alert—DMT RELEASE DETECTED.

Come on. Come on.

Inside the tank, Helena is dying, her brain dumping the last of the chemical that will fling her back three decades into a memory.

The lead soldier is coming toward Barry, screaming something that he can't understand over the ringing in his—

Blood is dripping from his nose, melting little burgundy holes in the snow.

He looks around at the dark evergreens, their branches sagging under the weight of a recent storm.

He looks at Helena, her hair different from the last time he saw her, in their basement lab in the Sonoran desert. It's now equal parts white and red. She's wearing it long and pulled back into a ponytail, and her face looks somehow harder.

"What day is it?" he asks.

"April 16, 2019. Second timeline anniversary since I died in the tank at DARPA."

They're standing in snowshoes in a glade on a mountainside, overlooking a city on a plain, ten miles distant.

"That's Denver," Helena says. "We built our lab here so I could be close to my parents." She looks at him. "Nothing yet?"

"It feels like I was in our home in Tucson literally seconds ago."

"Sorry to say you just shifted from one shitty April 16, 2019, to another."

"What are you talking about?"

"We failed again."

Their first meeting at the Portland bar. For a second time. The claims of clairvoyance. He fell in love with her even faster, because she seemed to know him better than he knew himself.

The memory rush is more intense this time.

Almost painful.

He collapses in the snow as the past twenty-nine years with Helena hit his brain like a train of memories.

They spent the decade before technology was sufficient to build the chair studying space-time, the nature of matter, dimensionality, and quantum entanglement. They learned everything they could about the physics of time, but not enough. Not nearly enough.

Then they explored methods of traveling back into memory without using the tank, searching for a faster way. But absent the sensory deprivation, all they accomplished was killing themselves again and again.

Next come the memories that break him.

Losing his mother again.

Fights with Helena over not having kids (that must have been infuriating for her the second time around).

The sex, the love, the beautiful love.

Moments of exhilaration from knowing they were the only two people in the world fighting to save it.

Moments of horror from the same realization, and the knowledge they were failing.

And then he's fully merged. The Barry with memories of all timelines.

He looks at Helena. She sits beside him in the snow, staring a vertical mile down toward the city with the same thousand-yard stare she's had for the last year, knowing this day was coming unless a miracle occurred.

Holding this new timeline up against the last, the change in

Helena is disconcerting, this version of her a slight degradation from the previous iteration, most evident in the quieter moments.

Less patience.

More distance.

More anger.

More depression.

Harder.

What must that have been like for her, reliving a relationship from the beginning, with all the knowledge of its weaknesses and strengths, before it even started? How was she even able to connect with him? With his naïveté? It must have been like speaking to a child sometimes, because, though he's technically still the same person, the perspective gap between who Barry was five minutes ago and who he is now with all of his memories is a yawning chasm. Only now is he truly himself.

He says, "I'm sorry, H."

"For what?"

"It must have been maddening, living our relationship again."

She almost smiles. "I did want to murder you on a semi-regular basis."

"Were you bored?"

"Never."

The air is heavy with the question.

"You don't have to do it again," he says.

"What do you mean?"

"With me."

She looks at him, hurt. "Are you saying *you* don't want to?"

"That is not what I'm saying. Not at all."

"It's OK if you are."

"I'm not."

"Do you want to be with me again?" she asks.

"I love you."

"That is not an answer."

"I want to spend every life with you. I told you this last week," he says.

"It's different now that you have full memories of every time-line. Isn't it?"

"I'm with you, Helena. We only scratched the surface on the physics of time. There's so much more for us to learn."

He feels his phone vibrate in the pocket of his parka. This last hike together to their favorite spot was worth it, but they should leave now. Return to civilization. Watch the world remember and then get the fuck out before the soldiers come for them, even though he's doubtful he and Helena would be found so soon. They lived under new identities this time around.

Helena takes out her phone and unlocks the home screen.

She says, "Oh God."

Struggling onto her feet, she takes off running in her snow-shoes, moving awkwardly back down the trail.

"What are you doing?" he asks.

"We have to go!"

"What's wrong?" he shouts after her.

She shouts back, "I will leave you!"

He clambers up and takes off after her.

It's a quarter mile downhill through the fir trees. His phone keeps buzzing—someone lighting him up with texts—and despite the massive footwear, he reaches the trailhead in less than five minutes, crashing into the hood of their Jeep, breathless and sweating through his winter gear.

Helena is already climbing in behind the wheel, and he scrambles into the passenger seat, still wearing the snowshoes as she cranks the engine and tears out of the otherwise empty parking lot, the tires spinning on the icy pavement.

"What the hell, Helena?"

"Look at your phone."

He digs it out of his jacket.

Reads the first lines of an emergency text on the home screen:

Emergency Alert
BALLISTIC MISSILE THREAT INBOUND TO MULTI-
PLE US TARGETS. SEEK IMMEDIATE SHELTER. THIS
IS NOT A DRILL.
Slide for more

"We should've seen this coming," she says. "Remember their UN statement on the last timeline?"

"'Any further use of the chair will be seen as an act of war.'"

Helena drives too fast through a sharp curve, the tires sliding on the snowpack, the ABS braking kicking in.

"If you wrap the Jeep around a tree, we'll never—"

"I grew up here, I know how to fucking drive in snow."

She guns it on a straightaway, densely packed fir trees rushing past on either side as they scream down the mountain.

"They have to attack us," Helena says.

"Why do you say that?"

"For all the reasons we talked about when I was at DARPA. Everyone's worst-case scenario is that one country sends someone back half a century and unwrites the existence of billions. They have to hit us with everything they've got and hope to destroy the chair before we use it."

Helena turns on the radio and pulls out of the entrance to the state park. They've already descended a couple thousand feet, and the only snow on the ground consists of melting patches in the shade.

"—interrupt this program. This is a national emergency. Important instructions will follow." The terrifying sound header of the Emergency Alert System blares inside the Jeep. "The following message is transmitted at the request of the US government. This is not a test. The North American Aerospace Defense Command has detected the launch of Russian and Chinese intercontinental ballistic missiles. These missiles are expected to strike numerous targets on the North American continent within the next ten to fifteen minutes. This is an attack warning.

I repeat. This is an attack warning. An attack warning means that an actual attack against this country has been detected and that protective action should be taken. All citizens should take cover immediately. Move to a basement or interior room on the lowest floor of a sturdy building. Stay away from windows. If outdoors or in a vehicle, head for shelter. If none is available, lie flat in a ditch or other depression."

Helena accelerates to a hundred miles per hour on the country road, the foothills falling away behind them in the side and rearview mirrors.

Barry leans down and starts to unbuckle the straps that attach the snowshoes to his snow-encrusted hiking boots.

When they merge onto the interstate, Helena pushes the engine to its breaking point.

After a mile, they enter the outskirts of the city.

More and more cars are pulled over onto the shoulder, doors left open as drivers abandoned their vehicles in search of shelter.

Helena hits the brakes as the road becomes log-jammed across all lanes of traffic. Hordes of people are fleeing their cars, hopping the guardrail, and tumbling down an embankment that bottoms out at a stream running heavy and brown with snowmelt.

"Can you get through to the next exit?" Barry asks.

"I don't know."

Helena pushes on, dodging people and driving through a handful of open car doors, the front bumper of the Jeep ripping them off in order to pass. The exit ramp to their turnoff is impassable, so she maneuvers the Jeep up a steep, grassy hill and onto the shoulder, finally squeezing between a UPS truck and a convertible to reach the top of the overpass.

In contrast to the interstate, the avenue is practically empty, and she burns down the middle of it as another alert blares through the speakers.

Their lab is in Lakewood, a western suburb of Denver, in a redbrick building that used to be a firehouse.

They're just over a mile away now, and Barry stares out the window, thinking how odd it is to see so little movement anywhere.

No other cars driving on the road.

Hardly any people out.

By his estimation, it's been at least ten minutes since they heard the first emergency alert broadcast.

He looks over at Helena to say what he's already said before, that he wants to do this again with her no matter what, when through her window, he glimpses the brightest light he has ever seen—an incandescent flower blooming on the eastern horizon near the cluster of downtown skyscrapers, so intense it burns his corneas as it overtakes the world.

Helena's face becomes radiant, and everything in his field of vision, even the sky, is robbed of color, blanching into a brilliant, searing white.

He's blind for five seconds, and when he can see again, everything happens at once.

All the glass in the Jeep exploding—

The pine trees in a park straight ahead bending so far sideways their tips touch the ground—

Structural debris from a disintegrated strip mall streaming across the road, blown by a furious wind—

A man pushing a shopping cart on the sidewalk flung fifty feet through the air—

And then their Jeep is flipping, the scrape of metal against pavement deafening as the shockwave blows them across the road, sparks flying into Barry's face.

As the Jeep comes to rest against the curb, the noise of the blast arrives, and it is the loudest thing he has ever heard—world-ending loud, chest-crushing loud—and a single thought rips through his mind: the detonation sound wave reached them too quickly.

A matter of seconds.

They're far too close to ground zero to survive very long.

Everything becomes still.

His ears are ringing.

His clothing singed all over with fire-ringed holes that are still eating through fabric.

A receipt in one of the cup holders has combusted.

Smoke pours through the vents.

The Jeep is resting on the passenger side, and he's still buckled into the seat, at a sideways attitude to what's left of the world. He cranes his neck to look up at Helena, who's still strapped in behind the wheel, her head hanging motionless.

He calls her name, but he can't even hear his own voice in his head.

Nothing but the vibration of his larynx.

He unbuckles his seat belt and turns painfully to face his wife.

Her eyes are closed and her face is bright red, the left side of it covered in glass-shrapnel from the window.

He reaches over and unbuckles her seat belt, and as she falls out of the seat onto him, her eyes open and she takes a sudden, gasping breath.

Her lips move, trying to say something, but she stops when she realizes neither of them can hear a thing. She lifts a hand turned red from second-degree burns and points at the glassless windshield.

Barry nods, and they climb through, struggling finally onto their feet to stand in the middle of the road, surrounded by devastation only fathomed in nightmares.

The sky is gone.

Trees turned to skeletons and molten leaves drifting down from them like fire-rain.

Helena is already stumbling up the road. As Barry hurries after her, he notices his hands for the first time since the blast. They're the same color as Helena's face, and already forming blisters from the white-hot flash of thermal radiation.

Reaching up to touch his face and head, he comes away with a clump of hair.

Oh Christ.

Panic hits.

He comes alongside Helena, who's limp-jogging now over the pavement, which is covered in smoking debris.

It's evening-dark, the sun invisible.

Pain is encroaching.

In his face, his hands, his eyes.

His hearing returns.

The sound of his footsteps.

Car alarms.

Someone scream-crying in the distance.

The god-awful silence of a stunned city.

They turn onto the next street, Barry figuring they're still a half mile from the firehouse.

Helena stops suddenly, bends over, and vomits in the middle of the street.

He tries to put his hand on her back, but when his palm touches her jacket, he instinctively pulls it away in pain.

"I'm dying, Barry. You are too."

She straightens, wipes her mouth.

Helena's hair is falling out, and her breathing sounds ragged and painful.

Just like his.

"I think we can make it," he says.

"We have to. Why would they hit Denver?"

"If they unleashed their full arsenal, they're striking every major city in America, thousands of warheads, probably hoping they get lucky and take out the chair."

"Maybe they did."

They move on, closer to ground zero by the looks of the towering cloud of ash and fire, still roiling and pluming in the indeterminate distance.

They pass an overturned school bus, the yellow turned black, the glass blown out, voices crying from within.

Barry slows down and starts toward it, but Helena says, "The only way you can help them is for us to get home."

He knows she's right, but it takes everything in his power not to at least try to help, even with a word of comfort.

He says, "I wish we'd never lived to see a day like this."

They jog past a burning tree with a motorcycle and its driver blown into the branches, thirty feet up.

Then a woman staggering hairless and naked in the middle of the street with her skin coming off like the bark of a birch tree and her eyes abnormally large and white, as if they'd expanded to absorb the horror all around her. But the truth is, she's blind.

"Block it," Helena says, crying. "We're going to change this."

Barry tastes blood in his mouth, pain slowly encompassing his world.

It feels like his insides are melting.

Another blast, this one much farther away, shakes the ground beneath them.

"There," Helena says.

The firehouse lies straight ahead.

They're standing in the midst of their neighborhood, and he barely noticed.

Because of the pain.

Mostly because it doesn't look anything like their street.

Every house built of wood has been leveled, power lines toppled, trees blow-torched and stripped of every hint of green.

Vehicles have been strewn everywhere—some flipped onto their roofs, others on their sides, a few still burning.

It's raining ash and fallout that will give them acute radiation poisoning if they're still in this hellscape by nightfall.

The only movement anywhere is from blackened forms writhing on the ground.

In the street.

In the smoldering front yards of what once were homes.

Barry feels a surge of helpless nausea as he realizes these are people.

Their firehouse is still standing.

The windows are shattered-out, gaping-black eye sockets, and the redbrick has been turned the color of charcoal.

The pain in Barry's face and hands is exquisite as they climb the steps to the entrance and move inside over the front door, which lies cracked and flattened across the foyer.

Even through the pain, the shock of seeing their home of twenty-one years like this is devastating.

Weak light filters in through the windows, revealing a place of utter ruin.

Most of the furniture has simply exploded.

The kitchen reeks of natural gas, and in the far corner of the building, smoke trickles through the open doorway to their bedroom, where the flickering of flames is visible on the walls.

As they rush through the house, Barry loses his balance in the archway between the dining and living room. He clutches the side of the archway to stop himself from falling and cries out in pain, leaving behind a handprint of blood and skin where he palmed the wall.

The access to their secure lab is another vault door, this time in the walk-in storage closet of what used to be the home office. The door itself is wired to the rest of the house, so using the keypad entry is out. Helena opens the flashlight app on her phone and sets the five-digit combination manually in the semidarkness.

She reaches for the wheel, but Barry says, "Let me."

"It's fine."

"You still have to die in the tank."

"Fair enough."

He steps to the door and takes hold of the three-spoked handle, groaning with agony as he strains to crank the wheel. Nothing's moving but the layers of skin he's stripping away, and a horrifying thought occurs to him—what if the heat of the blast fused the innards of the door? A vision of their last day together—cooking slowly from thermal radiation in the burned-out husk of their home, unable to reach the chair, knowing that they failed. That when the next shift happened, if it ever did, they would either blink out of existence altogether or into a world of someone else's making.

The wheel budges, then finally gives way.

The locks retract and the door swings open, exposing a spiral stairwell leading down into a lab that's nearly identical to the one they built in the desert outside of Tucson. Only here, instead of digging into the earth, they lined the stone basement of the old firehouse with steel walls.

There's no light.

Barry leaves part of his hand on the wheel as he pulls it away and follows Helena, corkscrewing down the stairs in the meager light of her phone's sustained camera flash.

The lab is strangely silent.

No humming of the fans that cool the servers.

Or the heat pump that keeps the water in the deprivation tank at the steady temperature of human skin.

The phone light sweeps across the walls as they move toward the end of the server rack, where a power bank of lithium ion batteries is the only thing glowing in the lab.

Barry goes to a panel of switches on the wall that transfers power from the electrical grid to the batteries. He faces another moment of pure terror, because if the blast damaged the batteries or connectors to any of the equipment, this is all futile.

"Barry?" Helena says. "What are you waiting for?"

He flips the switches.

Overhead lights flicker on.

The servers begin to hum.

Helena is already easing down into the chair at the terminal, which has begun its boot-up sequence.

"The batteries will only give us thirty minutes of power," she says.

"We have generators and plenty of gas."

"Yeah, but it'll take ages to reroute the power."

He sheds his fire-burned parka and snow pants and takes the chair beside Helena, who's already typing on the keypad as quickly as her scorched fingertips will let her, blood running out of the corners of her mouth and eyes.

As she begins to strip out of her winter clothes, Barry goes to the cabinet and takes the only remaining skullcap that has a full charge. He powers it on and places it carefully on top of his wife's head, which is blistering over.

The second-degree burns on his face are entering the arena of excruciating. There's morphine in the medical cabinet, calling to him, but there's also no time.

"I'll finish positioning the skullcap," she says. "Just get the injection port."

He grabs a port and turns it on, making sure the Bluetooth connection with the terminal is online.

In sharp contrast to her nuclear-sunburned hands, Helena's forearms are creamy and smooth, protected from the initial flash by her parka and several layers of shirts and thermal underwear. It takes him several tries with his ruined fingers to thread the IV into her vein. He finally straps the port to her forearm and heads for the deprivation tank. The water is a degree and a half cooler than the ideal 98.6, but it will have to do.

He lifts the hatch and turns to face Helena, who's stumbling toward him like a broken angel.

He knows he looks no prettier.

"I wish I could do this next part for you," he says.

"It's only going to hurt a little while longer," she says, tears running down her face. "Besides, I deserve this."

"That isn't true."

"You don't have to walk this road with me again," she says.

"I'll walk it as many times as it takes."

"You're sure?"

"Completely."

She grips the side of the tank and swings her leg over.

When her hands touch the water, she cries out.

"What is it?" Barry asks.

"The salt. Oh my God . . ."

"I'll get the morphine."

"No, it might fuck up the memory reactivation. Just hurry please."

"OK. I'll see you soon."

He closes the hatch on his wife, floating in agony in the saltwater.

Rushing back to the terminal, he initiates the injection sequence. As the paralytic drug fires, he tries to sit down, but the pain is so all-encompassing he can't stay still.

He heads through the lab and up the spiral staircase, through the office and the fire-bombed remnants of his and Helena's home.

Back outside on the steps of the firehouse, it's as dark as night and raining flecks of fire from the sky.

Barry descends the steps and walks out into the middle of the street.

A burning newspaper blows across the pavement.

On the other side of the road, a blackened figure lies in the fetal position, curled against the curb in its final resting place.

There is the whisper of hot wind.

Distant screaming and groans.

And nothing else.

It seems impossible that less than an hour ago, he was sitting in a snowy glade at ten thousand feet, overlooking Denver on a perfect spring afternoon.

We have made it far too easy to destroy ourselves.

He can barely stand anymore.

His knees buckle; he collapses.

Sitting now in the middle of the street in front of the firehouse, watching the world burn and trying not to let the pain overwhelm him.

It's been several minutes since he left the lab.

Helena is dying in the tank.

He's dying out here.

He lies back on the pavement and stares up into the black sky at the fire raining down on him.

A bright rod of agony knifes through the back of his skull, and he registers a wave of relief, knowing that means the end is coming, that DMT is flooding Helena's brain as she tunnels back into the memory of her walking toward a white-and-blue Chevy as a sixteen-year-old girl with her entire life ahead of her.

They will do all of it again, hopefully better next time.

And the motes of fire gradually fall slower and slower, until they're suspended all around him in the air like a billion lightning bugs—

It's cold and damp.

He smells the salt of the sea.

Hears waves lapping at rocks and bird cries carrying over open water.

His vision swings into focus.

There's a ragged shoreline a hundred yards away, and mist hovers over the blue-gray water, obscuring the spruce trees in the distance, which stand along the shore like a line of haunted calligraphy.

The pain of his melting face is gone.

He's sitting in a sea kayak in a wetsuit, a paddle across his lap, wiping blood from his nose and wondering where he is.

Where Helena is.

Why there are no memories of this timeline yet.

He was lying in the middle of the street in front of their firehouse in Denver just seconds ago, watching in agony as the sky rained fire.

Now he's . . . wherever he is. His life feels like a dream, flitting from one reality to the next, memories becoming reality becoming nightmares. Everything real in the moment, but fleetingly so. Landscapes and emotions in a constant state of flux, and yet a twisted logic to it all—the way a dream makes sense only when you're inside it.

He dips an oar into the water and pulls the kayak forward.

A sheltered cove slides into view, the island sweeping up gently for several hundred feet through a forest of dark spruce, interspersed with the white brushstrokes of birch trees.

On the lower flanks of the hill, a house sits on an expanse of emerald grass, surrounded by smaller buildings—two guesthouses, a gazebo, and down by the shore, a boathouse and pier.

He paddles into the cove, picking up speed as he approaches land, running the kayak ashore on a bed of crushed rocks. As he hauls himself awkwardly out of the cockpit, a single memory drops—*sitting at that bar in Portland as Helena climbed onto the stool beside him for the third time in their odd, recursive existence.*

"You look like you want to buy me a drink."

How strange to hold three distinct memories of what is essentially the same moment in time.

He moves barefoot across the rocky shore and into the grass, bracing for the tidal wave of memories, but they're late today.

The house is built on a stone foundation, the wood turned driftwood gray by decades of salt and sun and wind and punishing winters.

A massive dog comes bounding toward him through the yard. It's a Scottish deerhound, the same color as the house's weathered siding, and it greets Barry with slobbering affection, coming up on its hind legs to meet him eye to eye and lick his face.

Barry climbs the steps to the veranda, which boasts a commanding view of the cove and the sea beyond.

Opening the sliding-glass door, he steps into a warm living room built around a freestanding stone hearth that rises up through the heart of the house.

The small fire burning on the grate perfumes the interior with the scent of woodsmoke.

"Helena?"

No answer.

The house stands silent.

He moves through a French country kitchen with exposed beams and bench seating around a large island topped with butcher block.

Then down a long, dark corridor, feeling like a trespasser in someone else's home. At the far end, he stops at the entrance to a cozily cluttered office. There's a woodstove, a window overlooking the forest, and an old table in the center of the room sagging under stacks of books. A blackboard stands nearby, covered in incomprehensible equations and diagrams of what appear to be intricately forking timelines.

The memories arrive in a blink.

One moment nothing.

The next, he knows exactly where he is, the full trajectory of his life since Helena found him, and exactly what the equations on the blackboard mean.

Because he wrote them.

They're extrapolations of the Schwarzschild solution, an equation that defines what the radius of an object must be, based upon its mass, in order to form a singularity. That singularity then forms an Einstein-Rosen wormhole that can, in theory, instantaneously connect far-flung regions of space, and even time.

Because his consciousnesses from the previous timelines are merging with his consciousness on this one, his perspective of their work during the last ten years is paradoxically and simultaneously brand-new and intimately familiar. He sees it, both with fresh eyes and a total loss of objectivity.

He spent much of this life studying black-hole physics. While Helena was right there with him in the beginning, these last five years, as April 16, 2019, drew closer with no breakthrough in range, she started to withdraw.

The knowledge that she would have to do this all over again simply broke her.

On the window glass overlooking the woods, the fundamental questions he wrote in black magic marker many years ago still taunt him, unanswered—

What is the Schwarzschild radius of a memory?

A wild notion . . . when we die, does the immense gravity of our collapsing memories create a micro black hole?

A wilder notion . . . does the memory-reactivation procedure—at the moment of death—then open a wormhole that connects our consciousness to an earlier version of ourselves?

He's going to lose all of this knowledge. Not that it was ever really more than a theory—an attempt to pull back the curtain and understand why Helena's chair did what it did. None of his knowledge means anything without scientific testing. Only in the last couple of years has it occurred to Barry that they should bring their equipment to the CERN laboratory in Geneva, Switzerland, and kill someone in the tank in the presence of the Large Hadron Collider particle detectors. If they could prove the appearance of the entrance to a micro wormhole at the moment someone died in the tank, and a wormhole exit at the moment their consciousness respawned in their body at an earlier point in time, they might begin to understand the true mechanics of memory return.

Helena hated the idea. She didn't believe the knowledge payoff was worth the risk of their technology getting out in the wild again, which would almost certainly happen if they shared their knowledge of the chair with the scientific community at the LHC. Besides, it would take years to convince the powers-that-be to give them access to a particle detector, and years on top of that, plus teams of scientists to write algorithms and software to pull the physics data out of the system. At the end of the day, it was going to be far more difficult and time consuming to study the particle physics of the chair than it was to actually build the thing.

But time is what they have.

"Barry."

He turns.

Helena stands in the doorway, and the shock of seeing this iteration of his wife, in contrast to the previous two, sounds an alarm inside of him. She looks like a disintegrating version of the woman he loves—too thin, her eyes dark and hollowed out, her orbital bones a touch too pronounced.

A memory takes hold—she tried to kill herself two years ago. The white scars running down her forearms are still visible. He found her in the old claw-foot tub in the windowed alcove with a view of the sea, the bathwater turned the color of wine. He remembers lifting her nearly lifeless, dripping body out of the water and setting her on the tile. Frantically wrapping her wrists in medical gauze just in time to stop the bleeding.

She almost died.

The hardest part was there was no one she could talk to. No psychiatrist with whom she could share the burden of her existence. She only had Barry, and the guilt of not being enough for her has been eating him away for years.

In this moment, staring at her in the doorway, he is overcome by his devotion to this woman.

He says, "You are the bravest person I've ever known."

She holds up her phone. "The missiles launched ten minutes ago. We failed again." She takes a sip from the glass of red wine in her hand.

"You shouldn't be drinking that before you get in the tank."

She polishes off the rest. "It's just a nip to calm my nerves."

It's been hard between them. He can't remember the last time he slept in her bed. The last time they had sex. The last time they laughed at something stupid. But he can't begrudge her. For him, their relationship begins each iteration in that Portland bar, when he's twenty-one and she's twenty. They spend twenty-nine years together, and while each loop feels brand-new to him (until they reach this doomsday moment and gain memories of the prior timelines), from her perspective, she's been with the same man for eighty-seven years, reliving, over and over, the same stretch of time from twenty to forty-nine years old.

Same fights.

Same fears.

Same dynamic.

Same . . . everything.

No real surprises.

Only now, in this brief moment, are they equals. Helena tried to explain before, but finally he understands, and this knowledge reminds him of something Slade said in his hotel lab, just before his death—*Your perspective changes when you've lived countless lives.*

Perhaps Slade had a point. You can't truly understand yourself until you've lived many lives. Maybe the man wasn't completely raving mad.

Helena steps into the room.

"You ready?" he asks.

"Can you fucking relax for a minute? Nobody's sending a nuke into the coast of Maine. We'll get Boston, New York, and Midwest fallout, but that's hours away."

They've fought about this exact moment—when it became clear in the last couple of years that they weren't going to find a solution in this loop, Barry advocated for killing this timeline and sending Helena back before the world remembered its violent end on the previous timeline, and suffered a new one again on this one. But

Helena argued that even the slightest chance no false memories would return was worth letting it play out. And more important, she wanted, if only for the briefest window of time, to be with the Barry who remembered all timelines and everything they'd been through together. If he was honest with himself, he wanted that too.

This is the only moment in the entirety of their shared existence when they can truly be together.

She comes over to the window and stands beside him.

With a finger, she begins to erase the writing on the glass.

"This was all a waste, huh?" she says.

"We should've gone to CERN."

"And if your wormhole theory was proven right? Then what?"

"I stand by my belief that if we could understand how and why the chair is able to send our consciousness back into a memory, we would be in a better place to know how to stop the false memories."

"You ever considered the possibility that it's unknowable?"

"Are you losing hope?" he asks.

"Oh honey, it's long gone. Aside from my own pain, every time I go back, I destroy the consciousness of that sixteen-year-old girl walking out to the truck into her first moment of real freedom. I'm killing her over and over and over. She has never gotten the chance to live her life. Because of Marcus Slade. Because of me."

"Then let me carry the hope for both of us for a while."

"You have been."

"Let me keep carrying it."

She looks at him. "You still believe we'll find a way to fix this."

"Yes."

"When? The next iteration? The thirtieth?"

"It's so strange," he says.

"What?"

"I walked into this room five minutes ago and had no idea what those equations meant. Then I suddenly had memories from this timeline and understood partial differential equations." A fragment of conversation from another lifetime flickers in the neuronal structure of his brain. He says, "Remember what Marcus Slade said when we had him at gunpoint in his lab in that hotel?"

"You do realize, from my perspective, that was almost a hundred years and three timelines ago."

"You told him that if the world ever knew of the chair's existence, that knowledge could never be put back. Just what we're fighting against now. Remember?"

"Vaguely."

"And he said you'd been blinded by your limitations, that you still weren't seeing everything, and that you never would unless you had traveled the way he had."

"He was crazy."

"That's what I thought too. But the difference between you on that first timeline, and you now—it might be driving you mad, but you've mastered whole fields of science, lived entire lives the first Helena never would've dreamed of. You see the world in ways she never did. It's the same with me. Who knows how many lives Slade lived, and what he learned? What if he really did figure some way out? Some loophole around the dead-memory problem? Something you'd need however-many-more of these loops to figure out for yourself? What if this whole time, we've been missing something crucial?"

"Like what?"

"I have no idea, but wouldn't you like to ask Slade?"

"How do you propose we do that, Detective?"

"I don't know, but we can't just give up."

"No, *I* can't give up. You can tap out anytime you want and live your life in blissful ignorance that this day is coming."

"You've really come to think so little of my presence in your life?"

She sighs. "Of course not."

A paperweight rattles on the table behind them.

A crack spider-webs across the window glass.

The low rumble of a distant blast shudders through their bones.

"This is some kind of hell," she says, dark. "Ready to come down to the lab and kill me again, darling?"

Barry is no longer in the subterranean lab on his and Helena's island off the coast of Maine, but sitting instead at a familiar-looking desk in a familiar-looking room. His head hurts with a sensation he hasn't experienced in some time—the behind-the-eyes-throbbing of a deep hangover.

He's staring at a witness statement on a computer screen in front of him, and while there are no memories of this timeline yet, he's realizing, with a mounting horror, that he's on the fourth floor of the 24th Precinct of the NYPD.

West 100th Street.

Upper West Side.

Manhattan.

He's worked here before. Not just in this building. On this floor. In this spot. And not a desk *like* this one. This exact desk. He even recognizes the ink stain from a ballpoint pen mishap.

He pulls out his phone, checks the home screen: April 16, 2019.

The fourth timeline anniversary of Helena dying in that DARPA lab.

What the hell?

He rises out of his chair—substantially heavier than he was in Maine, Colorado, and Arizona—and inside his jacket, he feels the heft of something he hasn't worn in ages—a shoulder holster.

An eerie silence has overtaken the entire fourth floor of cubicles.

No one typing.

No one talking.

Just a stunned silence.

He looks over at the woman across from him—a cop he remembers, not from this timeline, but the original, before time was fractured by Helena's chair. She's a homicide detective named Sheila Redling, who played shortstop for their softball league. She had a wicked arm, and was the best drinker on the team. Blood is running out of Sheila's nose and down her white blouse, and the look on her face is unquestionably that of a woman in a state of sheer terror.

The man in the next cubicle over has a bloody nose as well and tears running down his face.

A gunshot explodes the pin-drop silence on the other side of the floor, followed by gasps and shrieks rippling across the maze of cubicles.

There's another shot, this one closer.

Someone screams, *"What the fuck is happening? What the fuck is happening?"*

After the third shot, Barry reaches into his jacket to pull his Glock, wondering if they're under attack, but he can't see any threats in his vicinity.

Just a sea of bewildered faces.

Shelia Redling stands suddenly, draws her weapon, puts the gun to her head, and fires.

As she drops to the floor, the man who shares a cubicle wall with her lunges out of his chair, grabs her gun from the pool of blood, and puts it into his mouth.

Barry screams, "No!"

As he fires and falls on top of Sheila, Barry realizes this all makes some terrible kind of sense. His memories of the previous timeline are with Helena on the coast of Maine, but these people were in the midst of a nuclear attack on New York City, where they all died or were in the throes of an awful death, after having just suffered the same fate in the previous timeline, where another nuclear attack had just happened.

Now the memories of this timeline break like a crashing wave.

He moved to New York in his early twenties and became a cop.

He married Julia.

Climbed the ranks of the NYPD to make detective in the Central Rob-bery Division.

He lived his original life all over again.

And it hits him like a shot to the kidneys—Helena never came to him in that Portland bar. He has never met her. Never heard from her. For some reason, she chose to live this timeline without him. He only knows her in dead memories.

He pulls out his cell phone to call her, trying to remember her number, and realizes that it can't possibly be the same on this timeline. He has no way to contact her, and the helplessness of that knowledge is almost more than he can bear in this moment, thoughts tearing through his mind—

Does this mean she broke up with him?

Found someone else?

Finally had enough of living the same twenty-nine-year loop with the same man?

As more gunshots erupt around him and people start to flee the area, he thinks back to the last conversation he had with Helena at their home in Maine and his idea of finding Slade.

Stay focused on that. If the past lifetimes are any guide, you only have a limited amount of time before hell rains down on New York.

He shuts out the chaos and slides his chair toward his desk, waking his computer.

A Google search for "Marcus Slade" pulls up an obituary in the *San Francisco Chronicle*, detailing that Slade died of a drug overdose last Christmas.

Shit.

Next he searches "Jee-woon Chercover" and finds multiple hits. Chercover runs a VC firm on the Upper East Side called Apex Venture. Barry snaps a photo of the contact info off their website, grabs his keys, and rushes for the stairwell.

As he descends the stairs, he dials Apex.

"All circuits are busy, please try your call—"

He sprints through the ground-floor lobby, into the late afternoon, reaching the sidewalk of West 100th Street, short of breath, a new alert lighting up his phone's home screen:

> **Emergency Alert**
> BALLISTIC MISSILE THREAT INBOUND TO MULTIPLE US TARGETS. SEEK IMMEDIATE SHELTER. THIS IS NOT A DRILL.
> Slide for more

Jesus.

While he has memories of this timeline, his identity encompasses, fleetingly, all the lifetimes he's ever lived. Unfortunately, that multi-timeline perspective will end when the missiles hit.

He wonders—what if this is all that's left of his life?

Of everyone's life?

A half hour of the same endless, repeating horror.

Some kind of hell.

Fifteen floors up, in a building across the street, a window breaks, glass showering the pavement, followed by a chair and then a man in a pinstripe suit.

He crashes headfirst through the roof of a car, whose alarm begins a piercing shriek.

People are running past Barry.

On the sidewalks.

In the streets.

More men and women plummeting out of skyscrapers, because they remember what it was like to die in a nuclear attack.

A civil defense siren begins to scream, and people are flooding out of the surrounding buildings like rats and pouring into an underground parking garage to take cover.

Barry jumps into his car and starts the engine. Apex is on the Upper East Side, just across the park, barely six long blocks from his current location.

He turns out into the street, but all he can do is creep along through the hordes of people.

Barry lays on his horn, veering finally onto Columbus, which is only slightly less mobbed.

He drives against traffic and turns right into the first alleyway he comes to, speeding in the shadows between apartment buildings.

He fires his light bar and sirens and muscles his way across two more streets filled with frantic, hysterical people.

Then he's accelerating his Crown Vic down a walking path in Central Park, trying to call Apex again.

This time, the phone rings.

Please, please, please pick up.

And rings.

And rings.

There are too many people on the path ahead, so he veers off into North Meadow, ripping across baseball diamonds where he used to play.

"Hello?"

Barry slams on the brakes and brings his car to a stop in the middle of the field and puts the phone on speaker.

"Who is this?"

"Jee-woon Chercover. Is this Barry?"

"How'd you know?"

"I wondered if you'd call."

Last time Barry interacted with Jee-woon, he and Helena had shot him in Slade's lab as he lunged naked for a gun.

"Where are you right now?" Barry asks.

"My office on the thirtieth floor of my building. Looking out over the city. Waiting to die again, like all of us. Are you and Helena doing this?"

"We've been trying to stop it. I wanted to find Slade—"

"He died last year."

"I know. So I need to ask you—when Helena and I found Slade at the hotel, he alluded to there being a way to undo dead memories. Some different way of traveling. Of using the memory chair."

There's silence on the other end of the line.

"*You mean when you killed me.*"

"Yeah."

"*What happened after—*"

"Look, there's no time. I need this information if you have it. I've been on a thirty-three-year loop with Helena trying to find some way to erase the world's knowledge of the memory chair. Nothing's working. That's why we keep reaching this moment of apocalypse over and over. And it's going to keep happening unless—"

"*I can tell you this, and it's all I know. Marcus did believe there was a way to reset a timeline, so there would be no dead memories. He even did it once.*"

"How?"

"*I don't know the specifics. Look, I need to call my parents. Please fix this if you can. We're all in hell.*"

Jee-woon hangs up. Barry tosses his phone into the passenger seat and climbs out of the car. Sits down on the grass, rests his hands on his legs.

They're shaking.

His entire body is.

On the next timeline, he won't remember the conversation he just had with Jee-woon until April 16, 2019.

If there even is a next timeline.

A bird lands nearby and sits very still, looking at him.

The buildings of the Upper East Side rise above the perimeter of the park, and the noise of the city is much louder than it should be—gunshots, screams, the civil defense sirens, the sirens of fire engines, squad cars, ambulances—all blending into a discordant symphony.

A thought occurs.

A bad one.

What if Helena died in that four-year period between 1986 and 1990, before she was supposed to find him in Portland? Could the fate of reality itself really depend upon one person *not* getting randomly hit by a bus?

Or what if she decided not to do any of this? Just live her life and never build the chair and let the world destroy itself? It would be hard to blame her, but it would mean the next reality shift will be one of someone else's choosing. Or no shift at all if the world successfully annihilates itself.

The buildings all around him and the open field and the trees glow the brightest white Barry has ever seen—even brighter than Denver.

There is no sound.

Already the brightness is waning, and in its place comes an inferno rushing toward him through the Upper East Side, the heat excruciatingly intense, but only for the half second it takes to burn through the nerve endings in Barry's face.

In the distance, he sees people sprinting across the field, trying to outrun their final moment.

And he braces for the lava-colored wall of roiling fire and death to engulf him as it expands through Central Park, but the shockwave hits first, rocketing him over the meadow at an inconceivable rate of speed that's slowing.

Slowing.

Slowing.

But not just him.

Everything.

He retains consciousness as this timeline decelerates to a standstill, leaving him suspended thirty feet off the ground and surrounded by the debris from the shockwave—pieces of glass and steel, a police car, melting-faced people.

The fireball is stopped a quarter mile away, halfway across the North Meadow, and the buildings all around him have been caught in the moment of vaporization—glass, furniture, contents, people, everything but the melting steel frames exploding out like a sneeze—and the immense death cloud rising above New York City from the point of impact is paused a mile into its ascent in the sky.

The world begins to lose color, and seeing everything frozen as the time bleeds out of it fires his mind with questions—

If matter can neither be created nor destroyed, where will all this matter go when this timeline ceases to exist? What's happened to the matter of all the dead timelines they've left behind? Are they time-capsuled away in higher, unreachable dimensions? And if so, what is matter without time? Matter that doesn't persist? What would that even look like?

He has one last realization before his consciousness is catapulted from this dying reality—this deceleration of time means that Helena might be alive somewhere, dying in the tank right this second in order to kill this timeline and begin another.

And a glimmer of joy rides through him at the possibility that she lives, and the hope that, in this next reality, even if only for a moment, he will be with her again.

Barry is lying in bed in the semidarkness of a cool room. Through an open window, he can hear a gentle rain falling. He checks his watch—9:30 p.m. Western European Time. Five hours ahead of Manhattan.

He looks over at his wife of twenty-four years, reading beside him in bed.

"It's nine thirty," he says.

Her last life, she climbed into the deprivation chamber at approximately 4:35 p.m., Eastern, so they're fast approaching the fifth timeline anniversary of 4/16/19.

In this moment, Barry's perspective is of having lived a single lifetime. This one. Helena crashed through the door of his life when he was twenty-one in a Portland bar, and they've been inseparable ever since. Of course, he knows all about their four past lives together. Their work. Their love. How it always ends with her dying in the deprivation chamber on April 16, 2019, when the world remembers the existence of the memory chair and all the horror it wrought. The previous timeline they spent apart. She stayed close to her parents in Boulder, built the chair herself, and used it to improve her mother's quality of life once Alzheimer's took hold. But she never made any progress on stopping the onslaught of dead memories, which she swears will find him any moment now. She doesn't know what Barry did with his last life, and neither does he. Yet. In this one, they continued their pursuit of understanding how the brain processes dead memories, and delved further into studies of the particle physics surrounding use of the chair. They've even made a few contacts at CERN, whom they're hoping to use on the next timeline.

But the truth is, as in the past iterations of their life, they've made no meaningful headway toward stopping what's about to happen. They are only two people, and the problem they're facing is enormously complex. Probably insurmountable.

Helena closes her book and looks over at Barry. The noise of the rain pattering on the shingles of their seventeenth-century manor house is perhaps his favorite sound in the world.

She says, "I'm afraid that when your memories of the last timeline come, you're going to feel like I abandoned you. Like I betrayed you. I didn't spend the last timeline with you, but it's not because I didn't love or need you. I hope you can hear that. I just wanted you to live a life without the end of the world looming, and I hope it was a good one. I hope you found love. I didn't. Every day I missed you. Every day I needed you. I was more lonely than I've ever been in my many lives."

"I'm sure you did what you needed to do. I know this is infinitely harder for you than it is for me."

He looks at his watch as the time changes from 9:34 to 9:35.

She's told him everything that will happen. The headache, the temporary loss of consciousness and control. How the world will immediately begin to implode. And yet there's still a part of him that can't quite believe it will happen. Not that he thinks Helena is lying. But it's hard to imagine the troubles of the world could ever reach them here.

Barry feels a glint of pain behind his eyes.

Sharp and blinding.

He looks over at his wife. "I think it's starting."

By midnight, he is the Barry of many lifetimes, although the previous one, in New York City, is oddly the last to arrive. Perhaps because there are so many, the memories come more slowly than any of the previous anniversaries.

He breaks down crying in the kitchen with joy that Helena came back to him, and she sits on his lap at the small table and kisses his face and runs her fingers through his hair and tells him how sorry she is, promising that she will never leave him again.

"Holy shit," Barry says. "I just remembered."

"What?"

He looks up at Helena. "I was right. There's a way out of this apocalyptic loop. Slade did know how to stop dead memories."

"What are you talking about?"

"I looked Slade up in the final moments of the previous timeline. He died last Christmas, but I spoke to Jee-woon. He said Slade had gone back and started a new timeline that didn't cause any dead memories at the anniversary point."

"Oh my God, how?"

"Jee-woon didn't know. He hung up on me, and then the world ended."

A tea kettle whistles.

Helena goes to the range and takes it off the heat, then pours the boiling water over their tea-ball infusers.

"On the next timeline, until we reach the anniversary," Barry says, "I won't remember any of this. You have to carry this knowledge on with you."

"I will."

They stay up all night, and only when day breaks do they dare turn on the news. This is the longest they've ever let a timeline play out beyond the anniversary point. It seems as though every nuclear weapon on the planet has been fired, and every major city in the United States, Russia, and China hit. Even the metro areas of US allies were targeted, including London, Paris, Berlin, and Madrid. The closest strike to Helena and Barry was Glasgow, one hundred and eighty miles to the south. But they're safe for the moment. The jet stream is taking fallout east into Scandinavia.

They head out at dawn through the backyard to put Helena in the deprivation chamber. They bought this property fifteen years ago and renovated every square inch. The house is more than three hundred years old, and from the surrounding fields, the view is of the North Sea, where it edges in around the peninsula at the Cromarty Firth, and in the opposite direction, the mountains of the northern Highlands.

It rained all night, everything dripping.

The sun is still below the sea, but the sky is filling with light. Despite the horrors on the news, it all feels shockingly normal. The sheep watching them from the pastures. The cold quiet. The smell of wet earth. Moss on the stone walls. Their footfalls on the gravel walking path.

They stop at the entrance to the guesthouse, which they transformed into their lab, both looking back at the home they poured their lives into, which they will never see again. Of all the places they've made their home together, of all the lifetimes, Barry has loved this one most.

"We have a plan, right?" he says.

"We do."

"I'll come down with you," he says.

"No, why don't you go look out over the fields until it's done. You love that view."

"You sure?"

"I'm sure. That's how I want to leave you in this life."

She kisses him.

He wipes her tears.

In the next life, Barry walks with Helena toward the stable. The night air is sweet, and the rolling hills surrounding their valley are shining under the stars.

"Still nothing?" she asks.

"No."

They reach the door in the timber-frame barn and move inside, through a tack room, and then down a corridor of vacant stalls that haven't housed horses in more than a decade.

The entryway is hidden behind a pair of sliding doors. Helena punches in the code, and they descend the spiral staircase into a soundproofed basement.

The cell is enclosed on two sides by stone walls, and the other two by sheets of ultrastrong glass pocked with ventilation holes. Inside the cell, there's a toilet, a shower, a small table, and a bed, upon which lies Marcus Slade.

He closes the book he's been reading and sits up, staring at his captors.

In this timeline, they made their home in the countryside of Marin County, thirty minutes north of San Francisco, in order to be close to Slade and prepare for this exact moment. They abducted him before he could overdose last Christmas, and brought him back to the ranch.

Slade woke up in this cell beneath the barn, where they've held him ever since.

Barry pulls a chair over to the glass and takes a seat.

Helena paces the perimeter of the cell.

Slade watches them.

They haven't told him why he's here. Not about the previous timelines or the memory chair. Nothing.

Slade rises from the end of the bed and approaches the glass. He stares down at Barry, wearing sweatpants and no shirt. His beard is unruly, his hair an unwashed tangle, eyes both fearful and angry.

As Barry watches him through the glass, he can't help feeling pity for the man, despite what he did in older timelines. He has no idea why he's here. Barry and Helena have promised him on multiple occasions that they have no intention of hurting him, but those assurances undoubtedly rang hollow.

If Barry is honest, he's deeply uncomfortable with what they're doing. But between Helena's prescience and her building of the memory chair with its incredible capability, he trusts his wife implicitly. Even when she told him they needed to kidnap a man named Marcus Slade before he died of a drug overdose in his Dog-patch loft.

"What?" Slade asks. "Are you finally here to tell me why you're doing this?"

"In a matter of moments," Helena says, "you will understand everything."

"What the fuck does that . . ."

Blood trickles out of Slade's nose. He staggers back, gripping his temples, his face screwed up in pain, and now a stabbing, pulsating agony hits Barry behind the eyes, doubling him over in the chair.

The timeline anniversary has arrived, and both men groan as the prior lifetimes begin to catch up with them.

———

Now Slade is seated on the end of his bed. The fear is gone from his eyes. Even his body language has changed to reflect an inner confidence and poise that wasn't there before.

He smiles, his head nodding.

"Barry," he says. "Nice to see you again, Helena."

Barry is reeling. It's one thing to have been told what happened on all those other timelines, another entirely to own the memories of his dead daughter and of watching the world destroy itself again and again. Of dying in the middle of Central Park as a shockwave hit. He doesn't remember the last timeline yet. Helena has told him that it took place in Scotland, which was apparently where he came up with this idea, but the memories are coming in as slowly as an IV drip.

Barry looks at Slade and says, "Do you remember your hotel in Manhattan?"

"Of course."

"Do you remember the night you died there? What you said to Helena right before?"

"Might need a little refresh on that one."

"You told her that the dead memories of older timelines could be undone if she knew how to travel the way you did."

"Ah." Slade smiles again. "You two have built your own chair."

Helena says, "After you died in your hotel, DARPA came in and took everything. Things were OK at first, but on April 16, 2019, six timelines ago today, the technology broke out into the wild. There were memory chairs being used all over the world. The schematics were published on WikiLeaks. Reality began constantly shifting. I went back thirty-three years to start a new timeline, so I'd have a chance to find a way of stopping the dead memories. But they always come. The world always remembers the chair, no matter what we do."

"So you're looking for a way out of this loop? A reset?"

"Yes."

"Why?"

"Because exactly what I told you would happen happened. Pandora's box has been flung open. I don't know how to close it."

Slade goes to the sink, splashes water in his face.

He comes back over to the glass.

"How do we stop the dead memories?" she asks.

"You got me killed in one life. Abducted in another. So let me ask you—why would I help you?"

"Because maybe you still have a shred of decency?"

"Humanity deserves a chance to evolve beyond our prison of time. It deserves a chance at true progress. Your life's work was the chair. Giving it to humanity was mine."

Barry registers a wave of rage flooding through him.

"Marcus, listen to me," he says. "There is no progress happening. Right now, the world is remembering the existence of the memory chair, and those dead memories will trigger a nuclear apocalypse."

"Why?"

"Because our enemies think the US is altering history."

"Know what that sounds like to me?" Slade asks. "Bullshit."

Barry rises and moves toward the glass. "I've seen enough horror for a thousand lifetimes. Helena and I were nearly killed in Denver when the missiles hit. I watched New York City vaporize. Hundreds of millions of people have four distinct memory sets of dying in a nuclear holocaust."

Helena looks at Barry and holds up her phone. "The alert just came through. I have to get to the lab."

"Just wait a second," Barry says.

"We're too close to San Francisco. We've talked about this."

Barry glares at Slade through the glass. "What is this special way of traveling?"

Slade takes a step back and eases down onto the end of the bed.

Barry says, "I have lived almost seventy years to ask you this, and you're just going to stare at the floor?"

He feels Helena touch his shoulder. "I *have* to go."

"Hang on."

"I *can't*. You know this. I love you. I'll see you at the bottom of the world. We'll keep after the micro wormholes. I guess it's all we can do, right?"

Barry turns and kisses her. She hurries up the spiral staircase, her footfalls clanging on the metal steps.

Then it's just Barry and Slade in the basement.

Barry pulls out his phone, shows Slade the emergency alert, advising of a ballistic missile threat inbound to multiple US targets.

Slade smiles. "Like I said, you killed me, abducted me, you're probably lying to me right—"

"I swear I'm telling you the truth."

"Prove it. Give me evidence that's not a fake alert you could've sent to your phone. Let me see it with my own eyes or fuck off."

"We don't have time."

"I have all the time in the world."

Moving to the glass door in the cell, Barry takes out the key and unlocks the dead bolt.

"What?" Slade asks. "Think you can beat it out of me?"

Barry would certainly like nothing more than to bounce Slade's skull off the stone wall until there is nothing left.

"Let's go," Barry says.

"Where?"

"We'll watch the world end together."

They head upstairs, past the stalls, out of the barn, and climb through the long grasses of a hill until they're high above the ranch.

The moon is up, the countryside bright. To the west, several miles away, the dark sprawl of the Pacific is shimmering.

The lights of the Bay Area glitter to the south.

They sit in silence for a moment.

Then Barry asks, "What made you kill Helena in that first timeline?"

Slade sighs. "I was nothing. Nobody. I'd sleepwalked through life. And then I was presented with this . . . gift of an opportunity. To do it all over. Think what you will about me, but I didn't keep the chair to myself."

A ball of white-hot light blossoms near the Golden Gate Bridge, illuminating the sky and the sea brighter than the brightest mid-day. So blinding Barry can't help but look away. When he turns back, a shockwave is spreading across the bay and the Presidio, expanding toward the Financial District.

As a second warhead bursts over Palo Alto, Barry looks at Slade. "How many people do you think just died in that split-second flash? How many more will suffer an agonizing death from radiation poisoning over the next few hours if Helena doesn't reset this timeline? What's happening to San Francisco is happening all across America. To the major cities of our allies. And we're unloading our arsenal on Russia and China. This is where your grand dream has taken us. And it's the fifth time it's happened. So how do you just sit there knowing the blood of all these people is on your hands? You aren't helping humanity evolve, Marcus. You're torturing us. There is no future for our species after this."

Slade's face is expressionless as he watches two towers of fire climb into the sky like torches. The light grids of San Francisco, Oakland, and San Jose have gone dark, but the cities smolder like the remains of a dying fire.

The concussive blast of the first warhead reaches them, and at this distance, it sounds like a cannon echoing off the hillsides. It makes the ground tremble beneath them.

Slade rubs his bare arms. "You have to go back to what happened first."

"We tried that. Multiple times. Helena went back to 1986—"

"Stop thinking linearly. Not to the beginning of this timeline. Not even the last five or six. You have to return to the event that started all of this, and that's on the original."

"The original timeline only exists in a dead memory."

"Exactly. You have to go back and restart it. That's the only way to stop people from remembering."

"But you can't map a dead memory."

"Have you tried?"

"No."

"It will be the hardest thing you've ever done. You'll probably fail, which means you'll die. But it is possible."

"How do you know?"

"Helena figured out how to do it on my oil rig."

"That's not true. If she had, we would've—"

Slade laughs. "Try to keep up here, Barry. How do you think I know it works? As soon as we discovered the technique, I used it. I went back into a dead memory and reset the timeline just before she figured it out." He snaps his fingers. "And, poof, it erased her memories of the discovery. Hers and everyone else's."

"Why?"

"Because anyone who knew could do just what you're proposing now. They could take the chair away from me, make it so it never existed." He looks Barry in the eye, the firelight of burning cities glinting from his pupils. "I was nothing. A junkie. My life wasted. The chair made me into something special. Gave me a chance to do something that would change the course of history. I couldn't risk all that." He shakes his head, smiles. "And there's a certain elegance to the solution, don't you think? Using the discovery to erase itself."

"What's the event that started all of this?"

"I killed Helena on November 5, 2018, on the original timeline. Go back as close to that date as possible . . . and stop me."

"How do we—"

Another blink of light, a hundred miles to the south, lights up the entire sea.

"Go," Slade says. "If you don't make it to Helena before she dies in the tank, you won't remember what I just told you until the next—"

And Barry is up and running, sprinting back down the hill

toward the main house, digging his cell phone out of his pocket, falling, scrambling back onto his feet, finally dialing Helena's number.

He holds the phone to his ear as he runs toward the lights of their home.

Ringing.

Ringing.

The sound wave from the second blast reaches him.

The phone still ringing.

Going to voicemail.

He throws it down as he reaches level ground, sweat stinging in his eyes, the house straight ahead.

Screaming, "Helena! Wait!"

The house is a massive country home built alongside a stream that meanders through the valley.

Barry runs up the porch steps and bursts through the front door, yelling Helena's name as he races through the living room, knocking over an end table and spilling a glass of water that shatters on the tile.

Then down the east-wing corridor, past the master suite, toward the end of the hall, where the vault door to the lab has been left open.

"Helena, stop!"

He tears down the stairs toward the subterranean lab that houses the memory chair and deprivation tank. They have the answer. Or at least something to try that doesn't require another thirty-three years. The look on Slade's face, glowing in the light of distant nuclear fires, was not the look of a lying man, but of one who had suddenly come to terms with what he'd done. With the pain he was causing.

Barry comes off the last step into the lab. Helena is nowhere to be seen, which means she's already in the deprivation chamber. The terminal screens support this, one of them flashing the message in red: DMT RELEASE DETECTED.

He reaches the deprivation chamber, puts his hands on the hatch to pull it open—

The world grinds to a halt.

The lab bleeds of color.

He's screaming on the inside, he has to stop this from happening, they have the answer.

But he can't move, can't speak.

Helena is gone, and so is this reality.

He becomes aware of lying on his side in total darkness.

Sitting up, Barry's movement triggers a panel of light above him, dim at first, then slowly brightening, warming into existence a small, windowless room containing the bed, a dresser, and a nightstand.

He throws back the blankets and climbs out of bed, unsteady on his feet.

Goes to the door and steps out into a sterile hallway. After fifty feet, it emerges onto a main artery that accesses this corridor and three others while also opening on the other side to a living space one floor below.

He sees a full kitchen.

Table tennis and pool tables.

And a large television with a woman's face paused on the screen. He has some vague recognition of her face, but he can't conjure her name. The entire history of his life lurks just below the surface, but he can't quite grasp it.

"Hello?"

His voice echoes through the structure.

No answer.

He heads down the main hallway, passing a placard affixed to the wall beside the opening to the next corridor.

Wing 2—Level 2—Lab

And another.

Wing 1—Level 2—Offices

Then down some stairs and onto the main level.

There's a gently sloping vestibule straight ahead that grows colder with every step, ending finally at a door that looks complex enough to seal a spacecraft.

A digital readout on the wall beside it displays real-time conditions on the other side:

Wind: from the NE 56.2 mph; 90.45 kph
Temp: -51.9 °F; -46.6 °C
Wind Chill: -106.9°F; -77.2 °C
Humidity: 27%

His socked feet are freezing, and in here the wind carries the moaning quality of a deep-voiced ghost. He grasps the lever on the door, and following the visual instructions, forces it down and counterclockwise.

A series of locks release, the door free to swing on its hinges.

He pushes it open, and the coldest breath of air he has ever encountered blasts him in the face with a sensation beyond temperature. Like fingernails clawing away his skin. Instantly, he feels his nose hairs freezing, and when he draws breath, he chokes on the pain of it sliding down his esophagus.

Through the open hatch, he sees a walkway angling down from the station toward the icecap, the world cloaked in darkness and swirling with needles of snow that sting his face like shrapnel.

The visibility is less than a quarter mile, but by the light of the moon, he can just make out other structures in proximity. A series of large cylindrical tanks he suspects is a water-treatment plant. A swaying tower that's either some sort of gantry or a drilling rig. A telescope, folded down against the storm. Vehicles of varying size on continuous tracks.

He can't stand it anymore. He takes hold of the door with fingers already beginning to stiffen and forces it to close. The locks engage.

The wind downshifts from a scream to that sustained and ghostly moan.

He walks out of the vestibule and under the lights of the pristine and seemingly empty station, his face burning as it reawakens from the slightest touch of frostbite.

In this moment, he is a man without memory, and the sense of being adrift in time is a crushing, existential horror. Like waking from a troubled sleep, when the lines between reality and dreams are still murky and you're calling out to ghosts.

All he has is his first name, and an out-of-focus sense of himself.

At the seating area around the television, he sees an open DVD case and a remote control. He sits on one of the sofas, takes the controller, and presses Play.

On the screen, the woman is sitting exactly where he is, a blanket draped over her shoulders and a cup of tea steaming on the table in front of her.

She smiles at the camera and brushes a wisp of white hair out of her face, his heart kicking at the sight of her.

"This is weird." She laughs nervously. "You should be watching this on April 16, 2019—our favorite day in history. Your consciousness and memories from the last timeline have just shifted over. Or should have. With each new iteration, your memories are coming in more slowly and erratically. Sometimes you miss entire lifetimes. So I made this video— first, to tell you not to be afraid, since you're probably wondering why you're in a research station in Antarctica. And secondly, because I want to say something to the Barry who remembers all timelines, who's quite different from the one I'm living with now. So please, pause me until your memories arrive."

He pauses the video.

It is so quiet here.

Nothing but the roar of the wind.

He goes to the kitchen, and as he brews a cup of coffee, a tightness forms in his chest.

There's a storm of emotion on the horizon.

His head pounds at the base of his skull, and a nosebleed hits.

The Portland bar.

Helena.

Her slow revelation of who she was.

Buying this old research station at the turn of the millennium.

They refurbished it, then flew the chair and all its component parts down here on a privately chartered 737 that stuck a harrowing landing on the polar runway.

They brought a team of particle physicists with them whom they had apparently scoped out in a prior timeline, who had no concept of the true nature of their research. They drilled out 1.5 foot–diameter cores 8,000 feet deep into the polar cap and lowered highly sensitive light detectors more than a mile below the ice. The sensors were designed to detect neutrinos, one of the most enigmatic particles in the universe. Neutrinos carry no charge, rarely interact with normal matter, and typically emerge from (and therefore indicate) cosmic events such as supernovae, galactic cores, and black holes. When a neutrino hits an atom on Earth, it creates a particle called a muon, that's moving faster than light in a solid, causing the ice to emit light. These light waves caused by muons passing through solid ice is what they looked for.

Barry's theory, carried over from prior timelines, was that if micro black holes and wormholes were flashing in and out of existence when someone's consciousness re-spawned in an earlier memory, these light detectors would register the light waves caused by muons caused by neutrinos ejecting from the black holes and smashing into the nucleus of earthbound atoms.

They got nowhere.

Discovered nothing.

The team of particle physicists went home.

Six lifetimes pursuing a deeper understanding of the memory chair, and all they had managed to do was postpone the inevitable.

He looks up at the screen, where Helena is frozen mid-gesture.

Now come the dead memories of prior timelines. Their lives in Arizona, Denver, on the rugged coast of Maine. His life without her in New York City, their life together in Scotland. But there are still holes. He has flashes of the last timeline near San Francisco, but it's incomplete—he can't remember the last days of it, when the world remembered.

He presses Play.

"So you've remembered? Good. The only way you're watching this is because I'm gone."

Tears release. It's the weirdest sensation. While the Barry of this timeline knows she's dead, simultaneously the Barrys of the prior timelines register the pain of her loss for the first time.

"I'm sorry, honey."

He remembers the day she died, eight weeks ago. She had become almost childlike by that point, her mind gone. He had to feed her, dress her, bathe her.

But this was better than the time right before, when she had enough cognitive function left to be aware of her complete confusion. In her lucid moments, she described the feeling as being lost in a dreamlike forest—no identity, no sense of when or where she was. Or alternatively, being absolutely certain she was fifteen years old and still living with her parents in Boulder, and trying to square her foreign surroundings with her sense of place and time and self. She often wondered if this was what her mother felt in her final year.

"This timeline—before my mind started to fracture—was the best of them all. Of my very long life. Do you remember that trip we took—I think it was during our first life together—to see the emperor penguins migrate? Remember how we fell in love with this continent? The way it makes you feel like you're the only people in the world? Kind of appropriate, no?" She looks off camera, says, *"What? Don't be jealous. You'll be watching this one day. You'll carry the knowledge of every moment we spent together, all one hundred and forty-four years."*

She looks back at the camera. *"I need to tell you, Barry, that I couldn't have made it this long without you. I couldn't have kept trying* to stop the inevitable. But we're stopping today. As you know by now, I've lost the ability to map memory. Like Slade, I used the chair too many times. So I won't be going back. And even if you returned to a point on the timeline where my consciousness was young and untraveled, there's no guarantee you could convince me to build the chair. And to what end? We've tried everything. Physics, pharmacology, neurology. We even struck out with Slade. It's time to admit we failed and let the world get on with destroying itself, which it seems so keen on doing."

Barry sees himself step into the frame and take a seat beside Helena. He puts his arm around her. She snuggles into him, her head on his chest. Such a surreal sensation to now remember that day when she decided to record a message for the Barry who would one day merge into his consciousness.

"We have four years until doomsday."

"Four years, five months, eight days," Barry-on-the-screen says. "But who's counting?"

"We're going to spend that time together. You have those memories now. I hope they're beautiful."

They are.

Before her mind broke completely, they had two good years, which they lived free from the burden of trying to stop the world from remembering. They lived those years simply and quietly. Walks on the icecap to see the Aurora Australis. Games, movies, and cooking down here on the main level. The occasional trip to New Zealand's South Island or Patagonia. Just being together. A thousand small moments, but enough to have made life worth living.

Helena was right. They were the best years of his lives too.

"It's odd," she says. "You're watching this right now, presumably four years from this moment, although I'm sure you'll watch it before then to see my face and hear my voice after I'm gone."

It's true. He did.

"But my moment feels just as real to me as yours does to you. Are they both real? Is it only our consciousness that makes it so? I can imagine *you sitting there in four years, even though you're right beside me in this moment, in my moment, and I feel like I can reach through the camera and touch you. I wish I could. I've experienced over two hundred years, and at the end of it all, I think Slade was right. It's just a product of our evolution the way we experience reality and time from moment to moment. How we differentiate between past, present, and future. But we're intelligent enough to be aware of the illusion, even as we live by it, and so, in moments like this—when I can imagine you sitting exactly where I am, listening to me, loving me, missing me—it tortures us. Because I'm locked in my moment, and you're locked in yours."*

Barry wipes his eyes, the full emotional weight of the last two years with her, and the two months alone, pressing in on him. He only waited to experience this seventh timeline anniversary to see what it felt like to be a person with numerous histories. To fully understand himself. It's one thing to be told you had a daughter. Another entirely to remember the sound of her laugh. The first seconds of holding her. The totality of all the moments is too much to bear.

"Don't come back for me, Barry."

He already did. The morning he rolled over and found her dead beside him, he used the chair to go back one month to be with her a little longer. Then when she died, he did it again. And again. Killed himself ten times in the tank to put off the great silence and loneliness of life without her in this place.

Helena says, *"'Now he has departed from this strange world a little ahead of me. That means nothing. People like us, who believe in physics, know that the distinction between past, present and future is only a stubbornly persistent illusion.' Einstein said that about his friend Michele Besso. Lovely, isn't it? I think he was right."*

The Barry on the screen is crying.

The Barry of this moment is crying.

"I would say it was worth it to accidentally build a world-destroying chair because it brought you into my life, but that's probably bad form. If

you wake up on April 16, 2019, and the world somehow doesn't remember and implode, I hope you'll go on without me and live an amazing life. Seek your happiness. You found it with me, which means it's attainable. If the world remembers, we did what we could, and if you feel alone at the end, Barry, know that I'm with you. Maybe not in your moment. But I am in this one. My heart."

She kisses the Barry beside her and blows a kiss at the camera.

The screen goes black.

He turns on the news, watches five seconds of a frantic BBC anchor reporting that the mainland of the United States has been hit by several thousand nuclear warheads, and then turns off the television.

Barry moves through the vestibule, toward the door that keeps him protected from the killing cold.

He's with an ancient memory of Julia. In it, she's young, and so is he. Meghan is there, and they're camping at Lake Tear of the Clouds, high in the Adirondacks.

The moment feels close enough to touch. The smell of evergreens. The sound of his daughter's voice. But the ache of the memory hangs like a black cloud in his chest.

Lately, he's been reading the great philosophers and physicists. Plato to Aristotle. From Newton's absolute time to Einstein's relativistic. One truth seems to be surfacing from the cacophony of theories and philosophies—no one has a clue. Saint Augustine said it perfectly back in the fourth century: "What then is time? If no one asks me, I know what it is. If I wish to explain it to him who asks, I do not know."

Some days, it feels like a river flowing past him. Others, like something he's sliding down the surface of. Sometimes, it feels like it's all already happened, and he's just experiencing incremental slivers, moment to moment, his consciousness like the needle in the grooves of a record that already exists—beginning, middle, and end.

As if our choices, our fates, were locked from our first breath.

He studies the readout on the door:

Wind: Calm
Temp: -83.9 °F; -64.4 °C
Wind Chill: -83.9°F; -64.4 °C
Humidity: 14%

But on a night like this, of a restless mind and dreams of ghosts, time feels secondary to the true prime mover—memory. Perhaps memory is fundamental, the thing from which time emerges.

The ache of the memory is gone, but he doesn't begrudge its visitation. He's lived long enough to know that the memory hurt because many years ago, in a dead timeline, he experienced a perfect moment.

It doesn't matter what time it is. For the next six months, it's always night.

The wind has died, but the temperature has plummeted to an eyelash-freezing eighty below zero. The research station stands half a mile away, the only smudge of manmade light in the vast polar desert.

There are no land features to speak of. From where he sits, there is nothing but a flat, white plain of wind-sculpted ice stretching off toward every horizon.

It seems impossible, sitting out here all alone in the perfect stillness, that the rest of the world is going to pieces. Stranger still that it's all because of a chair accidentally created by the woman he loves.

She's buried in the ice beside him, four feet down in a casket he built of pine scraps from the woodshop. He crafted a little marker from the best piece of oak he could find and carved a little epitaph in the wood—his only purpose these last two months.

Helena Gray Smith
Born July 19, 1970, Boulder, Colorado
Died February 14, 2019, E. Antarctica
A Brave, Beautiful Genius
Loved by Barry Sutton
Saver of Barry Sutton

He looks out across the icecap.

Not even a breath of wind.

Nothing moving.

A perfectly frozen world.

Like it's outside of time.

Meteors streak the sky, and the Southern Lights have just begun to dance on the horizon—a flickering ribbon of green and yellow.

Barry peers over the edge of the hole beside Helena's.

He takes a frigid breath, then slides a leg over the side and lowers himself below the surface of the plain.

His shoulders touch the sides, and there's a space hollowed out between his hole and Helena's so he can reach through and touch her pine-box casket.

It feels good to be near her again. Or what was once her.

The dimensions of his grave frame the night sky.

Looking into space from Antarctica feels like looking into space from space. On a night like this—no wind, no weather, no moon—the smear of the Milky Way looks more like a celestial fire, brimming with colors you'd never see from anyplace else on Earth.

Space is one of the few places where time makes sense to him. He knows, on an intellectual level, that when he looks at any object, he's looking back in time. In the case of his own hand, it takes the light a nanosecond—one billionth of a second—to transport the image to his eyes. When he looks at the research station from half a mile away, he's seeing the structure as it existed 2,640 nanoseconds ago.

It seems instantaneous, and for all intents and purposes, it is.

But when Barry looks into the night sky, he's seeing stars whose light took a year, or a hundred, or a million to reach him. The telescopes that peer into deep space are looking at ten-billion-year-old light from stars that coalesced just after the universe began.

He's looking back, not just through space but through time.

He's colder than he was hiking out to their gravesite, but not cold enough. He's going to have to open his parka and remove some layers.

He sits up, pulls off the outer shell of his right glove, and digs into his pocket.

He takes out a flask of whiskey, kept somewhat warm by proximity to his body and the air trapped between layers of clothing. Out in the open, it's more than cold enough to freeze solid inside of a minute.

Next, he takes out the bottle of oxy. It contains five 20 mg tablets, and if they don't kill him outright, they'll certainly put him into a deep slumber while the cold finishes him off.

He opens the bottle and dumps the pills into his mouth, rinsing them down with several swallows of ice-cold whiskey that still feels hot when it hits his stomach.

He's been imagining this moment obsessively since Helena died.

The loneliness has been unbearable without her, and the world beyond has nothing left for him, should it even continue to exist. He no longer wants to know what will happen next.

He lies back in the grave, thinking he'll wait to open his jacket until he feels the first effects of the drug, when a memory comes.

He thought he had them all, but now the last moments of the previous timeline flash in.

Slade saying—

"You have to go back to what happened first."

"We tried that. Multiple times. Helena went back to 1986—"

"Stop thinking linearly. Not to the beginning of this timeline. Not even the last five or six. You have to return to the event that started all of this, and that's on the original."

"The original timeline only exists in a dead memory."

"Exactly. You have to go back and restart it. That's the only way to stop people from remembering. I killed Helena on November 5, 2018, on the original timeline. Go back as close to that date as possible . . . and stop me."

Holy fuck.

He remembers racing down the hill, into the house, screaming her name. His hands frozen on the deprivation chamber hatch as the timeline ended.

What if Slade was right? What if those old timelines are still out there? Take his memory of Lake Tear of the Clouds. He could see the faces of Julia and Meghan clearly. He remembered their voices. What if he could restart a dead memory by the sheer force of his consciousness breathing life and fire into the gray?

Is there a chance it might also skid everyone else's consciousness back onto that dead timeline as well?

And if he could return, not just to a prior timeline, but to the original, there would be no false memories from subsequent timelines, and none from earlier ones either.

Because there are no timelines that pre-date the original.

It'd be like none of this ever happened.

He already took the pills. Probably has a half hour, maybe longer, before the drug takes over.

He sits up in the grave, sharp-awake.

Thoughts racing.

Maybe Slade was lying, but isn't staying here, killing himself next to Helena's body as he drowns in the memory of her the same fetishizing of nostalgia he did with Meghan? Just another instance of longing for the unreachable past?

———

Back at the station, Barry grabs a skullcap and the tablet that remotely controls the terminal. He climbs onto the chair and lowers the MEG microscope onto the skullcap, which begins to hum softly.

He sprinted the half mile from Helena's gravesite to the station, and figures he has ten to fifteen minutes before the oxy takes effect.

He's lived the events of the original timeline several times over—Julia, Meghan, his daughter's death, his divorce, his life as a cop in New York City. In his mind, the dead memories overlay one another, each lifetime manifesting in his mind's eye as a gray, haunted tableau. But the older the timeline, the darker it becomes, like whiskey left in the cask. He finally circles the oldest timeline—darker than the moodiest film noir and carrying the palpable gravity of the original.

He wakes the tablet and opens a new file to record the memory.

He's running out of time.

He doesn't remember anything about November 5, 2018. It's just a date in his head from Slade, and from a conversation he had with Helena many, many lifetimes ago.

But November 4 is Meghan's birthday. He knows exactly where he was.

Barry presses Record and remembers.

When he's finished, he waits for the program to calculate the memory's synaptic number. It occurs to him that if the number comes back too low, he'll have to dig into the software and disable the firewall, and that's going to take more time than he has.

The tablet flashes a number.

121.

Just barely in the safe zone.

Barry affixes an injection port to his left forearm and loads the drug cocktail into the mechanism.

He keeps thinking he feels the first signs of oxy as he programs the memory-reactivation sequence at the terminal, but soon he's naked and climbing into the tank.

Floating on his back in the water, he reaches up and pulls the hatch closed over the top of him.

His mind going in a thousand different directions.

This is going to fail and you're just going to die in this tank.

Fuck the world, save Meghan.

Go back out there and die beside your wife like you've been intending for the last two months.

You have to keep trying. Helena would want this.

There's a subtle vibration in his left forearm. He closes his eyes and takes a deep breath, wondering if it will be his last.

BARRY

The world stands as still as a painting—no movement, life, or color—and yet, he is aware of his own existence.

He can see only in the direction he's facing, staring across an arrangement of tables west toward the river, the water almost black.

Everything is frozen.

Everything in shades of gray.

Straight ahead, a waiter—dark as a silhouette—carries a pitcher of ice water.

People occupy tables shaded by umbrellas, caught in moments of laughter, eating and drinking, holding napkins to their mouths. But there is no motion. They might as well be carvings on an urn.

Straight ahead, he sees Julia, already seated at their table. She's waiting for him, paused in a pensive, anxious moment, and he registers a terrifying fear that she will forever be waiting.

This is nothing like returning to a memory on a live timeline. That is a process of slowly embodying yourself as the sensations of the memory wash over you. You come *into* action and energy.

Here, there is none.

And it occurs to him—I am finally in a moment of *now*.

Whatever he is or has become, Barry registers a freedom of movement he has never known. He is no longer in three-dimensional space, and he wonders if this is what Slade meant by—*And maybe you never will, unless you can travel the way I've traveled.* Was this how Slade experienced the universe?

Impossibly, he turns around inside of himself and stares back through . . .

He doesn't know what it is exactly.

Not right away, at least.

He's caught at the leading edge of something that reminds him of a time-lapsed star path, only it's a part of him, as much an extension of his being as his arm or his mind, falling away and spiraling in on itself into a glowing, fractal-like form more beautiful and mysterious than anything in his experience. And he knows, on a level he cannot begin to explain, that this is his original world-line, and that it contains the breadth of his existence as formed by memory.

Every memory he has ever made.

Every memory that has made him.

But this is not his only worldline. Others branch off from this one, twisting and turning in on themselves through space-time.

He feels the worldline of memories where he saved Meghan from the hit-and-run.

A trio of minor worldlines, each of which ended in his death at Slade's hotel.

The subsequent lifetimes he and Helena lived in their attempts to stave off the end of reality.

Even the branches he created in their last life in the Antarctic— spokelike radials of memory forming the ten times he died in the tank to be with her again.

But none of those matter anymore.

The timeline he's on is the original, and he's accelerating upstream against the river of his life, crashing through forgotten moments, understanding finally that memory is all he's made of.

All anything is made of.

When the needle of his consciousness touches a memory, his life begins to play, and he finds himself in a frozen moment—

The smell of dead leaves and the cool bite of autumn in the city, sitting in the Ramble in Central Park, crying after signing his divorce papers.

Moving again—

Faster now—

Through more memories than he can count.

As numerous as stars—like staring across a universe that is him.

His mother's funeral, looking down into her open casket, his hands on hers and the cool stiffness of them as he studies her face, thinking, That isn't you. . . .

Meghan's body on the slab—her crushed-in torso covered in a black bruise.

Finding her on the side of the road near their house.

Why these moments? he wonders.

Driving through the suburbs on a cold, dark night between Thanksgiving and Christmas, Julia in the front passenger seat beside him, Meghan in the back, everyone quiet and content, watching Christmas lights through the windows—an exhale in the midst of life's journey, between storms, where everything has settled into fleeting alignment.

Ripped away again, now hurtling through a tunnel whose walls of memory are rifling down on him.

Meghan behind the wheel of his Camry, the back half punched through the garage door, her face red and tears streaming down it as she white-knuckle clutches the steering wheel.

Meghan's grass-stained knees after a soccer game, six years old, her face ruddy and happy.

Meghan's first wobbly steps in their Brooklyn studio.

What is the reality of this moment?

The first time he touches his daughter in a hospital room—his hand to the side of her tiny cheek.

Julia taking him by the hand, leading him into the bedroom of their first apartment, sitting him down and telling him she's pregnant.

Am I in my final seconds in the deprivation tank in Antarctica, reviewing my life as it slips away?

Driving home after his first date with Julia and the weightless elation of hope that he might have found someone to love.

What if this is nothing more than the last electrical firings of my dying brain? Frantic neuronal activity bending my perception of reality and conjuring random memories?

Is this what everyone experiences at death?

The tunnel and the light?

This false heaven?

Does this mean I've failed to restart the original timeline and the world is finished?

Or am I outside of time, being pulled into the crushing black hole of my own memories?

His hands on his father's casket and the stark realization that life is pain and always will be.

Fifteen years old, getting called into the principal's office where his mom sits on the couch, crying, and he knows before they even tell him that something happened to his father.

The dry lips and trembling hands of the first girl he ever kissed in junior high.

His mother pushing a shopping cart through the coffee aisle of a grocery store and him trailing behind, a piece of stolen candy in his pocket.

Standing with his father one morning in the driveway of their house in Portland, Oregon, the birds gone quiet, everything still, and the air as cold as night. His father's face watching the moment of totality is more impressive than the eclipse itself. How often do you witness your parents awestruck?

Lying in bed on the second floor of his grandparents' nineteenth-

century New Hampshire farmhouse as a summer storm sweeps in from the White Mountains, drenching the fields and the apple trees and pattering on the tin roof.

The time he crashed his bike and broke his arm when he was six.

Light coming through a window and the shadows of leaves dancing on the wall above a crib. It's late afternoon—he doesn't know how he knows this—and the tones of his mother's singing drift through the walls into his nursery.

My first memory.

He can't explain why, but it feels like the memory he's been searching for his entire life, and the seductive gravity of nostalgia is pulling his consciousness in, because this isn't just the quintessential memory of home, it is the safe and perfect moment—before life held any real pain.

Before he failed.

Before he lost people he loved.

Before he experienced waking to the fear that his best days were behind him.

He suspects he could slip his consciousness into this memory like an old man into a warm, soft bed.

Live this perfect moment forever.

There could be worse fates.

And perhaps no better.

Is this what you want? To drop yourself into a still-life painting of a memory because life has broken your heart?

For so many lifetimes, he lived in a state of perpetual regret, returning obsessively and destructively to better times, to moments he wished he could change. Most of those lives he lived staring into the rearview mirror.

Until Helena.

The thought comes almost like a prayer—*I don't want to look back anymore. I'm ready to accept that my existence will sometimes contain pain. No more trying to escape, either through nostalgia or a memory chair. They're both the same fucking thing.*

Life with a cheat code isn't life. Our existence isn't something to be engineered or optimized for the avoidance of pain.

That's what it is to be human—the beauty and *the pain, each meaningless without the other.*

And he's in the café again.

The waters of the Hudson turn blue and begin to flow. Color enters the sky, the faces of the customers, buildings, every surface. He feels the cool air of morning coming off the river into his face. He smells food. The world is suddenly vibrant, brimming with the sound of people laughing and talking all around him.

He's breathing.

He's blinking.

Smiling and crying.

And moving at last toward Julia.

EPILOGUE

<hr />

Life can only be understood backwards; but it must be lived forwards.

–SØREN KIERKEGAARD

BARRY

The café occupies a picturesque spot on the banks of the Hudson, in the shadow of the West Side Highway. Barry and Julia share a brief, fragile embrace.

"Are you OK?" she asks.

"Yeah."

"I'm glad you came."

The waiter swings by to take their drink orders, and they make small talk until the coffee arrives.

It is a Sunday, the brunch crowd is out in force, and in the initial, awkward silence with Julia, Barry pressure-checks his memories.

His daughter died eleven years ago.

Julia divorced him soon after.

He has never met Marcus Slade or Ann Voss Peters.

Never traveled back into a memory to save Meghan.

False Memory Syndrome has never plagued the world.

Reality and time have never unraveled in the minds of billions.

And he has never laid eyes on Helena Smith. Their many lifetimes together spent trying to save the world from the effects of the chair have been banished to the wasteland of dead memory.

There is no question—he can feel it in his bones.

This timeline is the first, the original.

Barry looks across the table at Julia and says, "It's really good to see you."

They talk about Meghan, what they each imagine she'd be doing with her life, and it's all Barry can do not to tell Julia that he actually knows. That he's seen it firsthand in a distant, unreachable memory. That their daughter would have been more vital, more interesting, and kinder than any of their speculation could begin to do her memory justice.

As the food comes, he remembers Meghan sitting at the table with them. Swears he can almost feel her presence, like a phantom limb. And while it hurts, it doesn't break him the way it once would have. The memory of his daughter hurts because he experienced a beautiful thing that has since gone away. Same as with Julia. Same as with all the loss he has ever experienced.

The last time he lived this moment with Julia, they reminisced about a family trip into the Adirondacks, to Lake Tear of the Clouds, the source of the Hudson.

And the butterfly that kept coming around made him think of Meghan.

Julia says, "You seem better."

"I do?"

"Yeah."

It is late autumn in the city, Barry thinking this reality is feeling more solid by the minute. No shifts threatening to upend everything.

He is questioning his memory of all the other timelines. Even Helena feels more like a fading fantasy than a woman he touched and loved.

What feels real in this moment isn't his phantom memory of watching a shockwave vaporize the Upper West Side. What feels real are the sounds of the city, the people at the tables all around him, his ex-wife, the breath going in and out of his lungs.

For everyone but him, the past is a singular concept.

No conflicting histories.

No false memories.

The dead timelines of mayhem and destruction are his alone to remember.

When the check comes, Julia tries to pay, but he snatches it away and throws down his card.

"Thank you, Barry."

He reaches across the table and takes hold of her hand, clocking the surprise in her eyes at this gesture of intimacy.

"I need to tell you something, Julia."

He looks out at the Hudson. The breeze coming off the water carries a cool bite, and the sun is warm on his shoulders. Tourist boats go up and down the river. The noise of traffic is ceaseless on the highway above. The sky crisscrossed with the fading contrails of a thousand jets.

"I was angry with you for a long time."

"I know," she says.

"I thought you left me because of Meghan."

"Maybe. I don't know. It was too much to keep breathing the same air as you in those dark days."

He shakes his head. "I think that if you and I could go back to before she died, even if we could somehow prevent it, you still would have gone your way, and I would've gone mine. I think we were meant to be together for a time. Perhaps losing Meghan shortened the life-span of us, but even if she had lived, we'd still be apart in this moment."

"You really believe that?"

"I do, and I'm sorry I held on to the anger. I'm sorry I only see this now. We had so many perfect moments, and for a long time, I couldn't appreciate them. I could only look back in regret. This is what I wanted to tell you: I wouldn't change anything. I'm glad you came into my life when you did. I'm glad for the time we had. I'm glad for Meghan, and that she came from the two of us. That she couldn't have come from any other two people. I wouldn't take back a second of any of it."

She wipes away a tear. "All these years, I thought you wished you'd never met me. I thought you blamed me for ruining your life."

"I was just hurting."

She squeezes his hand. "I'm sorry we weren't the ones for each other, Barry. You're right about that, and I'm sorry for everything else."

BARRY

The loft is on the third floor of a converted warehouse in San Francisco's Dogpatch, an old shipbuilding neighborhood on the bay.

Barry parks his rental car three blocks away and walks to the entrance of the building.

The fog is so dense it softens the edges of the city, laying a gray primer on everything and diffusing the globes of illumination from the streetlights, turning them into ethereal orbs. It reminds him, in some ways, of the color palette of a dead memory, but he likes the anonymity it provides.

A woman heading out for the evening opens the front door. He slips by her and into the lobby, heading up two flights of stairs and then down a long hallway toward Unit 7.

He knocks, waits.

No one answers.

He knocks again, harder this time, and after a moment, a man's soft voice bleeds through the door.

"Who is it?"

"Detective Sutton." Barry steps back and holds his badge to the peephole. "Could I speak with you?"

"What is it regarding?"

"Just open the door, please."

Five seconds elapse.

Barry thinking, *He's not going to let me in.*

He puts his badge away, and as he takes a step back to kick the door in, the chain on the other side slides out, and a dead bolt turns.

Marcus Slade stands in the threshold.

"How can I help you?" Slade asks.

Barry walks past him, into a small, messy loft with large windows overlooking a shipyard, the bay, and the lights of Oakland beyond.

"Nice place," Barry says as Slade closes the door.

Barry moves toward the kitchen table and picks up a sports almanac of the 1990s and then a huge volume entitled *The SRC Green Book of 35-Year Historical Stock Charts.*

"Little light reading?" he asks.

Slade looks nervous and annoyed. He has his hands thrust into the pockets of his green cardigan, and his eyes keep shifting back and forth, blinking at irregular intervals.

"What do you do, Mr. Slade?"

"I work for Ion Industries."

"In what capacity?"

"Research and development. I'm an assistant to one of their lead scientists."

"And what kind of stuff do you guys make?" Barry asks, perusing a stack of pages that were recently printed off from a website— *historical winning lottery numbers by state.*

Slade walks over and snatches the pages out of Barry's hand.

"The nature of our work is protected under an NDA. Why are you here, Detective Sutton?"

"I'm investigating a murder."

Slade straightens. "Who was killed?"

"Well, this is a weird one." Barry looks into Slade's eyes. "It hasn't happened yet."

"I'm not following."

"I'm here about a murder that's going to happen later tonight."

Slade swallows, blinks. "What does this have to do with me?"

"It'll happen at your place of work, and the victim's name is Helena Smith. That's your boss, right?"

"Yeah."

"She's also the woman I love."

Slade is standing across from Barry, the kitchen table between them, his eyes gone wide. Barry points at the books. "So you have all this stuff memorized? Obviously, you can't take them with you."

Slade opens his mouth and closes it again. Then says, "I want you to leave."

"It works, by the way."

"I don't know what you're talking—"

"Your plan. It works like gangbusters. You become rich and famous. Unfortunately, what you do tonight causes the suffering of billions and the end of reality and time as we know it."

"Who are you?"

"Just a cop from New York City." He stares Slade down for ten long seconds.

"Get out."

Barry doesn't move. The only noise in the loft is the ragged sound of Slade's accelerated breathing. Slade's phone buzzes on the table. Barry glances down, sees a new text from "Helena Smith" appear on the home screen.

Sure. I can meet you in two hours. What's the problem?

Barry finally starts for the door.

Three steps from it, he hears a *click*. And another. And another.

He turns around slowly and looks across the loft at Slade, who's staring dumbfounded at the .357 revolver he would've killed Helena with in several hours. He looks up at Barry, who should be lying on the floor right now, bleeding out. Slade levels the gun on Barry and pulls the trigger, but it only dry-fires again.

"I broke in earlier today while you were at work," Barry says. "Loaded the chambers with empty shell casings. I needed to see for myself what you were capable of."

Slade looks in the direction of his bedroom.

"There are no live rounds in the house, Marcus. Well, that's not exactly true." Barry pulls his Glock from his shoulder holster. "My gun is full of them."

The bar is in the Mission, a cozy, wood-paneled tavern called Monk's Kettle, its windows steamed up on the inside against the cold and foggy night. Helena has told him about this place in at least three of their lifetimes.

Barry steps in out of the mist and runs his fingers through his hair, which has been flattened by the dampness.

It's a Monday night, and late, so the place is nearly empty.

He spots her sitting at the far end of the bar, alone, hunched over a laptop. As he approaches, the nerves hit—far worse than he anticipated.

His mouth runs dry; his hands sweat.

She looks quite different from the dynamo he spent six lifetimes with. She's wearing a gray sweater that a cat or dog has pulled a hundred little nits out of, smudged glasses, and even her hair is different—longer and pulled back into a utilitarian ponytail.

Watching her, it's apparent that her obsession with the memory chair has fully consumed her, and it breaks his heart.

She doesn't acknowledge him in any way as he climbs onto the seat beside hers.

He smells the beer on her breath, and beneath it, the subtler, elemental scent of his wife that he would know anywhere, out of a million people. He's trying not to look at her, but the emotion of sitting beside her is almost too much. Last time he saw her face, he was nailing the lid onto her pine-box casket. And so he sits quietly beside her as she writes an email, thinking of all the lifetimes they shared.

The lovely moments.

The ugly ones.

The goodbyes, the deaths.

And the hellos, like this one.

Like the six times she came to him in that Portland shit-kicker bar when he was twenty-one years old, sidled up beside him, young, bright-eyed, beautiful, and fearless.

You look like you want to buy me a drink.

He smiles to himself, because she does not, in this moment, look remotely like she wants to buy a stranger a drink. She looks, well, like Helena—sunk deeply into her work and oblivious to the world.

The bartender comes over, Barry orders, and then he's sitting with his beer, asking himself the question of the moment—What do you say to the bravest woman you've ever known, whom you lived a half dozen extraordinary lives with, whom you saved the world with, who saved *you* in every conceivable way, but who has no idea you even exist?

Barry takes a sip of beer and sets down the glass. The air feels electrically charged, like just before a storm. Questions avalanching through his mind—

Will you know me?

Will you believe me?

Will you love me?

Scared, exhilarated, senses heightening, heart thrumming, he turns finally to Helena, who, feeling his attention, looks over at him through those jade-green eyes.

And he says—

ACKNOWLEDGMENTS

I could never have written this book without the infinite support of my partner in creativity and life (and sometimes crime) Jacque Ben-Zekry. Thank you for the thousand conversations (often sitting at our favorite bars) about this story and characters. Thank you for your patience when, at times, this book ruled our lives, and for your indispensable editorial contributions that made *Recursion* better in every way.

David Hale Smith, my ninja-cowboy-assassin literary agent, has been a tremendous advocate going on nine years. Brother, I'm so thankful to have you in my life.

And keeping it in the Inkwell Management family for a moment—high fives to Alexis Hurley, who is responsible for bringing my books to the wide world, to Nathaniel Jacks for your superb, fine-grain contract work, and Richard Pine for your steady hand on the Inkwell ship.

Angela Cheng Caplan and Joel VanderKloot—what can I say other than every writer should be so lucky as to have a team like you driving the battle tank through the madness of Hollywood.

I've been writing for a long time, and I have never had a better publishing experience than with the team at Crown. My editor, Julian Pavia, my publisher, Molly Stern, Maya Mavjee, Annsley Rosner, David Drake, Chris Brand, Angeline Rodriguez, and publicity extraordinaire, Dyana Messina, are simply the best of the best.

Double shout-out to Julian for challenging me to make this story every bit as big and surprising as it deserved to be. As the *reader* deserved it to be. Your commitment to beating this novel into submission matched mine, which is all a writer can ask from an editor. *Recursion* would be a shell of itself without your fearless editorial eye.

Wayne Brookes at Pan Macmillan in the UK—I'm over-the-moon to have you championing my work on the other side of the pond.

Rachelle Mandik did an exceptional copyediting job on the final manuscript.

Clifford Johnson, Ph.D., professor in the Physics and Astronomy Department at the University of Southern California, provided invaluable insight in the final stages of the manuscript. All mistakes, assumptions, and crazy theories are mine alone.

This was hands down the hardest book I've ever written, and I leaned more on friends than ever before when it came time to gather feedback. To say thank you to those priceless people who provided notes on *Recursion,* and to pay tribute to other friends and writers I greatly admire, some of their namesakes appear in the book as follows:

Barry Sutton = the inimitable Barry Eisler, who went above and beyond in his notes and helped me to drill down into the book's theme in a moment when I needed his counsel most.

Ann Voss Peters = the lovely and talented Ann Voss Peterson, who has made so many of my books better with her thoughtful insights, in particular the motivations behind my characters.

Helena Smith = the British dynamo thriller writer, Helen Smith, who incidentally has the greatest Cards Against Humanity reading voice in the world.

Jee-woon Chercover = Sean Chercover, the greatest-smelling writer I personally know, and one of my favorite humans.

Marcus Slade = Marcus Sakey, my brainstorming brother who helped immeasurably at various milestones along the path of writing this book.

Amor Towles = Amor Towles, genius writer of *A Gentleman in Moscow,* my favorite book of the last five years.

Dr. Paul Wilson = the great Dr. F. Paul Wilson, titan of sci-fi and horror, and abstainer of snake wine.

Reed King = Reed Farrel Coleman, Long Island's noir poet and the benevolent Godfather of the mystery community.

Marie Iden = Matt Iden, the D.C. novelist, admirer of BoJack (my dog), and perhaps the Washington Capitals' greatest fan.

Joseph Hart = the brilliant sci-fi novelist and Lord of the northern Minnesota wilds, Joe Hart.

John Shaw = Johnny Motherfucking Shaw, owner of the greatest eyebrow in the known universe, and one of our finest crime writers.

Sheila Redling = Sheila Redling, the wonderful West Virginia writer and one of the funniest people I know.

Timoney Rodriguez = Timoney "cool, cool" Korbar, the only non-novelist in this group, but an amazing producer/creator in her own right, and an all-around uber-human.

Heartfelt thanks also to Jeroen ten Berge, Steve Konkoly, Chad Hodge, Olivia Vigrabs, Alison Dasho, and Suzanne Blue, for taking the time to give me feedback at various stages during the writing process.

Hugs and kisses to my luminous children—Aidan, Annslee, and Adeline. You are everything that inspires me.

And finally, around Christmas of 2012, Steve Ramirez and Xu Liu, two neuroscientists at MIT, implanted a false memory in the brain of a mouse. The general framework of Helena's "memory chair" spring-boarded off their stunning achievement. I'm profoundly grateful to them, and to all scientists who have dedicated their lives to unraveling the beautiful mystery of our existence.